COPYRIGHT

BOUGHT BY SANTA

B. LYBAEK

CONTENT WARNING

Listen, I'm getting really bad at trigger warnings. What's a yuck for some is a yum for others. And what's upsetting to one is a craving for someone else. Writing this part feels like my own personal Mount Everest—an impossible task that has me tearing my hair out.

While I've done my best to list all the tropes and themes my team and I picked up on, everyone views content differently. Please read responsibly, and remember—your mental health always comes first.

Adult characters | Alphahole | Bondage | Bought FMC | Breeding | Captive/captor | Dark Christmas romance | Death | He falls first | Kinks | Knife/blood play | Mafia | MF romance | OTT j/p | Rags to riches | Sexual awakening | Sexual discovery | Somnophilia (light!) | Torture | Unaliving

FOLLOW

THANK YOU

Emma, my bestie, my pain in the ass, my eternal cheerleader. You're the one who knows exactly when I need tough love and when I need a margarita. Thanks for being my therapist, my hype woman, and my personal reminder to 'just hit send already!' Without you, I'd probably still be overthinking chapter one.

To my rockstar alphas and betas; Alisha, Bree, Jasmine, Jennifer, Kat, Nichole, Anoesjka, Dorothy, Lisa & Melissa. Honestly, without you guys, this manuscript would be one giant plot hole after another. I owe you my sanity and probably a few extra hours of sleep.

All that's left to say is; hoe, hoe, hoe!

DEDICATION

For the ones who know Santa's list isn't the only thing getting checked twice. This Christmas isn't about presents under the tree—it's about the kind of gifts that make you sweat and beg for more.

To those who thought Santa was just about sleigh rides and cookies… welcome to the dark side, where stockings aren't the only thing getting stuffed.

CHAPTER 1

The Santa

I sit, fingers interlocked, elbows resting on the mahogany table that's seen more silent threats than a courtroom. Across from me, sits my dad—silver-haired and eyes like steel traps—and at his side, Arthur Hatt. The former's arrival from York, England, isn't a social call; it's a testament to the severity of this dinner we're having.

Arthur watches me with piercing blue eyes, assessing, calculating. They don't miss the way my jaw tenses. I can't help but wonder if he enjoys this meeting.

The Hatt family, the original bloodline, command from their throne in old England, reigning supreme. They've been peddling flesh long before our ancestors set foot on American soil. The Knight family is the American extension, a power in its own right.

After all, every king needs knights to defend his kingdom.

The servers glide around us, replacing our dishes with an array of rich food that only muffle the tension at the table. Lobster bisque, truffle-infused mashed potatoes, and asparagus so vibrant it seems out of place in this world of muted threats. I take a sip of the Cabernet, its boldness a much needed contrast to the forced civility between myself, Dad, and Arthur.

"I hear your dad passed the reins over to you last year," Arthur says, shattering the blessed silence just as I bring the wineglass to my lips, ready to empty it. "Congratulations, cousin."

The mention of our familial status is ridiculous and has never meant a damn thing. "Thank you," I retort. "Your journey over the Atlantic is not taken lightly, cousin."

"I should hope not," he responds, the corners of his lips twitching into a semblance of a smile. "One does not simply traverse an ocean for trivial matters."

Dad looks between us, but instead of looking pleased the dinner is going well, he frowns. "Nicklas, you know why I passed the reins over to you last year," Dad says, his voice cutting through the clink of silverware. "Ruby's out of the picture, married off to that... what's his name again? Michael, that's it." His fork clinks against fine china as he cuts into his food.

I resist the urge to point out that Dad is the one who, ten years ago, sold my sister to her much older husband who doesn't fucking deserve her.

"She has her uses, of course. But she can't carry on the family. She's not even a Knight anymore, she's a goddamn Simmons," he shouts, slamming his fist into the table, making the surrounding stuff rattle.

If my sister's married name is that offensive, he should have said no when her husband demanded she change her last name.

"And Jack... well, we all know about him and his penchant for gambling." Dad shakes his head, emphasizing the disappointment and distaste of my brother.

I feel the weight of his gaze on me, heavy with unsaid expectations. The muscles in my jaw tighten as I resist the urge to challenge him right there. I want to scream that it's not just about running the family business; it's about being shackled to it.

"Jack's not unreliable, he's just..." My defense falls flat even as I speak it, the truth bitter on my tongue. Jack, with his easy grin and careless shrugs, is too much like quicksilver, impossible to pin down.

"Unpredictable," Dad finishes for me, his voice devoid of emotion. "Your brother's antics won't be tolerated much longer, you know. It's a stain on our family."

A server refills my glass, and I nod in thanks, trying not to think of Jack, whose easygoing nature has always been a foil to my own intensity. I can almost hear his laughter, see the green glint in his eyes—a mirror of Ruby's, but without the shadow of submission to another's will.

Ruby, with her sharp tongue and even sharper mind, relegated to arm candy for some old money mogul. She could have been a force to be reckoned with, our secret weapon. Instead, she's another piece on the family chessboard, sacrificed for strategy.

"An empire needs a firm hand," Dad continues, his gaze locked on mine. "You've got that grip, Nicklas. Don't let it weaken."

The weight of his expectations feels like a yoke around my neck, heavy and unyielding. But I don't bow down. "Never," I say, my voice low and steady. A promise or a threat, it's hard to tell—even for me. The taste of power is complex, layered with both the sweetness of victory and the bitter tang of isolation.

"Good." Dad nods, satisfied, yet his eyes remain cold, calculating.

Arthur nods and makes a sound of approval at Dad's harsh words and even harsher assessment of my siblings. "So, I guess it all comes down to you, Nicklas," Arthur cuts in. "You need to secure the continuation of the Knight empire."

My fingers grip the edge of the table until my knuckles whiten. Secure the empire. A polite way of saying breed, produce an heir, or watch everything we've built crumble to dust. A legacy forged in shadows and whispered fears, demanding a continuation of its dark lineage.

As we sit among the grandeur of the dining room, the air heavy with the scent of truffle oil and the underlying iron tang of blood ties, I feel the weight of centuries bearing down on me. It's not enough to lead; I must also breed, weave new threads into this tapestry of corruption and power.

"Rest assured, the legacy of the Knights will forge ahead." There's a promise in my words, one coated in ice and fire—because if there's one thing I've learned, it's that power respects only more power.

"Good." Arthur leans back in his chair, the ghost of a smile playing on his lips. "Because if you do not uphold this tradition, there are others who will," he pauses, letting the threat hang in the air like mist over a battlefield. "And the Knight name could very well fade into obscurity."

The idea scrapes against my insides like a blade. Fade into obscurity? Never. I may despise the shackles they've placed upon me, but I will not be the one to break centuries of dominion. The Knight name will not wither under my watch.

"Then I'll do what's necessary," I say, my voice a low growl of commitment. The heat of the wine in my veins is nothing compared to the fire of determination that burns within me. I will secure an heir. I will cement our reign.

"See that you do," Arthur's tone is final. "Before Christmas would be preferable. I'm in the country until then, and I'd like to know it's happening before I return to England."

The dinner continues, but every mouthful is now laced with the acrid flavor of duty. The opulence of the meal, the perfection of the presentation, it all seems grotesque when juxtaposed with the stark reality of my purpose.

I clench my jaw, a muscle twitching in my cheek as I fix my gaze on Arthur. The air around us is thick with the delicious food on our plates, but it's the stench of expectation that chokes me. I lean back in my chair; the leather creaking under my weight, and try to find the words that won't betray my seething reluctance.

Taking a measured breath, I feel the constraints of destiny tightening around me. This isn't just about continuing the bloodline; this is about power, control, the unyielding grip we have over, not just New York's shadowy corners, but all of America.

"You'll get your heir before Christmas," I finally say, the words heavy like lead on my tongue.

Around me, the conversation carries on; they're talking about the death of Arthur's dad, Uther, due to poisoning almost three years ago. As I consider how to continue the lineage, their words become nothing more than background noise.

It's mid-November already, so I don't have long to find someone to impregnate. It would all be a lot easier if I was actually in a relationship, which I'm not. It's not that I have trouble finding women to spread their legs for me, but not one has lasted more than one night—two at most.

But now I'm supposed to find someone I can stand having around for at least nine months…

Well, fuck me!

CHAPTER 2

The Breeder

The cheerful strains of "Jingle Bells" reach me before I even push open the front door of Ability Acres, the care home where my sister lives. It's like stepping into another world—one where the weight of my problems can't follow. At least, that's what I keep telling myself.

"Hi, Carolina!" greets Nancy at reception, her eyes crinkling with genuine warmth. She's part of the reason coming here doesn't feel so heavy. I offer a smile, pushing down the ever-present anxiety that threatens to claw its way up my throat.

"Hey, Nancy," I say, the words a little more breathless than I'd like. "How's she doing today?"

"Willow's been buzzing all morning, dear. You know how much she loves this day."

I nod, my heart hitching a bit because I do know—I know too well. November thirtieth isn't just the day we decorate for Christmas; it's our shared moment of joy that I cling to, year after year.

I head down the hallway, passing staff members adorned in Santa hats, their smiles as bright as the tinsel lining the walls. The scent of cinnamon wafts from the kitchen, and for a moment, I let myself be carried away by the festive atmosphere.

Pushing open the door to her room, she's already ready, waiting for me with that bright smile that outshines the cheap, flickering fairy lights strung around her bed. Her eyes, the color of fresh earth after rain, light up at the sight of me. "Caro!" she exclaims.

"Hey, Will," I say, closing the distance between us with quick strides.

My sister—appearance wise, she's almost my twin, with the exception that her hair is practically white, whereas mine is blonde—is parked by the window in her wheelchair, a blanket draped over her legs.

The accident, a memory etched in sharp relief against the canvas of our lives, stole not only our dad's life, but her use of those legs when she was barely twelve. Dad was walking her to school when a guy lost control of his car, too busy texting. Heroically, our dad pushed Willow out of the way, taking the brunt of the impact on himself. He died instantly, and my vibrant sister was bound to wheels. But she never let it dull her spirit.

My sister's voice pulls me from the morbid and tragic trip down memory lane. "Ready to make the tree beautiful?" she asks, gesturing excitedly to the small artificial Christmas tree perched on a table beside her.

"Always," I respond, the corners of my mouth lifting into a genuine smile as I retrieve the box of ornaments from the closet. "And you haven't changed your mind on the color scheme again?"

She giggles. "No, and I promise I won't. At least not this year," she jokes.

We work together, Willow handling the delicate baubles, passing them to me with care. I stretch to hang them, weaving between the synthetic branches, filling in the gaps with glistening reds and golds.

"Higher, Caro! It has to be perfect," she directs, her laughter like wind chimes in the crisp winter air. And despite everything—the crushing weight of responsibility, the gnawing fear of tomorrow—I find myself laughing too, caught up in the magic we're creating.

I loop a silver garland around the top of the Christmas tree, but my mind's tangled tighter than these decorations. Money—or the lack of it—claws at me, a relentless beast with an insatiable appetite. I shove step up. I dropped out of school and took whatever jobs I could get to support myself and Will. Mom used whatever little money Dad and the insurance left us to support her new habits, so it was up to me to get the money to pay for Will's special needs treatments, and find a facility she could live in.

It hurts me to the core that I can't live with my sister, but none of the places I can afford are wheelchair friendly. Trust me, I've done extensive research. But no matter how much I looked and begged for the calculator to give me the results I wanted, there was no way I could afford her medical bills, a sufficient home, and feed the both of us. So, a home was the only affordable solution.

Looking at my sister, it's clear she misses our parents. I've always done my best to shield her from how cruel our mom became. "Hey, don't look so sad, Will," I chirp, forcing my tone to sound extra happy. "She *does* love it. You know they're here with us, in spirit." It's a line I've recited every holiday season since the accident, a mantra to soothe the ache of absence.

"Sometimes, I can almost hear her singing carols," Willow whispers, her smile tinged with nostalgia. She reaches out, her fingers dancing over a red bauble adorned with glittering snowflakes—a remnant from childhood Christmases that somehow survived the years.

"Well," I say, hesitantly, taking my sister's hand. "We can go caroling if you want."

Will scrunches up her face. "Har har, you know I'm tone deaf. You're the one named after the tradition so you should do it."

She isn't wrong. Mom's water broke while she and Dad were caroling on December thirteenth almost twenty-seven years ago, which is how I earned my name. Most people think it's because I was conceived in one of the Carolina states, but nope. Luckily, that's not the story accompanying my name.

The room seems to hold its breath, the air thick with unspoken words and memories that cling like cobwebs. We are the last Sterlings, clinging to each other in a world that has been anything but kind.

"Caro, promise me something?" Willow's brown eyes lock onto mine, earnest and searching.

"Anything, Will."

"Promise we'll always find a way to keep our traditions alive. No matter what."

My heart clenches, a vise of responsibility tightening around it. The thought of failing her, of watching the light in her eyes dim because I couldn't keep our world afloat, terrifies me more than anything else.

"Always," I say, and I mean it with every fiber of my being. Because in the end, it's not the money or the desperation that defines us. It's the love between two sisters, fighting against the cruelty of life.

Although it takes most of the afternoon, because Will has made me change the placement of everything a thousand times over, I finally place the last ornament. A bright red bauble which catches the soft glow of the fairy lights.

I step back, the scent of pine and cinnamon wrapping around me like a warm hug. The twinkling lights cast dancing shadows on Willow's face, illuminating her wide smile that's as comforting as it is heartbreaking.

"Looks perfect," I murmur, my chest swelling with a pride that momentarily eases the gnawing anxiety lodged deep in my belly.

"Better than perfect—magical," she insists, her voice ringing with a joy that belies her confinement to the wheelchair. The accident may have stolen her mobility, but not her spirit.

I bend down, plugging in the small electric kettle by her bedside. "Hot chocolate?" I offer, even though it's more statement than question. Tradition dictates it, and heaven knows we cling to those.

"Yes, please," she replies, her anticipation palpable as I mix the cocoa powder and marshmallows into the steaming water. We sip our drinks, the sweetness of chocolate and the burn of heat a sharp contrast to the chill seeping through the windowpane.

"Caro…" Willow begins, her tone shifting, "You'll come back soon, right?"

"Of course," I answer too quickly, the lie bitter on my tongue. Each visit costs something I can barely afford—time, money, hope—but I push that aside, focusing on the warmth spreading through my fingers

"Love you more," I reply with a half-hearted smile and slip out into the cold.

Back in the silent confines of my small studio, the once merry jingles of Christmas music now sound mocking. Bills are strewn across the kitchen table like a deck of cards dealt by fate—a losing hand. I sit, the weight of numbers and overdue notices pressing down on me.

I close my eyes, allowing myself this moment of vulnerability. My breath hitches, the fear and panic clawing at my insides. How much longer can I keep this up? How much longer before everything crumbles?

The room is suffocating, walls closing in, filled with the ghosts of our parents and the relentless pressure to provide for Willow. To give her the life she deserves—one that doesn't end within the confines of a care home room.

Letting out a shaky breath, I try to piece together a plan, any plan, that doesn't involve selling pieces of my soul or poking holes in prophylactics in vain attempts at securing an anchor in this storm. But as always, I come up with nothing. I'm a high school dropout without qualifications for anything. I only have one thing to offer; my body.

I stand in the middle of my cramped studio, eyes shut as I paint the fantasy once more; grand ballrooms, silken gowns, a life where Willow laughs free of worry. It's a dream spun from desperation, woven with threads of hope and longing. My fingertips graze the cold windowpane, imagining it's the smooth marble of some opulent mansion. The frosty touch sends a shiver down my spine, but it's not from the chill.

"Carolina Sterling, you will be the belle of every ball," I mutter, the words a vow to the night. "You'll find that golden ticket."

I snap my eyes open, the reality of peeling wallpaper and looming shadows crashing back. The fantasy fades, but it leaves behind a fierce resolve. No more tears, I decide. They solve nothing. Action—deceptive, sly, desperate action—is what's called for now.

Moving to my closet, I rummage through hangers until I find *the* dress. Red, daring, a whisper of fabric that promises sin and salvation all at once. A tool, nothing more, despite its allure. As I inspect the tags, still firmly attached, a smirk pulls at my lips. "One night only," I remind myself. "Wear it, charm them, return it."

It's a calculated risk, an investment in a future I'm clawing toward with everything I have. Each time I play this game, the stakes mount higher, the fall closer. But there's no room for doubt.

"Tomorrow, they'll see only what you want them to see," I say, practicing the tone of a woman who's never known the suffocating embrace of poverty—a woman who doesn't exist.

I lay the dress out, then turn to the mirror, studying my reflection. The blonde hair, the curves—they're my weapons in this masquerade. I practice smiles, tilts of the head, soft laughter. A mask of allure over the steel of determination.

I can't let myself slip, can't let the sparkle in my eyes dim to reveal the dread beneath. I must be all charm, all grace. Because somewhere in that crowd is a man with pockets deep enough to lift us from this mire. And I will find him.

After hanging the dress back in my closet, I reach for my laptop and power it on. It's time to make some money.

CHAPTER 3

The Santa

I watch from the kitchen window as Ruby and her husband pull into the drive. The December chill bites at the glass, but it's nothing compared to the icy grip tightening around my heart. I see him shove her—not rough enough to draw attention, but enough for me to notice.

My fists clench, knuckles white, a familiar surge of protectiveness rising within me like bile. I stride out the front door, the cold air slapping against my face, sharpening my senses. Asphalt crunches under my polished shoes as I close the distance between us. Ruby looks up, our eyes meet—a fleeting moment of silent understanding.

"Ruby," I greet her with a nod, then turn to her husband. His smug smile grates on my nerves. With a swift motion, I grab him by the collar and slam him against the car, metal groaning under his weight.

"Listen carefully," I snarl, my voice low, lethal. "You will treat my sister with the respect she deserves."

He sneers, unaffected by my show of strength. "She's mine, Nicklas. Bought and paid for. I can do what I want with my property."

The words hit me like bullets, fueling the fire in my veins. But I hold back, maintaining an ironclad façade. I can't afford to lose control, not here, not now. "Property?" I repeat, words laced with venom. "She is a

Knight, and if you ever—" I cut myself off, releasing him with a shove. No need for empty threats; he knows what I'm capable of.

"You okay?" I ask Ruby, ensuring my tone is even, controlled.

"Fine, Nick," she replies, her voice doesn't tremble, but her eyes betray her, reflecting a storm of emotions. They're glassy with unshed tears, and she sniffles softly. But then, right in front of me, she transforms; rolling her shoulders back and raising her chin. "Never better." The smile on her lips is fake.

"Good," I say, ignoring that we both know it's a lie. "Let's not keep Dad waiting."

As we walk inside, I feel the weight of my father's expectations bearing down on me. The need for an heir, for continuing the family legacy—it all rests on my shoulders. And yet, here I am, caught up in my sister's plight, unable to extricate her from a life she never chose.

I'm still simmering with fury when Dad joins us, his presence like a chill draft. "Is there a problem here?" he asks, eyes flickering between Ruby's practiced smile and my taut jawline.

Ruby's husband steps forward, smoothing his suit jacket. "No issue at all," he lies smoothly.

"Ruby?" Dad turns to her, eyebrows raised in expectation.

She shakes her head, her voice just a whisper. "No, Dad. Everything's fine." Her eyes dart to me, pleading silently for support I can't openly give.

I notice the tremble in her hands, the way she avoids meeting our father's gaze. The rage inside me burns hotter, but I keep it caged behind a cool exterior. This isn't the time or place. My sister needs me to be strong, not reckless.

"Let's eat," Dad commands, dismissing the tension as if it's nothing more than a wisp of smoke.

The dining room is a spectacle of wealth and power; crystal glasses catch the light with every flicker of the chandeliers above, casting prismatic colors across white linen tablecloths. Silverware gleams beside porcelain plates, each setting worthy of royalty. Servers move with silent efficiency, pouring wine and offering up platters of delicacies meant to impress.

But the opulence tastes like ash on my tongue. Jack should be here, his easy laughter and irreverence a counterpoint to the stiff formality. His absence is a gaping hole at the table, a reminder that he wasn't invited—a slight from Dad that I can't ignore.

"Jack had other commitments," Dad says nonchalantly when I bring up his absence. His voice is devoid of any warmth.

"Convenient," I mutter under my breath, and for the second time tonight, I ignore an obvious lie. My brother is only busy because I made sure of it, not wanting him to feel left out. Huh, so I suppose it's not a lie after all.

Dad rises from his place at the head of the long mahogany table. He clears his throat, commanding silence with an ease that speaks of decades ruling our entire family. The crystal chandelier above casts a warm glow over the dining room, rich with the scent of roasted meats and spiced wine.

"Today," Dad begins, his voice reverberating off the gilt-edged walls, "marks the day we lost my beloved Sienna, a woman of grace and strength."

I glance at Ruby across the table, her green eyes dim with unshed tears. She's trying to maintain composure under the weight of his gaze. It's December first—her birthday, and the anniversary of our mom's death. A cruel twist of fate that has never been allowed to go unnoticed or unmentioned.

"Her passing, giving birth to our youngest," he continues, an edge of steel in his tone, "was a sacrifice for this family." His words are a dagger disguised as a memorial. I know it's meant to remind us all of Ruby's debt—a life for a life.

"Here's to Sienna, whose legacy we uphold every day." Glasses rise around the room, but the toast feels hollow, laced with the subtle accusation that always simmers beneath the surface on this day.

"Happy birthday, Ruby," I murmur when the clinking of crystal ceases, just loud enough for her ears only. Her lips twitch into a fleeting, grateful smile before resuming their flat line.

Dad sits back down, gesturing for the servers to refill our glasses and bring more food. As courses come and go, I play my part, nodding along to conversations about influence and power, exchanging pleasantries that mask the turmoil beneath.

With every bite and sip, I feel the walls closing in, the expectations suffocating. Yet outwardly, I am calm—commanding even—as I navigate through the intricacies of our family's politics. It's a game of chess where the pieces are made of flesh and bone, and I'm a grandmaster playing for the highest stakes.

"Nicklas," Dad's voice slices through the post-toast murmur, "the matter of your heir. We need assurance that the future of the Knight family is secure." His eyes, sharp and assessing, fix on me.

"Everything is in place," I say, my voice a low drawl of confidence I don't feel. "The right measures have been taken. There will be an heir." My heart hammers against my ribcage, betraying the calm façade I present.

"Good, good," he nods, seemingly placated, yet I can tell he senses the edges of my fabrication. "We trust you won't delay."

Under the table, my fist clenches tight, nails digging into my palm. The heir situation isn't remotely 'under control', but admitting that would mean showing weakness—an impermissible act in our world. And so, I weave the narrative they expect to hear, a tapestry of lies that must hold strong under scrutiny.

"Timing," I add, "is everything. And the timing will be perfect." I punctuate the sentence with a sip of scotch, letting the burn in my throat anchor me to the lie.

"Very well," he says, turning back to his plate, his attention moving on as if discussing nothing more significant than a business transaction.

But then, in our family, heirs are just that—transactions. And I am the broker in a deal where the currency is blood and legacy.

The crystal chime of fine china sings a melancholic tune as the last course of our somber feast is served. Every bite of dessert feels like ash in my mouth, the sweetness a stark contrast to the bitterness that swells within me. I keep my eyes trained on the flickering candlelight, counting the seconds, waiting for this night to be over.

Dad and Michael, Ruby's husband, are in the middle of a stock trade debate when the dining room doors crash open. Jack strides in, his chest heaving, face flushed from sprinting. The room snaps to attention, the air suddenly thick with tension.

"Nicklas, there's a situation." Jack's voice is urgent, a sharp edge to his usually relaxed tone.

I stand abruptly, the chair scraping against the polished floor. A cold rush floods my veins, sharpening every sense. I see Ruby flinch at the commotion, her eyes wide and fearful.

"Talk to me," I demand, practically dragging my brother into another room.

"Someone's been siphoning funds—large amounts, undetected until now. We've got a mole."

"Damn it." I taste acid at the back of my throat. In our world, a mole doesn't just mean stolen money; it's a direct threat to our dominion, an insult that demands retribution. "Where's the breach?" I ask, already mentally cataloging potential weak points in our operation.

"East docks account. It's bad, Nick. We need to handle this now."

Wanting to spare Jack from having to look at our dad more than what's absolutely necessary, I tell him to go wait in the car. Then I return to the others. "Dinner is over, I've got to go," I announce.

"Nicklas, your brother can—" my father begins, but I cut him off with a raised hand.

"Business before pleasure, Dad. You taught me that," I say, a shadow of irony in my voice. We both know tonight was never about pleasure.

Without waiting for a response, I stalk out of the room, joining my brother in the car. As we head for the garage, the chill New York night air bites at my skin, but it's nothing compared to the fire burning within me.

"How did you catch him?" I ask my brother.

He chuckles darkly. "After going through the accounts, I noticed a small amount disappearing around the third Wednesday of every month. The offshore account it went into is owned by one of our shell corporations—"

"You've got to be fucking kidding me." Who in the hell would dare not just to steal from us, but to be that reckless and downright stupid?

Jack shakes his head. "That's the thing... I don't think who I caught is the real thief. I think it's a fall guy."

I mull over his words for a few moments, and the more I do, the more feasible it sounds.

This betrayal—it's personal. An attack on the Knights, on the empire my mom died for exactly twenty-eight years ago, on everything I've sworn to uphold and expand. It's fucking insulting just how personal it is.

The city speeds by in a blur of lights and shadows, but I barely register it. My focus narrows to the task ahead. "Who do you think the puppeteer is?" I grind out, every muscle tensed with lethal intent.

"Could be anyone from the Russians to the Italians. Hell, it might even be someone in our inner circle," Jack replies, his voice steady but grim. "But whoever it is, they've got connections. This isn't small-time thievery."

"Connections that could hurt us." It's not a question. The thought of vulnerability in my empire makes my blood boil, a dangerous heat simmering just under my skin. "I'll contact the three. Get them to use their contacts."

The three... well, it's not their official title or anything. They're just the three biggest crime lords who answer to me; Dominic, Lee, and Sergei, three men that have earned my trust and loyalty.

"Yeah, good idea." Jack pauses, then adds, "We need to send a message, Nick. No one betrays the Knights and lives to tell the tale."

"Damn straight." I agree, a cold resolve settling over me like armor. My mind races through the inventory logs, financial reports, faces of every single person who's ever pledged loyalty to me. A traitor lurks among them, and tonight, they will learn what it means to cross me.

"Do you think it could be—"

I hold up my hand, silencing Jack before he can finish that sentence. "It's not Sergei, Lee, or Dominic. Anyone but any of those three."

Letting it go, Jack checks the rearview mirror for tails. "East docks are coming up."

"Slow down when we turn the corner. I want a silent approach. Make sure your piece is ready." My own gun feels heavy against my hip, by now, it's like an extension of myself. One I never go anywhere without, not even to dinner at my dad's house.

"Always is." Jack taps the holster under his jacket, the subtle click of the safety a dark promise.

"Remember, we get in, we find the mole, and we make an example. No hesitation." The steely tone of my voice reflects the iron in my will. There can be no weakness, not with so much at stake.

"Understood," Jack confirms, his readiness palpable in the confined space of the car.

I take a deep breath, letting the icy air sharpen my senses, the adrenaline coursing through my veins. As we near the docks, the scent of saltwater and diesel fuel assaults my nostrils, a pungent reminder of the dirty work that awaits.

"Cut the lights," I command as we slip into the cloak of darkness that shrouds the docks. Jack obeys without a word, and we glide forward like predators stalking prey.

"Let's park here, out of sight." I point to a shadowed alcove between two warehouses, the perfect spot for our ambush.

Jack maneuvers the car with practiced ease, killing the engine as we settle into position.

"Check your gear. Once we step out of this car, there's no turning back." I pat down my own kit, ensuring everything is in place—the knives, the gun, the cuffs. Tools of persuasion for convincing a rat to sing.

"Ready." Jack's response is curt, mirroring my own unyielding determination.

I nod curtly, opening the door to step out into the night. Every cell in my body vibrates with the need for retribution, for control, for the absolute certainty that after tonight, the name Knight will be synonymous with untouchable.

Together we advance into the darkness, toward the reckoning that awaits. Jack at my flank, silent as death. The icy wind off the harbor is biting, carrying with it the stench of decay and old secrets. We approach the dilapidated storage unit where our mole—a traitor to the family—waits bound and gagged.

Even if the guy proves to be nothing more than a dupe, he'll pay the ultimate price tonight.

"Nick, remember we need him talking," Jack mutters, his voice barely a whisper against the howling wind.

"Talking's the easy part." My lips pull back in a grim smile. Making him survive what comes after—that's the tricky piece.

We reach the door, and I push it open with a measured force. Inside, dull light flickers from a swinging bulb, casting eerie shadows on the walls. The mole, a once-trusted lieutenant named George, squirms on a metal chair, duct tape criss-crossing his mouth, wrists secured behind his back.

My heart thrums, a rhythmic drumroll to the impending violence. I step forward, yanking off the tape, and his pleas spill out, desperate and garbled.

"Please, Nicklas, I didn't—"

"Save it for someone who gives a damn," I snap, cutting him off. My hands are steady as I select a knife from my kit, its blade gleaming ominously. "Who else is involved?" I demand, pressing the cold steel against his throat just enough to see a bead of blood.

"Nobody, I swear," he gasps, but the tremor in his voice betrays his lie.

"Wrong answer." I press harder, letting the fear seep into his bones. It's all about control—making him realize that every breath is a privilege, granted by me.

"Okay! Okay!" His eyes bulge, wild with panic. "There are others… but I don't know names. They contacted me anonymously."

I scoff, not for one second believing that the fucking rat doesn't know more than that. Realizing he needs further convincing, I cut his shirt from his torso before slamming the knife into his shoulder, taking a sick enjoyment in his pained howls and cries.

"Is that all you know?" I ask as I pull the knife out, slowly so he feels every inch.

His breathing is ragged, and despite the freezing cold, sweat beads on his forehead. "Meetings… they happened at night, always in different locations. Encrypted messages," he rushes out.

I pat his cheek condescendingly. "See, that wasn't so hard, was it?"

"How many?" Jack asks from behind me.

"I-I—"

Sensing that George is about to lie again, I interrupt him. "Don't lie to my brother," I sneer. "Just because I have other places to be tonight, doesn't mean I won't keep you alive until I have more time to make you regret ever crossing me."

"Please!" he screams, his eyes wild. "I… I don't know anything—"

"Do you know the locations?" Jack cuts in. The way George averts his gaze is very telling. "Give them to me."

"An old bar, The Filthy Oar. A parking garage on West End…" George continues, voice faltering.

Jack's fingers fly over a tablet, noting everything down with ruthless efficiency.

I'm pretty sure George has told us everything he knows, so I mumble, "Good boy." I hesitate long enough to see hope bloom on his face, and then I slam the knife into his stomach, slicing downwards so his guts spill out on the floor.

"Was that really necessary?" Jack asks dryly. "Now we need cleanup."

I shrug, "We're going to need that, regardless. Just email them so we can leave."

"Already on it, brother." Jack's response is clipped, filled with the same urgency coursing through my veins.

We exit into the night, the air thick with the promise of a storm brewing. I can feel the weight of the family name on my shoulders, a mantle forged in blood and secrecy. Jack's busy typing on the tablet as we head back to the car.

As we slide into the seats, the engine roars to life, mirroring the turmoil inside me. The docks fade behind us, but the darkness lingers, whispering of treachery yet to be uncovered.

"Next steps?" Jack asks.

"We hunt every last one of these rats down," I snarl.

CHAPTER 4

The Breeder

The pulsing beat of the club's music vibrates through my heels, up my legs, as I weave through the crowd. Each step is confident, a calculated sway designed to draw gazes. My dress clings to every curve—a shimmering second skin that I'll return by tomorrow's light, its price tag a hidden whisper against my thigh.

I scan the room, hunting. Not for pleasure—no, this is pure strategy. I need someone with deep pockets, a man who can't resist a damsel dressed in glitter and false promises. At the bar, I see exactly the kind of man I'm looking for. He's got that look, all sharp suit and sharper eyes. Money. His ring finger is naked, and he's alone.

"Is this seat taken?" I ask, my voice dipped in honey. I place my clutch on the bar, making it clear I'm here to stay.

His gaze travels up from my stilettos, slow and appreciative. "It is now," he says, a corner of his mouth ticking up.

"Thanks." I ease onto the stool beside him, crossing my legs. The slit in my dress parts, a deliberate tease. "What's a guy like you doing all alone on a night like this?"

"Looking for trouble," he smirks, turning to face me fully.

"Careful," I tilt my head, "Trouble has a way of finding you first."

"Then I must be lucky tonight." His eyes hold mine, a challenge flickering within. But he doesn't know I'm playing a different game.

"Maybe we both are," I respond, warmth spreading through my body—not from the drink he slides my way, but from the play. This is it, the dance I know so well.

"Tell me," he leans in, close enough that I catch the scent of his cologne, "what's your name?"

"Carolina," I say, letting the name roll off my tongue like a secret. "And you?"

"Does it matter?" he counters, and there's amusement in his voice.

"Only if you want me to scream it later," I quip, and his laugh is a low rumble that suggests he might just take me up on that offer. My eyes stray to my black clutch. There are three condoms in it, and I've poked holes through the foil of each one. Yeah, I'm that desperate to land a rich man.

I touch his hand, an accidental-on-purpose brush that sends a clear signal. He leans closer. "Tell me, Carolina, do you believe in Christmas miracles?" he asks, eyebrow cocked.

"Only the kind that comes wrapped in greenbacks," I reply, all brash honesty cloaked in flirtation. Because beneath the glamor, the desperation claws—I need this, for Willow, for me.

"Then let's see if I can't make a believer out of you," he says, and I can feel the night shift, the stakes raising with each breath.

"Try me," I challenge, because I've got nothing left to lose. And tonight, maybe, just maybe, I'll win something worth keeping.

After a few martinis, we move over to one of the couches. No longer limited by the awkwardness of sitting at the bar, I rest my hand on his thigh and run it up and down—close enough to his member to know he isn't indifferent to my advances.

"You're really something," the guy rasps, wrapping his long fingers around my wrist and pulling my hand onto his hardness. "Are you just teasing me, Carolina?"

Tilting my head to the side, I flutter my lashes. "The only teasing I do involves expensive lingerie," I purr.

He looks at me through hooded eyes, and just as I think he's going to finally kiss me, he leans back, putting more distance between us. "Is that so?" he questions.

I swallow the sigh threatening to spill free. But seriously, how long must we play this game? We should already be at his... wherever he lives. "It is," I rasp.

He nods to himself, seemingly lost in thought for a moment. Then he stands abruptly. "I need to take a piss." My nose scrunches in distaste at his crudeness. "But if you're still here when I come back, I'd love to take you home and find out what kind of lingerie you're wearing."

I nod eagerly as I watch him walk away. Even smiling sweetly when he turns around to check if I'm still waiting on the couch. Ah, now I get it. This guy thinks I'm going to make a run for it. Maybe he's been burned in the past, but I'm not going to do that. He's exactly the type I'm looking for, and I intend to take full advantage of him tonight.

While he's gone, I pull my phone out of my clutch. My thumb hovers over the glowing screen, the pulsing beat of the club fading into the back of my mind. I type quickly, words to Willow.

> *Me: I love you, sis. I promise I'll visit again soon *pink love heart**

The message sends, and for a moment, my heart stills. She's the reason I'm here—the reason I do anything. My sweet sister is everything I no longer believe in. She's kind, gentle, and she's just... she's one of those people that just continues smiling no matter what life throws at them.

When the guy returns, he does a double-take, his eyes widening as though he can't believe I'm still here. Well, believe it mister.

"Are you ready to show me your lingerie?" he asks as he sits back down. He grins in an obnoxious way that makes it clear he thinks he's being cute.

"Are you ready to earn the privilege?" I volley. If I'm reading him right, I can't be too eager. Leaning closer, I move my hand up his inner thigh, purposefully stopping just before I reach his crotch. "Or is that too *hard?*"

He swallows thickly and cants his hips so his erection grazes my hand. "It's definitely hard, alright."

"So what are we waiting for?" I purr.

My words seem to break the control he has on himself, because he shoots out of his seat, dragging me with him. I almost stumble on my heels in my attempt at keeping up with him as we weave our way toward the exit.

After getting our coats, we step outside. The frigid air slaps my cheeks, painting them with a rosy hue that belies the darkness churning inside me. I glance up at the night sky, searching for stars but finding only the void. It's fitting, somehow.

We stay outside the club for almost half an hour, long enough for my hands to start shaking. As we wait for cabs to drive by, more and more people join us, making it clear this is going to turn into a bloodbath.

As though he's reading my thoughts, my date says, "I don't live that far. Do you mind if we walk?"

I shake my head and give him a blinding smile as I let him lead me through the mostly empty streets.

The city's pulse fades behind us, replaced by the eerie quiet of streets less traveled. He's navigating with a confidence that doesn't match the knot of apprehension tightening in my gut. "Are you sure this is the right way?" My voice is steady, betraying none of the anxiety that claws at me.

"Shortcut," he grins. "Trust me."

I don't. But I nod, feigning ease. He doesn't look like a psycho, but I still slide my free hand into my purse, palming the pepper spray in case I need it.

The buildings here are cloaked in shadows, their stories untold and uninviting. We turn another corner. "Almost there," he promises, but the darkness seems to swallow his words.

Then, they're there—two figures looming out of the night like omens. They stand beneath a flickering streetlight, dressed as Santa Claus, their beards unnaturally white against the backdrop of the urban wasteland. But these aren't the jolly old elves of childhood tales; their eyes are cold, their stances predatory.

"Shit," I whisper, my breath fogging into the air. He follows my gaze, the atmosphere charged with sudden tension.

"Who—" he begins, but the Santas move.

One steps forward, reaching into the depths of his red coat, and my blood runs ice-cold with anticipation. Fear seizes me, a merciless grip that tightens around my throat. The festive costumes are a grotesque mockery, and my instincts scream that these men are harbingers of violence.

"Let's go!" I hiss, panic giving my voice an unfamiliar edge. But it's too late—the false cheer of their apparel can't mask the danger, and I know, I just know, we've stumbled into a nightmare before Christmas.

The tallest Santa's hand emerges, not with a candy cane or a toy, but with the cold glint of a gun. My body freezes, a deer in headlights, as he levels it at a man kneeling on the pavement. The other Santa looms over him, a judge passing down a sentence.

"Please…" the kneeling man's voice is a choked sob.

That's when it happens; my date's hand leaves mine abruptly. "Fuck this," he rushes out. I don't know why I'm surprised when he takes off, but I am.

Although every cell in my body urges me to flee with him, my legs betray me, refusing to move, shackled by the visceral terror gripping me.

My heart pounds out a frantic rhythm, a discordant drumbeat urging me to flee. But my body doesn't obey; it's as if my feet have grown roots into the ground, anchoring me to this nightmare.

Panic claws at my throat, sharp and desperate.

What the hell do I do?

What can I do?

Shit, if only my legs were working…

I'm about to die here in this filthy alley, I just know it. Although I can't see the Santas' faces, I can see their eyes. As I look from one to the other, I almost wish I couldn't. The dark orbs are empty, not a modicum of sympathy to be found.

I really am about to die here.

CHAPTER 5

The Santa

The chill of the December night doesn't bother me. Not when there's work to be done. I adjust the faux beard, a ridiculous accessory but necessary. Jack stands beside me, his own Santa accessories equally ludicrous on his towering frame, both of us hidden in plain sight. We're not wearing this shit to spread holiday cheer, but to make sure no one sees our faces.

Jack chuckles, a low rumble in his throat. "Should've brought some elves for the full effect."

I scoff, focusing on the task at hand. The thief thought he could steal from the Knight family and live to tell the tale. He was wrong.

This is the last accomplice to the rat we killed in the warehouse earlier tonight, and he is about to learn the same lesson. The pathetic, backstabbing fucker is shaking like a leaf. He pleads, sobs, but his fate is sealed. My gut clenches with a dark satisfaction. Fear is a tool, and I wield it expertly.

"Please… I didn't know who the money belonged to. You have to believe me," he whimpers.

"An excuse as thin as the ice you're skating on," I retort, my voice cold enough to freeze hell over. I can almost taste his dread. It fuels me.

"Let's wrap it up. I've got places to be," Jack says, impatience seeping through his usually laid-back tone.

"Patience, brother." I step closer to the sniveling man, reveling in the power I hold over life and death. "Let's ensure he understands the consequences of crossing us."

"Understood, understood! Please…" His words dissolve into another round of useless begging.

"Silence!" My command echoes off the brick walls encasing us. The man's mouth snaps shut, his body quivering. "Your cooperation now is meaningless. You've already chosen your side."

"God, please—"

"God can't help you here," I laugh.

The alleyway reeks of fear, a stench that's almost sweet to my senses. "Please," he tries again, looking up at me with eyes wide like a deer caught in headlights. Pathetic.

"Please?" I echo, my tone dripping with mock sympathy. Turning to my brother, I ask, "Do you think he deserves mercy?"

Jack chuckles, the sound deep and menacing. "After making us waste time having to track him down? I don't fucking think so."

Something about Jack's words sparks something in my mind. This hasn't been a waste of time. Hell, it hasn't even been drawn out. I absentmindedly scratch my cheek under the beard.

"What's up?" Jack asks, almost like he can sense my brain working hard to piece shit together.

The thing is, I'm not sure there's anything off. Right now, it's only a feeling… fuck, barely. It's half a feeling if anything. It just seems too… easy.

First the thief led us to one accomplice, and he neatly led us to the next one. Neither of the men we've hunted down needed much prompting, and the person they gave up was exactly where described. Fuck, not just that. They were… alone and defenseless.

Surely, it can't be this easy.

Shaking my head, I refocus on the man in front of me. "Any last words, then?" I ask, the cold metal of my gun pressing against the guy's temple. He sputters, begging, but it's all white noise. "Last chance to stand up and die like a man instead of on your knees like the filth you are." My words are cruel, but I don't have any sympathy for disloyal bottom feeders. Especially not those who run and kneel, too weak to face the consequences of their actions like a man.

A single gunshot shatters the silence. His body slumps, lifeless.

"Fuck's sake," Jack gripes. "Couldn't you have shot him anywhere but the head? Cleanup won't be happy about the mess." My brother's upper lip curls in distaste as he eyes the blood, fractured skull, and brain matter.

"Let them—"

I'm interrupted by a scream; a sharp, piercing guttural sound that cuts through the aftermath. My head snaps in its direction.

"Shit, who—" Jack starts, already moving toward the source.

Whipping around, I spot her—a woman, her eyes wide with terror. She's beautiful, even in fear. Blonde hair tumbling in disarray, curves hugged by her thin dress despite the December's chill. Hmm, she must have been in one of the clubs nearby. Her chest heaves with rapid breaths, her blue eyes wide and fixed on the fresh corpse.

"Mine," I growl, claiming the right to handle the unexpected complication myself. Without taking my eyes off her, I advance, each step measured, predatory. Her terror is palpable, and something within me stirs, a primal urge I haven't felt in years.

"Who are you?" she demands, trying to mask her fear with bravado.

I let out a dark chuckle. "Wrong question, Kitten," I reply, stepping closer, watching as she instinctively retreats. "You should be asking what I'm going to do with you now."

"Please, I won't say anything, I swear!" she cries out as I close the distance between us.

"I know you won't," I smirk.

My hand snaps out, fast as a whip, encircling her delicate throat. She gasps and drops her clutch as my grip tightens just enough to show her I'm in control, that her air depends on my whim. Her pulse beats wildly under my fingers, a trapped bird frantic to escape. She flails against me, all nails and spitfire.

A kick lands on my shin, surprisingly strong. It draws a chuckle from deep within me. Impressive. Most crumble in fear; she fights like a hellcat, and damn if it doesn't turn me on. No, it's more than that. Her survival instinct is strong, and I'm in fucking awe.

"Feisty, aren't you?" I muse, enjoying the flare of defiance in her eyes.

"Let me go!"

Her nails scrape against my skin, and I look down to see blood pebble where she's digging her claws into me. A sinister smile tugs at my lips. Her spirit, though futile, impresses me—it's been a long time since anyone dared to defy me. Still with my hand around her throat, I push her backwards until her back hits the wall.

I ease my grip on her as her struggle slows, causing confusion to flicker across her features. She's trying to work out the angle, why I haven't snuffed her out like her alleyway companion. Good. Let her mind race. Fear mixed with curiosity—it's a potent cocktail.

"Who are you?" she asks again.

Her eyes widen as I lean so close my breath fans across her face, flexing my hand around her throat. "Your worst nightmare or your sweetest dream," I reply. "Depends on how you play your cards."

At my words, she begins to fight again, trying to break free. But nothing she does has any effect on me. "Stop fighting," I rasp, squeezing harder, her life hanging by a thread, my thread. Her eyes plead, a silent prayer for mercy that only makes me want to tighten my grasp further.

"Kill her and let's move on," Jack urges, but I'm not done with her yet.

"Quiet," I snap, my decision made in the blink of an eye. She's more than just a witness now. My heart races with possibilities as her consciousness fades, her body going limp in my arms.

"Please," she rasps, tears brimming, ready to fall. "I—I have a sister…"

I almost laugh. A sister. An anchor to this world. Leverage. "You really shouldn't have told me that," I grin. My thumb presses harder against her windpipe, not to end her life, but to make her unconscious.

Her chest heaves for air that won't come, and her eyes are losing their fire, flickering with the realization that her life rests in my hands. I can see the moment she understands—she's mine now. Her body slumps, giving in to the darkness clawing at the edges of her vision.

"Fuck, Nick, what are you doing?" Jack's voice is a distant echo.

"Trust me," is all I offer as I watch the last bit of consciousness slip from her face. I'm not usually one for gambling. But this woman, she's a bet I'm willing to make.

"Better have a damn good reason for this," Jack grumbles behind me.

"Let's move," I command, grabbing the purse she dropped before I scoop her up. Her head lolls against my arm. She's soft where I am hard, light where I am darkness.

This is no ordinary woman. She's a fighter, a survivor; the very answer to a prayer I never even made. We stride back to the car, the night air cold against my skin. Her warmth seeps into me. I place her gently on the backseat, tugging her purse under her arm.

"Got the cleanup crew on the line," Jack mutters, phone to his ear.

"Good." My response is terse, my focus on the unconscious woman behind me. Her blonde hair fans out across the seat, a halo of innocence in a world that's anything but. "Make sure they get everything."

Jack climbs into the car, and as soon as the door is shut and we're moving, he turns to me. "Who is she, Nick?" Jack asks, eyeing the woman with a mix of curiosity and caution.

"The future," I reply, my mind already racing through plans and possibilities.

The drive to Jack's place is tense, his confusion clear as day. He wants answers, but I'm not ready to share my thoughts. Not until I know exactly how this intriguing stranger fits into my world—the world where I reign supreme, where everyone bends to my will. Except for her. Not yet.

"Care to explain now?" Jack probes once more as he exits the car at his house.

"Later," I reply curtly, my mind already racing ahead.

Driving back to my home, I spend more time checking on her in the rearview mirror than looking at the damn road ahead of me. Luckily, she remains unconscious, not even stirring when I carry her through the front door. Without hesitating, I bring her to my bedroom, laying her down on my bed.

I stand over her, this woman who has potential to be both a pawn and a prize in my twisted game. My eyes trace the soft rise and fall of her chest as she sleeps, oblivious to the storm about to break over her head. The vulnerability in her relaxed features belies the spitfire I've glimpsed—a flame I'm eager to stoke.

Minutes tick by as I stand there watching her. Watching the rise and fall of her tits with each breath, her shapely legs where the dress has ridden up. She's lost one of her shoes somewhere, and one of the straps on her dress is torn.

I lick my lips, my breathing turning ragged as I sit down next to her. I place my hand on her chest, feeling the steady beat of her heart. My dick stirs as I trace my fingers across her breast, finding her nipple easily enough.

Hmm, I need to see her without her clothes on. I never go into business without knowing all the facts, and tonight won't be any different. I do my best not to disturb her as I slide the strap off her shoulder, moving so I can pull the dress down her body, revealing her sexy, black lingerie.

Her curves flow seamlessly from her full, rounded breasts to her slender waist, and back out to her hips. Childbearing hips. I grin at the thought. I suppress a groan as I notice one nipple peeking out through the cup in her strapless bra. Little minx was dressed to impress, and, yeah, I'm fucking impressed.

Needing to see all of her, I roll her to the side and unclasp her bra. No longer caring about disturbing her, I roughly pull the bra off her. Her lush tits fall free. "Damn," I growl, my cock throbbing in my suit pants.

I can't resist palming, kneading the heavy flesh. If—no, *when*—I have my way, these will look so good swelling with milk. Her breathing intensifies, sounding haggard, and it's making me smirk. Does she know I'm touching her? Judging by her beaded nipples, she likes my touch.

Standing, I push her back onto her back and hook my thumbs into the delicate lace of her thong. I slide the scrap of fabric down her legs, cupping her calves so I can push her legs apart. As the apex of her thighs is no longer hidden, I see she's completely bare. Her pink folds beckon to me, and I run a finger through them. Fuck, she's wet.

"I wonder how you taste," I muse out loud, my voice husky with want.

Sinking down to the floor, I pull her to the edge so I can sample her. My mouth waters as I pull the faux beard down before darting my tongue out, teasing her clit. Then I continue downwards until I find her wet entrance. Her taste hits me like a freight train of the best kind. I can't resist lapping at her hole, licking up her arousal while I use my free hand to rub myself through my suit pants.

Just as I'm about to come, I stop. Not because my morals tell me to, fuck that. I'm not a good guy. I stop because I still have more research to do. Now that I know her body is up to snuff, I can move ahead to the next phase.

I get up from the floor and pull her further up the bed so her head is resting on my pillow. Then I go to get one of my button-up shirts and put it on her. It's a shame it hides her delicious body, but I'll see her naked again soon enough.

As I pick up her discarded clothes from the floor, I notice the tag is still on her dress and underwear. Interesting.

Pulling my phone out, I call Marco, the head of my security. After we took care of the thief and most of his associates, I ordered my team back here, knowing Jack and I could easily take care of the last one. Just as I'm about to get annoyed Marco isn't picking up, there's a knock on my bedroom door. I turn around to find him standing there.

"Sir?" he questions. His lips twist into a wry smile as he eyes the purse in my hand. "Black suits you. Maybe I can borrow that on my next night out."

Chuckling, I point at the sleeping woman. "Keep watch," I command. His answering nod is stiff, military. "No one touches her. And I need you to get me the moment she wakes up."

To his credit, Marco doesn't ask any questions. "Understood boss." His voice is a low rumble.

Her blonde hair fans out on the pillow, making her look like an angel, but I know better. Angels don't survive in my world—they get devoured.

And yet, I find myself wanting to use, maybe even protect, this one.

"If anything happens to her, you answer to me." My tone leaves no room for doubt.

"Of course."

Without a word, I clasp his arm before leaving my bedroom, trusting Marco to keep the woman contained and safe while I do some background checks.

Alone in my office, I empty her purse—or clutch; I think that's what Ruby calls these things—onto my desk. Various items fall out; her phone, some makeup, a compact mirror, and three fucking condoms. I pick the foil wrapper up, studying it in the light. At first I don't see anything, but as I look closer, I notice small holes. A grin spreads across my face as I confirm all three condoms are damaged.

When no ID falls out, I look inside. There's a small zipper in the lining, and as I unzip it, I see her driver's license tucked away in there. Carolina Sterling. The name rolls off my tongue as I say it out loud.

Using the software we use to run background checks on everyone we come into contact with, I rapidly type Carolina's name in the search bar. Information flows across the screen. She's twenty-six years old and lives alone. Her financials are a disaster, last-ditch efforts written between the lines.

Hmm, considering that her Cam Girl site, one owned by my family, seems to be a big hit, that makes no sense. I allow myself to get distracted long enough to see everything she's doing online. It seems she's not only uploading pre-recorded videos of herself in the shower and getting dressed, but she's also taking custom requests. None of the content is overly sexual, more teasing.

Entering the website with my owner credentials, I look through all the info that isn't available to the public. Carolina's contact information, previous auctions she's done for her used underwear and even a date. The money she's earned from this isn't insignificant, so why the hell is she living in one of the worst neighborhoods?

As I dig deeper, I find the reason for her lack of money. She has a monthly expense to a home for the disabled, and it seems her sister, Willow Sterling, twenty years old, lives there. I scoff in distaste. What kind of person doesn't even personally care for their family?

Then again, a woman who keeps her tags on her clothes and pokes holes in condoms doesn't have much of a conscience. Something doesn't sit right with me about that. When Carolina mentioned her sister, she sounded desperate, and not just to save her life. There was more to it, like she was fighting for her sister rather than using her as a bid to gain her freedom.

I lean back, considering the woman unconscious in my bed. She's desperate, willing to do anything for her sister. That's something I can use.

Continuing my search, I find that Carolina's dad, Shaun Sterling, died in the same hit-and-run that left Willow disabled. Their mom, Luna, died not too long ago from an overdose, it looks like Carolina and Willow are each other's everything, which is perfect.

Carolina's got fire, I saw it in her fight. It amuses me, impresses me. And those curves, that blonde hair—it's all a bonus. I need an heir, desperately, and she's looking for financial security.

Two birds, one stone. There's a tightness in my chest that wasn't there before, an anticipation of what's coming.

My lips curl into a half-smile at the thought. I know she'll put up one hell of a fight. I can already imagine the fire in those blue eyes when she wakes up here, in my home. The way she'll arch under my touch, defiant even as she succumbs to the inevitable.

I'm Nicklas Knight. I get what I want, and I want this hellcat to carry my heir.

CHAPTER 6

The Breeder

My eyes snap open, and my heart slams against my chest with the force of a runaway train. I'm not in my cramped studio, nor am I curled up on the crumb-infested sofa that doubles as my bed more often than not. No, this is some sort of... palace?

Opulence drips from every corner of the room—the kind you see in those period dramas Willow loves to devour, her wide eyes reflecting the light of impossible dreams. Silk sheets caress my skin, cool and smooth like the quiet whisper of a promise. Plush pillows cradle my head, but their softness feels like a mockery when I tug at my wrists and find them bound to the bed's ornate posts.

I twist as much as possible, managing to lower the sheet covering me. As I look down at my body, I kind of wish I hadn't bothered because I'm no longer wearing yesterday's dress. I'm wearing a man's button-up shirt. Anger and humiliation flare within me at the thought of someone undressing and dressing me while I wasn't conscious.

"What the hell?" My voice is a snarl that echoes off the high walls. The furniture around me is straight out of a fairytale—a wardrobe that could house a thousand gowns, a vanity with a mirror so large it could reflect all of my failures.

I strain against the restraints, my body twisting, seeking freedom. The silk rope bites into my skin, a reminder of the direness of my situation. I can't afford to be here—literally. This isn't part of the plan. The plan is to find a rich husband, someone who'll look past my façade and shower Willow and me with security, not... whatever twisted scenario this is.

My mind races back to the night before, the lavish club where I'd hoped to snag a wealthy bachelor with my tight dress and practiced smile. But now? Now I'm caught in a web, and I don't even know where the spider is.

My breath comes in shallow gasps as I take in the sheer size of the room again, the height of the ceiling that makes me feel small and insignificant. Despite the roaring fireplace, I feel cold, and a shiver runs down my spine.

"You're finally awake."

His voice cuts through the silence, low and commanding, startling me. Even without seeing him, I know he's one of the men from last night, and with my luck—or lack thereof—he's probably the one I watched shoot someone in cold blood.

I can feel his presence loom closer, though I refuse to show the fear clawing at my insides. Instead, I lift my chin defiantly, meeting the shadowed gaze of the man still wearing the Santa hat and beard.

"I need the bathroom," I whine as I twist like a contortionist on the bed.

Unable to look away, I follow him with my eyes as he moves over to me and undoes the restraints. Before I can thank him, he fists my hair, pulling me up so I'm seated. "Don't try anything," he warns, his tone low and menacing.

"I won't," I whimper as he intensifies his brutal hold on my hair.

"Good," he clips. Then he roughly pulls me to my feet, shoving me toward the adjoining bathroom.

When I try to close the door, he laughs darkly and shakes his head. "You're not going to watch me pee," I hiss, crossing my arms over my chest. Shit, even my bra is gone. What did this man do to me while I was sleeping? No, wait... I wasn't sleeping. He fucking choked me until I became unconscious. Thoughts of me trying to fight him off come rushing back, almost overriding my need to pee. Almost.

He rolls his eyes. "I'm not going to leave you alone, Hellcat. Either you pee with the door open, or you can piss yourself."

The pressure on my bladder intensifies, and I can see he's not going to budge. Bowing my head in shame, I walk over to the toilet and sit down. Hiding my face in my hair, I peek at him. At least he has the decency to look away while I do my business.

As soon as I'm done, I wash my hands and splash some cold water on my face. I avert my gaze from the mirror, not wanting to know what I look like. Superficial as it is, I can't feel good or strong if I don't look the part. And right now, I know I have to be looking like a mess.

Once I switch off the water and dry my hands on a towel that's so soft I want to run it across my skin, the guy grabs my arm and forces me back to the bed. This time, he doesn't bother to tie me up.

"Are you going to let me go?" I ask, hopeful.

"Shh. We have much to discuss, Carolina," he coos, and I flinch at the way he casually uses my name, a perverse intimacy in a situation devoid of any warmth.

I want to ask him how he knows my name, but the stubborn part of me refuses to acknowledge that. The room is silent except for the crackling of the fireplace, the flickering flames casting dancing shadows across the walls. I should be screaming, fighting tooth and nail, but instead, I'm eerily calm, survival instincts kicking in. I need to be smart about this.

"Like what?" I ask, trying to sound indifferent.

The man rubs the back of his neck. "Like your finances," he says. He paces at the foot of the bed, his presence large and threatening even while wearing the ridiculous Santa hat and beard.

"There's not much to talk about," I admit scornfully.

He chuckles. "New York is expensive, isn't it, Carolina?" He pauses, his tone laced with mockery. "Especially when you're paying for your sister's facility."

I freeze, every muscle tensing. How does he know about my desperation? The money for Willow's care? The air thickens around me.

choking me. I'm an open book to him; my carefully crafted façade crumbles. "What do you want?" I croak.

Rather than answering me, he stops moving, studying me like he's committing every movement I make to memory. "You need money," he says. "And I need an heir."

What the actual hell? Surely this man can't be for real. "An heir?" I echo. "You want to… to… breed me like a bitch in heat?"

The man throws his head back and laughs loudly. "That's not how I was going to phrase it, Hellcat. But sure."

Hating that he knows all these things about me while I know nothing about him, I ask, "Who are you? What's your name?"

A knock sounds, and the man opens the door. A smartly dressed woman walks in with a tray in her hands. "Where do you want the food, sir?" she asks.

He points at the foot of the bed. "There's fine."

She nods curtly, and places the tray on the mattress. My stomach lets out an embarrassingly loud growl as the scents of food hit my nostrils. Oh my God, it smells delicious.

"Hungry?" he asks sardonically as soon as the woman's gone again.

I nod eagerly, watching as he moves over to a chair in the corner and pulls it to the foot of the bed. Taking his time, he makes himself comfortable, crossing one leg over the other while steepling his fingers together. "Well, what are you waiting for? Dig in."

Wasting no time, I reach for the silver dome and remove it to reveal a plate filled with freshly cut and peeled fruit, scrambled eggs, bacon, and bread. Forgetting all about manners and appearances, I pick up the silver fork and start shoveling very unladylike sized portions into my mouth, barely chewing before the next bite.

There's another knock, but I don't look up, too focused on the food. When I finally feel like my stomach isn't eating itself, I lean back, daintily wiping my mouth with the cloth napkin the cutlery was wrapped in. "Thank you," I breathe.

He chuckles. "You're very welcome. Thirsty?"

I look up at him from beneath my lashes to see him holding out a crystal glass filled with what I assume to be orange juice. "Yes," I admit, taking the glass from his outstretched hand.

Now that I'm no longer focused on basic necessities like needing the bathroom, hunger and thirst, I scramble back up the bed and lean against the headboard. My eyes flick around the room, and just as I'm about to ask why I'm really here, a thought hits me, making my blood run cold. "Y-you didn't poison the food, did you?" My voice wavers.

He lets out a booming laugh. "I can assure you that if I wanted you dead, I wouldn't poison you," he laughs, like that's meant to make me feel at ease.

"Right," I mutter, mostly to myself. "You'd shoot me in the head like the guy last night." As soon as the words are out of my mouth, I slap my hand across my lips. Shit, I shouldn't have said that.

Amusement sparkles in his dark eyes as his tattooed hand cups his chin. "I wouldn't dream of shooting someone as beautiful as you in the head," he rasps.

What the hell do I even say to that? Feeling like I can't just ignore it, I mumble, "Umm… thank you."

He waves me off with a tattooed hand, sitting straighter. "Don't mention it." When I let out a heavy sigh, he stands abruptly. "I think we've talked enough for now. You should rest."

I shouldn't feel disappointed that my captor tells me he's going to leave me alone, yet I am. Not because I want his company—good riddance—but because I don't feel as though we've done a lot of talking. I mean, I'm still not completely sure what it is he wants from me, and I hate not knowing.

Before I can tell him that I've never felt more awake, and that I want more answers, he strides into the adjoining bathroom, closing the door behind him. I grumble something sarcastic about him getting privacy in there and when I hear his chuckle, I know he heard me. Good.

It doesn't take long before he reemerges with a basket filled with items I can't see. Though I can imagine it's filled with things that can be used as a weapon, which I suspect is the reason he wouldn't let me pee in peace.

"I'll be back later. Feel free to shower and look around the bedroom, but don't walk out that door. In fact, don't touch it at all." With those words, he leaves the bedroom, locking the door behind him.

I huff out an annoyed breath. What was the point of telling me not to touch the door when he's locked it? It feels like a test, one I can't afford to fail. So no matter how much it calls to me like a beacon, I tell myself to ignore it.

Now that he's gone, I suddenly feel exhausted beyond belief. But I refuse to go back to sleep without at least cleaning my body. So I take him up on the offer to shower.

In the bathroom I find everything I need already waiting near the sink. Towels, a brand new toothbrush still in its packaging, shampoo, conditioner, and even some lotions and deodorant. Not wanting to think too much about what that means, I tear the shirt off and take what I need with me into the shower, ignoring the gigantic corner jacuzzi for now.

After I'm clean and dry, I leave the bathroom with only a towel wrapped around me since I don't have any clothes. I was just going to wrap the sheet around me, but what I find is so much better.

On the bed there's a pile of clothing waiting for me. Everything from underwear to jeans, even a very nice, deep-red negligee. With the fire still going, I don't need the sweater in the pile, so I opt for a pair of sleeping shorts and a tank top.

Once I'm dressed, I climb back into bed, hiding my head beneath the sheet. Although my mind should be exploding with thoughts, it's not. It's almost like the overload of everything has rendered me unable to think at all. Closing my eyes, I let myself drift off to sleep, knowing there's nothing else I can do to pass the time.

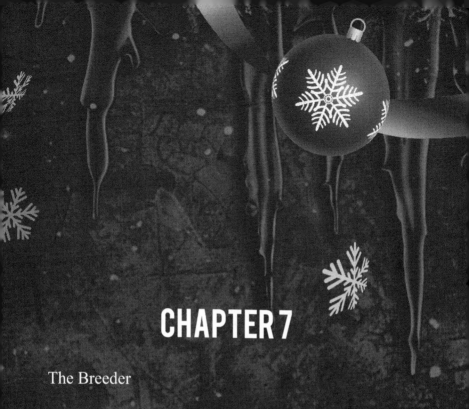

CHAPTER 7

The Breeder

Blinking awake, I feel groggy and… I don't know. Uneasy, I guess. I sit up and reach for the lamp on the bedside table, switching it on. Although I'm still alone, I feel like I'm being watched. It wouldn't even surprise me if there are cameras in here so the psycho Santa can keep an eye on me.

Scoffing at the idea, I get out of bed, needing to stretch. The way my muscles creak and protest tells me I've been sleeping for longer than I should. After freshening up in the bathroom, I walk over to the large bedroom windows and pull the curtains back.

"Wow!" I whisper, completely awestruck at the view that greets me of Central Park, blanketed in fresh snow, glowing under the city lights.

The trees are dusted in white, shimmering like jewels against the night sky. Not only is the view breathtaking, it's so… majestic. The snowy expanse of the park stretching out beneath me, making everything feel beautifully still and surreal. It's like the whole city is wrapped in a winter spell, and I can't look away.

A bitter laugh escapes my lips as I realize I've gotten what I wanted—at least partly. Assuming Santa isn't going to let me go, then, for now, I live in a prestigious area, one I've lusted after for years.

Talk about getting your wish delivered in a twisted way.

I take one last look at the winter wonderland below before turning away from the darkness. I wish I knew how long I've been here, how long I've slept the first and second time. But without any clocks in sight, there's no way to gauge the passing of time.

Sure, it's dark outside, but that hardly tells me anything this time a year. When he made his outrageous proposal, it felt like we were talking for hours, but in reality, it might only be minutes.

A sad laugh bubbles up my throat, but I swallow it down. It doesn't matter if it's been days or weeks, because the only person who'll miss me is Willow. And she's… well, she's not exactly able to throw herself into a rescue mission.

My thoughts stray to Willow as I look out of the window. I need my phone so I can text her, let her know I'm okay before she starts to worry. If it's still the weekend, she'll be busy with arts and crafts at the care home, so there's a chance she hasn't noticed my absence yet.

I whip around as the door opens, and the guy strides into the bedroom. He's carrying a tray with a bowl of something that looks like pasta, and a bottle of water.

"Do you always sleep this much?" he asks, walking over to the vanity table where he places the food.

I just shrug before asking a question of my own. "What day is it?"

"Sunday," he replies.

Shit. "I need to call my sister," I rush out, my voice high with the growing panic I feel. "She'll worry and I have to… please. I'm all she has."

"I've texted your sister," he says, gesturing at his food. "She's fine."

I pin him with my stare. "I said I need to speak with her," I all but growl.

"Eat first," he says, like that's more important than Willow. "You can talk to your sister later. You must be starving." The way he takes care of my needs is… daunting. I almost think I'd prefer if he were shouting and threatening me.

"Yeah," I confirm. "I am."

Since I believe his earlier words about not wanting to poison me, I accept the food and water without any objections.

While I eat, I pretend not to notice the way he's studying me. But I can feel his eyes on me, burning into my skin. I hate the way my body reacts under his stare. I hope he can't see the way my nipples tighten.

"Stop watching me," I huff.

"No." That's it, that's all he says.

Scoffing, I do my best to tune him out while I finish the huge plate of food. Once I'm done, I shuffle over to the bed and sit down at the edge. "Tell me more about this deal you mentioned," I say, swirling my hand in the air in a 'go-on' motion.

He sits down in the same chair at the end of the bed he had sat in earlier. "Straight to business, huh?" His voice is dark and deliciously husky.

I nod. "Why not? It's not like I have much of a choice." Licking my lips, I let my eyes trail the length of his impressive body, the suit he's wearing isn't hiding how built he is.

When our eyes lock, he raises a brow, and I shrug. I don't care if he's seeing me checking him out. I'm caught in-between a rock and a hard place, so sue me for trying to find any redeeming qualities about this shit show that is my life.

"You want to breed me," I remind him, like he could have forgotten what he said earlier. "Tell me what it is you want from me, exactly."

"I want everything from you, Carolina," he answers, and the simplicity of it terrifies me more than any threat could.

His words echo in my head, a heavy weight that threatens to crush me. And yet, beneath the fear and the fight, there's something else—a flicker of curiosity about the man hiding beneath a bushy beard. But I push it down, lock it away.

"I'll make it easy for you to choose," he croons. "Your options are death or carrying my heir."

Although I had already worked that out for myself, hearing it said out loud so casually is an entirely different matter. The room spins, and I fight to keep my composure. Death—a word that hangs over me, a shroud waiting to fall. My mind flashes to Willow, her smile, her laughter. She's all I have left.

"Death?" My voice trembles despite my best efforts to sound defiant.

He leans closer, his head cocked as if examining prey. "Yes, that's one option." I can't read his face, but his eyes—they glimmer with a predatory glee. What sick game is this? "Choose wisely, Carolina." His voice drops to a whisper, a devil's caress. "I'm not known for my patience."

Unable to sit still any longer, I get off the bed and walk over to the fireplace. I know I shouldn't turn my back on him, but… oh, who am I kidding? This man has all the power whether I'm facing him or not.

I need a minute to process all of this, and I can't do that while looking at the fake bushy beard. Dread pools in my stomach. Death or a deal with the devil himself? My life, Willow's future, it all hangs in the balance.

Knowing he has me beat, I sigh and turn back around to face him, squaring my shoulders. "Give me the details," I demand, trying to mask the quiver in my voice with bravado. "What does giving you an heir entail?"

"Smart girl." He straightens up, nodding approvingly. "Always best to know what you're agreeing to. The devil is in the details, after all."

No, the devil is here, in this room, looking at me like he's contemplating all the ways he wants to use me.

I glare at him, my fear mingling with anger. The need to protect Willow gives me courage, or perhaps its reckless desperation. Whatever it is, I cling to it. "Just tell me already." My eyes burn into his, searching for any hint of humanity, but finding none.

The tension coils tighter, a spring ready to snap. I'm trapped, bound by circumstance, my fate intertwined with a man hidden behind a festive disguise and sinister intentions. I have to make a choice. For survival. For Willow. For the glimpse of hope that still flickers, stubborn and persistent, within me.

He stands up and walks over to where I'm standing, and I catch the scent of pine and something darker, like a snow-covered forest hiding predators. The room is silent, save for the crackling fire and my ragged breaths. His next words are ice, chilling the air between us. "Ten million dollars to bear my child." The sentence hangs heavy, a guillotine poised to sever my future from my past. "And you must conceive by Christmas."

A cold sweat drenches my skin. Ten million dollars. The sum echoes through my mind like the chime of a cursed bell, each toll weighing down on my chest. I should be repulsed, terrified at the thought of carrying the child of a man who is synonymous with danger, whose very presence sends shivers crawling up my spine.

"Think about it, Carolina." His voice slices through my spiraling thoughts, every syllable laced with power. "You wouldn't have to poke holes in condoms anymore."

My heart stammers at his knowledge, and I hate him for reminding me of my own desperation. He's observed my darkest moments, seen through the façade of the sophisticated life I've pretended to lead. It's as if he's peeling back my layers, leaving me exposed and vulnerable.

The money he offers is life changing, too much to decline on the principle of morals I don't even have. Ten million dollars would secure both mine and Willow's futures; it would be a sanctuary in a world where we have none.

It gnaws at me, this choice between swift damnation and cruel salvation.

"Is that even possible?" The question slips out before I can censor it, my mind grappling with logistics over morality.

There's a gleam in his eyes, a predator sighting its prey. "It is," he confirms.

"Christmas," I whisper, the word a mingling of dread and wonder. It's insane, impossible, and yet…

The room feels too small; the walls pressing in. My sister's face dances before my eyes, her smile the beacon guiding me through this tempest. What am I willing to sacrifice for her? My body? My soul? It's not even a question, I was already willing to become pregnant to ensnare a rich man. This way, I at least have a guarantee of money.

A tremble courses through me, a leaf caught in a storm, as I lift my gaze to meet his obscured one. "And what makes you think I'd agree to this madness?" My voice is a whisper of defiance, but my heart betrays me with its frantic beating.

"Because, Carolina," he starts, his tone void of mockery. "You're a survivor. You'll do anything for your sister. And deep down, you know I'm your best option."

He's right, and the realization tastes bitter on my tongue, a pill too large to swallow. Yet, amid the fear and reluctance, a tiny spark ignites within me—the possibility of a future without the constant struggle, the endless worry.

I take a deep breath, watching him as he folds his arms across his chest. Though his eyes are cold, there's a flicker of something hidden in the depths, something I've also heard hints of in his voice. "You need this," I breathe, finally realizing the magnitude of the situation. "You're trying to turn the tables on me, making it sound like I'm the only one who's desperate."

His eyes crinkle with amusement, but he doesn't speak.

Feeling bolder, I lift my chin. "I have conditions of my own."

His broad shoulders shake with unshed laughter. "I expected nothing less," he chuckles darkly.

"I won't be your prisoner," I demand, sucking my bottom lip between my teeth. "And you'll pay all my expenses for December, including Willow's care—"

He interrupts me with a scoff. "We can call you my guest if that makes you feel better. But you will live here with me, share my bed, and only do what I allow." His tone makes it clear this isn't up for discussion. "And, yes. I'll pay for strangers to take care of the sister you're too busy to look after yourself."

My hands ball into fists, and I suck in a sharp breath of air. His assessment, though wrong, hurts. The truth is that I can't take care of my sister by myself. I want to, so damn much. But the shitty studio I'm renting isn't exactly disability friendly, not that I'll tell him that. Let him think I'm a cold-hearted monster.

"I have work to do," I say, inwardly cringing as I think about the money I've already lost out on.

"No, you don't," he says. When I open my mouth to argue, he presses his index finger against my lips. "I've deleted your Cam Girl site and shut down your account for good."

"You what?" I screech, angered beyond belief. "You had no right to do that, and I need the money."

He just shrugs. "No, you don't. Take my offer and you'll never want for anything again."

My entire body shakes with anger, and, yeah, humiliation. I'm not proud of the way I've been making money. Though I'm not exactly embarrassed either. I've done what I could, what was needed. I refuse to feel bad about that.

The thing is, as great as his offer is, and no matter how amazing ten million sounds, it isn't going to last me forever. Not in New York, and not with everything Willow needs. And what about taxes? And… I bet there are things I haven't even thought about yet.

"You're thinking too hard," Santa observes, dryly. "If you say no, that's it. There'll be no second chance for you."

Sighing, I consider if I should ask for more money, but before I can even come up with an amount to counter with, he speaks again.

"I'll throw in an apartment. One for you and your sister. One where you never have to pay rent again."

Well… shit. I can't say no to that. "Wait, what happens if I don't become pregnant before Christmas?" This is something I need to know before I can even consider it. If he's just going to kill me anyway, that's a lot of pressure to put on my poor womb.

"What do you mean?"

Meeting his gaze straight on, I roll my shoulders back, feigning confidence. "I still want to be paid, and I want your word I get to walk away from you. Alive."

He tilts his head to the side, eyeing me curiously. "Deal. If you're not pregnant by Christmas, I'll pay you two million for your troubles, and you'll be free to leave."

Looking down at my bare feet, I pretend to ponder this. In reality, I've already agreed in my mind. But he doesn't need to know he has me, so I bide my time while shifting my weight from one foot to another.

Although I'm acting calm, I'm anything but. My mind is racing, trying to come up with ways to escape. At the same time, I'm trying not to entertain those stupid thoughts. There's no escaping this. It's happening whether I want it or not.

Maybe I should… no. I need to accept this. "Okay," I finally whisper, feeling as though I'm signing my life away. "I'll do it." I raise my head, looking into his dark eyes.

He nods. "Just so we're clear, the deal is that I pay you ten million dollars to conceive and carry my heir. If you're successful, I'll pay for everything you need until one year after giving birth. At which time you'll walk away with the full ten million. Obviously, you'll never be permitted to see the child again. If you're unsuccessful, I'll pay you two million, give you a place to live, and you get to walk away, free to live your life free of me."

"Okay," I repeat.

"One more thing," he says. "If you ever tell anyone about this deal or about me, your sister will pay the price. I'll make her suffer in ways you can't even imagine, Carolina. Is that clear?"

Tears gather in my eyes, making me blink furiously to stop them from falling. "Yes, I understand," I croak around the ball of emotions in my throat.

My heart beats a staccato rhythm, matching the seconds slipping away. I'm hyper-aware of him as he stands before me, a menacing Santa in this perverse holiday tale.

"In that case," he rasps. "Time to unveil the man behind the myth." His fingers hook beneath the white beard as he takes a step back, putting more distance between us.

The fabric peels away from his skin with a whisper, and I find myself holding my breath. The hat follows, a slow reveal that feels like unwrapping the most twisted of Christmas presents. And then, there he is—a real life Adonis if I ever saw one. I can't help but gape. His features are sharp, carved from stone by a skilled sculptor. There's a ruggedness to him that no amount of civilization could tame.

"Do you know who I am?" His voice is thick with amusement, eyes glinting with something unrecognizable.

Shaking my head, I continue to study him; a scar slashes across his face—a jagged line that starts at the bridge of his nose and carves a path down his cheek. It's a flaw that enhances rather than detracts, adding to the dangerous allure of the man who now owns me.

"No. Should I?" I ask, swallowing harshly as I answer his question with one of my own. My eyes trace the contours of his face, the ink-black hair, the predatory gaze. He's not just handsome; he's devastating. Which is fitting since he holds the power to ruin me, wipe me from the face of the earth without anyone but my sister and uncaring mom even knowing I ever existed.

His smirk tells me he enjoys my discomfort. But there's also an intensity in his gaze that holds me captive, even without the restraints. It's as if he's searching for something within me, some sign of acquiescence or maybe something else.

"It wouldn't be good for you if you did." His approval sends an unexpected shiver down my spine. "But you can call me Nicklas."

"Nicklas." I taste his name on my tongue, paying close attention to the way the organ rolls to speak it. Then an unbidden giggle slips out as I eye the discarded costume. "You've got to be kidding me. Nicklas... Nick... Saint Nick... Santa."

The glint in his eyes is a mixture of dark amusement and a predator. "Ho, ho, fucking ho," he deadpans, flashing me a smile that's all teeth.

This is it—the turning point of my life. I've struck a deal with the devil himself. Ten million dollars. One child. A future secured for me and Willow. Questions whirl through my mind. Can I really go through with this? What does it make me? Am I a victim or a willing participant? The answers elude me, lost in the depth of Nicklas' dark eyes.

"Come over here," he commands huskily, holding his hand out to me.

Before I can fully process his words, my body obeys, moving closer to him. As soon as I take his hand, he pulls me flush against him. "Wait," I squeak, surprised by his nearness. Nicklas' body is as hard as mine is soft, and he smells incredible. Without meaning to, I sag against him.

"Look at me." I tilt my head back and look up at him. "Normally, I seal business deals with a handshake. But I think a kiss is more fitting for our arrangement."

I open my mouth to protest, but before I can utter a word, he bends and fuses his lips to mine in a hard kiss that leaves me breathless. Our lips move together, and when his tongue licks along the seams of my lips, I immediately open up to him, unable to resist.

As he kisses me like he's trying to possess me, I mewl into his mouth. I slide my hands up his strong arms, winding them around his neck. Every part of me is pressed against him, and it feels… amazing.

CHAPTER 8

The Santa

The glow of my phone barely cuts through the darkness in the bedroom. I've been awake for hours, but enjoyed Carolina's nearness too much to get out of bed. Her soft breathing is a steady rhythm in the silence. I tap out a text to Dr. Carmichael, one of the Knight family doctors.

> Me: Dr. Carmichael, I need you at the penthouse this afternoon.

She's used to receiving communication from us at all hours, so I'm not surprised when she replies to my message almost immediately.

> Doc C: Of course. What's it regarding?

> Me: I need a full health and fertility check on someone.

> Doc C: Is mid-afternoon okay?

After confirming that's fine, I untangle Carolina, who has her leg thrown across mine, and get out of bed. After wearing the Santa beard and hat around her for a couple of days, I almost feel naked without it. I can't stop smirking as I shower and shave.

The woman agreed to my proposal without ever seeing me. Not that my looks should matter, yet there's a primal satisfaction to be found in her positive reaction. There was no way to mistake the way her pupils dilated and the flaring of her nostrils. Oh yes, she liked what she saw.

As usual, I dress in one of my custom-tailored suits, and as I pull my belt through the loops on the pants, I wonder what it would be like to use the leather on her round ass. Just because our agreement is about producing my heir, doesn't mean we can't enjoy ourselves while doing it.

Leaving the bathroom, I head straight for the kitchen, where I run into Marco. "Good morning, sir," he greets me.

"Marco," I rumble as a way of greeting. "I have a few errands to run this morning, so I need you to look after Carolina."

He nods. "Understood." Clearing his throat, he looks toward my bedroom door. "Is she still asleep?"

"She is," I confirm. "There's no need to wake her up. But if she gets up, please make sure she gets breakfast as quick as possible. Let the kitchen staff know."

If Carolina wakes up, she won't be alone. There are constantly people in my apartment. Marco and at least one other from my security team, cleaners, and my chefs. At any given time, there are at least five people in here, and that's not counting the ones in the lobby of the building or outside.

"I'll make sure to keep an eye on her. Would you like an hourly update?" This is why Marco's my favorite. He's always proactive and thorough in his tasks.

Running a hand down my face, I nod. "Yeah."

He turns back to his coffee, quietly giving me the space he knows I prefer. I pull my phone out and read the most recent text from Jack.

Jack: Dude, what the hell are you up to? Why aren't you answering?

I roll my eyes and read through the ten texts he's sent me since I took Carolina home. I decide to answer one of the other ones, one that asks about her.

Me: She's fine, and yes, she's still here.

Jack: Why? Are you up to some kind of kinky role-play that requires a captive?

Me: If I am, that's none of your business. But I'm actually about to head to her place to pick up some things. Wanna meet me there?

When he asks for the address, I send it to him, arranging for us to meet there within the hour. I knew Jack wouldn't be able to resist joining me. I wish I could say it's because he's a loyal brother, which he is, but it's also because he's a curious fucker.

Before leaving, I go back to the bedroom to say goodbye to the woman sleeping in my bed. She might be asleep, but that doesn't mean I'll leave without telling her so. She's still deep in slumber, now sprawled across the bed, almost starfishing. The sheet is only covering half of her body, her naked tits on full display.

Even though I didn't go further than kissing her yesterday, I insisted she sleep naked. She might as well get used to it. Once the doc has given her the all-clear, I want access to her beautiful cunt at all hours of the day.

I lean down, my lips brushing her forehead in a feather-light kiss. It should feel innocent, but nothing about the way I react to her is. My hand moves of its own accord, slipping beneath the sheet that covers her lower half. The warmth of her skin against mine sparks a jolt of desire that shoots straight to my dick.

Guilt? None. Remorse? Doesn't exist in my world. I'm a man who takes what he wants, and right now, I want her. My fingers trace the curve of her pussy, and she shifts in her sleep, a soft moan escaping her lips, when I slide a finger between her folds and into her wet heat.

"Fuck," I mutter under my breath. "You're fucking soaking." The need to wake her, to take her here and now, is overwhelming. But I resist. There's a plan—a purpose to all of this, and I won't be derailed, not even by my own primal urges.

I withdraw my hand reluctantly, the mix of her heat and my cold resolve leaving me both frustrated and focused. I need to get out of here before I lose the fight against myself.

When I lift my hand to my mouth, intending to lick my fingers clean, I notice blood smeared across the digits and the heel of my hand. The scent of copper fills my nostrils, grounding me in the reality of the situation. I need to clean up.

As I wash my hands in the bathroom, watching the blood swirl down the drain, I wonder if I should wake her up so she can clean up. Ah, fuck. I have nothing for her here. No tampons, no… nothing. Well, that settles it. I'll let her sleep and pick up whatever she needs before I return.

With one last glance at her peaceful form, I leave the penthouse, the echo of the door clicking shut, a finality that resonates deep in my bones. I make my way to the underground garage, where I pick my armored SUV. The neighborhood Carolina lives in—*lived* in—isn't a good one, so I might as well take precautions.

During the drive, I text Ruby, asking her for advice on what to buy for Carolina. I know my sister will probably want to know more details, but all she needs to know is that I need period products. She can do what she wants with that information.

Since it's still early, I know it'll be at least an hour before she's awake enough to answer, which means I hopefully only have to deal with one sibling at a time.

Speaking of siblings, Jack's already there and waiting as I pull up to the rundown building Carolina's studio is in. A Cheshire grin splays across his lips as I exit my vehicle. "Morning, bro," he greets. "I have to say, this is one of the lousiest places you've ever taken me."

I return his smile with a forced scowl. "Shut up," I grumble.

The street reeks of piss and other bodily fluids, making me scrunch up my nose in disgust. It's one thing to endure the stench when torturing someone, but when it's so potent outside, it's fucking bad. We quietly walk into the building together. According to the info I found, Carolina's studio is in the back on the ground floor.

"Got a key?" Jack asks when we stand outside her door.

Instead of answering him, I kick the door in. There's no point in being delicate, because this shithole needs to be leveled to the ground. A place like this isn't for living, it's for existing. "Don't need one," I smirk.

If I thought the stench outside was bad, this is worse. The small studio is coated in a scent of decay, desperation.

"Jesus, Nick," Jack mutters from behind me, his voice laced with disbelief. "You weren't kidding about the shithole."

I barely hear him. My eyes scan the room, taking in the peeling wallpaper, the single naked bulb that casts a sickly yellow glow over everything it touches. The small couch in the middle of the room is barely held together by the stained fabric, and the springs are exposed. Clothes are neatly folded in a corner, a mix of cheap fabrics and faded colors.

"Christ," I mutter. "Nothing of this is worth fucking saving." Even as I say it, I know I have to at least make an effort to look around.

Although Jack nods his agreement, he begins to move items, stuffing whatever clothes that seem worth saving into a duffel bag he found in the corner. My gaze falls on a small photo frame, the glass cracked. It's Carolina and a girl, younger, smiling. Willow. I clench my fist, feeling an unexpected pang.

My hellcat is doing all she can for her sister, even living in this dump. Clearly, I judged her too harsh when I learned the sisters aren't living together.

The more I look around, the more I hate knowing she lived here. Mold spreads across the small windowpane and ceiling, which should be enough to make it unlivable. Despite the state of the place, it's clean. Knowing that the mother of my heir has spent time trying to keep this place in good shape angers me. She deserves more.

"I think we're done." Jack's voice breaks my reverie.

Looking around, I grab a few folders and the crumbled picture from the shattered frame. "Yeah, I think so too," I agree. "Let's get out of here."

We leave the studio, the door hanging ajar. I turn back, pulling out the lighter I always carry out of habit. The flame flickers to life, casting dancing shadows over my tattooed hand.

"Whoa!" Jack exclaims, holding up his hands. "I get you want to burn this dump to the ground, but people live here."

I nod slowly, he's right. Neither of us have any problem killing those who deserve it, but the innocent people living in this building haven't earned my wrath. With a sigh, I run a hand down my face and pull out my phone.

Marco answers on the first call. "Boss?" he inquires.

"How's she doing?" I ask. As promised, he's sent me hourly updates, and both confirmed she was still in bed. I listen intently as he lets me know she's still asleep. "Good, keep it that way. Look, I'm at her studio now and the place needs to go. Burn it to the fucking ground."

"Sure thing," he agrees, as usual, not asking any questions.

"But make sure everyone is evacuated first," Jack adds. "Anyone with kids can be placed in one of our hotels until you find more permanent solutions."

I shoot my brother an incredulous look. What the hell is this? Some Hallmark Christmas miracle? Fuck no. Jack arches his eyebrow, silently daring me to contradict him. "Fine. Do it," I huff.

Without looking back, we walk out to our vehicles, and I quickly throw the bag with Carolina's few belongings onto the passenger seat. When I close the door, I find Jack studying the street. "You know," he says, pointing to a building further down. "We could get rid of all of it and build some new shit."

"To what end?" I ask, genuinely curious. "We're not exactly do-gooders. Besides, the people here aren't likely to be able to pay the kind of rent we charge."

Jack scratches the scruff on his chin. "Ruby wants us to do more charity to improve our image. Lately, there hasn't been enough to offset the negative whispers. If we keep it up, the police can't keep looking the other way no matter how much we pay them."

"I get it," I say. "If we restore the neighborhood, we could run it at a loss to help out."

"I'll talk to Ruby," Jack confirms. "She'd love to get involved."

He isn't kidding; this is exactly the kind of thing our sister would get a kick out of. And, honestly, if it gets her away from her creep of a husband for a few hours a day, it's worth it. "You do that," I agree.

Turning to face me, Jack pins me with his stare. "You know Dad wasn't kidding, right? He wants you to produce an heir like last year."

"I know," I confirm. "I got it handled."

He narrows his eyes at me. "So that's why you're wearing shining armor?" Jack's eyes glint with mischief as he leans against my sleek black vehicle, arms folded across his chest.

I glance at him, feeling a surge of possessiveness that's too intense for the short time I've known Carolina. "I am a Knight, after all," I confirm. "She's going to give me an heir."

None of us mention the fact I should make sure I get three, mostly because I don't believe in the family superstition. The fact that my dad lost his two brothers, that my grandpa lost his two sisters, and that my great-grandpa lost one of each proves nothing.

There's no such thing as a curse that kills off two of the three children fathered by the Knight Leader. There. Just. Isn't.

Jack chuckles, shaking his head. "Does she even know about this plan of yours?" Jack arches an eyebrow, the sunlight reflecting in his green eyes.

"She does. I made her an offer too good to refuse." My hand clenches at my side, the image of her asleep in my bed flashing through my mind. Possession coils tight within me.

He lets out a low whistle and stands up straight. "Damn, you're serious, aren't you?" He claps me on the shoulder, his laughter fading. "I hope it works out because I don't want to have to take over." His voice becomes solemn, and I know he hates the thought as much as our dad does.

"Don't worry," I assure him, pulling him into a hug. "This won't be your burden. I promise, Jack."

We say our goodbyes, and I wait in my car, watching him drive away before I check my phone to see if Ruby has answered my text. She has.

Ruby: Are we just going to gloss over the fact you don't need to know for yourself?

Ruby: Hello?!?!?! Don't fucking ignore me!

Ruby: Fine, be that way. If it's someone you actually give a damn about, just buy every product in the shop since you can afford it. Everyone needs a different absorbency.

Ruby: You should also get some chocolate, comfy socks. Maybe a heating pad? Dude, you're seriously making me go through my own stuff here.

Ruby: Right, okay, even though you're clearly ignoring me, I'm the best little sister, so here's your shopping list: every size tampon—branded. No cheap shit. Get the pads with the highest absorbency (indicated by drops on the packaging!!), at least one blanket, some fluffy socks, fluffy pajamas (nothing tight or sexy!), and... whatever you think will make her comfortable.

I roll my eyes as I read the last of my sister's texts. Just what the actual fuck? This all sounds like shit you'd buy for someone who's terminal, not someone who has to go through this shit once a month.

My annoyance doesn't last long, though. It's nice to see my sister's personality peek through the words. So much better than the timid version I see when Dad or Michael are around.

Me: Sorry, was with Jack. Thanks for the list. You're right, you're the best little sister!

Ruby: Who's it for?

Me: I'm going through a tunnel and can't answer.

I chuckle out loud as her immediate reply comes in.

Ruby: Whatever. I'll grill Jack for info!

I chuckle to myself, having no doubt Jack will spill everything. Ruby is persistent, and it's usually easier to give her what she wants than fight her.

Me: Are you busy today?

Ruby: God no. Do you need anything? Please say you do. You know I can't go anywhere without you or Michael saying so.

My heart contracts at the reminder of the life she's living. Life... I snort to myself. That isn't fucking living, it's surviving.

Since what I need is too hard to explain in a text, I send my sister a voice message, asking her to contact Ability Acres, the care home Willow Sterling is staying in. I'd go there myself, but I want to get back to Carolina. Besides, Ruby is much better at this stuff. She's used to dealing with businesses, and can undoubtedly charm her way inside if she pretends she's a potential investor.

Ruby: You got it.

Placing my phone in the holder, I tear away from the curb and head toward the nearest shop. Fuck, I don't even know what kind of shop I should go to. A drug store could help with the actual period products, but I doubt they sell the rest my sister demanded I buy. Since I don't usually do my own shopping, I'm kind of at a loss for where to go.

I keep driving until I come across one of the big chains. Unbothered by the people shouting at me, I park in the disabled zone and stride into the store. The fluorescent lights of the place are harsh, clinical, but I'm not here for ambiance. I'm here for Carolina.

Tampons first. I scan the aisle, rows upon rows of feminine products, staring back at me like an army ready for battle. Regular, super, overnight, what the hell do these even mean? I grab an assortment of both tampons and pads, not skimping on quantity.

Next, chocolate. Not just any chocolate—I pile up the fanciest looking ones, the ones wrapped in gold foil and promising exotic flavors. Dark, milk, with almonds, sea salt, caramel fillings. If there's a hint of pleasure to be found in their taste, Carolina will experience it.

I'm not sure why I care so much, and I refuse to examine it. Instead, I keep going. My basket's getting heavy, but I don't stop. Heat pads, fluffy socks, a silky robe that looks like it'll feel like heaven against her skin.

Aromatherapy candles, bath bombs that smell of lavender and jasmine, a plush blanket that begs to be curled up in—at least that's what the smiling woman on the sign claims. I add a giant teddy bear for good measure, its soft fur under my fingers reminding me of the way Carolina's hair felt when I brushed it aside.

"Anything else?" the cashier asks, raising an eyebrow as the conveyor belt overflows.

"Is there?" I challenge, daring him to suggest I've missed something. But he shakes his head, ringing up the items with a kind of reverence reserved for the absurd.

"Taking care of someone special?" he tries to make small talk.

"Something like that," I reply curtly, swiping my card without flinching at the total.

After loading the bags into the vehicle, I rush home, eager to see Carolina again. By the time I pull into the garage, I feel a sense of urgency.

Huh, that's not usually how I react. Then again, how would I know? Carolina is the first woman that isn't family to set foot in my home. Sure, I've had an abundance of one-night-stands in my life, but I've either fucked them at their place, or one of the Knight owned hotels.

Elevator doors open, and I step into the penthouse, the bags crinkling in my arms. It's a bizarre sight, me laden with comforts instead of weapons or threats. Luckily, Marco doesn't comment on it as he greets me, instead he tries to take some of the bags. But I shake my head and head straight for the bedroom.

"Wait," he calls after me. "You should know that—"

"Not now," I growl. "Whatever it is, it can wait until later."

Pushing open the bedroom door, I find Carolina is no longer in bed. The water's running in the bathroom, so after putting down the bags, I knock softly. When she doesn't answer, I push the handle down to find she's locked herself inside. "Carolina," I call out, slamming my fist against the door. "Open up right fucking now."

"I'm in the shower," she shouts back.

Her dismissal angers me. "Open. The. Damn. Door." The water shuts off, and a moment later, she unlocks and opens the door. "What's the matter?" I ask as soon as I see her face, taking her hand and pulling her to me.

She looks up at me through wide eyes filled with fear, and… is that shame? "I-I'm so s-sorry, Nicklas," she stutters. "I'll fix it. I promise."

My eyebrows furrow in confusion. "Fix what?" I question, gently cupping her face. She flinches like she thought I was going to hurt her. "What the fuck's going on?" My tone becomes harsher. She tries to pull away from me, but I don't let her. Instead, I place my hands on her hips.

Her face is ashen. "I… umm… I got my period," she whispers, like she's afraid to say the words out loud. "The sheets are ruined. And I know they're expensive. I'm so sorry. I'll pay for new ones." Her rushed admission is too much, and I can't hold my laughter back.

"You think I care about a little blood?" I question. "I got everything you might need," I tell her, pointing at the bags on the floor.

"Oh!" Her mouth forms into a cute O as she frowns. "You knew?"

I nod. "Found out just before I left. Look, I didn't know what you needed, so I got some of everything." Letting go of her, I bend and pick up the two bags with the period shit and the two with clothes. "Why don't you go clean up, and I'll make sure breakfast is waiting when you come out?"

"Okay," she agrees softly.

She takes the bags from me and disappears back into the bathroom. As the lock slides into place, I shout, "Don't ever lock me out, Hellcat." She lets out a squeak, but unlocks the door immediately.

Satisfied, I turn toward the bed and the bloodied sheets. Instead of asking one of my staff to change the bed, I strip it, knowing Carolina would hate knowing someone else had done it.

I gather the dirty sheets under my arm and pick the remaining bags up, and leave the bedroom. I run into one of the cleaners and hand her the dirty sheets, asking her to put fresh ones on once Carolina's done in the shower.

CHAPTER 9

The Santa

I stand by the door, arms crossed over my chest, as the doctor enters the room in my penthouse reserved for medical stuff. Dr. Carmichael doesn't waste a second; she's all business as she immediately begins setting up, preparing for the tests she's about to conduct. Efficiency is what I pay for, and her swift movements reassure me that Carolina is in capable hands.

"Good afternoon, Mr. Knight," Dr. Carmichael greets with a curt nod, not even flinching at the cold aura I emanate.

"Doctor," I reply, my voice clipped, my gaze never wavering from Carolina, who lies exposed on the examination table, vulnerability etched into every line of her body—yet so deliciously enticing.

Dr. Carmichael raises a delicate brow as she looks at Carolina. "You must be Miss Sterling," she observes, snapping on gloves with practiced ease.

Carolina pushes herself up, so she's resting on her elbows. "What gave it away?" she snaps, blowing a stray strand of hair out of her eyes.

Since the good doc texted me when she was on her way and what to expect, I had time to get Carolina into the room and onto the examination table. She was surprisingly agreeable until she found out I wasn't going to leave her and the doctor alone. In fact, I think she's still pissed about that.

"Miss Sterling, we're going to begin with an ultrasound, followed by a series of blood tests, to assess your fertility levels. I'll also do a pregnancy test," Dr. Carmichael explains, her tone professional, detached. It's the detachment I appreciate most; emotions have no place in my world unless I'm the one evoking them.

Carolina lies back down and throws her hands up in the air. "Have at it, doctor. But you should know I'm bleeding from my vagina, so a pregnancy test isn't necessary." Turning her head toward me, she shoots daggers through her eyes, making me bark out a surprised laugh at her crassness.

"Are you certain you're on your period?" Dr. Carmichael asks, unbothered by Carolina's words. "Or is there a chance it's another form of vaginal bleeding?"

My hellcat gnaws on her bottom lip. "Well, I'm pretty certain. My womb feels like it's being sliced open with a dull knife, and the cramps are definitely real."

I soften my gaze, regretting I didn't buy any painkillers. "Do you have anything for her pain?" I ask the doc, not wanting Carolina to suffer through pain unless I'm the one who's dolling it out.

She nods. "I do. Remind me before I leave." Turning to Carolina, she gestures to her feet. "Please place your feet in the stirrups," she commands.

Carolina's eyes flicker toward me again, a silent plea for privacy, but I don't budge. I stay behind the doctor, wanting to see everything she's doing. My presence here isn't about intimidation; it's a reminder of our arrangement. She's mine, and every part of this process belongs to me, too.

"Nicklas, please..." she starts, "at least stop eyeing my vagina—"

I cut her off with a sharp look. "I'm staying," I clip, the words laced with an edge that should tell her to let it go right the fuck now.

Carolina's mouth snaps shut, the tension in her jaw betraying her frustration. The doctor doesn't miss a beat, turning on the ultrasound machine, the soft whirring noise filling the silence.

As the cool gel spreads across Carolina's stomach and the transducer glides over her skin, images flicker on the monitor. I can't decipher them, but I don't need to. Dr. Carmichael's steady commentary tells me all I need to know. Ovaries, follicles, womb—all words that spell out the future heir to my empire. Carolina's discomfort is irrelevant; this is about legacy.

"Everything appears normal," Dr. Carmichael concludes, stripping off her gloves with a professionalism that matches my own approach to business. "Do you want to put on some clothes?" Even though the question is clearly meant for Carolina, both women look at me.

When I nod, Carolina moves behind the privacy curtain, and I promptly follow her. I get she doesn't want the doctor to watch her get dressed, but that doesn't mean she gets to hide from me. She looks up as I approach, but doesn't say anything. I watch as she picks up the pajama pants I got her, reaching into the pocket for something. My body tenses, readying myself in case she tries anything stupid.

"Do you mind getting me some toilet paper?" she asks, exasperation coating her words.

"What's in your hand?" I ask, pointing at the one that's clearly clenched around something.

"It's nothing. Can I have some toilet paper, please?"

"Show. Me. What. You. Are. Holding."

Huffing, she opens and shows me the tampon. "It's just a fucking tampon, Nicklas. Now, are you going to get me some toilet paper or not?" she snaps.

I get her some toilet paper and wet wipes, watching as she wipes herself before placing the tampon inside her. I don't know why, but Carolina's period fucking excites me. It feels like a secret layer I'm peeling back, one, judging by her awkwardness, she's never shared with anyone.

Fuck, I like knowing I'm her first.

Once Carolina is dressed, she sits back down on the table, never looking away from me as the doctor draws blood and rambles on about the tests. "I'll send the blood samples to the lab immediately. You should have the results within a couple of hours," she explains when she's done.

"Ensure it's sooner," I say, my impatience clear. Dr. Carmichael nods, understanding the unspoken threat in my tone, and quickly packs up her equipment.

As Carolina sits up, she pins me with a glare. "What's the rush? I'm on my fucking period, Nicklas. I can't conceive anything for a week, anyway."

Right, she has a point there, not that I'm going to admit that. "I don't like waiting," I snap. "The sooner I know whether you're a viable candidate, the better."

I don't miss the smile on Dr. Carmichael's lips, though she has the good sense to wipe it away when she notices me watching her. "Here are the painkillers." She goes to hand Carolina the jar, but I quickly snap it from her hand. "Take care, Miss Sterling," she says, giving Carolina a brief, impersonal smile before exiting the room.

With the doctor gone, my attention shifts entirely to Carolina. I should punish her for openly defying me, but I have no intention of doing that. I like her spark and defiance, it's stoking a fire within me, making the power I hold over her even more intoxicating. Knowing she's mine for the next month is fueling the primal urge that simmers beneath my tailored suit.

Whether it's only for December or the next year and nine months, I will have her, completely and thoroughly, and nothing—not her comfort or her protests—will deter me from what I want.

"What happens if I'm unable to carry a child?" Carolina asks, her voice small.

I close my eyes for a brief moment, not willing to even entertain that thought. "You are," I growl.

"But what if I'm not?" she insists.

The sterile smell of antiseptic lingers in the air, hell, I can smell it on her skin. I frown, not liking the way it smells on her, it's hiding the scent that's all her. "Get up," I order, ignoring her question.

Carolina hesitates for a fraction of a second before obeying, rising from the table with a grace that belies her inner turmoil.

"We'll get the results today, then you'll see I'm right," I say, keeping my voice devoid of emotion. The timetable is a dangling carrot for both of us, a timeline that holds more than just medical data—it holds our fate, entwined and uncertain.

Carolina's eyes flicker to mine, a storm of emotions clouding the blue depths, but she remains silent. I take her hand and lead her back to the bedroom and into the ensuite bathroom. The need to cleanse and claim her flesh is overwhelming.

"Shower with me," I rasp. It's not a request, and we both know it.

Carolina hesitates, her lips parting slightly as if she might protest. I see the defiance sparking in her gaze, the bratty resistance that tempts me like a red flag to a bull. "I… Nicklas, I—" Her words falter under the weight of my stare.

"Don't test me right now, Hellcat," I interrupt sharply.

She swallows hard, her bravado crumbling as she realizes the futility of arguing with me. Slowly, she nods, acquiescing to my demand, and I move over to the spacious shower, turning on the water. The sound reverberates against the marble, a rhythmic beat that seems to pulse with our heartbeats. Steam begins to rise, cloaking the room in a warm mist that clings to my skin.

"Undress," I instruct, peeling off my own clothing with deliberate slowness, never breaking eye contact. She complies, revealing the curves and softness that haunt my dreams, making me burn with a desire I've never known before her.

As we step under the hot cascade, I close the distance between us, relishing the initial shock of water on my skin. I watch her closely, noting the way her breath catches and her hardened nipples show how her body responds to my proximity.

"Turn around," I growl, needing to touch her, to wash away the remnants of anyone else's hands on her.

The steam clings to my skin as I watch Carolina under the spray of the shower, her blonde hair plastered to her delicate shoulders. She's a vision of vulnerability, and it stirs something primal within me.

I reach for the body wash on the ledge, pouring a generous amount into my palm before pressing myself against her back. My hands find her hips, my fingers splaying over the softness there, and I hear her breath hitch.

"Relax," I command, the word a low rumble in her ear. My touch is firm as I massage the lather into her skin, tracing the curve of her waist and up to the swell of her breasts.

She leans into me, her head tilting back, giving me access to the column of her throat. "Nicklas," she moans.

Bending down, I lick the length of her neck. "Yes, Hellcat?" For good measure, I pinch her nipples, making her arch her back and push her ass against my hard cock. I spin her around to face me, my gaze devouring the sight of her flushed cheeks and parted lips.

My hands roam lower, and I reach between her thighs, finding the string of her tampon. Without hesitation, I pull it free and carelessly toss it into the corner. Her gasp is sharp, and her body tenses.

"W-we shouldn't… I mean… I'm bleeding." She bows her head like she's feeling ashamed.

"Look at me," I growl. When she doesn't obey, I move a finger under her chin and force her to lift her head. "You're mine, Carolina. I've bought the right to every inch of you, even your blood."

There's a flicker of something in her eyes—fear, excitement, need. It's all there, mingling in the blue depths. But then she wordlessly melts against me as the blood mingles with the water, swirling down the drain.

My thumb brushes over her clit, eliciting a moan that vibrates through her body. It's a sound that grips me, that makes me want to hear it again and again. "Don't stop," she moans as she runs her hands across my shoulders and down my chest to my abs. She caresses every groove, like she's committing my body to memory.

I growl with approval as she reaches my cock, fisting the shaft. I don't care that she can't close her hand around my girth, her touch is all that matters.

While she slowly jerks me off, I slide two fingers into her wet heat. Knowing the wetness is caused by a mixture of her natural lubricant and blood makes me fucking feral.

"You like that?" she purrs, working her hand along my shaft with a deliberate slowness.

"Harder," I rasp, thrusting into her hand. "Squeeze me harder."

As I curl my fingers inside her, hitting her walls, I claim her lips in a hard kiss that's filled with need. I suck her bottom lip between my teeth, biting the tender flesh as I've seen her do countless times. Our mouths move together with an urgency that's both wild and inevitable.

I taste the sweetness of her lips, the heat of her tongue, and it's everything I crave. As we kiss, our bodies press closer, the boundaries between us blurring until I'm not sure where I end and she begins.

My fingers piston in and out of her, and I make sure the heel of my hand presses against her swollen clit. "Purr for me, Hellcat," I growl against her lips.

She throws her head back and moans loudly. "Oh, yeah. Right there."

What the fuck kind of men has she been with in the past? If anyone buys that performance, I dare say they've never really felt what sex *can* and *should* be like. The moans coming from her are so fucking fake I can barely stand it. As is the way she bites her lip and looks up at me from beneath her lashes.

It's all practiced, staged.

I still my hand. "Is that really what you think I want?" I taunt as I pull my fingers from her bloody cunt.

"What?" she volleys. "W-what did I do?"

Moving my hand to the nape of her neck, I squeeze until she whimpers in pain. "I don't care what fucking limp-dicked shitheads you've spread your legs for in the past, Carolina. But when you're with me, I never want you faking anything."

Her eyes widen. "I wasn't—"

Without warning, I shove my red fingers into her mouth, intending to shut her the fuck up before I lose my patience. She cries out and tries to get away from me, but I tighten my hold on the back of her neck, holding her in place.

"This thing between us is real," I roar, angry she dares fake anything with me. "I am paying good money for your womb, Carolina. And I expect you to do your part."

She gags as I ruthlessly shove my fingers down her throat. She garbles and moans, and I'm pretty sure she tells me to go fuck myself. Maybe I should fuck my hand. At least that would be real and not whatever she thinks she's doing.

When tears stream down her cheeks, I pull my fingers out of her mouth and let her breathe again. "I-I'm sorry," she sobs, her knees buckling.

I chuckle, darkly. "Are you?" I question, not believing her for one second.

She stares defiantly at me, and I raise a questioning eyebrow. "No," she hisses, angrily swiping at her tears. Her tone makes it clear her sobs were as fake as her moans. "You've bought my vagina, but not my pleasure. That shit you have to earn."

A sinister smile stretches across my lips. "Is that so, Hellcat?"

Fuck, she's sexy when she's angry and making demands.

Mimicking my words, she retorts, "Yes, that's so."

I let out a cruel laugh while I tangle my fingers in her long, blonde hair. Then I force her down on her knees, ignoring her whimpers and hisses of pain. "I was going to make you come so hard," I growl.

She rolls her eyes. "That's what they all say," she smarts.

As much as her bravado and spirit turn me on, it also pisses me right off. I'm tempted to make her come just to prove how easily I can do it. The only reason I don't is that after throwing that shit in my face, she has to earn the right.

"Stay on your knees," I rasp while stroking my hard cock. "Since there's no point in fucking you yet, you can swallow my cum. Open your mouth and stick your tongue out."

The Breeder

Anger and humiliation flash in my eyes as I do as he says. He tightens his grip on his cock and starts stroking himself faster. I close my eyes, refusing to look at him.

"Look at me, Carolina," he commands in a deep, gravelly tone. When I shake my head, he pulls at my hair until I can't take the pain anymore, and I finally open my eyes. "If I tell you to do something, you fucking do it."

Without warning, he shoves his cock into my mouth, and I try my best not to gag at the sudden intrusion. I move my hands to his thighs to steady myself, but he uses his free hand to slap them away.

He pumps into my mouth with wild abandon, and I can tell he's close to coming. I want to weep with joy as the taste of his pre-cum spreads in my mouth. It's a hell of a lot better than the disgusting taste of my period.

Ugh, gross!

"Make me come," he growls, thrusting deeper into my throat.

My eyes water and I feel like retching, but I do as he says. He grunts and groans above me, his movements becoming more erratic by the second. I try not to think about what's happening and focus on just making him come quickly.

After what feels like an eternity, he finally releases into my mouth with a loud moan.

He pulls out and looks at me like I'm a bug under his shoe. Then he pushes me away from him. "Clean yourself up, you're getting blood everywhere," he sneers before striding out of the bathroom without another word.

I collapse onto the floor, tears streaming down my cheeks as I try to catch my breath. How did things get so out of control? How did I end up in this situation? I know the answer—desperation. Desperation for money.

The money isn't even to live an extravagant life, it's so Willow and I can both survive. And now here I am, selling my body to a man who doesn't see me as anything other than a vessel for his child.

But despite everything that's happened today, there's still a part of me that refuses to give in completely. He might be renting my womb, but no matter what he's saying, he doesn't own my pleasure or my actions.

I might have agreed to lie on my back and spread my legs for him whenever he wants me to, but that's it. He doesn't get to make me come or dictate how I act.

Maybe I should have insisted on a legal contract between us. Then again, can you even get contracts for this shit? We could probably find one for surrogates and amend it to fit our situation.

CHAPTER 10

The Breeder

After the bathroom fiasco, I barely see Nicklas for the next week. He only comes into the bedroom when it's time for bed, which is always absurdly late, and then he's gone before I wake up. We don't talk or touch, or anything. We just sleep in the same bed as the strangers we are.

Wait, that's not true. He did tell me that because of my lies, he wouldn't let me speak to Willow, or even let me leave the confines of the bed and bathroom. Since he refused to answer any of my questions, I can only imagine that by lies he meant my fake moans.

The truth is that I did it because I thought it was what he wanted. Every guy I've ever been with has only cared about their own pleasure while making it clear they expected me to be deep in the throes of passion while they fumbled to find my clit.

Nicklas was nothing like that, though. His fingers were steady, and he knew exactly what he was doing. My moans were authentic. I wasn't faking them—exaggerating, sure. But I didn't outright fake anything.

Now, the fucker is punishing me for doing what I thought he wanted, what has always been expected of me. I want to scream and cry from the unfairness of it all. And maybe I would if it wasn't because I'm doing my best not to let him see how much it's getting to me that I can't speak to Willow.

I'm pulled from my thoughts as the subtle click of the lock sounds too loud in the otherwise quiet room. I'm on my feet before I even register moving, the soft whisper of silk against my thighs as I pad across the room toward the sound. My heart races, not with fear, but with an aching hope that it's him.

Maybe I'll even apologize just to end this solitude hell.

But it's just the silent housekeeper with her tray of food and stoic face, pushing through the doorway. The disappointment is a physical pang, and I swallow it down, trying to engage with the only other human I've seen in days.

"Good morning," I say, forcing brightness into my voice. She doesn't respond, doesn't even meet my eyes as she sets down the tray. The clink of porcelain and silver is the only answer I get.

"Can you tell me what day it is?" I try again, my voice catching.

But of course she doesn't. She's more drone than human, an impassive statue in a maid's uniform. I swear Nicklas is sending her to me just to piss me off. Because the way she ignores me is grinding on my nerves.

As she turns to leave, I reach out, touching her arm. "Please, I just want to hear someone's voice. Why won't you talk to me?" My voice wavers, and I'm seconds away from losing it.

She shrugs me off, and the door snicks shut behind her. My hand hovers in the space she left, trembling. This silence is suffocating. These walls are too perfect, too sterile. I need something real, something raw.

"Fuck you, Nicklas!" I scream as loud as I can.

When I'm met with nothing but silence, I pick up the tray and hurl it at the locked door.

"You see that?" I shout. My arms are outstretched as I spin around in a circle, just in case he has cameras in here and can see me. "If you want me to eat, come tell me yourself. Don't send your staff. Fucking coward!"

I wait for as long as I can, but nothing happens. As the minutes tick by, I'm starting to feel ridiculous for being so dramatic and desperate. But I'm not sure I can stomach spending another day locked in this room, staring at the same four walls. I'm going stir crazy here.

With nothing else to do, I walk to the window. The city sprawling beneath like a kingdom at my feet, yet I'm no queen—just a pawn in Nicklas' baby-making game. The only kindness afforded to me is the spectacular view.

In some ways it's better, in others it's a lot worse. While I can use the daylight to estimate the days passing me by, I'm also reminded of the freedom the people walking about probably take for granted and that I envy.

I've walked by this area many times, admiring the apartments from the outside. Even though the men I look for are rich, this is next level. Like serious money—*old money.*

The realization makes me feel... I don't know how to describe it. Like an insignificant bug caught in a web. Yeah, I think that's the best descriptor my brain can summon right now. I already knew these things, but seeing and feeling it is very different from drawing the conclusion in a darkened room.

I sigh and turn away from the window, unable to stomach looking at it anymore. It's all too much. So I head into the bathroom and run a shower. Feeling dirty, I scrub at my skin until it's red and sore. It's a bad habit I've had for years. Whenever things get too much, I need pain to sort through my thoughts.

Once I'm done, I dry off and wrap the soft towel around my body as my gaze lands on the electric toothbrush Nicklas uses. I don't know why it happens, but the second I look at it, I remember his words. No, not his words per se—his actions. He pushed me away and punished me because he was disgusted by the way I've conditioned myself to act to a man's touch.

Picking up the toothbrush, I push the power button. A smile creeps across my face as I feel the vibrations in my hand. Maybe this is what I need; to explore and discover all by myself.

I know it's not normal that I've never masturbated, yet I haven't. To me, sex has always been a transaction where the guy's pleasure was part of the exchange. Never mine. And until Nicklas, I've never thought too much into it. It just was.

But since my period is gone, and the doctor declared me fertile, noting in her email to Nicklas that she didn't see any issues preventing pregnancy, I might as well try to make my time with him... pleasurable.

I make my way back into the bedroom and as soon as I reach the massive bed, I lie down and make myself comfortable. Still fisting the toothbrush handle in one hand, I use the other to discover every inch of my body. I palm my breast, pinch the nipple, and run my digits all over my torso.

Spreading my legs, I run the bottom of the handle across my sex, and gasp when I make contact with my clit. "Oh!" I'm surprised at how good it feels.

Spurred on, I circle my nub until my legs shake and my breath turns ragged. Holy shit, the vibrations are something completely different. Something I can't believe I never knew. As my orgasm crashes over me, I feel like a kid in a toy store; excited for more and definitely not able to control myself.

I guide it lower, biting my lip to stifle a moan. The sensation is electric, sending waves of pleasure coursing through me. My hips rock, instinctively seeking more, chasing the high. I close my eyes, letting go of thoughts, of worries—letting go of everything but this moment and the delicious pressure building inside me while I fuck myself with the buzzing handle.

Panting, I allow my imagination to conjure images of Nicklas watching me with those dark, intense eyes. Would he be angry? Or would that possessive streak of his flare at the thought of me using his things to satisfy myself?

Maybe he'd take his long and thick cock out and stroke it while watching me. Shit, maybe he's doing that right now. Instead of feeling shame, I feel triumph as the sounds falling from my lips are completely organic.

I stop moving my hand, allowing the plastic handle to rest inside me. Then I force myself to recognize the difference between the sounds I'm making now, and the ones I've always forced in the past. If I had my phone, I'd probably record myself so I could really compare mental notes on my performance.

I shake my head at my stupid thoughts. I'm here to give Nicklas an heir, not for anything else. But even as I think that, I know it's not that easy. The other day he was willing to fuck me despite my cycle, it was the fakeness of my moans that turned him off.

So if I want to walk away with ten million dollars at the end of this, I need to be good enough for him.

Although I'm no longer in the mood, I bite down on my bottom lip and force myself to continue. I work the handle in and out of my pussy. Every time I feel myself slipping into my old ways, wanting to make exaggerated noises, I stop and start over. Honestly, it's more exhausting than sexy because every time I stop, I rob myself of the orgasm that's so close I can practically taste it.

While Rome wasn't built in a day, it's true that practice makes perfect. My legs are shaking, my hips undulating as I fuck myself as fast and hard as I can. I'm almost sobbing with need and my pussy is pulsing. It only takes a few more thrusts, then the pleasure hits me so hard I cry out.

"Fuck. Fuck. Shit. Yes!" I'm barely aware of my words as tears fall from my eyes. Not from sadness, but from… I don't actually know. The sheer intensity, maybe. All I know is that black spots dance in front of my eyes, and I'm beyond exhausted.

As soon as my breathing returns to normal, I want to curl up and take a nap. But as I look down at my body, I can't bring myself to do it. My thighs are glistening and sticky with my arousal, I need another goddamn shower.

My legs feel like jello as I make my way back to the bathroom. When I reach the sink, I don't avoid looking at my reflection like I've done the other times. No, this time I meet my own gaze, my lips curling upwards in a smug grin. I'm feeling extremely proud of myself.

That's when I notice I'm still clutching the damn toothbrush. The handle is completely covered in my juices, and I'm just about to rinse it. But then I think better of it. And instead, I just slam it down on the pristinely white sink.

I don't know if Nicklas will be able to see what I've done, but I hope not. Damn, I wish I'd thought about doing this while I was still bleeding.

If for no other reason, then retaliation for him shoving his bloody fingers into my mouth.

Oh well, live and learn. It's still nice to imagine him brushing his teeth with my arousal all over the handle.

CHAPTER 11

The Santa

"You good, boss?" Marco drawls as we walk into my home.

My shirt clings to my skin, the fabric heavy with the scent of gunpowder and sweat—a stench from tonight's dealings. "Never better," I grin.

"You look it," Macro retorts, chuckling.

Tonight, we acted on a tip from Dominic, and it wasn't fruitless. Seven guys were waiting for me, Jack, and Marco as we went to get our shipment of goods. Luckily, Dominic and his men laid in wait to turn the table on the guys that tried to ambush us.

Something about it feels… off. If it wasn't for the tip we got just an hour ahead of time, Jack would have been there alone.

Before I can tell Marco what I'm thinking, we're interrupted by one of Marco's men. I think he's the one who was on Carolina duty today. "Marco! There you are. Look, I need to…" He trails off and his eyes widen as he spots me. The guy looks like he's about to piss himself with fear.

I look at Marco and silently raise an eyebrow. Christ, if the guy can't handle seeing the blood splatters on us, he's in the wrong fucking line of business.

"Well?" Marco prompts, folding his arms across his massive chest. "Out with it. What's so important?"

Since the guy is new, I decide I don't need to be here for whatever he has to say. It's Marco's domain, and I know he'll fill me in if I need to know. "Laters," I throw over my shoulder.

"I-it's about the woman." He sucks in an audible breath. "Carolina."

My head snaps in his direction. "What about her?" I snarl, immediately on edge. "Did something happen?"

I'm pretty sure I would have heard about it sooner if she'd escaped, and I can't imagine any of my men doing anything to her. They're too fucking scared of me to violate my orders.

When the guy lets out an honest to God whimper instead of answering me, I close the distance between us. My hand shoots around his neck and my fingers dig into his throat. "Speak!" I roar.

All color disappears from his skin, and he's as pale as the fucking moonlight. He opens his mouth as if to speak, but the only sound coming out of his useless fucking mouth is some garbled wheezing.

"Not that it's any of my business," Marco drawls lazily. "But if you want answers, you might want to stop squeezing his throat."

Right.

I immediately let go, and the guy crumbles to his knees, folding like a sack of potatoes. Pathetic. I crouch in front of him and fist my hand in his light hair. "Don't make me ask again," I snarl menacingly.

The guy looks up at Marco, and it's almost comical the way he begs for mercy with his eyes. "It wasn't my fault," he cries. "I did my job like I was supposed to—"

"What wasn't your fault?" I demand.

Marco sighs and walks over to us. When he reaches me, he squeezes my shoulder. "Let me talk to the kid alone, boss."

"No!" My breathing is ragged as anger thrums through my veins. "He knows something. And I want to know what it fucking is."

"He can't tell you if he's too scared to use his words," Marco calmly says. "So take a few steps back and pretend you got something better to do."

Huffing, I let go of the guy and stand up to my full height. I shoot

Marco a glare as I do what he says, backing up enough to give the two of them some semblance of privacy. A part of me wants to run to the bedroom and see what the fuck Carolina's done. But another, the cold and calculated part of me knows I need to bide my time. Whatever the answer is, I have a feeling I won't get the answer without the guy telling it to Marco.

It feels like hours pass before Marco tells his guy to go home, and then he comes over to me. His deep frown lines tell me I won't like whatever he just found out.

"Spit it out," I snarl.

Shaking his head, he clasps both of my shoulders. "No."

"No?" I echo.

"I want you to do two things for me, boss."

Snorting, I look at him. His expression is grave, which tells me more than any words could. Marco isn't messing around. "What do you want me to do?" I ask, forcing myself to chill the fuck out.

"Watch the security camera that's monitoring your bedroom, and when you're done—"

"Marco!" I shout, not in the mood for his games.

"And when you're done, remember you're the one who told the kid never to take his eyes off the girl."

As I stand there, opening and closing my mouth like a damn idiot, Marco turns on his heel and disappears. Well, fuck! I run a tattooed hand through my dark hair, willing myself to go to the bedroom instead of following him.

I tread softly on the floor, the door creaking open just enough for me to slip inside. The moonlight spills over Carolina's form. Her blonde hair a halo against the dark pillowcase. For an instant, the sight of her, so vulnerable and serene, nearly siphons away the day's violence. *Nearly.*

Although I want to wake her up and make her suck me off again, I leave her to sleep and head into the adjoining bathroom. Closing the door, I switch on the light. I begin to undress, knowing I need a shower before climbing into bed. The blood on my clothes and hands isn't mine, and I won't let anyone else touch her.

The quiet clink of my cufflinks as I toss them onto the marble countertop on the sink echoes loudly in the otherwise silent room. Once I'm naked and have kicked my bloody clothes into the corner, I step into the shower and clean myself off.

Thoughts about when I had Carolina on her knees make my cock perk up, and I'm tempted to whack off. But no. She has to be nearing the end of her cycle, so I need to save all my cum for my hellcat.

Finished with my shower, I dry off and I walk over to the mirror. I run my hand along my jaw, the scruff there isn't out of control yet, so I decide to leave the shaving for another couple of days. I reach for my toothbrush, and that's when I feel it—the stickiness coating the white plastic handle.

I bring it up to my nose and inhale deeply. Her scent envelops me; it's sweet and… "Ohh, you naughty kitten," I growl as soon as I realize it's her arousal I can smell.

Even while she was bleeding, I could smell her desire through the coppery scent of her blood. Knowing it's on my toothbrush feels like a live wire snapping against my skin, igniting a surge of desire.

Remembering the guy that looked like he was about to be violently sick by the mere thought of telling me what he saw, I retrieve my phone from my suit pants, and pull up the security feed from the bedroom. It doesn't take long to find what I need, and my cock pulses as I watch my hellcat masturbate with my toothbrush.

So. Fucking. Hot.

With another growl, I pick up the handle and throw the bathroom door open, uncaring about the sound. Carolina jerks up in the bed, her head darting left and right as she searches for the sound.

"Nicklas," she breathes as her gaze lands on mine.

I stride over to the bed, propping one knee up on the mattress as I reach for her. My large, tattooed hand closes around her delicate chin and I tilt her head so she has to look up at me. "Got something you want to tell me?" I rasp.

Her nostrils flare, but she doesn't say anything until I show her the stained plastic handle. "I-I…" She clamps her lips together and looks off to the side.

I lean down, close enough to feel her breath ghosting across my lips.

"Carolina," I coax, my voice barely above a whisper, yet laced with authority. "You better fucking answer me."

She sighs. "I didn't want to disappoint you again," she whispers softly.

My mind drifts back to the video, and I mentally curse myself for watching it without sound. "Disappoint me?" I question, arching an eyebrow. "How so?"

Despite the darkness, I notice the flush creeping along her cheeks. "You said I was fake," she admits. "So I… ahh." She pauses and licks her lips. "I didn't want you to call off our arrangement."

I'm stunned silent, my hand falling from her face. What the hell? I know I've been a dick, keeping my distance after I forced her to suck my cock. But I never said anything about canceling our agreement.

"So you, what?" I rasp, needing her to tell me what went through her pretty head.

The video plays on a loop in my mind's eye, and I remember the look of frustration, bordering on anger at times, that crossed her face more than once. It made her look like she was concentrating hard and didn't get the outcome she wanted.

She swallows hard, her eyes tracking to mine. I see the questions there, the quick calculation as she tries to work out what I want to hear. The air between us crackles with unspoken promises, each breath we take entwining our fates further. Her scent wraps around me, sweet and heady, mingling with the darker notes of my own desire.

"Say something," I say, my voice low, knowing full well she's caught in the snare of my presence.

"Something," she whispers defiantly, but there's a tremor in her voice that betrays her nonchalance.

"Smartass," I retort, though there's no malice behind the word. It's an acknowledgment of her spirit.

Carolina sighs audibly. "I was trying not to fake my moans." She shakes her head. "It was harder than I thought it would be."

This has my interest, and I want her to keep talking. "Go on," I rumble as I lift her arms above her head and pull her tank top off. I should fucking spank her for wearing clothes in bed when I've told her not to.

Instead, I push her down so she's lying on her back, looking up at me. She sucks in a breath as I crawl all the way onto the bed, positioning my body between her spread legs and placing my arms on either side of her head to keep my weight off of her. Bending my neck, I suck one of her pert nipples into my mouth, sucking and nibbling at the sensitive flesh.

"Oh!" she gasps.

I let go of her nipple. "Keep talking." When she nods, I pepper kisses all over her chest.

"Umm… I'm not sure what to say," she admits.

"Why did you fake it?" I ask, looking up at her.

She rolls her eyes and huffs. "Are you sure you want to hear about other guys?"

The mere thought of someone else touching her has my temper flaring, but I lock it down as tight as possible. "If I must," I grind out through gritted teeth.

"Fine. Okay. I wasn't even aware I was fake moaning with you, okay?" She scoffs at herself at how stupid that sounds. "It's something men have expected for years, so I guess you can say it's become second nature." I don't tell her I'd already figured that part out for myself.

I move further up the mattress so the tip of my cock rubs against her clit. The moans coming from her as I rut against her are anything but fake. They're deep and so fucking raw.

Our lips crash together in a fervent tangle, hungry and urgent. I taste the remnants of her defiance, sweet and heady, and I can't get enough. She opens up to me, her moans swallowed by my mouth as our tongues dance to a desperate rhythm.

Her hands roam over my bare chest, nails grazing my skin, leaving trails of fire in their wake. "God, Nicklas…" Carolina gasps against my lips, and the sound of my name from her is both a torment and a pleasure. It's a lit match to my control, and I press closer, driven by a need that only she can satiate.

"Tell me what you want," I demand.

"I want you to make me come."

Groaning, I tug at her nipple. "How do you want to come? Do you want me to use my hand? My mouth? My cock?"

"Y-your cock," she whispers.

I snake my hand between us, sliding my fingers underneath her panties and through her wet folds. "Are you still bleeding?" I'm pretty sure she isn't since the toothbrush isn't covered in blood.

"No," she answers.

Slowly, I slide two fingers inside her, testing her walls, reveling in her heat. Her wetness coats my hand, a testament to her arousal, and the sight of my digits disappearing inside her only makes my cock throb harder.

I'm a man possessed as I pump my fingers in and out of her hot channel, curling them just so—knowing exactly where to hit to make her moan. "Nicklas," she mewls, her nails digging into the sheets. "Please!"

I reward her with a devilish grin before leaning down to tease her aching nipple with my tongue, grazing it lightly before sucking. "Please, what?"

"Make me come," she moans.

My fingers piston in and out of her cunt. My cock aches as I watch her writhe beneath me, her perfect tits flushed and hard as she begs for more. This woman, my captive, is utterly amazing. Not only does she still want our deal, not that she ever had a choice, but she even wanted to do better. Knowing that makes my heart contract and my cock swell.

Her cunt squeezes my fingers tightly and her legs shake around me. "That's a good kitty," I praise. "Purring for me so prettily."

"Nicklas! Oh my God! I can't... I need... Nicklas!"

When she bucks, I move my hand to her pubic bone and hold her down while I mercilessly fuck her harder with my finger until she screams my name in ecstasy. Wetness leaks from her core, making it impossible to keep my desire for her at bay.

Without a word, I pull my fingers from her core and line my cock up against her swollen folds. "Ready or not," I growl as I thrust into her. "Here I fucking come."

Carolina cries out and bows off the bed. Her hips meet me thrust for thrust as I hammer into her over and over. I groan her name. "Fuck. You feel so good wrapped around me."

My hellcat mewls approvingly as her hands cup her bouncing tits. "Yes. Right there."

I fuse our lips together again, biting and licking her tongue. Every nerve ending comes alive, and it doesn't take long before my nuts draw up and I'm ready to spill my seed. Although I'd love to see my cum on her creamy tits, I stay inside her cunt.

"Make yourself come," I demand, my voice low and filled with gravel.

Carolina moves her hand between us, and I can feel her circling her clit while I slam into her so hard she keeps moving up the bed. Uncaring, I follow her and keep my ruthless pace until she cries out. Fuck, the way her inner walls squeeze me like a vise is too much. I thrust once more, and that's all it takes before I come with a roar.

"Carolina! Fuck!"

I keep fucking her through my orgasm, wanting to prolong the intense feeling. Christ, fucking Carolina is unlike anything I've ever done before. She's so responsive and pliable. Perfect.

As soon as her pussy relaxes, I pull out of her and slide backwards. Then I push my fingers inside her, stopping my cum from leaking out of her.

"Grab the pillow and put it under your hips," I instruct.

"Nicklas," she breathes. "I don't think I'm ovulating—"

"Do it," I bark, not willing to negotiate.

I might not know everything there is to know about the female body and its cycles, but that doesn't mean I'm willing to waste my jizz. Any chance, no matter how small, is worth taking. We remain like that until I'm satisfied that one of my swimmers has had ample time to reach her uterus.

Then I lie down next to her, pulling her close so her head rests on my chest. "You've managed to surprise me tonight," I admit. "Not many people can say that."

"Good or bad?" she challenges, and I can hear the smile in her tone.

"Good," I confirm. "So fucking good that I'll give you your phone back tomorrow."

She squeals. "Really? Can I call Willow? I just need to know she's okay. Please, would that be okay?"

I chuckle, loving how eager she is. "Of course. It's your phone, you can do whatever you want."

"But?" she asks, undoubtedly hearing the warning in my tone.

"I've cloned it. I'll know everything you do, Carolina. And if you do something stupid, Willow will be the one to pay the price."

CHAPTER 12

The Breeder

Happy tears prick at my eyelids and my heart pounds a fierce staccato against my ribs as I finally close my hands around the sleek device in my hand. My fingers tremble as I swipe to unlock the phone.

It might only have been a week, but the time cut off from Willow is something I feel in my soul. Now, I'm finally about to talk to my sister again.

"Remember, Kitten," Nick's voice cuts through my anticipation, a dark melody that sends shivers down my spine. "I'll be listening to every word."

I nod, unable to trust my voice, acutely aware of his towering presence behind me. His breath is warm on my neck, a stark contrast to the chill of the room. The thought of him monitoring our conversation taints my excitement with a drop of poison. But I won't let him steal this moment from me. Not this one.

"But do you *have* to be right there?" I ask, irritated. "If you've cloned my phone, you can listen from anywhere."

Stupid as it sounds, now that I'm out of the bedroom and in his spacious living room, I feel more vulnerable. It doesn't make any sense since I'm still locked up. But it feels more daunting to be in a space I'm not familiar with. Especially this one. Everything is so fancy and shiny, making me scared I'll break something priceless.

Nicklas sits down next to me on the couch. He cups the nape of my neck, squeezing until I whimper and look at him. "Can I trust you?" he asks, his tone ominous.

Ignoring the sliver of fear running down my spine, I huff, "You said that if I fuck up, my sister will pay the price, and you said that for a reason."

"Which is?" he clips.

"You know I'll do anything for her," I admit. "So you know I won't put her in danger."

A pregnant silence falls over us like a suffocating blanket, and I know it's because I haven't answered his question.

"Yes," I say softly. "You can trust me."

The words are barely out of my mouth before he slams his lips to mine, kissing me roughly. The scruff on his face makes my skin burn, and each swipe of his tongue makes my pussy contract.

"Nicklas," I whimper.

I feel myself relaxing as our lips and tongues continue to move together, and before I know what the hell I'm doing, I've twisted on the couch and thrown one of my legs over both of his. With a growl, he lets go of my neck and palms my hips, lifting me onto his lap with ease.

My fingers rake down the front of his shirt, eagerly tugging at the fabric until it's free of his suit pants. Then I snake my hands underneath the fabric so I can feel his skin. He's hot and hard. A surge of feminine pride races through me as his abs tense when I slide my hands over them. I love knowing he isn't indifferent to my touch.

Nicklas tangles his fingers in my hair, tilting my head to the side so he can deepen the kiss. Gyrating my hips, I moan into his mouth when his rigid length hits my clit just right. "God!" I hiss. I'm so lost in our making out that I can't focus on anything but the need building inside me.

Using his grip on my hair, he forces my head backwards while looking up at me through hooded eyes. "You have to stop," he groans, sounding like that's the last thing he wants me to do.

"I don't want to," I admit. I barely recognize my own voice. It's husky and thick with need.

He lets out a deep chuckle. "Are you going to make your sister wait while I fuck you?" My cheeks flush hot with guilt for allowing myself to forget about Willow. "That's what I thought," he smirks as his thumb runs across my tender lips.

Needing to compose myself, I place my hands on his shoulders and force myself to breathe deeply. I'm not aware that I'm watching his scar until he takes my hand and presses my fingers against the marred flesh.

"How did you get that?" I ask, running my fingers along the length of it. Up close it looks intimidating as hell. It tells that someone got close enough to injure him, but he lived to tell the tale.

I'm surprised when he answers. "Let's just say I had a disagreement with someone I considered a friend." There's zero emotion in his tone.

Staring into his dark eyes, I notice the gold flecks around his irises. They create a beautifully hypnotizing pattern. If I didn't know better, I could almost fool myself into believing he's opening up to me. After all, the eyes are said to be the window to the soul, and if that's true, then Nicklas is allowing me more than a peep right now.

"I didn't know you had friends," I quip, breaking our intense eye contact.

He chuckles. "I don't anymore. But once, I did, and it almost cost me my life."

Swallowing thickly, I brazenly cup his cheeks, running my fingers along the roughness of his scruff and up his smooth skin. "I'm glad you're alive," I admit.

Nicklas moves so quickly I let out a startled yelp. Before I know what's happening, he pushes me off his lap and stands up. "Of course you are." His tone is smooth but his glare is so intense I squirm inwardly. "You stand to make a lot of money from our arrangement, and all you have to do in exchange is spread your legs for me."

I don't know why his cold words surprise me, but they do. Hell, they do more than that. They cut me deeper than I like, and I realize I've let this monster get under my skin. Squaring my shoulders, I absentmindedly run a hand through my hair, finger-combing the tresses back into submission.

Although I try my best not to watch him tuck his shirt back into his pants, I can't make myself look away. Every minute in this man's presence is like playing with fire. He's the proverbial flame, and despite my best attempts, I'm the moth drawn to its undoing.

"I want a contract," I snap, surprised by my words.

"What?" Nicklas bites out.

Refusing to back down, I get to my feet, hoping he can't see how badly my legs are shaking. "You heard me," I say, glad my voice holds steady. "I want a legally binding contract between us."

To my surprise, Nicklas throws his head back and laughs. "Are you sure that's what you want?" When I nod eagerly, he smirks. "Be careful what you ask for, Hellcat. But I'll take care of it."

"You will?" I ask, stunned he's giving in so easily.

"Absolutely," he confirms.

I gnaw on my bottom lip and ponder his words. Something about the way he suddenly shut down and his reaction now doesn't sit right with me. Although it's beyond tempting to try to dig deeper, I don't want to risk him taking my phone back.

"Thank you," I say, even though I'm not sure I should thank him. "Can I call my sister now?"

He smiles, but it doesn't reach his eyes. "I'll leave the room while you talk to her," he says. "But remember, I'll be watching. One wrong move, and—"

Waving my hand in the air, I interrupt him. "Yeah, yeah. You'll make her pay, and I'll regret ever being born. I get it," I hiss. It's probably not a good idea to talk to him like this, but I can't stomach listening to him threaten Willow. "I said you can trust me, Nicklas. Give me the chance to prove it."

He doesn't say anything else, just strides out of the room, leaving me alone with my thoughts and phone. With him gone, I sit back down on the couch before I unlock the phone. When I open the message thread between me and my sister, I'm taken aback.

"What the hell?" I murmur, feeling more violated than I can put into words.

There are messages from me that I've never sent, and messages from Willow that I've never read. Sure, I knew Nicklas had done something like this to keep my sister from realizing I was... well, not missing... but... unavailable. But seeing it is something different altogether.

I swallow down my desire to hunt his ass down and slap him. Mostly because I know I can't do that. So before I can let my temper get the better of me, I press the video icon on my sister's name and wait.

It rings once.

Twice.

Three times.

Then my sister's beaming face pops onto my screen. "Caro!" she squeals.

"Will," I half-sob, half-laugh. "How are you?"

"I'm doing great."

I nod along, loving listening to Willow when she's talking about something she loves. I don't think she realizes she's practically shouting and her arm gestures are almost erratic. That's my sister for you; exuberant and passionate.

"That sounds great," I laugh as she finishes telling me about the fifty baubles she's crammed into her room since I left. "Did you stick to the same colors as we used on the tree?"

"No. I was going to go with the blue and white, but then my friend convinced me to pick red. 'Tis the season and all that." She laughs so hard tears form in her eyes and roll down her cheeks.

My sister's laugh is so infectious I join in even though I don't get it. Red is a traditional color, sure, but it's not a funny color by any stretch of the imagination. "What gives?" I laugh. "I'm missing something, aren't I?"

Will turns her head and looks at something—or someone—I can't see. "Do you wanna say hi?" she asks.

"Sure," a woman says.

"I want you to meet my new friend," Will explains. "I think you'll like her." She reaches off-screen, and before I can say anything, her friend steps into view.

The woman is poised with an elegance that feels out of place. Her raven-black hair is styled to perfection, not a hair out of place, and her emerald green eyes flash with an unspoken warning. Whoever she is, she's so beautiful it's impossible not to feel inferior in her presence—even if said presence is through a camera.

"Ruby, this is my sister, Caro." Willow's words are proud, but they barely register.

"Hello, Caro," Ruby says smoothly, her voice laced with an edge that doesn't match her cordial smile. "I've heard so much about you. I'm Ruby."

"Hi-hello," I stammer, making a complete fool of myself. The woman rubs me wrong, she makes me feel like she's assessing me for weak spots. For my sister's sake, I keep my face neutral, my smile plastered on even as my mind screams in silent alarm. "Nice to meet you." I manage to keep my tone light.

"Likewise," Ruby replies, her gaze unflinching, almost challenging. "As fun as this is, Willow and I have to go. We're going ice skating—"

"Ice skating?" I sputter in surprise. My sister is in a fucking wheelchair.

Ruby raises a black eyebrow, her gaze instantly becoming glacial. "Yes, is that so hard to believe? Your sister might have certain physical limitations, but that doesn't mean she can't have some fun."

The words hit me square in the chest, making guilt and anger flare to life. I know damn well what my sister is capable of.

"She didn't mean it like that, Ruby," Will says, defending me. "She's just being overprotective." Then my sister turns to me. "Ruby has arranged for the rink to be mostly empty so she can push me around. Come on, don't say I can't go, Caro."

I open my mouth to answer but no words come out. I just stare at the two women, unsure of what to say. "Wear a scarf," I say, knowing full well how lame that sounds. "And, umm… have fun."

When my gaze lands on Ruby, she begrudgingly nods. "I'll take good care of your sister. At least for as long as you take care of my brother." The warning in her tone is so badly masked I wonder how Will isn't hearing it.

Her brother? Ah, shit… now that she's said that, I can see the familial resemblance in the eyes, chin, and... aura.

"Wait what?" Will asks. "Caro, do you know Ruby's brother?"

I pinch the bridge of my nose. "I do," I admit. "Look, I'll tell you about it another day. But for now, the two of you should hit the ice."

We say our goodbyes, and as soon as I've ended the call, I fly up from the couch. "Nicklas!" I shout, not giving two shits who might hear me as I stomp toward the door he disappeared out of.

Gah, this place is so big I'll need a freaking map to navigate it. After opening the third door without finding him, I hear a pained scream. My blood runs cold and I consider turning back, but since I've clearly not learned my damn lesson about curiosity even after being in the alley that led me to Nicklas, I go to push open the next door, but before I can even touch the handle, someone grabs my shoulder and spins me around.

"You shouldn't be here."

CHAPTER 13

The Santa

The screams echo through my torture room, a cacophony that usually blends into the background of my world. But not today. Today, each cry stokes the fire in my gut, a fury ignited by the thought of someone else's eyes on Carolina.

"Please, Mr. Knight, I didn't mean to—I swear!" The man strapped to the chair is barely recognizable now, his face swollen and streaked with blood. I lean in close, my breath steady against his battered ear.

"You saw something you shouldn't have," I growl, my fingers tightening around the pliers.

"But you... you told me to watch her!"

I give him a sharp nod. "I did, and that's the sole reason you woke up this morning." My breathing is deep, ragged both from excitement and from wrestling him into the chair. I cup my jaw; the spot, where he got a lucky punch in, throbs. "And you repaid me by telling others what you saw."

Rumors and hushed whispers don't remain hushed for long in a place like this. If the damn kid had just kept his mouth shut about what he saw, I wouldn't have to kill him. Send him away, probably. But I'd let him live as a favor to Marco.

"P-please," he cries, squeezing his eyes shut. "I don't want to die."

He shudders, and when I look down, there's a wet patch at the front of his pants that wasn't there a minute ago. Fucker pissed himself.

"Then you should have kept your mouth shut," I say, my tone completely devoid of sympathy. "You knew she wasn't there for your pleasure, yet you looked at hers. You looked at the mother of my heir. *My* hellcat. Mine. *Not yours.* M.I.N.E!" I roar out the last part, losing myself in the maddening anger.

He whimpers, a sound that grates against my nerves. My grip doesn't falter as I yank another nail free, his howl filling the space between us. It's a warning to others, a testament to my wrath.

Suddenly, the door bursts open, and Marco joins us. He doesn't even glance at the mess I've made of his nephew. What can I say; he's loyal, and he knows the kid fucked up yesterday.

"What is it?" I snap, locking eyes with Marco.

"Found Carolina snooping around," he drawls. "She was trying to find you."

I let out an audible sigh. "Damn her curiosity," I curse. "Did she hear or see anything?"

Marco inclines his head slightly. "Heard a scream. But other than that, nothing. I took her back to the kitchen where the staff is keeping an eye on her."

Despite wanting to take my time with this guy, I pick up my knife and, in a quick, fluent motion, I slice his neck open. His scream immediately turns garbled. Panic's written all over his face as he claws at his neck, uselessly trying to stifle the blood flowing from the cut.

"I'll get someone to clean this up," I say. I might be a bastard, but I'm not so cold as to expect Marco to do it.

Ever loyal, he says, "I'll take care of it. I brought him in and vouched for him. With all due respect, this is my mess." His tone is grave, and I know it's because he feels like he's failed me rather than the loss he should feel.

I clasp his arm. "This isn't your fault, Marco. And I don't blame you in the slightest. You're a good man, and I don't want you to think otherwise. Your position here is safe."

He visibly relaxes at my words. "I'll still take care of it since I need to come up with something to tell my sister, anyway."

I leave Marco with a promise of paying for any expenses his family needs. Normally, I only offer this to my most loyal men when they die or get seriously injured in my service. But special circumstances call for special solutions. Marco's worth it.

Before going to the kitchen, I dip into one of the spare bathrooms and take a quick shower and change clothes. Carolina's already seen me kill a man, but that doesn't mean she needs to know what goes on behind the closed doors of my penthouse.

My phone vibrates just as I round the corner to the kitchen. Pulling it out, I see it's the contract I requested for Carolina's services. My lips twist up into a wry smile and anticipation thrums through my veins. I hope she knows what she asked for.

Carolina's sitting at the kitchen island, eating fried eggs, bacon, and some buttered bread. I watch as she reaches for her cup which undoubtedly contains coffee. Oh, this is so fucking on. My hellcat is about to regret asking for a contract.

"Put that down," I growl menacingly.

Her spine stiffens as her hand freezes mid-air. "W-what?"

My smile is still in place as I walk to her side and take the cup from her hand. Then I turn to Greta, one of my trusted employees. "Please take Miss Sterling's plate. She's done for now."

"Of course," Greta replies easily.

"The hell I am," Carolina seethes. "I've barely eaten."

I ignore her outburst and continue talking to Greta. "I've sent you an email with the food and drinks Miss Sterling is allowed. Only items on the list are approved."

Greta gives me a stern nod before making herself scarce. I turn to Carolina, whose eyes are shooting daggers at me. "Don't worry, you won't go hungry," I say calmly, like that's the issue.

"You do not get to fucking dictate what I put in my body," my hellcat hisses. "You're going too far, Nicklas."

"Am I?" I ask, quirking an eyebrow. "You wanted a contract between us, Carolina. So I took the liberty of having one drawn up."

She folds her arms over her chest. "I won't sign anything that gives you control over my body."

I chuckle darkly. "What did you think would happen, hmm? You're to conceive my heir, so it only makes sense we do what we can to guarantee a positive result."

She opens her mouth, probably to chew me out, but then she shuts it again. Knowing I've rendered her speechless, I reach for my phone and pull up the digital contract. Then I forward it to her and point at her phone resting on the kitchen island.

"You should read that," I say when it vibrates against the marble.

Her eyebrows shoot up her forehead as she unlocks the phone. "How do you know my email?" she demands.

I shrug. "There isn't much about you I don't know," I assure her.

"How?" she whispers.

Smirking, I walk over to her and place my finger below her chin, tilting her head back so she has to look up at me. "You gave it all to me willingly." I run my thumb across her soft, luscious lips. "When you signed up on my Cam Girl site."

She gasps. "W-what?"

Chuckling, I revel in her obvious discomfort and embarrassment. Red blossoms on her cheeks and down her neck. "Did you know that 'Cam' isn't short for 'Camera' but for 'Camelot'?"

"Camelot?" she asks, her tone confused.

"Indeed," I confirm, grinning. "We are Knights, after all."

She shakes her head and mumbles something under her breath, but continues to read. While she does, I move behind her, gathering her long hair in my hand and moving it away from her neck. Then I lower myself so my lips ghost across her skin, reading over her shoulder.

CONTRACT FOR CONCEPTION OF HEIR

Date: ___ day of _____, 2024

Parties: Nicklas Knight ("Mr. Knight") and Carolina Sterling ("Ms. Sterling")

Purpose: Ms. Sterling agrees to conceive an heir for Mr. Knight by natural means under the following terms.

1. Duration and Conception Deadline

Effective from December 1, 2024, until one year after the child's birth or if conception fails by December 25, 2024.

2. Payment Terms

Successful Conception:

All expenses covered from December 1, 2024, until one year after the birth.

$10,000,000 upon the child's birth.

Lifetime housing with all expenses paid.

Unsuccessful Conception:

All December 2024 expenses covered.

$2,000,000 payout.

3. Living Arrangements and Obligations

Residency: Ms. Sterling will live with Mr. Knight from December 1, 2024, until one year after birth if conception is successful.

Availability: Ms. Sterling will be available to Mr. Knight at all times during the contract.

Exclusivity: All intimate relations are exclusive to Mr. Knight. This includes orgasms; Ms. Sterling is only allowed the orgasms Mr. Knight bestows on her.

Restrictions: Ms. Sterling will only perform activities approved by Mr. Knight.

4. Dietary Restrictions

Fertility Diet: Ms. Sterling agrees to consume only specified foods to promote fertility.

Amendment Upon Pregnancy: Diet will be adjusted to suit pregnancy needs.

5. Parental Rights and Contact

Waiver: Ms. Sterling relinquishes all parental rights upon the child's birth.

No Contact: No contact with Mr. Knight or the child after one year post-birth. Breach results in damages.

Residency: Ms. Sterling will not reside in New York or neighboring states indefinitely post-birth. Housing will be provided in an alternative state or country.

6. Confidentiality

Both parties agree to maintain strict confidentiality regarding the contract and pregnancy.

7. Governing Law

This Contract is governed by the laws of the State of New York and by the Knight family.

Signatures:

Nicklas Knight

Date: _____

Carolina Sterling

Date: _____

I know the exact moment my hellcat is done reading because she leaps off the chair and away from me like my touch is burning her. She spins around so fast the hair I only just managed to let go of, whips her in the face.

"What the fuck, Nicklas?" she screams like a banshee. "What. The. Actual. Fuck."

Tilting my head to the side, I watch her. She's trembling, her hands are balled, and her nostrils flare with every inhale. Her barely controlled anger makes me smile. That's it, Kitten. Let it out, I silently beg.

CHAPTER 14

The Breeder

I stand there, my hands clenched into fists at my sides, the phone with the contract in my fierce grip. The audacity Nicklas has to present me with such terms—it's not just insulting, it's vile. My breath comes out in sharp, heated bursts, each exhale a silent scream against the injustice of it all.

"Is there a problem, Carolina?" Nicklas' voice is infuriatingly calm, a stark contrast to the storm raging inside me.

"Problem?" The word is a hiss through my teeth. "You think trapping me with this… this breeding contract is acceptable?" I can't keep the tremor from my voice, anger and disbelief waging war within me.

The room seems to sway as I fight to control the shaking that takes over my body. Anger surges through my veins like wildfire, consuming any semblance of composure. I want to tear the contract to shreds, to throw it back in his face, but I know what's at stake—my sister, my future, everything I've worked for.

"Well, you wanted a contract, and I obliged. This is for our mutual benefit." His dark eyes are unyielding as he stares me down. "And now you know the seriousness of my world."

Mutual benefit? What a cruel joke. There's no benefit here for me, only chains disguised as clauses. His world—a world of shadows and cold-hearted deals—is swallowing me whole, and the thought chokes me with dread. "Benefit?" I spit the word out. "This isn't a partnership; it's ownership!"

Nicklas stands unmoved, his tattooed arms folded across his chest like steel bands. For a moment, I see the flash of something in his gaze— pride, possession? It only fuels my fury. "Ownership is a strong word," he rebukes, his tone holding an edge of warning.

It's fucking accurate, that's what it is. My heart pounds against my ribs, a frantic drumbeat echoing my inner turmoil. Nicklas Knight is many things, but stupid isn't one of them. He can't possibly believe I'll allow him to reduce me to a broodmare. Can he?

"Then find a better one," I challenge, my body trembling, not just with anger now, but also with a fear I refuse to acknowledge. Fear that he might be too powerful to resist, fear that he'll break more than just my will.

"Careful, Carolina. You're not in a position to make demands," he warns, his voice a low rumble that reverberates through the tension-laden air.

"Neither are you to make such vile propositions," I counter, knowing full well the danger of provoking him. But I can't help it—the flame of defiance burns too brightly, even against the tide of my own trepidation.

The air between us crackles with the intensity of our standoff. I'm acutely aware of every breath he takes, the way his nostrils vibrate slightly with barely suppressed irritation. He's a predator, and I've just bared my throat to him. But I won't back down—not when so much is on the line.

"Sign the contract, Carolina," he commands, his voice leaving no room for argument.

"No," I volley, shaking my head. "No way."

"Carolina!"

"Nicklas," I say, mirroring his tone. "What's good for one is good for the other."

"Meaning?"

Lifting my phone, I unlock it and point at the contract. "Everything I have to do, you do, too."

He throws his head back and lets out a booming laugh. "You want to own my pleasure, Kitten? Is that it?"

Instead of letting him distract me, I shrug. "Among other things."

Stretching, he steeples his fingers together behind his neck. "State your terms then, Carolina. Show me your claws."

"You can only eat and drink the things you allow me to eat and drink," I say dryly. When he doesn't object, I grow bolder. "If I have to be available for your pleasure, you have to be available for mine. And—"

"Is that so?"

Ignoring his interruption, I carry on. "And I don't like the exclusivity clause." I keep my tone haughty and lift my chin.

His eyes darken until they're almost black. "What's your problem with that clause? Don't tell me you want to fuck other men." The way he says it makes it clear my answer better be no. "Because while you were on the phone with your sister, I killed the last man that watched what's mine. And I'll fucking kill every single person in Manhattan if that's what it takes for you to understand you're mine."

He fucking did what? "What are you talking about?" I argue. My voice doesn't falter, which is good. I don't want him to know how much his words are affecting me.

"That got your attention, hmm, Kitten?" He smirks knowingly. "When you decided to use my toothbrush to get yourself off, I had someone watching you—"

"Oh, my God!" I cry out. I'm so goddamn stupid. I knew there was a chance Nicklas was watching, but I don't think I ever thought anyone else might be.

"No reason to be embarrassed," Nicklas coos. Fucking coos. "He's dead now."

My breath hitches as I realize that must be the pained scream I heard. Jesus, a man's dead because of me. Because of... fuck. Why did I ever think I could go toe-to-toe with a man I saw murder another in cold blood? I need to stop antagonizing him and just get this month over with.

"Talk about overreacting," I force myself to say. I take a deep breath, willing my body to stop shaking. At least while I'm in the same room as Nicklas. "I have no interest in anyone else. In fact, fucking somebody who isn't you is the farthest thing on my mind." My tone is monotone, like I'm reading a script.

"So why fight the exclusivity?" he asks, his tone sharp like he doesn't believe me.

Lord, he's being dense. "Because the same rules aren't laid out for you. I'm not okay with the double standard. Especially not when you're fucking me bare," I retort, almost screaming again.

His lips twitch into an almost smile. "So you want the same rules for me as I've laid out for you?"

"Yes!"

When his smile grows into a full-blown smirk I feel like I just got played, and his words prove me right. "Alright, once again, I'll give you exactly what you ask for. Equality, Kitten. So if I don't knock you up, you can pay me two million for the orgasms."

Oh, fuck. He's right, I hadn't completely thought this through at all. I know he sees it as his words register on my face. "You manipulative fucker," I hiss, my voice strangled. It's true what he says, he's giving me exactly what I'm asking for. And in the process, he's twisting it like an evil Genie. While still somehow managing to make it so it's no less than what I've demanded.

Even though I feel like crying and kicking like a petulant child, I unlock the phone in my hand. My hand shakes as I sign digitally. With each stroke of my name, I feel the walls closing in around me. It feels like a sentence, a binding that tightens around my very soul.

"All done," I sneer, angry I got played by… well, by myself.

My signature on the page feels like defeat, a heavy weight anchoring me to this new, terrifying reality. My mind races, frantic for an escape that doesn't exist. I'm caught in Nicklas Knight's web, and every fiber of my being rebels against it.

Unable to help myself, I add, "Happy now?" The words are venomous, spat out as I glare at him with all the hatred I can muster. But he just watches me, dark eyes glinting with a cold satisfaction that chills me to the bone.

"Ecstatic," Nicklas replies, a cruel smirk twisting his lips. His voice is low and smooth, like the purr of a lion that has cornered its prey. It sends shivers down my spine, but not the good kind.

I need to get out of here, away from his predatory gaze. I whirl around and stride toward the door, desperate to reclaim even a shred of control over my life. But before I can reach the sanctuary of solitude, his hand wraps around my arm, ironclad and unyielding.

"Where do you think you're going?" The question is rhetorical; we both know I'm not going anywhere he doesn't want me to.

"Let go of me, Nicklas," I snarl, trying to wrench my arm free, but his grip only tightens, pulling me back until I'm flush against his solid chest. Heat radiates through the layers of our clothes, a stark contrast to the ice in his voice.

"First things first, Carolina." His breath fans hotly against my ear, causing an involuntary shudder to travel through me. "Since I don't plan on relying on the stork to find me, it's time to get down to business."

Without warning, he pushes me forward and bends me over the table, the polished wood cool beneath my palms. The forcefulness of his movements leaves me breathless, heart hammering in my chest. His body hovers over mine, a cage of muscle and power trapping me in place.

"Time to earn your money," he growls, and the raw possessiveness in his tone terrifies and thrills me all at once.

"Is this what gets you off? Power?" I spit the words out, trying to keep the tremor from my voice. Anger swirls within me, a tempest that threatens to consume us both.

"Power," he confirms, his voice a rough whisper that reverberates through the room. "And you, my little hellcat." As if to punctuate his words, he grinds against me, letting me feel his hard length. The clothes between us don't do a damn thing, and the movement makes my clit tingle and my nipples pucker.

The acknowledgment sends a jolt through me, unwanted arousal blooming deep in my belly. I hate that he affects me, hate that my body betrays me in his presence. But I refuse to let him see it, to give him the satisfaction of knowing he can elicit such a response from me.

"Go to hell," I manage through gritted teeth, though my resolve falters with each thrust of his hips against my ass.

His laughter is dark, rich, and utterly maddening. "Oh, my sweet kitten, we're already there. And you're mine to burn with."

My heart pounds in my chest as he roughly tears through the fabric of my pants, the sound of ripping material echoing through the room. I thrash against him, my mind screaming rebellion, but my body betrays me with its trembling.

"Stop!" I snarl, even as his fingers trail with maddening precision over my skin, igniting a fire that threatens to consume me from the inside out. His touch is skilled, too knowing, finding that ache within me and coaxing it to a fever pitch.

"Never," Nicklas replies, his breath hot against my ear. Every brush, every stroke is a declaration, a branding of ownership that I can't escape.

I hate him for this, for the way my body opens up to him, soft and willing despite the fury boiling in my veins. The pleasure mixes with my anger, a toxic cocktail that sets my senses ablaze. It's wrong, so wrong, but my hips betray me with their involuntary tilt toward his touch.

"Damn you," I gasp as he circles my clit, the friction building a coil of tension deep within me. My nails dig into the wood of the table, trying to anchor myself in the midst of this storm he's unleashed.

"Say you want it," he commands, his voice a dark whisper that sends shivers down my spine.

"Fuck off," I breathe out, defiance and desire warring within me. But with each expert caress, my resistance crumbles, my inner walls clenching in anticipation.

"Beg me to make you come."

"No!" My resolve falters—dissipates—as he removes his hand from my pussy. "P-please make me come," I moan, hating myself a little more for giving in to him.

"Such a good kitten," he murmurs, and then he pushes his fingers inside me.

The digits piston in and out of me, and the sloppy sounds coming from my pussy are so loud they drown out my moans and gasps. This man plays my body like he's known it for years rather than days. He expertly takes me right to the precipice, but instead of denying me the pleasure building inside me, he sends me crashing over the edge.

"Nicklas!" I scream his name as my pussy contracts around his fingers. "Yes. Yes. Yeeessss!" I'm barely aware of my words as I rock my hips against his hands, wanting more of him inside me.

While I'm recovering from my orgasm, he turns me around so I'm facing him. He uses his foot to lower my pants and underwear, and I awkwardly kick them off. The clang from his belt and sound of his zipper being lowered reach my ears only a moment before he frees his long, rigid, and thick cock.

I've seen a lot of dicks in my desperate hunt for financial freedom, but I can't say I've ever paid much attention to any of them. Some were short, some thin, and some crooked. But they were all just hard lengths. Nothing like Nicklas' which is… I hate admitting it, but even seeing it is a turn on.

"Look at it," he orders, like my eyes aren't already glued to it. I watch as he lazily strokes himself. "Do you see how hard I am for you, Carolina? My cock is fucking weeping and it's all because of you." He runs his finger along the slit and brings it up to my lips. Before I can fully process what I'm doing, my tongue darts out and licks the salty wetness from the pad of his digit.

"Mhmm," I moan, surprised that I don't hate the taste at all.

I'm so lost in the moment, I don't realize Nicklas has moved until he places his large, tattooed hands on my buttocks and lifts me up onto the table. "Wrap your legs around me," he demands huskily.

I quickly do as he says, impatiently digging my heels into his sculpted ass. Then I lean back on my elbows and look up at him, licking my lips with anticipation as I feel the tip of his cock against my opening. I whimper as he painfully slowly inches into me, stretching me to fit his huge dick.

"Christ!" I pant, breathing through my nose at the sting following his slide into my body. "I need a second." I'm not trying to be difficult or prolong it, I really do need a moment to adjust to the size of him.

"Almost there," he rasps. He leans forward and moves my hair away from my face. "You're doing so well, Carolina."

Then he fuses our lips together in a maddening kiss. All the sensations have my toes curling and I feel like I'm about to burst with… I don't know what. Sensation overload? If that's even a thing.

I barely have time to brace myself as he breaks the kiss and slams the rest of the way into me. "Fuck!" he groans. "Too. Damn. Tight."

He palms my hips in a bruising hold, and then our bodies move together in a furious rhythm, a collision of anger and lust. I claw at his back, wanting his clothes out of the way. But he just chuckles and continues to fuck me, so I move my hands under his shirt, digging my nails into his flesh, marking him as he marks me.

The table creaks beneath us, a testament to the raw force of our fucking. This isn't gentle or loving; it's primal, a battle for dominance that neither of us can win. We're locked in this dance of destruction, each thrust a strike, each cry a surrender. My thoughts scatter, lost in the haze of sensation that Nicklas draws from me. There's pain and pleasure, hate and something perilously close to ecstasy. I can feel every inch of him, claiming me, owning me in ways I never thought possible.

"Look at me," he growls, and I do, meeting his gaze. There's no softness there, no mercy—just the fierce triumph of possession. And yet, buried deep in those dark eyes, I see a flicker of something more, something that speaks to the raw need we both feel. "Your cunt is squeezing me so tight. If I didn't know better, I'd almost think you were a virgin."

Obviously, that's an impossibility since he's already had me. Maybe he thinks it's a compliment, but I refuse to thank him for noticing I'm doing my Kegel exercises. "More. I need more," I admit through gritted teeth, the word torn from me by the relentless drive of his hips.

His movements grow erratic as we spiral toward release. The world narrows down to this moment, to the searing heat between us, and when he moves a hand between us and flicks my clit, I come apart, shattered by the intensity of my climax.

"Nicklas!" I cry. "I'm… I'm… I can't. I—" My orgasm steals my words, making it impossible to speak.

After a few thrusts, Nicklas follows, his own release a hot rush that seals me to him in the most intimate of ways. "Fuck! Carolina!"

The aftermath clings to my skin, a sheen of sweat and the musk of rough, unbridled sex. My chest heaves, trying to reclaim the breath that Nicklas has stolen with his relentless pace, his dominating presence leaving no room for anything but submission. He half collapses on top of me, we're both breathing hard. Without thinking, I wrap my arms around him, holding him tightly against me as I fight to get my breathing under control.

My brain still feels like mush as he straightens while still inside me, and I try to gather my scattered senses, but then I see his hand move—a glint of something metallic in his grasp. Nicklas' fingers are deft as he retrieves what looks like a small plug from his pocket, and without a word, he positions it against me.

"Stay still," he commands, his voice a low rumble that reverberates through the silence of the room. I tense, a fresh wave of defiance battling the exhaustion that threatens to claim me. But the way he looks at me, dark eyes burning with an insatiable need, confirms that this is non-negotiable, so I just roll my eyes.

I whimper as he pulls out of me. The coolness of the plug contrasts with the heat of my flesh, and a shiver runs up my spine as he pushes it inside me. "Don't even think about taking it out," Nicklas warns, his tone brooking no argument. He's staking his claim in the most primitive of ways, ensuring his seed remains where he believes it belongs.

I bite back a retort, knowing any words now would be as useless as they are unnecessary. This man, this force of nature, doesn't just break wills—he forges them anew, in the fires of his own desires. The plug is a weight within me, a foreign object dictating my body's rhythm. Every movement reminds me of its presence, of him, and of the undeniable truth that I am inexorably tied to Nicklas Knight.

His fingers trail lazily over the curve of my hip, a possessive touch that speaks of promises and threats all wrapped into one. The room is silent save for our breathing. "Remember who you belong to," he rasps, leaning close enough for his breath to caress the skin on my neck.

I don't respond, but my body betrays me with a tremor that speaks volumes. I hate how much I want him, even now, even after everything.

As Nicklas steps back, straightening his suit with an air of nonchalance that belies the intensity of moments before, I'm left with the echo of his touch, the fullness inside me, and the irrefutable knowledge that there's no turning back from the precipice upon which we stand.

His hand finds the plug, adding some pressure to it. "This should help give my swimmers the best chance," he says simply, satisfaction lacing his voice like a vise around my heart.

"When can I take it out?" I ask as I sit up on the table. I know he just said I shouldn't take it out, but surely he doesn't mean I have to wear it forever.

"You can't," he growls. "I'm the only one allowed to remove it."

Although I should rage, should scream at the walls and at him for the way he keeps taking it further, I do nothing. Because beneath the anger, beneath the fear, there's a thread of dark anticipation—a yearning for the tempest he brings, a craving for the chaos that is Nicklas Knight.

He keeps his hand on the bottom of the plug, as though he's making sure I'm not going to try to push it out. I mean, seriously?! If I wanted to do that I sure as hell wouldn't try while he's watching.

Nicklas finally lets go, taking my hand and helps me off the table. When I bend to reach for my discarded clothes, he slaps my ass so hard I let out a yelp. "What the hell?"

Chuckling, he lifts me up, my legs automatically winding around his waist. "You don't need clothes right now," he growls, bending so he can lick the length of my neck.

While he carries me into the bedroom, I notice a few people peeking around walls and through doors, like they're trying to figure out if it's safe to come out. Shit, I never thought about his staff when he spread me out on the table, but considering what happened to the last person who saw me in the throes of passion, maybe I should have.

I still don't know how I feel about that. On one hand, I'm horrified Nicklas is so cavalier about other people's lives. But on the other hand, I'm secretly flattered. Yeah, maybe he isn't the only one who's messed up.

As Nicklas gingerly lays me down on the bed, he follows, rolling onto his side. His hand immediately moves back between my thighs to cup the plug again. Whether to feel it's still there, or show that he owns me, I don't know, and I'm not sure I care.

There's something about it that makes me feel so indescribably wanted—needed—that I revel in it.

"About your concerns," he says, his voice filled with gravel. "You're the only one who gets my fingers, my mouth, and my cock."

I turn my head, staring at him as it takes me a moment to catch up. Oh, right, he's talking about what I said before signing the contract. "Really?"

An angry rumble bursts through his lips. "Are you questioning me, Hellcat?"

Rolling my eyes, I huff. "Of course I'm questioning you. It would be stupid of me not to."

He quickly moves to his back, pulling me on top of him so I'm straddling his hips. I moan softly as I feel his hard length between us, pressing against the plug and my clit. "You're anything but stupid," he says, almost sweetly. But then, as if to prove he isn't sweet, he tears at my shirt until it rips open. "I'm yours, and only yours."

CHAPTER 15

The Santa

I lean over the desk, my fingers drumming an impatient rhythm against the mahogany as Marco lays out the terms on the tablet. Every word he speaks is crucial—each clause a blade to carve out our future dominance in New York's underbelly.

"Profit margins will skyrocket once we finalize this." Marco's voice is all business, a low murmur that only I am privy to. The air in the office is thick with the promise of power, and it crackles around us like static electricity.

But before I can respond, the door opens to reveal Ruby standing there. "Hi Nick," she greets before turning to the other man in the room. "Marco."

"That was quick." It's barely been a couple of hours since I texted her and asked her to come over. After fucking my hellcat on the table yesterday, she told me what Ruby's been up to, and about the threat on Willow. "What do you think you're doing with Willow?" I ask, cutting straight to the point as I sweep my hand through the air toward an empty chair.

Needing no further prompt, she strides into my office and takes a seat. "Whatever do you mean?" she asks, her tone innocent but her facial expression anything but.

Sighing, I steeple my fingers together. "Stop the games, Ruby. Carolina told me that you threatened her."

Ruby rolls her eyes. "I did no such thing." She crosses one leg over the other. "I simply reminded her—"

"Ruby!" I interrupt, not in the mood for her games. "Spare me your games and just tell me what the hell you're doing."

"Fine," she relents. "I did as you asked, I offered a donation to the place and took the opportunity to meet Willow. She's... she's an interesting person, you know. I actually like her."

I'm surprised by her sincerity; Ruby doesn't like many people, but judging by her tone, and the small smile grazing her lips, she does indeed like Carolina's sister.

"So I've spent some time with her. I'll admit I didn't expect to like her, but I do."

I nod. "So why did you threaten her?"

She rolls her eyes again. "I thought that's what you wanted, Nick. Why else ask me to go there if it wasn't to help keep your chosen pussy in check?"

Even though that's not what I want, or need, her reasoning makes sense. And if I'm honest with myself, it is why I asked Ruby to check the place out. "Fine," I relent. "But no more games. Leave Willow alone."

My sister pouts. "I like spending time with her, Nick. She's a breath of fresh air. She's so... positive."

Narrowing my eyes, I lean closer. "No more threats, Ruby. Especially not to Carolina. If I hear you've crossed me, I'll—"

"You'll what?" she volleys, anger rolling from her as she balls her hands into fists. "I told you that I only did it because I thought that's what you wanted. If you don't want me thinking for myself you should stop giving me vague instructions."

I let out a dark chuckle. "You got it," I agree, glad I don't have to finish the empty threat. We both know there's nothing I won't do for her.

Besides, it makes me feel like a shit to even threaten her. Especially, when the only thing I could take from her is what little freedom she has. Ruby only goes where she's told, which I suppose is what's expected of a Mafia princess.

"Can I ask you something, Nick?"

"No," I reply curtly, already knowing I don't want to hear whatever is on my sister's mind.

Ignoring me, she asks anyway. "What are you doing with Carolina?"

I keep my face schooled in indifference, though inside, a primal possessiveness claws at my chest. Carolina is *mine,* and no one has the right to question that—not even family. "Carolina is not up for discussion, Ruby," I say, my tone final.

"You can't be serious." She crosses her arms, her every word laced with venom. "Carolina has all but abandoned her sister. Her. Sister. In that cold home. Is that really the kind of woman—"

"Enough!" I shout, unable to temper my anger. "Not that Willow's situation is any of your business, but it's temporary."

Ruby huffs, and I see her resolve waver just for a second. She knows better than to cross me when it comes to matters of the family, so this must be important for her to challenge me in my own home. "Come on, you know I'm right," she argues. "She's not good enough for you."

Studying my sister, I narrow my eyes, trying to find any clue as to what this outburst is about, but I don't find anything. "Not another word about Carolina," I growl.

To my surprise, my sister throws her hands up in the air, sighing audibly. "Nick… I just… it's her sister. No one should abandon family like that. How do you even know she's going to be a good mom—"

I don't give her the chance to finish her sentence. With a few steps, I walk around the table between us, gripping her shoulders so hard she winces. "What the hell has gotten into you?" I roar. "Why do you think it's okay to come into my home like this? To make demands?" Her eyes widen, and I can't say I blame her since I've never laid hands on her before. For Carolina, I'd fucking kill my own sister.

She opens her mouth, probably to spew more venom, but then she thinks better of it and closes it again. When I'm sure she's got the message, I let go, taking a step back from my sister. "Anything else?" I ask, forcing my tone to be cordial.

Lifting her chin, Ruby meets my gaze. "You're playing with fire,

Nick."

"Then let the flames come," I reply, a smirk tugging at my lips. "I'm not afraid of getting burned."

Ruby shakes her head as she slowly moves toward the door. "If you're that confident in your chosen pussy, why not bring her for dinner tonight?" Without waiting for my reply, she leaves, and I make a mental note to tell my people not to just let her wander into my home like this.

The door slams with the finality of a judge's gavel, and Ruby's exit leaves a cold void in its wake. I shift my stance, my hands flat on the mahogany desk, knuckles pale. Anger simmers within me, a controlled burn.

Shaking my head, I turn back to Marco, who's remained quiet during Ruby's brief visit. He knows better than to get involved in Knight family drama. Good man. "Make sure everything's set for the dinner tonight," I command, my mind already shifting gears.

"Of course, boss," Marco replies, his tone suggesting he understands the underlying urgency without question.

As he, too, exits, I sink into my leather chair, eyes closing briefly as I collect myself. How dare Ruby speak of my hellcat with such disdain? The thought ignites something feral inside of me. Carolina is mine—a raw truth that pulses through every vein.

Finder's keepers, and now that I've found her, and gotten a hint of her spirit, I want her to be the queen on my chessboard—*my* fucking chessboard. I don't know why I'm feeling so strongly about her after so few days together. I obviously don't really know her yet, but I know enough.

Every time I've challenged her, she's more than risen to the occasion. That excites me, and it makes me want her around for longer. Tonight's dinner with my dad and Arthur is the perfect time to show off my hellcat and see if she's up for yet another challenge.

My thoughts are interrupted by a soft knock. I straighten up, schooling my features into an impassive mask as the door opens. Carolina steps into the room, and even in her simplicity, she devastates my senses. Her blonde hair cascades like molten gold over her shoulders, those blue eyes holding storms of their own.

"Nicklas?" Her voice is soft but carries an edge of steel. I admire her for it.

"Carolina." I stand, moving closer. "There's been a change of plans for tonight."

"Oh?" She tilts her head, curiosity piqued.

"You're going to be officially introduced to the family," I say, watching her closely. "As mine."

Her eyes widen slightly, but she doesn't back down. "Yours," she repeats, tasting the word, gauging its weight. *"Your* what? Your breeder?" She cringes as she speaks the word, making me smile.

"Just mine," I confirm, each syllable a hammer striking iron, forging the bond between us. "And Carolina, wear something... memorable."

"Memorable how?" She challenges, her bratty demeanor rising to the bait.

"Something that screams you belong to no one else but me." My gaze locks with hers, a silent promise that tonight, I'll brand her soul with my touch.

"Umm..." She looks up at me, wringing her hands in front of her. "I don't own anything like that to wear," she admits, her voice soft.

That's true, I know from being in her home that anything she owns is very... modest. "Go shower," I chuckle, stepping forward so I can brush a tendril of her hair behind her ear. "I promise there'll be something to choose between when you get out."

She nods, a flicker of understanding passing between us.

"Oh, and Hellcat," I call after her. She pauses, but doesn't turn around to face me. Seeing her defy me at every possible turn, no matter how small, immediately has my cock waking up. "Don't wear panties."

"W-what?" she gasps, still not turning around, but I notice her shoulders tense.

"You heard me," I growl. "No. Panties."

Nodding again, she takes one more step away from me, and I'm tempted to let her go and watch on the security camera when she realizes the mistake she's about to make. Since I don't have time to play with her now, I call out her name again.

"You're allowed to remove the plug while you shower."

She doesn't answer, doesn't need to. And I'm content standing here, watching her walk away from me. My eyes are glued to the seductive sway of her hips, the way her ass moves with each step. I'm fucking hard again.

With a groan I turn around and reach for my phone on the desk, using it to text Marco so he can make sure the clothes for Carolina are brought into the bedroom.

During the week she was on her period, I bought a lot of clothes for her, including several dresses, anticipating her need for them. And just because I could, I had the tag removed from every single item. The clothes have been hanging on the rack in one of the spare rooms, but now it's time to move them into our bedroom so my hellcat can start using them.

At my dad's estate, I help Carolina out of her new coat, revealing the midnight blue dress that hugs her curves like it was sewn directly on her. It's an exquisite blend of elegance and provocation; long enough to be formal, yet with a slit up the thigh that promises sin.

The absence of her panties beneath is our secret, one that makes my cock harden every time I think about it. Of course, I had to check she'd followed my order before we came here, but I left her on the brink of release, knowing the next orgasm I give her will be so much sweeter.

Taking her hand, I pull her toward the dining room we're using tonight. It's not the same as the one I sat in with Dad and Arthur eleven days ago. That one is for family only, and since Carolina isn't family, yet, she's not allowed in there.

If you ask me, there isn't much difference in the rooms. It's all about power, the subtle play my dad loves.

High ceilings with exposed wooden beams give the space a rustic edge, while sleek, modern finishes bring an air of sophistication. A long mahogany table stretches beneath a striking chandelier, its glass and metal design both bold and elegant. The walls, dark and slate-like, are punctuated by oversized windows that frame the night outside, and a massive stone fireplace at the far end crackles softly, its warmth filling the room.

The blend of cool stone floors and deep-hued rugs beneath my feet adds texture and color, while large abstract paintings bring a modern touch. The room feels both expansive and intimate, designed to awe and envelop at once. It's a place where rustic meets modern in perfect harmony, every detail carefully chosen to impress.

Everyone is already seated; Dad at one end of the table, Arthur at the other. Ruby and her husband sit together with Jack on one side, the other empty, making it clear where we're expected to sit.

While I lead us over to our seats, I quickly introduce everyone to Carolina, or, more accurately, point out who they are and state their names. When I get to Arthur, he raises an eyebrow after I've said his name, and I get it. No one but a Knight or a Hatt is allowed to know who he is, but fuck it. Those rules don't count tonight. Why? Because I've fucking decided so.

My hellcat is above such rules, especially as the future mother to my first, and hopefully all, heirs. I meant what I told her yesterday; I'm hers, and she already knows she's mine.

Ruby's eyes narrow as Carolina takes her seat beside me, and her lips curl into a snarl. "So, this is your latest purchase?" Ruby's voice drips with disdain, an icy challenge that fills the room.

"Ruby," her husband's tone is a low growl, barely audible over the servers that immediately begin to place food on the table. "Enough."

Her cheeks flush with a mix of anger and embarrassment, but she doesn't back down. She never does. I can't help but admire her spirit, even as it grates against me. "No. I'm sorry, but this is not okay. Nicklas bought her services. How can we all just be okay with that?"

The tension in the dining room is a living thing, undulating through the air like smoke. Ruby's words hang heavy, and I can't help but tighten my grip on Carolina's thigh.

I stare at my sister for a long moment, my jaw clenching as I consider the myriad of ways I could put her in her place. But before I can decide on a course of action, I catch sight of Dad. His lips press into a thin line as he stares at us. That familiar disapproval etched across his face is like a cold splash of reality—Dad doesn't take lightly to risks that could threaten our legacy.

"Why is she here?" he asks, authority clinging to each word. His cold eyes stay on Carolina, who averts her gaze.

"Carolina is here because I want her to be," I say firmly, my voice a clear declaration. "She belongs at this table, by my side."

Dad's glower intensifies. "I asked why," he repeats. "You have more important things to do than flaunt your newest toy around."

"Carolina isn't just a guest," I declare, loud enough for all to hear, my fingers tracing idle patterns on her skin beneath the table. "She's the future of this family."

Across from me, Jack shovels another forkful of food into his mouth, seemingly oblivious to the show playing out before him. His indifference is almost comical compared to the rest of us caught in the undertow of family politics. It's as if he's made an art out of detachment, his role more shadow than substance within the Knight empire.

"Pass the salt, please," Jack mutters, reaching across the table without a glance in our direction. The trivial request falls flat in the thick atmosphere, yet somehow only heightens the absurdity of it all.

I turn back to Carolina, whose eyes are wide with quiet apprehension. "Should I leave?" she whispers.

"Absolutely not," I reply harshly. "You belong here. *You belong with me.*"

The tension in the dining room is thick enough to carve with a steak knife, but Arthur seems to find it all terribly amusing. From across the table, his eyes glint with undisguised mirth, soaking in the undercurrents of animosity like it's the evening's entertainment.

"Quite the family gathering we've got here," he drawls, lifting his wineglass in a half salute. "Never a dull moment with the Knights, eh?"

I'd bristle at the condescension if I wasn't so focused on Carolina beside me. She's rigid, her hands folded neatly in her lap like she's holding herself together by sheer willpower. I hate that she feels this way—on display, cornered by suspicion and judgment. My gaze cuts through the opulence of the room, daring anyone else to add to her discomfort.

As everyone fills their plates with the different meat, vegetables, and whatever else has been placed on the table, I take my hellcat's plate. "Let me," I say softly, reaching for the silver serving tongs.

There's a subtle shift in the air as I plate a delicate portion of roasted lamb onto Carolina's dish. It's not just about feeding her; it's an assertion, a silent declaration that she's under my protection. My thumb brushes against her hand as I pass her the plate, a fleeting touch that speaks volumes.

"Thank you," she murmurs, her voice barely above a whisper. But her eyes—those deep pools of uncertainty—lock onto mine with a fierce intensity that says more than words ever could.

Arthur watches us, his head tilted in curiosity. "You two seem quite… attuned to each other," he comments lazily. "It's fascinating."

As dinner progresses, I keep my attention on Carolina, ensuring her glass is filled with sparkling water instead of wine, pouring it myself to avoid any mistakes. She catches the gesture, a grateful gleam in her eyes that warms something inside me.

"I have a question," Arthur says. Everyone stops moving and talking the moment he opens his mouth, sending the room to a crashing halt. "How did you meet Sienna?" The question is clearly meant for Dad.

He clears his throat, wiping his mouth and taking a sip of wine before answering. "You know how," he almost growls.

"Indeed," Arthur agrees, smirking. "But I'd still like to hear your answer."

Dad gives a sharp nod. "I bought her at one of the Hatt auctions."

This isn't news to anyone at the table… well, I suppose it is to the woman at my side. I quickly lean in and whisper, "Sienna was my mom," just so she knows who we're talking about.

"And what about you, Michael?" Arthur asks, looking straight at Ruby's husband. "How did you come to be married to the lovely Ruby?"

Michael guffaws. "I bought her from Caspian." He nods in Dad's direction. "For more than she's proven worth," he adds on a grumble, and I clench my hands together, resisting the urge to drag him outside for that insult.

I might not always see eye-to-eye with my sister, and she might be a pain in my ass. But she's still my sister. "Careful, Michael," I growl.

"It seems there's a tradition for buying women," Arthur observes. "As far as I can see, there's no issue with Carolina's presence, or how she came to be here."

Now that the King has spoken, no one says anything to contradict him.

The food and wine still have Jack's undivided attention, and even Dad has turned away from the conversation. Deciding to follow suit, I begin to eat, but I almost immediately notice that Carolina hasn't taken as much as a single bite.

I put down my own cutlery and grab her fork, stabbing a cut piece of meat from my plate that I lift to her mouth. She wordlessly arches an eyebrow, but parts her lips, accepting the food. "Good, isn't it?"

She nods, and hums around the next bite I serve her; more meat with some potatoes and green vegetables. "Yes, thank you," she murmurs.

While I continue feeding the both of us, I don't pay attention to anyone else, or the conversation that sounds in the background. My sole focus is on the beautiful woman next to me, making sure she gets enough to eat.

Once our plates are empty, and everyone has had enough, the servers appear, clearing out the table before carrying in the dessert. Unlike the main course, the chocolate torte is plated.

The silver dessert spoon glimmers in my hand. Her breath catches when I lean in, my lips brushing her earlobe. "Open up," I command softly, offering her a bite of the decadent dessert.

She complies, her eyes locked with mine, vividly blue and brimming with a wildness that speaks to my very soul. As she savors the rich flavor, I let my free hand drop beneath the table, settling on her bare thigh again.

"Nicklas," she murmurs, a tremor in her voice as my fingers inch higher, higher, and higher. I don't stop until I feel the heat from her cunt and the plug connecting with me.

With deft fingers, I remove the plug from her pussy, loving that I can feel wetness literally gush from her opening. "What's the matter? Don't you like torte?" I deadpan, feeling the heat of her as I stroke her gently.

Carolina squirms under my touch, but it's pure pleasure that lights her gaze—a flame that reflects my own burning desire. I love how she responds to me; it's a heady power knowing I can unravel her so completely.

We're playing a dangerous game, one wrong move away from exposing our intimacy to prying eyes. But risk is part of the thrill—in business, in life, in this moment. Every gentle caress sends a message to her, to them, to the very air we breathe—I am hers, and she is irrevocably mine.

Her breathing quickens, her chest rising and falling in an erratic rhythm as I slide my fingers in and out of her tight, slick cunt. The tight coil of her arousal winds tighter, squeezing my digits as I delve deeper.

"Nicklas…" Carolina gasps, barely audible.

I cast a warning glance at her, my movements relentless. I won't stop until she comes all over my fingers. And then, oh then, I'll wipe it on the torte and feed it to her right in front of my family. Luckily, they're all engrossed in their own conversations, too busy to pay us any attention.

As I coax her toward climax, I watch her struggle to maintain her façade of indifference. She bites her lip; her knuckles white where they clutch at the tablecloth. And then, with a shuddering breath, she surrenders, her body quaking silently as waves of pleasure crash over her.

I remove my fingers and push the plug back inside her. Then, just as I promised myself, I smear her cream on the remaining torte. Before feeding her any, I take a bite myself. "Mhmm," I groan. "Delicious." Carolina's cheeks are flushed with the aftermath of her release. My possessive gaze lingers on her, drinking in her vulnerability, her strength, her undeniable beauty.

She parts her lips, her tongue darting out to lick her lips. "You didn't just do that," she whispers. Then she straightens her back, meeting my gaze. "D-did it taste good?"

A wicked smile takes over my lips. "Oh, Hellcat," I rasp, moving closer to her as I position more torte on the fork and push it into her mouth. "You have no idea."

My cock is painfully hard, and I can't fucking wait for this evening to be over so I can bury myself inside her, feel her weeping sex tighten when she comes around me. I'm pulled from my thoughts when her hand cups my length, stroking it.

"Let me help you with that," she purrs, looking up at me with a smile that's pure lust.

I wrap my fingers around her wrist, squeezing until she whimpers in pain, betrayal replacing her smile. "If I'm not coming inside you, I'm not coming," I insist, almost unkindly. "All my jizz is for your cunt."

"You're attending on behalf of the family, right?" Dad's voice is loud enough to garner my attention.

"Of course I am," I reply smoothly, absentmindedly kissing the palm of Carolina's hand.

I don't need to ask him to repeat the question to know what he's talking about. As the head of the Knight family, there are events to attend, and December is one of the busiest months for keeping up appearances, for mingling, and for making people forget all the bad shit we're involved in.

"Good," Dad says. His cold gaze flicks from me to Carolina and back to me again. "You shouldn't let anyone distract you from your duties. Especially not a woman." I frown, not liking the thinly veiled threat in his tone.

CHAPTER 16

The Breeder

I am freaking bored out of my mind.

There, I said it.

Sitting on one of the stools in the kitchen, I twirl a lock of my hair around my index finger while humming to myself. I've tried making small talk with Greta, I've learned that's the name of the woman who brought me food when I was locked in the bedroom, but she's only giving me one-word answers.

"Tea?" she asks, which I suppose is her way of asking if I want more tea.

I shake my head. "No, thank you." What's the point of hanging around one of the few people I see around here when she won't talk to me?

As I shift on the stool, I wince when I accidentally drag the bottom of the plug between my legs against the hard surface. But despite the initial discomfort, it quickly morphs into lust, making my clit throb.

Damn this thing, and Nicklas' orders to only wear skirts or dresses without panties. Then again, it feels sexy and forbidden to walk around commando like this. Okay, so maybe I don't hate it entirely.

It's been two days since the odd dinner with Nicklas' family. Where

I thought it was a disaster, Nicklas saw it differently. At least, that's what he told me when we got home. Home... what a joke. I might live here for now, but my home it is not.

Yesterday, I spent the day with Willow. I visited her in the care home, and then we went to this little cafe nearby for hot chocolate. Our first outing together in years. Not because she can't go out, of course she can. But I've never had money to spare, not even on something as simple as getting a hot beverage.

But thanks to Nicklas already having paid all my bills, I do have a bit of cash. And since he insisted on having one of his men drive and follow me, I didn't have to worry about spending money on transportation. Thankfully, the guy stayed at a discreet distance, so I didn't have to explain his presence to Willow.

But ugh, I did have to tell my sister about Nicklas, all thanks to Ruby and her... meddling. Since I neither can, nor want to, explain our arrangement, I kept it simple by saying I've gotten a new job. I mean, it's not exactly a lie. Actually, it's completely true since he's paying me to use my womb. A bit like a rent agreement.

I snort to myself, hating how clinical it sounds, especially when every interaction between us is everything but. If I thought I'd just need to spread my legs while he pumped away, I'm proven sorely mistaken. Nicklas is... intense. And with every touch, I feel like he's awakening something inside me. Maybe he is.

Reaching for my phone on the kitchen island, I check the time again. It's barely ten in the morning, and with Willow busy on some outing with the care home today, I have no idea how to spend my time. But I can't stand Greta's judgmental glances anymore, so I push the cup away and get off the chair.

"I'll... umm... see you later." She doesn't even acknowledge my words, just continues whatever she's doing at the sink.

With boredom clawing at my mind, I decide it's high time I explore the expanse of Nicklas' penthouse. As I leave the kitchen, the air becomes laced with the scent of sandalwood, a constant reminder of my wicked Santa's presence.

Room by room, I wander with a sense of curiosity sharpening my senses. The modern art pieces adorning the walls are striking—a blend of bold colors and abstract shapes. I can't quite understand them, but there's something captivating about their chaos.

The living area transitions into a gallery of sorts, and I find myself standing before a painting that snatches my breath. It's a dark, tempestuous sea with a single beacon of light shining through the storm. Does this reflect the turmoil beneath Nicklas' stoic façade?

I wander aimlessly through the penthouse, my fingertips grazing over sleek surfaces and plush fabrics. Nicklas' home is a trove of distractions, with so many more rooms than I ever imagined.

Some doors are locked, but instead of lingering in front of those, I quickly leave them behind. Since I've seen him kill one man in cold blood, and he's admitted to killing another just for watching me get myself off, I'm too scared of what I could possibly find.

Reaching a room sequestered at the back of the apartment, I push open the door. It creaks with disuse, a stark contrast to the rest of Nicklas' meticulously kept domain. The air inside tastes stale, heavy with secrets and silence. Dust motes dance in the slanting light as I step forward, curiosity piqued by this neglected space.

A loose floorboard underfoot gives me pause. Kneeling down, I pry it open with more eagerness than finesse. Beneath lies a collection of papers and a diary, aged leather cracked and worn. It's an intimate artifact, one that seems out-of-place amid the sterile legal documents.

The diary belongs to a Sienna Knight... Oh! As I continue leafing through the yellowed and worn papers, I remember she was Nicklas' mom.

May 15th, 1996

I still can't believe it!! I'm pregnant again!

I took the test this morning, and there it was, clear as day. I feel like the luckiest woman alive, but also a bit nervous. This is the third, the one that completes the magic number.

The Knight family always says three is the key.

One heir isn't enough. Fate can be cruel, and it seems like there's always tragedy waiting to strike, but with three, we stand a chance.

Caspian says it's some old superstition, but it's hard not to think about it now.

We already have two wonderful boys, and now, I'm hoping with all my heart that this one's a girl.

A little girl to balance out the chaos, to bring something new to our lives. I'm already imagining her, hoping she'll be the one who changes everything, the final piece to our family's puzzle.

Here's to hoping fate is kind this time.

"Three," I murmur, tracing the words with a finger.

I continue to flick through the diary at random, drawn to the scrawled confessions like a moth to a flame.

August 22nd, 1996

She's kicking up a storm today. A tiny flutter, as if she's saying hello.

It's incredible to think I'll be holding her in just a few months.

I've chosen her name: Ruby. It feels perfect, strong and vibrant, just like I imagine she'll be. I'm already dreaming of her nursery, soft pastels with touches of deep red, maybe a little ruby gemstone tucked somewhere special.

I can't wait to meet you, Ruby. You're already

my everything.

I devour the entries, each one painting a picture of the Knight's enigmatic empire. The Hatt family looms over the narrative like specters, their presence a constant reminder of the power that binds Nicklas to this grand, yet shadowed existence.

My mind swirls with newfound knowledge, the pieces of Nicklas' puzzle slowly fitting together. Understanding dawns, and with it, a fierce determination to learn more—to see beyond the man of iron and ice, to the vulnerabilities he guards so ruthlessly.

"Three," I find myself saying as I finish yet another entry highlighting the magic number. Three children for survival, for power, for continuation. A shiver runs down my spine—this isn't just about being provided for; it's about being irrevocably woven into the tapestry of an empire.

I'm on the floor, the rough texture of the old carpet biting into my skin through my thin dress, but I hardly notice. The diary's yellowed pages whisper secrets with every turn, and I'm lost in the world of Nicklas' mother—a woman whose strength seems to have bled into the very fibers of this hidden book.

I close the diary and clutch it to my chest. The contract Nicklas drew up only mentioned one heir, so what does that mean? Does he not believe in this superstition? Or is he planning to have other women—better women—conceive the last two heirs? For some reason, that thought makes me angry.

The air changes, shifts with an energy I've come to recognize as Nicklas. My heart stutters, thudding against my ribs like it's trying to escape. I lift my head, and there he is, standing over me—a dark shadow against the dying light filtering through the window.

"Nicklas," I breathe out, and his name feels like a brand on my lips, powerful and possessive.

"Kitten, what have you found?" His voice is a low rumble, vibrating through the room. It's commanding, yet laced with an eagerness that's almost palpable.

"Your mom's diary," I admit, feeling like a thief caught red-handed.

But instead of anger, there's an intense curiosity in his gaze—as if he's seeing me for the first time.

"Let me see." He doesn't ask; he never does. His large hand envelops mine, gently prying the leather-bound book from my grasp. The heat from his touch races up my arm, igniting a fire that spreads through my body.

"Nicklas…" I start, feeling as though I should explain myself. But he's already pulling me to my feet, his hands firm on my waist.

"Look at me."

I do, and I'm caught in the storm of his dark eyes, so full of questions and a hunger that mirrors my own. It's a look that says he's as enmeshed in this connection as I am, whether he likes it or not—whether I like it or not.

"Now that you know more about my family, it's only fair you tell me something about you."

I clear my throat. "What do you want to know?"

"Tell me what drives you," he says, and there's something raw in his command—a need to understand the woman in his arms.

"Survival," I confess, the word torn from somewhere deep inside me. "For me, for Willow."

"Survival," he echoes, and it's not a question but an acknowledgment of our shared reality. The pull between us intensifies, magnetic and undeniable.

Feeling braver now that he hasn't scolded me for snooping, I ask a question of my own. "Who's going to carry your other two heirs?" When he arches an eyebrow, I continue. "Your mom wrote about needing three heirs. You've only paid me for one." Try as I might, I fail at keeping jealousy from bleeding into my tone.

Of course, Nicklas hears it, it's evident in the Cheshire grin splitting his lips. "Are you jealous, Kitten?" He moves his hands from my hips, wrapping his arms tightly around my back, and I melt into him.

My soft breasts flatten against the hard ridges of his chest, making me wonder if he can feel my hardened nipples poke into him through our clothing. The bra I'm wearing isn't padded, and the thin fabric of my dress barely counts as a barrier. So, maybe?!

"No," I say, answering him with a shake of my head. "Not jealous. Just…" I don't know what I am. No matter my tone, I'm not jealous. It's more like… no one likes to be replaced, or knowing they're going to be.

"Would you like to give birth to all my kids?" Nicklas asks, cupping my chin and forcing me to look up at him. "Is that what this is about?"

I lick my lips as I ponder the question. Is that what I want? I don't think it is… but maybe. "I don't know," I admit on a whisper.

"You need to be patient," he replies cryptically, bending so his breath is hot against my ear. "All in due time." And though his words are a reprimand, they're also a vow—one I intend to hold him to.

"Teach me patience, then," I say, my tone teasing but my intent serious. Nicklas smirks, a dangerous gleam in his eye.

"Careful what you wish for." His fingers trace the curve of my waist, setting my nerves alight. "You might just get it."

His lips crash against mine with a passion that ignites a fire within me, his hands possessive as they roam my body, grabbing the soft globes of my ass and squeezing, kneading. With each movement, the plug inside me is jostled, and my sex feels like it's on fire.

Swiftly, he removes the plug, eagerly replacing it with two fingers.

"Nicklas," I gasp, my breaths coming in short bursts as he deepens his exploration, his mastery over my body absolute. "Oh, God!"

"You've no idea how much I want you," he growls, his voice laced with a dark promise.

Then he scoops me up, effortlessly carrying me from the room cluttered with secrets and whispers of the past, into a chamber that promises decadence and surrender.

This bedroom is alien compared to ours—chains dangle from the ceiling like twisted vines, sex toys lay on display like forbidden fruit, and at the center is a sex swing. A. Sex. Swing.

In one corner, is an ancient and imposing bed. The dark wooden headboard catches my eye first, with a sword intricately carved into its center, every detail sharp and deliberate. Four tall bedposts rise at each corner, draped in heavy burgundy fabric that cascades down like a protective curtain.

The air is thick with the scent of old wood and echoes of history. This bed… I feel like I've already seen it somewhere, though that's impossible. As I nibble on my bottom lip, I realize where I've seen it—in my mind's eye. Sienna Knight described it in one of her diary entries. This is the marital bed, the bed on which every heir is meant to be conceived.

I swallow hard, my heart hammering against my ribcage. The sight of the chains, the enormity of the bed, it all sends a shiver down my spine, not of fear, but of anticipation. Nicklas senses my hesitation, his touch gentle yet firm as he reassures me without words, guiding me toward the bed.

"Are you ready to play, Kitten?" he rasps, making me shudder in his hold.

CHAPTER 17

The Breeder

As soon as I nod my acquiescence, punctuating it with a needy whimper, he lies me down on the bed. "Spread your arms and legs," he commands.

Doing as he says, I spread my limbs until my body is forming an X on the silk sheets. The saying 'X marks the spot' comes to mind, making me grin.

Said grin is wiped from my lips when Nicklas casually pulls a knife from the inner pocket of his suit jacket, the light reflecting on the blade as he gently lowers it until it's touching my collarbone. My breath hitches.

"Do you trust me?" he asks solemnly.

I swallow harshly. "N-no," I reply.

He chuckles and slides the knife down until it catches on the dress. Then, he moves it beneath, slicing the fabric as he continues the downwards movement, splitting the dress in two. I realize I'm holding my breath when he wedges the tip of the knife between the cups of my bra, yanking until that, too, falls open.

"Nicklas," I half gasp, half moan. I barely recognize my own tone, and my thoughts are a swirl of fear and lust.

"Move your arms above your head, Kitten," he rasps. "And put your wrists together."

Again, I follow his demand without hesitation. As soon as my arms are where he wants them, he shuffles around the bed and leans over the bed, reaching for me. I feel more than hear it as he guides my hands into some kind of restraint. I angle my head so I can see what he's doing.

Clearly, I didn't notice everything about this bed, because I didn't see the built-in restraints at the head. I experimentally test the leather by pulling, but there's no give at all. It doesn't hurt, though, all thanks to the soft lining on the inside.

While I'm focused on my hands, Nicklas slides chains around my ankles. They're not as tight as the leather around my hands, but there still isn't a lot of give.

"Look at you," he praises, his dark gaze reflecting my expression of excitement. "You're so beautiful like this. I could stare at you for hours."

"Please don't," I murmur, really hoping he isn't just going to watch me.

Rather than answering me, he removes his suit jacket, neatly folding it before slowly unbuttoning his shirt. As I lie there, naked and waiting, it's maddening how much time he wastes on undressing. Don't get me wrong, I love the view, even lick my lips as he unbuckles his belt, and I swear my pussy contracts at the swooshing sound when he pulls the leather from the loops on his pants.

"Nicklas!"

He chuckles, his tattooed hands opening his pants, and I shudder as the black trail of hair on his lower stomach comes into view, knowing exactly where that leads. The show he's giving me is such a turn on I feel I could come from the lightest touch.

After what feels like hours, but were probably only minutes, he's finally naked. I shamelessly drink in every ridge of his body; from his shoulders to his feet, and everything in between. It's hard not to get stuck on his long, thick cock, and the pre-cum beading at the tip.

"Look at you," he murmurs, circling the bed like a predator. "So willing to surrender to me."

Surrendering to Nicklas feels natural, necessary even. My body responds to his proximity, to the dominant energy he exudes. There's no room for fear, only a deep, aching need.

He traces a finger down my arm, and it leaves a trail of fire in its wake. He pulls out a feather tickler from the drawer and runs it over my sensitive skin, eliciting involuntary shivers. My breath hitches as he explores, learning what makes me gasp, what makes me squirm. Much to my disappointment, he stays completely away from the apex of my thighs, only grazing the surrounding areas.

"Please..." I don't even know what I'm pleading for—his touch, his possession, his everything. All I know is that I'm teetering right on the edge. My body is slick with sweat and arousal, and I'm desperate to come.

"I told you to be patient." With a swift movement, he spins me to my stomach, helping me regain my balance as my arms and legs twist. My restraints feel tighter, but it's still not too uncomfortable, or even painful. "Have you ever come from pain before?" he asks, his voice husky.

"P-pain?" I stutter, my heart beating harder at his question. "I-I don't want pain."

His large hand runs across my exposed backside, he nudges one finger into the crevice of my ass cheeks. I tense as the tip finds my puckered opening. No, surely he doesn't mean... I swallow, feeling embarrassed but also so, so aroused by the thought of him taking me *there*.

"Stop," I beg.

"You don't get to deny me," he corrects me sharply. Before I can process what he's doing, his hand disappears, and the next second, there's a sharp crack as he slaps my ass.

"Ouch!" I cry out.

"Never."

Slap!

"Do."

"Nicklas!" I howl.

Slap!

"That."

Slap!

"Again."

I writhe, uselessly trying to avoid the unforgiving slaps as he rains them down, but it's not happening. Tears stream down my face as he ruthlessly spanks my ass, my breath is coming in ragged, shallow bursts. He keeps going, and each time his palm connects with my skin, I jolt.

"Nicklas!" I scream, not sure I can take any more.

I hide my face in the sheets, tensing as I wait for more pain to come, but it doesn't.

He gingerly begins to stroke the abused skin, his soothing touch both making it better and worse at the same time. Better, because I think I crave knowing he won't hurt me again—worse, because I'm scared to relax if more pain is to come.

"W-what did I do?" I hiccup, my sobs muffled by the sheets. "W-what d-did I do w-wrong?" He bends, kissing my throbbing backside, the scruff making me whimper even more as it feels rough against the sore skin.

After releasing my wrists and ankles from the restraints, he lies down next to me as I cry. I want to curl into a ball, but I'm scared to make the wrong move. I tense as something cold and wet hits my abused ass, then his hand appears, carefully rubbing it into my skin.

"Don't ever deny me again," he growls, anger coating his words. "You do what I say, when I say it. Is that understood?"

Even though I've signed a contract that basically states just that, I balk against saying the words out loud, so I press my lips together.

"Say you understand me," he barks, the words so different from the feather-light touch of his hand on my burning flesh.

"No!" I refuse on a hiccup. "I won't say it. Not now. Not fucking ever."

I wait with bated breath, telling myself to prepare for more pain, but it never comes. It's confusing when he chuckles and pulls me flush against him, his erection nestled in the crevice of my ass. "I love when you fight me, Hellcat. But there's a time and place. And this isn't it."

This isn't a fucking game, it's my life. I'm not defying him for his entertainment, just as I didn't sign the contract for his pleasure. I signed to give myself and Willow a future, and I fight him when I'm unable to bow to his will. It's all about survival for me.

"What does it matter?" I huff, surprised to find I'm gradually relaxing more and more the longer we lie here. "You take what you want, do what you want, no matter what I say or do."

He's quiet for so long, I don't think he's going to answer me. "It's a good question," he finally says, sounding like he's giving some serious thought to the answer. "I don't know why, Carolina. Only that it's important to me."

I don't know what to make from his words, but I find myself looking for a hidden meaning. Maybe it's because he's a man who always has to take what he wants. Could that be why he wants me to give it to him freely?

"Ask me," I croak, my voice hoarse from all the screaming.

"What?"

"Ask me for what you want," I say, my voice steadier now.

A squeal leaves me when he moves, grabbing my hips and positioning me on top of him. I wince, leaning forward as much as possible as to spare my ass cheeks. My long, blonde hair falls in a curtain around us as I bend my neck and look down at him.

"Why do you want me to ask you for what I already own?" he rasps.

I resist the urge to roll my eyes. "Because you want me to give it to you. But I can't give you anything you demand, that's still you taking. So if you don't want that, you need to ask for it."

When he lifts his hand, I can't help flinching, and his eyes darken, anger pooling in their depths. "I'm not going to hurt you like that again, Carolina. Never," he vows. "I'm so sorry."

Refusing to say it's okay when it's not, I bite the inside of my cheek, trying not to tremble. But it's hard, and I don't just mean his cock between my legs. The intensity and anger rolling off him is enough to drown me, fighting it feels like fighting the pull of a current.

He rears up, wrapping his arms around my back, resting his forehead against mine. "I mean it," he murmurs. "I'm sorry."

I get the feeling he hasn't apologized to many people in his life, and it makes me feel special to know I'm one of the few. "Okay," I say, still mindful not to say the action was okay.

He sighs deeply, still not looking away from me. "I still want to fuck you." His length twitches between us, punctuating the words, and my pussy answers with a flutter.

Whether my head is in the game or not, there's no denying my body wants this. Badly. "Me too," I sigh. Admitting that feels wrong, like I'm fucked up for wanting him after what he did to me. "But I don't want you to hurt me again."

Maybe it's stupid of me to say that since it got me in trouble the last time I did, but if he hurts me again, I'll know his apology means nothing, and that his words aren't to be trusted. Not that I should trust him, regardless.

He stretches so his forehead is no longer level with mine, and then he freaking licks the sweat from my forehead and eyebrows. What the hell! "I'll always want to hurt you, and I know you can take it, Hellcat. But no, I won't let my temper get the better of me again."

With boldness I don't know where it comes from, I push him down so he's lying flat on his back. Gyrating my hips, I drag my drenched slit along his thick, throbbing shaft. "I said no," I hiss. "No more pain."

"And I told you not to deny me," he growls.

I open my mouth, ready to argue more, but he rears back up, capturing my lips in a scorching kiss. His tongue wrestles mine into submission as he licks at every corner of my mouth. My hands are on his shoulders, and when he cups my sore ass too hard, I hiss while instinctively digging my nails into his skin.

He growls, kissing me harder, and I moan into his mouth, the burn on my backside morphing into a level of pleasure I didn't even know existed. It hurts, yes, very much so. But each painful throb makes my inner walls contract. We're caught in a vicious circle, one where more pain means more pleasure, and more pleasure means more pain.

"Nick—" Another moan cuts me off.

"I need to be inside you," he rasps.

"Yes," I agree. Then I reach for his length, wanting to put him inside me, but he stops me.

"Not on the bed."

I lean back, blinking in confusion. "But this is the bed where we're meant to conceive your heir," I say, dumbfounded.

He doesn't question how I know that, probably figures it's from the diary. Or maybe he has read it and knows for certain. "There's something else I want to try today," he says.

Carefully, I climb off him, doing my best to jostle my ass as little as possible. I've never noticed how much you use it or move it until trying to avoid it, which is basically impossible.

Once we're both standing, he takes my hand and leads me over to the sex swing, his eyes darken with desire as he looks between me and it. "Are you up for it?" I'm surprised he asks.

"I-I think so."

He helps me into it, apologizing again when I hiss out a breath as I sit down on the leather strap. When I reach for the handles above me, he stops me. "No, I want you to lie back."

My eyes widen, and I gulp, not reveling the idea of putting any trust in him or his ability to keep me from falling. "Can't I just—"

"No!" he growls. "I want you vulnerable and spread out for me."

With a sigh, I tighten my hold on his forearms, slowly leaning back until the second leather strap stops me. My breath comes out in quick puffs, sweat beads on my forehead, and a sliver of fear runs down my spine.

"Mhmm, Carolina," he groans, his eyes glued to my pussy. My legs are resting on his shoulders, giving him easy access. "So fucking pretty."

I preen under his heated gaze and words. My back arches on its own, drawing his dark eyes to my peaked nipples. "Touch me," I beg, suddenly needing his hands on me.

When he moves, stepping closer, I dig my nails into his forearms, scared I'm going to fall down. "I've got you," he assures me, and I see the truth in his dark orbs—Nicklas won't let me fall, and if I do, he'll either catch me or plunge with me. "Hold on tight, Hellcat. I'm going to raise you. But you're not going anywhere. Trust me."

I try to relax as he reaches up, pushing a button on the chain holding the swing. Even though he's told me what's coming, I scream in surprise when the chain tightens, pulling me up until my pussy is level with Nicklas' hard cock.

"Are you wet?" he asks, already rubbing the tip of his dick against my drenched opening.

I'm not just wet, I'm soaked—in a place that's far beyond turned on. I'm freaking needy; needy for him, for the pleasure he's promising me.

As he finally pushes inside me, I cry out, the sensation so intense while I'm balanced above the ground. His hands move to my hips, grasping them firmly. Instead of thrusting, he pulls me toward him, sheathing his hardness inside me.

"Fuck!" he growls.

"Nicklas," I moan. "Oh my God!"

The more we move, the more I relax, almost forgetting that I'm hanging up here. All I can focus on is the glorious feeling of his cock inside me, stretching. He continues to talk dirty to me, telling me how much he loves the feel of my cunt, the way I squeeze him. Each word makes me feel bolder, and… treasured.

No longer scared to fall, I let my hands fall from his arms so they dangle at my sides. His approving groan is the perfect reward. He picks up the pace, moving me faster and harder, our skin making slapping sounds every time we connect.

"Ahh, fuck. I'm not going to last much longer." He furrows his brows like he's trying to stop himself from coming.

I squeeze my inner muscles around him. "Come," I demand. "Fill me with your cum. Fuck your heir into me."

Giving up on moving me, he palms my tits as he impales me harder. Each thrust pushing me closer to the edge of oblivion. The swing moves with us, a pendulum of carnal rhythm, each sway amplifying the sensations until I'm lost in a sea of ecstasy.

"Your wish is my command," Nicklas growls, kneading my breasts deliciously hard.

"Nicklas!" I cry out as waves of pleasure crash over me, his name a sacred incantation that binds us together.

"Mine," he declares, his own release chasing mine, a testament to the depth of his possessiveness.

In the stillness that follows, the only sound is our labored breathing. We bask in the afterglow, skin glistening and hearts racing. Lying in the cradle of the swing, I'm held aloft not just by its sturdy straps but by the strength of what grows between us—something fierce and tender, something that might just be love.

When my body begins to feel uncomfortable, and I need to move, Nicklas lowers the swing but orders me to put my legs in the air. I do as he says, watching as he goes to get the plug. As soon as it's back inside me, he helps me up. My legs feel like jelly, and he helps steady me. Then he retrieves his shirt and boxer briefs, handing me both to put on.

"I don't want to risk anyone seeing what's mine."

While I put it on, I eye him. "I don't want anyone seeing what's mine either," I clarify, pointedly staring at his naked chest. He might be wearing pants, but his upper body is just as enticing as his lower one.

He grins as he shrugs his suit jacket on. "This will have to do."

Together, we walk back to our bedroom, and I let him guide me into the bathroom where he begins to fill the massive corner bathtub. Thanks to the multiple taps, it doesn't take long before it's half filled. We undress each other, and I find that I like doing that to him. It's like opening a present.

"Get in," he commands, his voice low and husky, the dark allure that he exudes wrapping around me like a silken shroud.

I obey without hesitation, slipping into the steaming bath. The water embraces me, warm and comforting, and I sink deeper, letting it lap at my collarbones. Nicklas watches me for a moment with those intense eyes before joining me in the tub, the water displacing around his powerful form.

He's close now, so close that I can see the flecks of gold in his dark irises. Without a word, he takes a soft sponge and begins to wash me. His touch is gentle yet possessive, reminding me of who I belong to.

"Lean back," Nicklas murmurs, guiding my body against his. He massages shampoo into my hair, his fingers skillful and tender. The scent of jasmine fills the air, and I close my eyes, giving myself over to the sensations—the heat of the water, the glide of his hands, the steady beat of his heart against my back.

While I let him wash my hair, I feel something inside me shift and bloom. It's terrifying and exhilarating all at once. He rinses my hair, the water caressing my scalp in rivulets.

"You'll learn to trust me," he says suddenly.

"Maybe," I allow, not mentioning that I did trust him when I let him fuck me in the swing.

"Good," he says, satisfaction lacing his voice. "Because every part of you is mine, Carolina. To protect, to pleasure, to impregnate."

After we're done, and we've dried each other off, he asks me to wait while he goes to get something from the bedroom. While he's gone, I do my best to shut my brain off, which is harder than it sounds. But right now, I don't want to think. I just want to feel—to be present in the moment.

When he returns, he's holding a small velvet box. "Will you wear this?" he asks as he opens it to reveal a beautiful diamond ring.

"Nick is that—"

"There's a party coming up, and I want you to wear this." His gruff tone betrays the urgency he feels.

"Why?" I ask. My heart is hammering in my chest, making it hard to breathe.

"Because I asked nicely," he smirks. "Do you accept the ring?"

I don't know why I end up agreeing, but with a nod and a whispered, "Yes," I do. My lips part as he slides the ring onto my finger where it fits perfectly—like it was made for me.

CHAPTER 18

The Santa

The chill of the December air is nothing compared to the icy command that accompanies my entrance into the lavish Christmas party. The scent of pine and the soft tinkle of crystal are mere backdrops to the electric hum of New York's elite acknowledging my presence. I scan the room, a predator among sheep.

"Nicklas Knight," someone murmurs with a mix of reverence and fear. They know who I am, what I represent—the unyielding force of the Knight family.

I'm barely aware of the decorations, the garlands heavy with shimmering baubles and the grand tree towering toward the frescoed ceiling. My focus narrows on Carolina as she clings to my arm, still not at ease around other people. But as mine, she'll have to get used to it sooner or later.

The deep red dress she's wearing tonight, hugging her figure, flowing down to the floor and swooshing softly around her feet with each graceful step. The front is cut daringly low, held together by nothing more than a simple gold clasp that matches the glint of her jewelry, teasing the edge of elegance and allure.

But it's the back of the dress that truly captivates me. It dips dangerously low, skimming just above her waist, leaving her back bare and smooth. The way the fabric clings, then cascades, is both classy and undeniably sexy. It's a dress that demands attention, a perfect blend of sophistication and seduction, and on her, it's nothing short of stunning.

My hellcat, my kitten, as graceful as any feline.

Every man's gaze she attracts feels like a challenge to me, and the possessive beast within stirs, never asleep for long. Carolina looks up at me, her red lips curving in a knowing smile, a silent affirmation that she's here for me—only for me.

Servers appear, one holding a tray with sparkling drinks, another two carrying hors d'oeuvres like stuffed mushrooms, smoked salmon, baked brie bites, feta and watermelon, mini crab cakes, and a lot of other small bites I can't name.

I take a glass of champagne for myself. "Do you have any water?" I ask, nodding toward Carolina.

"Come on," she whines, batting her lashes as she looks up at me. "Can't I even have one glass of champagne tonight?"

Bending down, I claim her lips in a slow, deep kiss. "One," I rasp when I pull back. "But only one."

The smile she gives me is totally worth it, and it makes me want to beat my chest with my fists for being the reason it's splitting her lips.

Since I lost my temper with her a couple of days ago, I've done everything in my power to make her smile—which is one of the reasons we're here tonight. Among the guests is an esteemed doctor I want to introduce Carolina to.

We mingle for a bit, talking to people I don't care about. Carolina seems interested, and she even lights up as she shakes the hand of a few celebrities. None of them impress me, but as long as she keeps smiling, I'll put up with it.

"Why don't we dance?" I ask, filled up with the fake pleasantries.

Her eyes widen. "You dance?"

I throw my head back and laugh loudly. "Oh, Kitten," I smirk as I pull her toward the dance floor. "Let's see if you can keep up." I hand both our glasses off to one of the servers, noting that Carolina's wasn't even half empty, so she can have another one later.

The live band begins the next song just as I lead Carolina onto the dance floor, her hand soft in mine. We glide into a waltz, my hand firm on her back, guiding her effortlessly. The room fades as we move together, perfectly in sync.

"You're making this so easy," she laughs, happiness making her blue eyes sparkle. "I guess it's true what they say, the perfect partner really makes a difference."

The moment the tango begins, everything sharpens between us. I pull Carolina close, our bodies nearly colliding, the air thick with tension. Her eyes meet mine, blazing with challenge, daring me to take control. The music is relentless, driving us with every beat, demanding precision and passion.

"You've seen nothing yet," I rasp, determined to show her more.

My hand tightens on her back, and I lead her into a sharp turn, our movements quick and forceful. She matches my intensity, pushing back with just enough resistance to make the dance a battle. I dip her low, holding her suspended just above the floor, her breath catching as she hovers in that precarious moment. There's a flash of trust, but also defiance, as she waits for me to pull her back up.

The music pushes us harder, and we respond with fierce, deliberate steps. Each pivot is a test, each movement a clash of wills. I can feel the tension coiling between us, a power struggle disguised as dance. Her hand grips my shoulder, tighter now, as we drive through the final sequence, the air around us crackling with energy.

As the last note hangs in the air, I pull her close, our bodies flush, our breathing ragged. The tension doesn't release—it lingers, heavy and electric, a reminder of the raw, powerful connection we've just forged on the dance floor.

We're both breathing heavily, and it has nothing to do with our fast movements. I once heard that a real tango is like foreplay, and that's exactly how it feels with Carolina.

When the music shifts to a slow jazz number, I draw her even closer, our steps turning into a gentle sway. My fingers trace the edge of her dress, and she rests her head against my chest. The party buzzes around us, but in this moment, it's just us, moving together as one.

"Are you enjoying yourself?" I croon into her ear.

Tilting her head, she looks up at me. "Oh, yes. Very much so." The way she looks at me is everything.

She's seen my beast, yet she's so trusting. It's fucking humbling, and it makes me want to do better by her. I don't mean that I'll stop being the ruthless asshole I was born to be, that'll never change. But I mentally vow to always treat her like the queen I want her to be.

When she's had her fill of dancing, I take her hand and we walk off the dance floor. I make sure to cover her body with mine so she isn't jostled or pushed by the many bodies nearby.

We're almost at the bar when someone walks in front of me. "Nicklas Knight, as I live and breathe. How are you doing?" he greets.

"Valentine Grant," I reply, pulling Carolina to my side. "I'm well, thank you. Have you met Carolina Sterling, my wife to-be?"

I smother down a laugh at Carolina's shocked expression, pleased when she quickly rearranges her face into a more suitable mask. "Pleasure to meet you, Valentine," she sing-songs, shaking his hand.

"The pleasure is all mine, Carolina. Look, would you mind if I speak to your fiancé alone?"

She discreetly shoots me a questioning look, and I make a mental note to reward her for that later. "Go ahead," I say, nodding at the bar. "Why don't you go get us some drinks?"

As soon as she's gone, Valentine pulls me into a conversation about donations for Holloway University, where he teaches criminology. While we talk, part of my mind stays tethered to Carolina. I watch her laugh, her eyes lighting up the room more than any chandelier could. Since it's other women she's talking with, I don't see the need to interrupt her fun.

Then he approaches—some asshole I've never seen before.

The moment that sleazy grin spreads across the stranger's face as he lays a hand on Carolina's bare shoulder, my world narrows to a single point of white-hot rage. My conversation with the esteemed Valentine Grant fades into the background as I fixate on her—the flicker of discomfort in her eyes, the way she shifts uneasily.

"Excuse me," I mutter, cutting him off mid-sentence without a shred of apology. The distance between me and Carolina closes with swift, determined strides. My heart drums a furious beat echoing the possessive roar in my veins. *She's mine.*

I reach the interloper, take his wrist in a vise grip, and wrench it away from her skin, pushing him back with enough force that his feet stumble to regain balance. "Keep your damn hands off her," I growl, the threat in my tone unmistakable and deadly. He tries to laugh it off, the sound brittle and high-pitched against the thrumming tension in the air.

"Easy there. I was just being sociable," he chuckles nervously, but there's a quiver to his voice that betrays his fear. His gaze darts around, seeking an ally or an escape.

"Wrong move," I hiss, stepping closer until he's forced to look up at me. "She's not for you. Never will be."

A collective breath seems to be held by those nearby, their faces drawn tight with anticipation of violence. The rich and powerful of New York City might thrive on scandal, but they know better than to interfere with a Knight's wrath.

"Nicklas," Carolina chimes in, her touch light on my arm, though I barely register it over the pounding of blood in my ears. She's trying to soothe the beast, her presence both a balm and a blaze. "Let's not cause a scene," she says, her voice steady but edged with urgency.

"He touched what's *mine.*" I can't keep the snarl from my lips, even as I feel her gentle squeeze, a silent plea for restraint.

"Please," she whispers, leaning in, her breath warm against my neck, her scent enveloping me. It's the only thing that reels me back from the edge, reminding me of what I stand to lose if I give in to the darkness that always lurks just beneath the surface.

"Fine," I relent, the word more a growl than anything else. But I don't take my eyes off the man who dared to lay a finger on her. He knows now, unequivocally, that Carolina is untouchable—except by me.

My blood's still boiling, the noise of the party fading into a dull, inconsequential roar. With one nod directed at the corner, I seal the man's fate. Marco slips out of the shadows from where he's been guarding us. He quickly spots the man who touched Carolina.

"Let's have a chat," he growls, steering the man away with an iron grip.

There's a ripple of silence as they pass, and eyes dart away, refusing to meet mine. Everyone here knows better than to interfere with Knight business.

"Hey," Carolina murmurs, pausing until I give her all my attention. Her eyes lock onto mine, fierce and fiery. "I'm okay, and I'm not going anywhere."

"Damn right you're not," I growl, still too angry to fully appreciate the magnitude of her words.

"Come with me," she says, tugging at my hand, leading me away from the crowd that's too afraid to speak, too enthralled to look away.

I let her pull me to a secluded corner, the shadows embracing us like the darkness in my own soul. My chest heaves with each ragged breath, the urge to unleash violence still coursing through my veins.

"Nicklas," she whispers, pressing close. Her touch is supposed to be soothing, but it ignites another kind of fire within me.

"You should keep your distance," I warn, trying to steady myself, but she's undeterred.

With a boldness that both infuriates and arouses me, she slides my hand under the hem of her skirt, guiding it until I can feel the cool metal plug nestled inside her. "Feel that?" she murmurs, her breath hot against my ear. "I'm yours. Only yours."

That single reminder is a fuse lit to dynamite—my possessiveness flares, transforming the anger into voracious desire. My thumb brushes against her, feeling her body's response to the plug, to my touch. The soft sigh that escapes her lips is a melody to my savage need.

"Kitten," I rasp, my other hand gripping her chin, pulling her gaze to mine. "You're playing with fire."

She smiles, a daring curve of her lips that tells me she wants to get burned. "Then let me feel the heat."

It's a challenge, a plea, and I'm powerless to resist. I'm Nicklas Knight—I take what I want, and right now, all I want is her. The world fades away as I claim her mouth. She tastes like sin and redemption, and I'm a man starved for both.

"Nick," she gasps between kisses, "make me yours. Again and

again."

Fuck, I love the way she said that. "Trust me," I growl, "by the end of tonight, there won't be a soul alive who doesn't know you belong to me." And I seal that promise with another kiss that leaves us both breathless and wanting more. Always more.

She sighs. "I can't wait until the end of the night."

I can't help but marvel at the brazenness of her as her deft fingers work my zipper with a sense of urgency that matches the frantic beating of my heart.

"I need this. We need this," she whispers, her voice thick with desire.

The cool air hits my hard cock as she frees me from the constraints of my suit pants and boxer briefs. Her hand wraps around me, pumping once, twice—firm and sure. It's an echo of how she grips my world: boldly and without reservation.

"Hellcat," I warn, my voice a low rumble, "don't waste what's meant to be buried inside you." My mind is awash with images of her swollen with my child, carrying the heir to the Knight legacy.

She drops to her knees, her eyes locked onto mine, filled with a hunger that mirrors my own. The sight of her, ready to worship me with her mouth, sends a surge of primal satisfaction through my veins. When her lips encircle the head of my cock, it's all I can do not to lose myself completely.

"I won't waste a single drop," she mumbles against me, sending vibrations straight to my groin.

"Fuck," I groan, one hand fisted in her golden hair, guiding her, though she needs no direction.

Her mouth works magic, her tongue swirling and teasing until the pressure builds into an undeniable force. I can feel every inch of myself pulsating for release, and when it comes, she takes it all, every drop, her throat contracting around me.

But we're far from done. As she rises, her kiss is fierce, claiming, and I taste myself on her—marking territory in the most intimate of ways. With a slick transfer, she passes back the cum she'd gathered, and the act sears itself into my memory. A carnal communion; a seal of possession.

"Get under my dress," she huskily commands, her voice laced with determination. "Push it back into me. I want every part of you."

And like the beast I am, I obey, sinking to my knees before her. Our roles reversed, yet both in control, both consumed by our acts. Her bare skin greets my touch, and she moans as I pull the plug out of her. She's showered without the plug since I last thrust my cum into her hot cunt, so the only moisture is her arousal.

I do my best to gather as much of my cum as possible on the tip of my tongue before thrusting into her wet opening. This would all be so much easier if she was lying down, or maybe hanging upside down, but hey, I'm not complaining.

The sounds she makes as I fulfill her request, pushing my cum into her, is a symphony to my soul. "God, yes," she breathes out, her body meeting each of my movements with a desperation that speaks volumes of her commitment.

She grinds her slick cunt along my face, gasping when the tip of my nose hits her clit. Grabbing her hips, I urge her to move faster, to fuck my face until she gets herself off, and she does. She grinds all over my face, covering me in her juices and my cum, and I don't fucking care one bit.

When she comes, her sounds are so muffled I'm convinced she's shoved her fist into her mouth to keep quiet. My hellcat isn't normally this quiet, and the thought that she's restraining herself for me has me instantly hard again.

After sliding the plug back into place, I crawl out from under the skirt of her dress. I rearrange my pants, tucking my cock away. Then I take her hand, intending to lead her to the bathroom so we can both clean up. But she has other plans, and before I can take one step, she tugs her hand free and cups my face.

"What are you—" I'm interrupted when she raises to her tiptoes and brazenly licks my cheeks and forehead.

"Mhmm," she purrs.

"Carolina!" I hiss. "If you don't stop right now, I'm going to bend you over and fuck you right here."

She lets go of me, but instead of looking contrite, she looks like she's actually considering it. I chuckle and drag her into the bathroom. Switching the tap on, I gather water in my hands, but before I can splash it across my face, she switches the water off again.

"Don't wash me away," she orders, folding her arms across her chest.

"Excuse me?"

She shakes her head. "Nuh-uhh. Unless you want me to remove the plug and wipe myself clean, you'll walk back out there with my pussy juices all over your face."

Fuck me, that's... that's... everything.

When we emerge back into the party, the air crackles around us—charged with our shared possessiveness. My arm wraps around Carolina's waist as I guide her through the crowd. People part for us, their gazes curious and wary, knowing better than to intrude.

I quickly spot the man that's the reason I left Jack and the three to do some dealings alone so I could accept tonight's invitation, and I lead us over to him.

"Carolina, this is Dr. Alan Hargrove," I introduce, my tone commanding respect.

"It's an honor to meet you," she says warmly, her voice steady despite the earlier storm of passion.

"Please, the pleasure is all mine," Dr. Hargrove says, taking her hand into his wrinkled one. "What can I do for you two?" Even though the question is aimed at both of us, his eyes never leave mine and crinkle with amusement.

"Dr. Hargrove specializes in neurology," I continue, ensuring he understands the importance of what I'm about to say. "My sister-in-law-to-be, Willow Sterling, she's paraplegic. I want you to make her your priority."

Dr. Hargrove nods, his eyes flickering with recognition. "Of course, Mr. Knight. Is this a recent development?"

"No, it's not," Carolina answers. "My sister was injured when she was twelve, which was eight years ago."

"Oh, dear," Dr. Hargrove replies. "May I ask what happened?"

Although I've read all the facts and could answer, I want to hear the story from the woman at my side.

"Our dad was walking Willow to school when a drunk driver came toward them." Despite the emotion in her voice, Carolina looks regal as she lifts her chin and continues. "Dad managed to push Willow out of the way, but the car hit and killed him. Unfortunately, when he pushed my sister out of the way, she stumbled down some stairs and landed in an awkward position that left her paralyzed from the waist down."

Dr. Hargrove nods as he listens intently. "I see, that sounds serious. Is the paralysis due to a spinal cord injury?"

"Y-yes," Carolina stutters.

I can see the answer written all over his features before he says anything. "In that case, I'm afraid there's nothing that can be done. I'll be happy to look at your sister's file, but it sounds like the nerve connections needed for movement and sensation have been disrupted." He pauses and runs a hand down his face. "Sadly, the current medical technology cannot fully restore these connections."

That's the answer I feared.

"Yeah, that's what I've been told," Carolina says, sounding wistful.

"Where's your sister staying?" he asks kindly, and when she tells him where, he smiles widely. "I'm familiar with Ability Acres. I can easily drop by and assess both your sister and her file if you want? It would be no trouble at all."

Carolina perks up at that, and she thanks him over and over, well, alternating between gratitude and questions. She's determined to get the best care for Willow, so when Dr. Hargrove mentions a private facility he's on the board for, she's all ears until she hears the monthly price.

"Make it happen," I order, shaking my head as she tries to argue with me about the price.

"It's too expensive," she insists, digging her nails into my hand that she's still holding, like that's going to deter me.

"If I may," Dr. Hargrove cuts in. "We do have some openings for people who can't pay—"

"No!" both Carolina and I interrupt simultaneously.

Turning to my hellcat, I use my free hand to peel her claws out of my flesh. "Hey, listen to me," I insist. "You could probably get one of those spots for people in need. But why take that from someone who really needs it when I can easily pay for it?"

Carolina huffs theatrically. "But *I* can't pay for it. She's my sister, so I should be able to."

"Sure you can," I grin. "You're my fiancée after all."

The shocked expression she makes is all I need to confirm that she didn't think I was serious when I asked her if she wanted the ring while she was getting ready for the party. Taking her left hand, I press down on the ring I gave her.

"I asked you if you accepted the ring, and you said yes," I remind her.

"W-what?" she sputters. "But this… it's just a ring. You didn't ask me to marry you."

Shrugging, I lean down and whisper in her ear. "I don't have to ask when you're already mine."

Despite rolling her eyes, she smiles, and it's not one of those fake ones she plasters on for other people. This smile reaches her eyes. "Fine," she says, trying to sound haughty. Then she looks at Dr. Hargrove again. "I guess I can afford the facility after all. How do I—"

"Marvelous," the older man laughs. "If you want, you and Willow can come by my office tomorrow. How does that sound?"

"Sounds good," I say, cementing the deal with a handshake.

Carolina is less reserved, and she throws her arms around his neck, hugging him tightly. "Thank you," she sobs so softly I'm barely able to hear it. "Thank you so much."

Since Dr. Hargrove is an old—emphasis on *old*—family friend, and has been nothing but loyal, cordial, and respectful toward me, I let it slide when he returns the hug. But only for about twenty seconds, which I think is extremely lenient of me.

CHAPTER 19

The Santa

I grip Carolina's hand tighter as we slide into the back of Marco's SUV, the night air crisp and biting against my skin. The city is a blur of Christmas lights and shadow, but my mind is darker than these streets, running through the events of the evening with lethal precision.

"Everything is handled, boss," Marco mutters from the driver's seat, his eyes meeting mine in the rearview mirror. His voice is low, laced with the promise of violence already carried out.

"Good," I respond curtly, my thumb stroking over Carolina's knuckles. She doesn't need to know the details—just that she's safe. That no one touches what's mine and lives without consequence.

"So I guess I should congratulate you two," he chuckles. "I hear you're now engaged."

I wait for Carolina to deny it, but to my surprise, she doesn't. "Thank you," she says, straightening her spine.

The rest of the car ride is silent except for the steady hum of the engine and Carolina's soft breathing. Her head rests on my shoulder, and I can feel the trust she places in me weighing heavier than any crown. She's mine to protect, to cherish, to breed. And her dedication tonight has only solidified my possessive need for her.

Once home, I dismiss Marco with a nod, knowing he understands the silence that hangs between us. He knows the unspoken directive—no loose ends.

I follow Carolina into our bathroom, watching her as she starts to remove her makeup and brush her teeth. Then I help her get the dress off, and because she asks nicely, I don't tear it from her body.

"So tired," she yawns, staring longingly at the shower. "But I feel like I need to clean up first."

"Absolutely not," I scoff. "We wear each other's juices with pride, Hellcat. Don't give up on me now."

The grin she gives me is absolutely lethal, and I fucking love it. "Fine," she relents.

Before she can leave the bathroom, I open the small cupboard above the sink and pull a white, rectangular package out. "I think it's time you take one of these," I say as I hand her the pregnancy test.

She bites her lip as she accepts it. "Wow," she breathes. "Yeah, I guess I should. We only have nine days left, right?"

"We have all the fucking time in the world," I lie on a growl.

This might have all started because I wanted an heir, and I still want one. Carolina, however, isn't just a hired womb, she's now my fiancée. It might not have happened in the traditional way, but who fucking cares? I don't, and so far it doesn't seem like she does either.

"Go on," I urge. "Pee on the damn stick."

"With you watching—" She cuts herself off, already knowing there's no point in arguing.

I don't turn around or look away; I watch her as she sits down on the toilet, and then she slides the stick between her thighs, covering it in her urine.

Hmm, I've never been into piss play, but right now, I'd consider letting her pee on me. There's something so insanely intimate about watching her like this, and greedy as I am, I want everything life has to offer with her.

Once she's done, she wipes herself and gets some extra toilet paper to lie the test on. Then she washes her hands while I set the timer on my phone for two minutes. We don't talk while we wait, we're both focused on the single line. I barely blink, too scared to miss the appearance of a second line.

But it never comes. Not when my timer goes off, or within the extra five minutes we wait. I take the test and throw it into the trash can. "We'll do another one tomorrow. I think I read that the morning is the best time."

There's no hiding the disappointment we both feel, but I feel guilty as she averts her gaze and just nods. "Yeah, fine. Whatever." Her shoulders slump as she leaves the bathroom and crawls into bed. "It might be a bit too early for a test to show." I'm not sure if she says it to herself or me.

Although I have things to do, I follow her, lying down next to her. I wrap my arm around her and pull her closer—her back against my front—and nestle my face against her neck. "Are you disappointed?" I ask.

"A little," she admits. "But mostly, I'm afraid you're disappointed in me. That you're not getting your money's worth."

"Fuck the money," I growl menacingly. "All I want is you, Hellcat. You and me, that's all that matters."

"Really?" she asks, hope bleeding into her voice.

I move her so she's lying on her back, hovering over her so she can see just how serious I am. "Yes, really. I fucking love you, Carolina—"

"You love me?" she gasps, her mouth forming an O.

Nodding, I answer, "I do. That's why I keep telling you that you're mine. It's why I put a ring on your finger."

"You love me," she repeats, only this time, it doesn't sound like a question.

Chuckling, I lie back down, pulling her against me again. "Forevermore," I vow.

She doesn't say it back, which is fine. She will eventually. There's no escaping me, and if she tries… well, I'll just have to tie her up until she gives up.

Carolina Sterling is mine.

Her body feels amazing against mine, and as her breath grows deeper and deeper, I almost forget that I need to stay awake. But as soon as I remember why I can't give in yet, my blood boils, running hot with the memory of that bastard's hands on her.

I wait until her breathing steadies, confirming her descent into dreams where I hope she's safe from the darkness that clings to my soul. Then I slip from the bed, my movements ghost-like as I make my way to my torture room.

He's there, tied to a chair, the remnants of fear and pain etched into his face. Good. He should be afraid.

"P-please," he starts, the tremble in his voice music to my ears.

"Shut up," I snarl, my hands itching to deliver the retribution burning through my veins. I circle him like a predator, each step measured, each breath filled with purpose.

"B-but—"

"You touched what is mine," I say, leaning close, my lips brushing his ear with deceptive softness. "For that, you'll pay."

He flinches away, straining against the bindings at his wrists and ankles. It's a pitiful sight, this creature who dared to encroach on my territory. Who dared to lay hands upon my queen.

"Why did you touch her?" I demand, my voice rumbling with contained fury.

"I-I—" he stammers.

Running out of patience, I silence him with a fist to his face. The sound of my knuckles connecting with his nose echoes in the dark silence.

"Answer me," I say, every syllable a threat of more violence to come.

"I d-didn't know!" he cries out, tears welling in his eyes. "I swear, I didn't know she was yours! I don't even know who you are."

The last part I believe, that he didn't know who I am is more likely than not having noticed Carolina arrived with me. "And do you know now?"

He shakes his head, shouting when I punch him again, and again, and a-fucking-gain.

"Oh, God... p-please," he whines, but his pleas only fan the flames of my wrath.

Pausing, I answer him. "Not God. Knight," I growl.

Then I continue to punch him; his nose and jaw break under my furious punches, but I don't stop—I can't stop. The basement echoes with the sickening crunch of retribution and the man's guttural cries as I mete out justice for the insult to what is mine.

For the next several hours, I extract my vengeance, every crack of bone, every whimper of agony a balm to my raging beast. He's gasping for breath, his eyes begging for mercy that will never come his way. His cries echo in the silence, a fitting soundtrack to the bloody tableau we've become.

When I'm no longer satisfied using my fists, I pause long enough to get clippers. I don't pay any attention as I shove every finger on the offending hand through the holes of the custom-built contraption, or when I use all my strength to sever the digits from his hand.

He screams and thrashes. His eyes rolling back into his head before he passes out. For fuck's sake.

"Marco!" I bark, and when he joins me, he's quick to hold the smelling salt under the guy's nose.

It takes longer than I'd like for the guy to come around, which tells me he's almost at the end of his limit. What a fucking waste of space.

"Hey!" I bark, snapping my fingers in his face.

Due to his broken jaw, he can't talk, which is probably for the best. I doubt his words would be more meaningful than the pitiful noises he makes.

"This is the end of the road for you," I tell him, my tone completely devoid of emotion. "If there's a next life, I hope you'll remember how this one ended. Never touch something or someone that isn't yours."

I reach for the gun Marco's holding, and after activating the silencer and removing the safety, I lift it, pointing it straight at his head.

"See you in the next life, motherfucker." With those words, I pull the trigger.

His body jerks, but there's no doubt he's dead.

"Damn," Marco whistles as he looks down at the mess I've made. "Guess I need to be careful about offering a hand to the future Mrs. Knight."

I grin at him. "As long as you offer first, we're good, my friend."

I instruct Marco to dispose of the broken body, and as always, he's a step ahead of me. "Cleanup will be here within the hour. I'll make sure they're thorough."

With a sharp nod, I pull my phone out to see if there's any news from Jack. There isn't. Although I know I should keep my head in the game and check in, I bid Marco goodnight and return to the sanctuary I share with Carolina, and after a shower, I crawl into bed, finding she hasn't moved since I left her.

CHAPTER 20

The Breeder

I'm trembling slightly as I push Will toward the sterile white door with "Dr. Alan Hargrove" etched in sleek, black letters. It's a stark contrast to the cluttered world outside, where Christmas decorations are sprouting like wildflowers.

"Chin up, Caro," Willow says, her voice a soothing balm to my frayed nerves. "We've got this, right?"

"Right," I echo, though my stomach knots tighter. We're here for her, but it feels like I'm the one unraveling.

As I knock on the door, I ponder how Willow always seems to be in such good spirits. It's untouchable, unlike mine that feels like I'm lost at sea. I need to toughen up, to stop being so obsessed about her getting better.

Really, who am I to decide what 'better' is? If she's not complaining, I have no right to.

The door opens, and I glance up at Dr. Alan Hargrove. "Hello again, Carolina." His silver hair crowns his head like a halo of wisdom, and his eyes are sharp as a hawk's. "And you must be the reason we're all here," he says to Will, a smile crinkling the corners of his eyes.

"Nice to see you again, Dr. Hargrove," I say, my throat tight.

"Hi there, Dr. Hargrove. Thank you for seeing me on such short notice." She greets him with the enthusiasm of someone who sees life as a glass perpetually full.

As he waves us into the room behind him, he says, "Please call me Alan."

In the adjoining examination room, I position the wheelchair so Will can move from her wheelchair and onto the examination bed.

The doctor's practiced hands are gentle as he checks my sister's reflexes. The tests unfold like a well-rehearsed play; a tap of the hammer here, a brush of fingertips there, each movement meticulous and measured. I watch, barely breathing, as Dr. Hargrove conducts a symphony of neurological assessments, from checking pupil dilation to testing muscle strength.

"Everything okay?" Will asks, catching the furrow in my brow. "I mean, I'm still paralyzed, right? Or can I suddenly walk on water?"

Dr. Har—Alan—laughs softly to himself before telling us he's done, and suggesting we sit down in his office to talk. He disappears to get us some drinks, and while he's gone, I help her back into the wheelchair, not that she needs my help. This is more for me, so I have something to do.

"I'm sure everything's perfect," I lie, my voice barely above a whisper. My heart yearns to believe it, even as it dreads the uncertainty.

"You always were a bad liar," she sing-songs. "But sure, sure. Perfect would be nice for a change."

While we wait for Alan to return, I ask my sister about Ruby. "Are the two of you still hanging out?" I ask, absentmindedly scratching my nose with my left hand.

"Wow!" she exclaims. "Hold on a fucking second, Caro. Why are you asking me about Ruby when you're carrying that diamond around?"

Shit, I hadn't thought about that. I don't even know how to explain everything to her. Or more accurately, I don't know where to start.

"Does this mean you're not just dating Ruby's brother?" she probes.

"Yeah," I sigh. "I guess I'm engaged to him."

Will scrunches up her nose. "You're engaged to a man I haven't met? How can that be when he doesn't have my approval?"

I burst out laughing at the forced disapproval in her voice. "Sorry," I laugh. "I'll make sure to rectify that as soon as possible."

Before we can say anything, Alan returns with three cups of steaming hot chocolate placed on a black tray. The scent luckily drowns out the clinical smell in here, making it less intimidating.

"Okay, should we dive right in?" he asks, looking straight at her.

"Let's do it," she agrees.

"Unfortunately," Dr. Hargrove begins with a sigh, "there have been no advancements in treatment that would improve your current condition, Willow."

I feel the sting of tears threatening to spill, but I blink them away furiously. It's not the news we hoped for, but it's the news we expected—somewhere deep down, at least. Willow, bless her, just nods with an accepting smile.

"Thank you for checking." Her voice is steady, but it's the slight tremor in her grip that betrays her disappointment.

"However," he continues, shifting his gaze between us, "as I told Carolina yesterday, there is a top-notch care facility here in New York City that you might consider. They specialize in patients with spinal injuries and offer state-of-the-art therapies that can significantly improve quality of life. They even have the option to live there with other patients if you want."

Will gapes. "Do you mean NREC? Oh my God, you totally do, don't you?"

He laughs good naturedly. "Yes, I'm talking about the NeuroRehab Excellence Center. I take it you have heard about it."

My sister practically bounces in her wheelchair. "Have I? I mean, yes, yes I have. It's like Neverland, a mythical place unless you have a butt load of money."

Alan laughs harder, even slapping his stomach. "That's the place. Your sister's fiancé was very insistent, so I've pulled some strings. There's a spot open for you if you want it."

Before Will can answer, I inject. "Umm, if this is something you'd rather take your time to—"

"No way," she almost shouts. "There's nothing to think about. That place is the dream. If I can get a spot there, I'll take it."

"Fantastic," Alan says.

Then she looks up at me, the light dimming slightly in her eyes. "I mean, can we afford it?"

"The spot we're holding for you is part of a program that helps those who need it. All your expenses will be taken care of," Alan lies smoothly.

Before I left this morning, I made Nick call ahead to make sure Will never finds out we're paying for her spot. Not that she isn't worth it, but I know my sister well enough to know she'd feel extremely uncomfortable. And now, since she seems to know a lot about the place, I don't regret that decision.

If the money wasn't for Will, I'd never accept after learning how many zeroes are needed just to cover the monthly expenses. But… for my sister, I'll swallow my pride.

"Actually, I'm headed over there within the hour. Would you like to come with me?" Alan asks her.

"Yes!" She fist pumps the air and smiles widely.

"Do you want me to come with you?" I ask.

To my surprise, she shakes her head. "No. If it's okay with you, I want to go by myself. But I'll totally call you later."

Hours after saying goodbye to Will and Alan, I'm back in Nick's apartment, sitting alone in the spacious living room. After checking my phone every minute for updates from my sister, I retrieved Sienna's diary, needing to know more about this family I've apparently agreed to marry into.

I still don't know how I feel about that.

Overwhelmed, confused, dizzy—like the earth is spinning too fast on its axis, and I'm just expected to keep up with it. But what's more is that I think I want to. I like what I have with Nick, and even though I probably shouldn't, I feel safe with him.

It's more than that, though. It's like every minute with him is an exciting exploration, a test of wills and strength. Despite not having any power of my own, I don't think I've ever felt more capable or strong than I do with him.

I know it makes no sense that I accepted his proposal—his claim— when I don't even know if I love him. Honestly, that's part of the thrill.

> *They expect us to be broodmares, nothing more.*
>
> *I feel the weight of their gaze, ever-present, calculating my worth by my ability to produce an heir...*

There's no date on the first fifty entries or so. I guess that makes sense since it sounds like she was locked up. Caspian's words from the family dinner echo in my head; Sienna was bought at some kind of twisted human auction. Yeah, of course she wouldn't know the date, and depending on how long she was held captive, maybe not even the year.

> *Today it happened. I was bought like I was an item to be bid on rather than a person.*
>
> *My new owner's name is Caspian, and he says I can call him that. The way he said it made it sound like a big deal, and I suppose it is. At the place they held us before the auction, they told us to never assume we were allowed to use our owner's name.*
>
> *The expectations are clear: I'm here to be his wife and to provide heirs.*
>
> *The weight of that expectation is heavy. They say it's vital for the family, for the legacy, but it feels like a lot to bear.*
>
> *What if I can't fulfill that role? What if*

something goes wrong? I'm afraid that failing to meet these expectations might mean more than just disappointment...

Then, I finally get to an entry with a date, but no year. Did Caspian not tell her what year it was? Or did she simply not want to commemorate it in her diary?

July 10th

Caspian seems to have a genuine interest in me, but can I trust that this is more than just a duty to him?

The way he talks about the future, it's as if there's no room for personal connection or genuine affection—just an obligation to produce heirs and maintain the family line.

I want to believe there's more to this, that there can be warmth and understanding between us.

I don't know what the future holds, but I'm trying to keep an open heart.

I hope that, somehow, we can find a way to make this work—not just for the sake of the family legacy, but for ourselves.

July 30th

Tonight, Caspian told me about his family, the burden of being a Knight.

He introduced me to his family. I don't know what I expected, but it wasn't for my owner's dad to force his hand between my legs, wanting to feel my hymen for himself. I almost threw up when he did it right in front of Caspian's mom, younger brothers, and... no, I won't think about it.

Caspian assured me it won't ever happen again.

We're getting married tonight, in secret. Once I'm his, he says no one can ever touch me again.

I retch as I read that entry over and over, my stomach churning more and more violently every time my eyes pass over it. Christ, should I be happy Caspian didn't do that to me when we had dinner with him only five days ago?

By now, the living room has become dark, but I'm too engrossed to get up and switch the light on. I grab my phone and use the flashlight app so I can continue reading.

August 5th

When Caspian told me about what it means to be the head of the Knight Mafia, he made it sound like a burden. But as he brutally murdered someone right in front of me for stealing some weapons, he was reveling in it. He looked... happy.

Oh, God, the horror didn't stop there. He killed everyone; wiped out an entire family in a single night. And he dragged me along to witness it all.

November 17th

Caspian laid his hands on me tonight. It's the first time he's touched me out of malice.

It was my own fault!

He's told me over and over that nothing is more important than the family business. I knew that, and yet I dared question him when he came home late.

I didn't mean to make him angry, I was just so disappointed because I'd arranged for a special night for us. But... he's right. I'm a stupid girl that needs to know my place.

The Knight family comes first, always. We women are expendable.

September 5th

Another miscarriage.

The disappointment is suffocating.

Caspian hardly looks at me now, his eyes always searching for something more, something I'm beginning to fear I cannot give.

I flip back to the previous entry, trying to figure out if it's the same year. Something tells me it isn't, especially since she hasn't mentioned other miscarriages or pregnancies. As I look closer, I notice papers have been ripped out, only leaving stumps in the spine.

December 24th

It's Christmas Eve, and instead of joy, there's a silent demand hanging in the air.

Three children for success—they say.

My womb has become a battleground, and I am both the warrior and the territory fought over.

Again, papers are missing, so I don't know if this is from the same year as the previous one about the miscarriage.

My heart clenches in sympathy, my trembling fingers running over the embossed initials on the cover as I close it. Sienna's pain resonates with my own fears. I close my eyes, envisioning her—an elegant woman trapped in a golden cage, her body a vessel for the Knight legacy.

Her words echo in my mind, painting a vivid picture of life married into the Knight family—expectations as high and unyielding as the skyscrapers that dominate New York's skyline.

My fingers absentmindedly trace the contours of my engagement ring, a stunning piece of artistry that seems to mock me with its weight. An intricate band of white gold twists around a diamond so large it easily catches the light from the screen on my phone, even after switching off the flashlight.

I need to understand the man I'm supposed to marry—the man who commands fear and respect in equal measure. My resolve hardens as I rise from the couch, the diary tucked under my arm, and find my way through the sprawling apartment that feels more like a fortress with each step. The hallways are silent, but I feel eyes on me, watching, always watching.

Finally, I reach his office, the door closed. I knock once, and as I wait for Nick to reply, I start wondering if he's even home. Most days, he disappears after breakfast. Sometimes he tells me about meetings he has, but that's mostly when he has to leave the apartment. I don't actually know what he's doing when he's here.

"Nick?" I call as I knock once more, but instead of waiting, I push the handle down.

Last night he gave me a damn engagement ring and said he loves me, I take that to mean I don't have to stand out here waiting for an audience.

CHAPTER 21

The Breeder

As I enter the office, I find him sitting at his desk, his hands interlaced behind his head. He's smirking like me being here is amusing to him, and for some reason, that rubs me the wrong way. "Took you long enough to make up your mind," he drawls, pointing at his laptop that's facing him.

I walk around the desk and look at the screen, which shows the place where I just stood while knocking. "You watched me?" I ask, incredulously. "So you knew it was me. Why didn't you say I could come in?"

Shrugging, he replies, "I shouldn't have to. You're going to be my wife, Kitten. Everything I own is yours, including my heart."

"But what does that mean?" I ask. "If you think that means I'll allow your dad to stick his fingers inside my vagina you better think again." For good measure, I slam Sienna's diary down on the desk.

Arching an eyebrow, he looks up at me with anger twisting his normally handsome features. "What did you just say?" His tone is low, dangerously so.

Instead of letting him intimidate me, I start rambling about the diary entries I've just read, repeating that I refuse to let Caspian or anyone else touch me. "And you can forget about selling me. I might be yours, Nicklas, but that's it. I'm not a toy you can share around, and I'm definitely not entertainment for the entire family."

The more I talk, the more worked up I get. As I continue to rant, my tone grows louder until I'm shouting at him. I know it's not actually him I'm upset with, yet I can't make myself stop. I have all these confusing feelings warring inside me, making it impossible to sort through anything. So instead of even trying, I just lash out.

"Are you done?" he asks when I pause to take a deep breath.

"Done?" I scream. "I'll show you fucking done."

I grab the nearest object—a heavy paperweight—and hurl it across the room. It shatters against the wall, pieces scattering across the floor, but he doesn't move, doesn't even blink. Unable to stop, I reach for anything within my grasp—books, pens, a glass that explodes into shards when it hits the ground.

Each crash echoes my own breaking heart. "Why won't you say something?!" I'm shrieking now, the words raw and ragged. My hands are trembling, tugging at my hair as if I can tear the pain out of my skull.

But he just sits there, behind his desk, his face a mask of stone. The silence between us is unbearable, choking me, and all I want is for him to react, to show me something—anything—that he feels this too. That he can see how desperately I need him to put me back together.

"Please, Nicklas," I whisper, my voice hoarse and broken. "Please, just... say something. Do something. I need you. I need you to care." I collapse onto the floor, my strength leaving me as the sobs take over, shaking me to my core.

My knees barely hit the floor before he's out of his chair, looming over me. Grabbing my arm, he pulls me onto my feet and quickly pushes me up against the wall. "Now you're done," he rasps, his eyes no longer uncaring. "You can accuse me of many things, and you'll probably be right. But the one thing you don't get to question is how much I care for you, Hellcat. I've told you that you're mine. I've told the world that you're mine. I've put a damn ring on your finger. What more can I do?"

"Tell me you won't let your dad—"

"Stop!" he roars. Anger rolls off him in palpable waves, but I refuse to cower. "I refuse to believe you actually want an answer to that."

"Why?" I scream back.

Lifting his hand, he wraps it around my throat and squeezes. "Do you know what I did after you fell asleep last night? I killed the sorry son of a bitch who touched you at the party. That's two men I've killed for you, Kitten. And you know what? I'll kill two a day, every hour, every fucking minute if that's what it takes for you to finally understand that you. Are. Mine!"

The way my breath hitches has nothing to do with his hold on me, and everything to do with the dark and alluring words he speaks. "You killed for me again?" I ask, licking my lips.

He nods. "And I'll continue to do it. But the one thing I won't fucking tolerate, is you basically asking if I'm going to allow my dad to touch you in any way. Ask me again, and I'll take it out on your ass."

I whimper—honest to God whimper.

A dark chuckle leaves him. "Maybe you want me to?"

Do I? I don't know, maybe… but no. That's not why I came in here. Shaking my head, I say, "Your mom's—"

"I know what it says," he growls. "I've read that damn thing end to end a thousand times. I know what happened to her. But that's her story and not yours."

Nodding, I do my best to process his words. "So none of it—"

Again, he interrupts me. "You're misunderstanding me, Kitten. Most of the things that happened to her after being bought by Dad will also happen to you. But I can guarantee you that one of them won't be me sharing you. Not with my dad, not with any-fucking-one." He adds pressure to my throat, making it so I can barely breathe. "Nod if you understand."

I eagerly nod, and as he slams his lips against mine, I pour all my fears, my insecurities, and everything in between into the kiss. I nip at his lips, breaking the bottom one. But I don't care, not even when he does the same to me and our blood mingles in both our mouths.

While we kiss, I claw at his clothes, eager to get them off. Not just because I'm so incredibly turned on and wet, but mostly because I want to feel him—need it, need him.

Nick's the one to break the kiss. We're both panting like we've run a marathon when he rests his forehead against mine, squeezing his eyes closed. "You know what I am," he rasps.

The air in Nicklas' office is thick with tension, a living entity that wraps around me like a vise. I stand before him, my heart thundering, demanding the truth about the blood that stains his hands and the dark empire he commands.

"Tell me everything," I say, my voice steady despite the tremor of nerves beneath my skin.

With a heavy sigh, he carries me over to the desk and sits me down on it. Then he sits back in his chair, the movement predatory, deliberate. His dark eyes lock on mine, revealing nothing and everything all at once.

"You want to know about the Knight family?" His question isn't really a question; it's an opening gambit.

"Yes." I swallow hard, bracing myself.

He slides the chair closer, and I fight the urge to retreat. This is Nicklas in his element—raw power, barely leashed. "We are the unseen hand that guides the underworld. Our reach extends far beyond what you can imagine, Carolina."

"Human trafficking," I say, remembering the scribbled words from Sienna's diary and the ones Arthur spoke at dinner. "You buy people." My words hang between us, heavy with implication.

"Once, yes. The world changes, and we adapt. Now, our endeavors are… different. Actually, there's still one place…" Trailing off, he shakes his head. "Doesn't matter. But our goal has always remained the same— to maintain control, to ensure our dominance."

"And the killings?" I press on, my pulse racing.

He chuckles. "Are you put off by them or intrigued?" He reaches out, his fingers brushing against my cheek.

I should recoil, but instead, I lean into his touch. A part of me revels in the danger he represents, drawn to the darkness like a moth to flame. It's a revelation that sends a shiver down my spine—not of fear, but of something far more complicated.

"Not put off. I'm… intrigued," I admit, licking my lips. "Especially not the ones you've done for me. It's… I think I like it." If he's going to be completely honest, it's only fair I am as well. And as messed up as it is, that's how it makes me feel.

"Everything I've done, I've done for the Knight legacy; for our future." His voice drops, a husky whisper that sends heat pooling low in my belly. "For you."

I look up into his face, seeing the raw honesty there. "And if I asked you to stop? To walk away from it all?"

"You wouldn't."

"But what if I did," I insist. I don't know what drives me to ask again. Maybe it's because of the words I read in Sienna's diary, a hidden need for more reassurance that her story won't be mine. "What if I asked you to stay home from a business thingy. Would you do it? Stay with me, I mean."

"I already have," he replies. "I've missed a lot of business to be with you. Ask me if I fucking care."

"Do you care?"

He lets out a mirthless and gruff laugh. "I should. The Knight family is supposed to come first. But I…"

As he seemingly struggles to find his words, I finish the sentence for him. "But you don't."

"I don't," he agrees. Then he sighs. "You need to understand that I can never let go completely. It's not just business. It's who we are—who I am. I am the Knight family, just as it is me."

Morality is a pesky thing, and right now, I'm torn between the morality I should feel, and the complete lack of it. I look at the man before me—a man willing to spill blood for power, yet who holds me as if I'm the most precious thing in his world.

"You're right," I confess. "I won't ask you to stop."

"Does this not scare you?" His question is soft, almost vulnerable.

"Should it?" I counter, a hint of my own bravado creeping into my voice.

"Most would run from this truth."

"I'm not most people," I reply, and it's true. The darkness doesn't repel me; it beckons, promising a depth of passion and devotion I've never known.

"Then let us be unapologetic in who we are," he says, closing the distance between us. His lips capture mine in a kiss that seals our fates, binding us tighter than any vow.

In this moment, I realize the gravity of our connection. With every brush of his lips, every whispered promise, I'm falling deeper into a world where morals are painted in shades of gray, if not black—a world where I belong, entwined with the enigmatic and dangerous Nicklas Knight.

He ends the kiss too fast for my liking, and I whine at the loss of his lips on mine. He stands before me, a dark god in his tailored suit, which looks good although I tore at it not too long ago. His eyes are blazing with intent, the hunger in his gaze is almost palpable and it sends shivers cascading down my spine.

"Take your dress off," he growls, his voice low and rough.

When I got back from taking Will to see Dr. Hargrove, I changed into a sexy, black dress, which now proves to have been a great idea. Without looking away, I slide the straps down my shoulders, licking my lips as I stand up as well. I pull the dress down until it pools at my feet.

My nipples are already hard, and he quickly pinches them, making me moan and arch my back as I unclasp my bra and discard it. I'm now standing in front of him, completely naked. His strong hands grip my hips, easily lifting me back onto the desk before spreading my legs apart as he leans in close.

His mouth hovering over mine, close enough I could stick my tongue out and lick the seams of his lips, still it feels too far away. The anticipation is maddening, but I don't have to wait long. He captures my lips in a searing kiss, demanding and possessive, and I melt into him, lost in the heat of our connection.

"Nick," I moan against his lips, "I need you."

"Every inch of you is perfection," he murmurs, trailing kisses down my neck and across my collarbone. At the same time, he reaches down and quickly removes the plug he still insists I wear.

Then he kneels before me, his head level with my core. My breaths come in short gasps as his tongue darts out, teasing at the sensitive flesh there. A moan escapes my lips, and he looks up at me, his eyes gleaming with satisfaction.

"Tell me what you want, Kitten," he commands, his voice laced with desire.

"Eat me out," I demand, the words tumbling from my lips in reckless abandon.

Without hesitation, he obliges, his mouth expertly working over me, sending waves of pleasure coursing through my body. I thread my fingers through his hair, holding him close, desperate for more.

"Fuck, you taste so good," he groans, his tongue dipping deeper, exploring every fold and crevice.

I lean back so I'm resting on my elbows, loving the way he looks up at me from between my legs. The look in his eyes is that of a man who's doing something he loves, and fuck if that isn't hot.

"Nicklas!" I gasp, teetering on the edge of ecstasy. "I'm so close."

He hoists my legs over his shoulders, adjusting his position so my ass is lifted off the desk. Then he pushes two fingers inside me, making me see stars with each pump. My orgasm is so close, I just need a bit more and then...

"W-what... why?" I cry when he retrieves his fingers. I'm immediately missing them inside me.

Then I feel them at my puckered opening, and this time I don't try to stop him. Not because of what happened last time, but because I get it. He wants to claim me everywhere, fill every hole I have—and I want the same.

"Relax for me, Kitten," he groans as he pushes his finger inside me.

I'm trying, I really am. But the intrusion feels so foreign it's damn near impossible when my body wants to clench automatically. "I'm trying." There's absolutely no enjoyment to be found in what he's doing, and I have to stop myself from moving away from his probing fingers. "It hurts," I hiss.

"Get on your hands and knees on the table," he commands, and I quickly do as he says, eager to stop the failed experiment.

Once I'm on all fours, he runs his hands from my shoulders to my ass cheeks, gently squeezing them. They're still sore from three days ago. Suddenly, his tongue is between my legs, lapping at my opening.

"Oh God!" I cry, arching my back, eager for more. I try to look at him over my shoulder, but I can't see him.

He continues to fuck my pussy with his tongue, and it doesn't take long before I'm shaking, barely able to keep myself upright.

"Come for me, Hellcat. Let go," he urges, his fingers joining his mouth in their relentless pursuit of my pleasure.

And then, I'm breaking apart, my body convulsing in bliss as I shatter beneath his touch. But Nicklas isn't done with me yet. While I'm coming down from my high, I feel his tongue licking from my drenched channel all the way back to my tight opening.

"Nicklas!" I gasp, embarrassed to have his tongue right there.

Undeterred, he licks the rim before hardening his tongue and working it inside my ass just as he slides two fingers into my weeping pussy. I'm on sensation overload, my brain shutting down as all I can do is feel what he's doing to me. And damn, it's so… filthily perfect.

I arch my back, eager to get him deeper, in both holes. When he removes his tongue from my ass and replaces it with a single digit there's no pain. Only a burning, uncontrollable need for more; more of him, more of the pleasure coiling deep in my stomach.

"That's it," he praises. "The sight of my fingers disappearing into your tight ass is pure perfection."

If this is what perfection feels like, I'm going to strive for it every single day for the rest of my life. I want to tell him how good it feels, but I can't make any words come out of my mouth, only garbled, nonsensical words that are really more like animalistic noises.

Nick picks up his pace, making the coil inside me intensify. It feels like it's growing, and I feel an overwhelming need to pee. "Wait… stop… I need to…"

Instead of stopping, he fucks me harder, adding a third finger to my pussy, and a second finger to my ass. This time the burn is exactly what I need to take me over the edge again. I cry out his name, mewl, and scream as my entire body tenses.

Then it releases, and I can't stop myself, I let go and liquid sprays from me like never before. What I thought was a need to pee wasn't that, it was something else entirely.

"Fuck!"

I'm barely aware of Nick removing his fingers from my openings, inelegantly shoving my legs wider as he… wait, what is he doing? I feel his lips close around my entire sex. Oh… he's drinking me down.

"Give me more," he demands, like I have any control over it.

I've never done that before, so I don't know if there's any way for me to control it. I still give it a try, pushing to see if more comes out, and it does. His appreciative groans and moans go straight to my pussy, making more wetness seep out of me. It's like a delicious and intense circle that just keeps looping.

"No more," I cry when it's finally too much. "P-please."

Even though I can't see or feel it, I just know he's smirking. "Are you sure?" he rasps, sliding out from under me.

I awkwardly move around so I'm on my back, my legs dangling over the edge of the desk. I look up at him, loving how dark and intense his eyes are. It makes me feel like he's all-seeing, which I've come to learn I love when it comes to me.

"Why? What do you have in mind?" I ask playfully, palming my breasts as I pointedly stare at the crotch of his suit pants. Even though the fabric is dark, there's no mistaking the wet patch. "Did you come in your pants?"

"No," he rasps. "But it was close. Christ, Kitten, when you squirted…" Trailing off, he closes his eyes, a rumble sounding from deep in his throat as though the mere mention is bringing out his feral side. "But I'll always save my cum for your pretty cunt. You know that."

I watch mesmerized as he quickly undresses. When he removes his pants, his cock springs free; it's so huge. Every time I look at it, I marvel at the fact that it fits inside me. It should be an impossibility, but luckily it's not.

"Get that inside me," I moan, pointing right at his rigid member, resisting the urge to lick my lips as it bounces with every step he takes closer to me. "Now."

Positioning himself between my spread legs, he leans down, placing his lips close to my ear. "Tell me what you want," he growls, his words vibrating against me.

"I want you to fill me with your cum. All of it. Shoot your load deep in my pussy," I gasp, lost in the whirlwind of sensation of his hardness pressing insistently against my core.

"Turn around," he orders, his voice thick with lust. "Brace yourself on the desk."

I obey, my mind cloudy with need. He positions himself behind me, his hardness pressing against my entrance. With one swift thrust, he fills me completely, eliciting a cry from my lips.

"Fuck, you feel incredible," he grunts, setting a punishing rhythm. Each stroke drives us further into a frenzy of passion and possession.

"Please, Nick, I need your cum inside me," I plead, my nails digging into the wood of the desk.

"Anything for you," he promises, his movements growing more frantic as we chase release together. "Come for me, now. Milk the cum from my balls with your cunt."

"Nicklas!" I scream as another orgasm rips through me, my walls clenching around him.

"Carolina!" he roars, his release hot and potent within me, marking me as his own.

We stay like that for a few moments, panting; the air charged with the intensity of our union. Slowly, he pulls away, turning me to face him, his eyes softening.

"Nothing has ever felt so right," he confesses, brushing a stray lock of hair from my face.

"Me too," I breathe out, still reeling from the depth of our connection.

Later, alone in the bathroom, I hold my breath as I wait for the result of the pregnancy test. The familiar single line appears, and my heart sinks. Negative, again.

"Damn it," I curse under my breath, fighting back tears.

Frustration and determination mingle within me. This isn't the end. I will bear Nicklas Knight's child, no matter what it takes. I glance at my reflection in the mirror—a woman transformed by a love as dark as coal, and a burning purpose.

If the Christmas deadline is non-negotiable, I'm running out of time.

So far, I've been too scared to ask in case the answer is 'yes'. Eight days left, is that even enough time? Wouldn't the test already show I'm pregnant if… I shouldn't be thinking like this.

"Next time," I promise myself. "Next time, it'll be positive."

As I exit the bathroom, I find Nicklas sitting on the bed. He's redressed in a clean suit, looking like he's about to… "Are you going out?" I ask, incredulity lilting my words.

"No, I'm not going anywhere. But there's some business I have to take care of. People will be coming over."

I put some extra sway in my step, deliberately trying to entice him. "Does that mean I have to go asleep alone?" I pout.

The time we've spent together is so short, yet I find that I've become addicted to this man. There's no other word for it. When we're not together, I miss him. And when we are, I crave him in ways I never knew existed. It's like his soul is now interwoven with mine in a tapestry that can't be undone.

"I'm afraid so, Kitten," he says, sounding like he isn't any happier about it than I am. "It shouldn't be more than a couple of hours."

"Fine," I sigh, crawling into bed and under the sheets. "Where will you be?" When he looks confused at my question, I clarify. "I mean, what room? I don't like not knowing where you are."

The grin splitting his lips is almost boyish, as though it pleases him immensely to hear. "We'll be in the meeting room. The one next to—"

"I know where it is."

After kissing me goodnight, promising to not be more than two hours, he leaves me.

CHAPTER 22

The Santa

Leaving Carolina naked in bed is harder than it should be. Normally, I revel in business, love the power that comes from ruling. Since my hellcat entered my life, I don't have the same thirst for it.

No matter how I feel I can't keep leaving it to others. I can't afford for anyone to realize how absent I've been, especially not with what Sergei found. So no matter how much I want to stay in bed with Carolina, business calls.

She's my addiction, making the blood rush in my veins just thinking about how she feels under my touch. I've never been one for obsession, always keeping control, but she makes me want to lose it.

Marco catches up with me as I make my way into the room we usually reserve for meetings like the one tonight. "Boss," he says, dipping his head.

"Is everything ready?" I ask, already knowing it is.

He nods and opens the door for me, flicking on the light. "It is. Some of the guests have already arrived. Is it okay to let them in now?"

I walk over to the floor-to-ceiling windows, watching the New York skyline that stretches in front of me. A testament to the empire I rule over, to the power I wield. "Get the rat first," I reply through clenched teeth.

Tonight's meeting is impromptu, and I don't like when things change like this. This is my domain, and I don't suffer fools or disrespect. The Russian we found sniffing around where he doesn't belong fits both categories, and tonight he'll pay the price.

Marco returns with the bound and gagged man. He is bleeding onto my rug from the multiple lacerations on his torso and face. One eye is completely swollen closed, his nose is broken, and when he opens his mouth to groan in pain, I notice several teeth are missing. One leg is broken so badly the bone is sticking out, and the opposite shoulder has clearly been pulled from its socket.

"Did you have fun?" I observe dryly, raising an eyebrow at Marco who just shrugs and grins.

"He told me there was nothing I could do to make him talk," he states. "And you know how much I like proving people wrong."

Yeah, that would totally do it. Marco takes things like that as a challenge, one he will never back down from.

I watch as he throws the man into the corner, chaining him to the radiator. Not that it's needed, I don't think he'll ever walk again. I mean, he'll never leave alive, sure. But even if I let him go, he'd have to drag himself out of here, or slither like the snake he is. I snort at how fitting that is.

"You can let the three in now," I say, eyeing Greta as she joins us, placing bottles of alcohol on the table, before getting the glasses from the corner cupboard. "Thank you." I give her a curt nod.

As soon as they're both gone, I crouch down in front of the man. He seems to be so far gone in his pain that he barely registers he isn't alone anymore. I run a finger down his face, making him flinch as I pull the gag out.

He lets out another pitiful moan. "P-please l-let me g-go."

His words are boringly predictable, so I shove the gag back into his mouth. Then I stand up and kick at his broken leg, which causes him to howl in pain. "You won't find any sympathy from me," I say coldly.

I sit down at the end of the table, taking my spot just as Marco returns with our guests. Each of them dip their head in a show of respect before taking their seats. The room is dimly lit, casting long shadows over the faces around me—men who hold power in their respective territories, yet all of them answer to me.

Across the table, the crime lords who answer to me sit with a mixture of tension and respect. Dominic, the leader of the East Side operations, wears a patch to hide the eye he lost. It's a reminder of a past betrayal that he handled with swift, brutal efficiency. His good eye darts around the room, always calculating, always watching.

Next to him is Lee, a man who built his empire with a mix of charm and fear. His suits are always impeccable, his manners flawless, but there's a coldness to him that makes even the hardest men wary. He smiles easily, but it never reaches his eyes.

And then there's Sergei, the Russian who caught the spy, presumably sent by one of his brethren. He's newer to this circle, but he's already proven his worth. His presence is like ice—calm, deliberate, and utterly ruthless.

I tell Marco to sit opposite me, at the other end of the table, so when Dad arrives, he tries to take the seat to my right. "No," I bark. "That's for Jack." As if on cue, my brother walks in, smirking as he shuffles into the chair I've reserved for him.

There's only one spot left, and it's not one of any importance which is exactly why I want Dad to sit there. It's also why he's not happy about it. "Surely—"

I interrupt him. "Just sit down so we can get started."

The scowl he sends my way is the same one that made me cower when I was growing up, but now it doesn't do a damn thing to me. That's not true, it amuses me.

I let the silence stretch for a moment, letting them feel the weight of it. This room, this table, is mine. They know it, and I don't need to remind them. The city outside is ours to control, but only if we stay in line—*my* line.

I lean forward, breaking the silence. "Let's get to business."

"Who is he?" Lee's voice is gravel mixed with silk, referring to the bound figure slumped against the wall.

Sergei leans forward in his chair, going straight for the vodka. "He's the reason we're here," he replies while filling his glass to the brim.

"A Russian spy," I state, my voice carrying the weight of my authority. "He was found lurking in our territory. Thanks to Sergei's quick thinking, we managed to get him before he could disappear."

Jack shifts in his seat, a predator ready to pounce. "What do we know? Has he talked?"

"Only enough to confirm his purpose." I tilt my head toward the man who dares not move, who knows any breath could be his last.

"He sang for me," Marco chuckles coldly. "And it wasn't pretty."

This earns a round of laughter from everyone at the table.

"Is that so?" Dominic laughs boisterously. "That might be the gravest offense of all."

Marco leans forward, his fingers steepled before him. "May I speak?" Even though he already has, I appreciate the question and I nod. "He confirmed he was sent here to spy on us, but he never told me exactly what he learned, how long he's been in your territory, or who sent him."

Lee growls. "Kill him."

Dominic and Sergei quickly rumble their agreements.

I drum my fingers against the table, considering the options. Just because there's only one outcome doesn't mean there's only one way to get there. "Sergei." He slants his head in my direction as I say his name. "Is it odd to you that he won't tell us who sent him?" Although I'm pretty sure I already know the answer, I have to ask.

"Not at all," he says, confirming my suspicion. "If he speaks—"

"But he'll die either way. So why not save himself the added pain?" Jack asks.

"As I was trying to say," Sergei continues. "If he speaks his family will more than likely suffer. There's a good chance they'll be left unharmed, hell, maybe even receive some kind of payment, if he doesn't sing like a canary."

I cup my cheek, feeling the scar beneath my thumb. There's no glorifying tale linked to the injury. I was betrayed after putting my trust in the wrong people, something I'll never do again.

Dad rolls his eyes. "If you need these..." Pausing, he gestures around the table. "… men to tell you what to do, you're not ready to lead. It's pathetic."

Inwardly, I bristle, but outwardly, I keep my expression neutral, careful not to show how much his attitude is bothering me. "And if my dad thinks I need him around to conduct business, maybe he shouldn't be here," I reply coldly.

No one says anything while I stare Dad down, refusing to blink first. The problem with a staring contest between the former and current leader is that neither wants to back down. But if I'm the one to do it, I'm showing everyone I'm the weakest. That isn't happening.

Dad looks away as Jack slams his fist into the table. "We should send them a message." I mentally make a note to thank him later. "No one spies on the Knight family and lives to tell about it."

"I agree," Sergei says, cracking his knuckles. "A bloody one."

"Agreed," I say, signaling Marco with a nod. He understands; this isn't just about punishment, it's about setting an example. No mercy for those who cross us.

I glance at the spy, his chest heaving beneath the tight ropes, his fear palpable. He's heard everything, yet can say nothing. Good. Let his mind paint the gruesome pictures of what's to come.

"Marco, move our guest closer," I order.

"Of course," Marco replies smoothly, already rolling up his sleeves.

The blade in my hand feels like an extension of my will as Marco holds the Russian's arm outstretched on the dark wooden table. The spy's eye, wide with terror, darts from me to the steel glinting under the lights. His muffled whimpers are the only sound in the room as I position the edge against his flesh.

"Any last words?" I ask, though the gag in his mouth makes the question rhetorical. No one betrays Nicklas Knight and lives to speak of it.

I slice down with precision. Blood spurts, staining the wood a deep crimson. The man's scream is stifled behind the gag as his hand falls onto the table. It's a clean cut—a warning to anyone who dares cross me.

"Package it," I command Marco, who nods without a flicker of emotion across his stoic face. He's seen this before; he's done this before. The severed hand is a message that cannot be ignored.

"Sergei," I call, and when he looks my way I continue. "The kill is yours."

He grins and inclines his head, knowing it's an honor, one I didn't have to give him. But we both know he's earned it. "Thank you," he says, coming to stand next to me. "Do you mind if I use my own weapon?"

"Not at all," I say.

Apart from Dad, I trust every single man in this room. We've bled together, and each and every one has bled for me. So I don't take their weapons when they come here, my one and only demand is that no one is allowed more than one.

Sergei pulls a small vial from the inner pocket on his suit jacket, the liquid a bright pink.

"Of course the Russian carries poison," Lee snorts derisively.

"But why is it pink?" Jack asks.

Unperturbed, Sergei removes the cork and places the small glass on the table. "Open his mouth," he instructs Marco, who looks at me for confirmation, so I give him an encouraging nod.

"This is Sergei's show," I confirm as I sit back down.

Marco traps the spy between his legs, and then he takes the knife I used to cut his hand off, using it to slice the gag, making sure to knick the corner of his lips as well. Then he shoves his hand into the man's mouth, grabbing hold of his tongue.

"Open wide," he barks.

The man does as he's told, and as soon as Marco's no longer holding his tongue, Sergei pushes the entire vial into the spy's mouth, making me wonder why he even bothered to remove the cork lid.

"Keep his head tilted up," the Russian instructs Marco.

Sergei puts one hand on top of the spy's head, clamping the other around his jaw. He repeats the motion until we all hear the bottle crunch. For a couple of moments, nothing happens. But then the spy's face turns pink; multiple shades of the color.

Using his remaining hand, he claws at his throat. He screams as he scratches at his flesh until it breaks. I've seen a lot of bad ways to die, but this has to be one of the most gruesome ones. Yet another reason to keep Sergei close.

"And that's why it's pink," Sergei says, winking at Jack.

"Nicklas," Caspian's voice slices through the room as Marco wraps the severed hand in cloth. "What of Carolina? Any news of an heir?"

I take the blade from the table where Marco left it. As I wipe the blade clean, feeling the weight of my father's gaze, I remind myself why I shouldn't just outright banish or kill him. "That's none of your concern," I reply, refusing to give him more than that. "And this isn't the time to discuss her."

"Are you testing her endurance? Her ability to adapt to our way of life?" He persists, his tone demanding.

"She's more than capable," I say, sliding the blade back into its sheath. "She'll bear my heir and that's the end of that."

"Make sure of it," Caspian presses, his eyes hard as flint. "We can't afford weakness in our lineage."

"Carolina isn't weak," I snap, the thought of her soft curves and fiery spirit igniting a possessive fire within me. "She's stronger than you know."

He snorts. "She's a woman, son. Of course she's weak." Dad's voice is clipped. "Especially with the way you're catering to her every whim—"

"What did you just say?" I snarl, interrupting him. "Are you keeping tabs on me?"

Dad shrugs as though the accusation is neither here nor there. "Not at all. But I have friends who were at that party. They all noticed that you were too busy with your toy to conduct business."

As Marco exits with the grisly parcel and barks at some of his men to come get the corpse, I do my best to keep my cool. But the more I feel my dad's eyes bore into me, the more I want to remind him who's in charge. And maybe I should, but respect can't and shouldn't be demanded—it has to be earned.

I glare at my father, the warning in my eyes as sharp as the blade I just cleaned. "Don't even think about Carolina," I say with a growl. "She's off limits to you."

"Off limits?" he scoffs. "She's your—"

"*Mine*," I cut him off, feeling a surge of possessiveness I've never known before I met her. My chest tightens. This woman has become my obsession, my every waking thought, and I'll be damned if anyone, even my own dad, tries to tell me what to do about her. "She's not your concern, and she's not your responsibility. So the next time you mention her name better be to greet her, or I'll take your tongue."

I'm aware that everyone is looking between us like a twisted ping-pong match, but I don't care. Backing down isn't even in my fucking vocabulary, and I refuse to do it just because he's my dad. I scoff because calling him 'Dad' is generous. He didn't take an interest in any of his kids until we were old enough to be introduced to the family biz.

That happened when I was thirteen, and from that day, he took over raising me—or as he called it; training me.

"Not. Another. Word," I warn him, and when he opens his mouth to argue, I wave him off. "Or I'll have Marco remove you. The only reason you're allowed at this table is because of my grace."

"Bullshit!" he sputters.

I make a show at looking at the men around the table. "No," I calmly reply. "It's not bullshit. Everyone here would happily volunteer to slit your throat. My ruling is the one thing keeping you alive. Remember that because the only thing keeping me happy is Carolina."

"What's that supposed to mean?"

Sighing, I roll my hand in the air in an 'are you stupid' motion. "It means that as long as I'm happy, I'm less likely to give into the constant pleas for you to be put out of your misery."

I don't know why it's taken me this long to stand up to him. I mean, I do know. Years of conditioning isn't to be scoffed at. He's succeeded in making me see him as the god of my world. But no more. Because I no longer need a god; not when I daily worship a goddess.

As if summoned by my thoughts alone, said goddess bursts through the door. She looks like a vision against the starkness of this bloodstained room. I rise, my chair scraping back, tension coils in my gut. Every muscle primed for action.

"Nicklas, I thought—"

"No women are allowed here. Leave!" Dad barks at her.

Instead of flinching at his harsh tone, she holds her ground, those wide eyes scanning the room, landing on me. In that split second, something primal within me snaps. I cross the space between us in two long strides, grabbing Carolina by the arm and pulling her close.

"Never speak to her like that again," I snarl at my dad, the menace in my voice unmistakable.

"Son—" Dad starts, but he's talking to my back.

Carolina's pulse flutters beneath my fingers. I can feel the heat of her skin through the thin fabric of her robe. With a firm tug, I draw her to my side, settling her onto my lap once I retake my seat. Her soft curves press against my hardened body, an intimate fit that sends a jolt straight to my cock.

"Everyone," I command, my tone leaving no room for debate, "this is Carolina. My future wife, my fiancée." The words roll off my tongue with an unwavering certainty. She's mine, and I want these men to know it.

The room reacts immediately. Heads bow, murmurs of respect circle among them—all but Caspian, who stands rigid, his jaw set.

"Congratulations," Marco says, breaking the tense silence as he returns. Obviously, he already knew, so his reaction is more to get the ball rolling.

"Thank you," I reply, my hand resting possessively over Carolina's thigh. I can feel the warmth of her through the layers.

"Welcome to the family," Jack adds, though his gaze lingers a bit too long for my liking. I squeeze Carolina's leg, a silent reminder that she belongs to me.

"Thank you," Carolina says softly. There's vulnerability there, and it strikes a chord deep within me.

As the meeting dissolves, I hold her close, reveling in her presence. Carolina—the woman who unknowingly walked into a mafia den but so far, she's taken it in stride.

"Come," I murmur, standing with her still in my arms. "We have much to discuss."

CHAPTER 23

The Santa

"Can we stay here?" she asks, tilting her head up to look at me.

I blink, not sure if I heard her right. "You… you want to stay in here?" I ask, dumbfounded.

Blood stains the floor, a mosaic of violence that's become as familiar to me as the tailored suits on my back. The room reeks of iron—the aftermath of asserting dominance within the Knight empire. I watch Carolina survey the scene, her gaze unwavering. She doesn't shy away from the gore; instead, she moves closer to me.

"I… that…" Pausing, she swallows thickly. "… are you hurt?" Her voice is steady, cutting through the silence.

I look down at my hands, smeared with blood—not mine. "I'm fine," I assure her, my tone leaving no space for further inquiry. But in this moment, something shifts inside me. Her concern, so raw and genuine, cracks the armor I've worn since I was thirteen.

"Sit with me," I command more softly than I intend, gesturing to the chairs that aren't splattered with reminders of today's necessity.

As we sit, I begin to unravel the threads of our existence here. "The men who just left… they're the pillars of our organization here in New York. Each one sworn to me, bound by blood or loyalty." My eyes flicker to hers, ensuring she understands the gravity.

"Keep talking," Carolina says, fingering the bow on her midnight blue robe without breaking eye contact.

"I—" My throat is dry, and all I want to do is to rip her clothes off. She looks entirely too sexy, and I both loathe and love that everyone saw her looking so sinful.

Carolina stands, pulling at the bow, shrugging the robe off to reveal the black lace underneath it—her nightgown, stopping just above her mid-thigh. The lace hugs her body, showcasing every curve with seductive precision.

Her long, blonde hair is ruffled, probably from sleep. She isn't wearing any traces of makeup, which, to me, that just makes her even more flawless as she stands in front of me. Her tongue darts out, and my cock hardens as I watch her lick her lips.

"Hellcat," I rasp, but she shakes her head.

"I said, keep talking, Nick."

"What do you want to know?"

Tilting her head to the side, she taps her long, slender index finger against her cheek. "Who were those men? I mean, I've seen your dad…" She shudders as she mentions him. "… Jack, and Marco before. But the others?"

I explain the other three to her. "Dominic, the one with the eyepatch, is the leader of the East Side operations. He mostly deals in weapons and drugs. Lee, the one with the pink tie, is… well, he built his business by whoring himself out. He gathered secrets, and once he had enough to force his way to the top, that's exactly what he did."

"Wow."

"Sergei is complicated," I say, continuing my explanation. "We should be natural born enemies, but he's come to earn my respect. I know he's loyal."

She nods slowly, and there's a shrewdness in her eyes, as though she's mentally creating files for each man, cataloging the info I'm giving her. "And you trust each of these men?"

"I do," I confirm.

"Should I?"

I can honestly say I never considered her asking that. "Do you want to?" I ask, unsure what I can say.

She hums softly. "I don't know. But if you trust them, it seems I should as well."

Although she makes an excellent point, I can't bring myself to say yes. When she burst in here, they were all respectful, sure. And yes, I trust them with my life, but I'm not sure I'll ever fully trust anyone else with hers.

I can't help but admire her boldness. In a room that has witnessed brutality, she stands completely undaunted, acting like we're discussing the season or where to go for dinner.

"Okay then," she says, nodding sharply. "For you, Nick, I'll try."

Before I can argue that I won't ask that of her, she pulls her nightgown over her head, showing me her gloriously naked body.

When I reach for my belt, she tuts as she moves closer. Once we're so close I can feel the swell of her tits against my chest, she pulls my shirt free from my pants. "I want to undress you tonight."

I watch her, the way she moves with a purpose, stripping away the layers of my power suit. My blood-stained hands rest at my sides; I'm transfixed by the sheer force that is Carolina Sterling. Her fingers work deftly on the buttons of my shirt, revealing inked skin beneath.

As soon as I'm naked, she slaps her hand against the table. "Lie down," she commands, and there's an authority in her tone, a fire in her eyes that matches the heat coursing through me. I do as I'm told, lying back on the cold, hard table where not too long ago decisions about life and death were made.

She climbs atop me, bare and unyielding. She rests on her knees first, smirking as she moves one hand between her legs to remove the plug. As soon as she has it between her fingers, she rubs it against my lips. I eagerly snake my tongue around it, loving the way she tastes.

"Mhmm," I groan,

Then she wraps her fingers around the base of my erect cock, angling it so she can lower herself onto it. "Tell me," she pants as she slowly takes me into her body, "about your empire."

"Our empire," I correct her. "It's all *ours,* Hellcat."

"Ours," she moans, throwing her head back as she takes more of me inside her. "What's my role in all of this?"

I groan, feeling her warm center press down onto me. "You're becoming the heart of it all."

"Your heart?" she asks, her body beginning to move in a rhythm that has my words catching in my throat.

"God, yes," I confess. The sensation of her riding me blends with the gravity of our conversation. "You've become my weakness, and yet, you're also my greatest strength."

I'm caught between awe and arousal as Carolina moves above me, her body a living flame that sears my skin. Each time I reach for her, she slaps my hands away, a silent command that stokes the fire within me. It's not just about pleasure; it's about power—the power she's claiming over both our bodies.

"No," she orders with each slap, her voice a whip that keeps me in line. "You've had the power for too long. Now it's my turn."

And I obey, because to see Carolina like this—unleashed, unfettered—is worth any restraint. I'm raw under her touch, under the demand in her eyes. She is the hurricane, and I am willingly caught in her storm.

Her movements intensify, and she leans forward, lips grazing my ear. "And what of your trust, Nicklas? Do you trust me?"

"Implicitly," I choke out, every bounce tightening the bond between us, forging it in passion and whispered truths.

With a fluid motion, she reaches for my knife on the table, its blade glinting ominously in the dim light. She positions it right against my neck, the cool metal a stark contrast to the warmth of her skin. It's a test, a challenge.

"Even with this?" she questions, pressing ever so slightly, her inner muscles clenching around me.

"Especially with that," I reply, my voice steady despite the danger. The knife doesn't waver; neither does her gaze. It's a dance with death, a testament to the trust that's grown between us.

"Good," she murmurs. "Because I need to know that when I bear your children, when I carry on the Knight legacy, it's with a man who trusts me as much as I risk for him."

"There's no one else I'd want to be the mother of my heirs. No one else I'd share this darkness with—" She silences me with a kiss, deep and claiming.

"Nick," she gasps, the knife still poised as a reminder of the balance between life and death we constantly tread. "I will give you everything."

"And I'll cherish it all," I swear, feeling the pressure build within me. Every stroke, every touch is a step closer to creating something eternal.

She removes the knife from my throat, throwing it over her shoulder. Our bodies move together, she rides me with a fervor that speaks of more than just lust—it's a merging of souls, an understanding that stretches beyond the physical.

The sight of her, head thrown back in abandon, bathed in the dim light filtering through the blinds, imprints itself into my mind. I'll remember this: the fierce woman who rides me, determined and yet tender, like she's carving out her place in my world—one thrust at a time.

"You can touch me now," she moans, holding up her tits like a delectable offering to me. Wasting no time, I reach for them, pinching and rolling her beaded nipples between my fingers. Her moans intensify, as does every movement of her hips. "I'm so close!"

She's not the only one. My nuts tighten just as warmth spreads at my lower back. "Carolina," I groan, unable to hold back as she climaxes, her cunt squeezing my cock hard, like it's trying to pull the jizz from my balls.

We're both panting, breathing so heavily it's all that can be heard as she collapses onto me. Her cheek presses to my chest. As I look down, I smile when I see the self-satisfied smirk curling her lips upward.

That wasn't just sex, that was a queen claiming her king—her Knight.

Her fingers trace patterns on my forearm, grounding me in the present. The touch is delicate but firm, just like her.

We lie there until our breathing returns to normal, our hearts no longer galloping. Then she pushes herself up, her long blonde locks falling around her face like a curtain. "That was really something," she says with a wide smile.

Reaching up, I grab her hair, twisting it around my hand. I pull so she's forced to bend her neck. "I hope you enjoyed the control, Hellcat, because you're the only one I've ever given it to."

There's a softness in her eyes that tells me she knows just how much she means to me. It's one thing to say I'll burn the world down for her, another to let her rule it in my place.

"What comes next?"

Her question hangs in the air, a specter that's haunted me since I took over the family business. The Knight legacy isn't just about power; it's about survival, continuation. A chill runs down my spine as I look into her eyes, seeing the same determination that drew me to her in the first place.

"Before anything else, there's something you need to know." My voice is steady, but inside, I'm a cacophony of nerves. "You'll have to complete a test."

"Test?" Her brow furrows, a mixture of confusion and defiance sparking in her gaze. "What kind of test?"

"A test of loyalty, strength, and resolve," I say, each word measured, heavy with unspoken implications. "That will determine if you're ready to stand by my side as my wife."

"Stand by your side, or stand behind you?" There's a challenge in her tone, one I both respect and desire.

"Beside me," I affirm, locking my jaw to keep my emotions in check. "Always beside me."

Her hand pauses on my skin, and I can feel her processing this new reality. She doesn't move away, doesn't cower. Instead, she leans closer, closing the distance between us, her breath warm against my ear.

"Then I'll pass it with flying colors," she vows, her voice laced with a fiery conviction that sets my blood aflame. "For us. For our future."

CHAPTER 24

The Breeder

I blink open my eyes to the muted sunlight filtering through sheer curtains, a soft glow that tells me I've slept longer than usual. The silken sheets whisper against my skin as I sit up. Nick's side of the bed is cold, sadly. One of these days, I'd like to wake up in his arms instead of just falling asleep in them.

A note rests on the pillow beside me, its white color all wrong against the deep crimson of the bedspread.

Come find me.

The words are scrawled in his bold, assertive handwriting, and something flutters low in my belly. It's not just the command that stirs me; it's the silent promise that lingers between the lines. Swinging my legs over the side of the bed, I reach for the robe draped across the nearby chair. I slip it on, tying it tight around my waist.

The hallway outside the bedroom is transformed, no longer just a passage but a statement. Rose petals—a trail of them—scatter across the hardwood in vibrant reds and blacks, leading me forward like a path in a dark fairy tale. My heart races with every step I take, the petals a sensual reminder of the man who waits for me, the man who demands my presence with nothing more than a note.

"Nick?" My voice comes out breathy, anticipation tugging at my lips as I call out for him, unsure of where this floral breadcrumb trail will lead. Each petal underfoot is a testament to the opulence he's surrounded by, to the world he's brought me into—one where desire and power intertwine.

I follow the roses, holding my breath as I near the doorway at the end of the hall. I know the room well even though I've only been there once. It's the room with the marital bed. Every part of me yearns for what awaits, for the touch of the man who has awakened desires within me I never knew existed.

Eagerly, I step inside, and without Nick to distract me, I take my time really surveying the room. The swing is pulled into a corner, chains still dangle from the ceiling. Despite the many toys and instruments, the bed remains the focal point of the room. The walls are as black as the sheets on the bed, making everything look grander and darker. I love it.

"Kitten," I hear his voice before I see him, deep and commanding, sending a shiver down my spine. "I'm glad you found my note."

Spinning around, I find him. His dark eyes alight with a possessive fire that makes my nipples pebble and my clit throb with want. Nick doesn't need to speak; his gaze alone beckons me closer, and I'm helpless but to obey.

"Today, I lead," Nick commands, his voice a caress against my earlobe as he leans closer. He steps around me, his presence predatory, and in his hand is a sleek vibrator, its black surface adorned with a single white snowflake. A shiver of anticipation laces through me, and I nod, silently giving myself over to him.

"Good girl," he murmurs, his approval sending warmth straight to my core. With deft fingers, he parts the silk of my robe, exposing me to his hungry gaze. The cold metal of the vibrator trails down my belly, all the way down to my core. "Are you wet for me?"

"Yes," I murmur, shuddering as he pushes the edge between my pussy lips. It's not a lie, I'm so turned on just from his voice that I can feel it. "So wet."

The sensation is startling, a delicious invasion that makes me gasp. Nick switches it on, and the vibration starts slowly, a tantalizing hum that sets my nerves alight. "Feel that?" he asks, his eyes locked onto mine. "That's just the beginning."

Tremors dance through me, and I'm unable to hold back my wanton moans. "J-just the beginning?" I don't even have the imagination to try to guess what he has in store for me. Each vibration creates a rhythm that matches my quickening pulse. My body responds instinctively, clenching around the toy. I moan again, lost in the swirl of sensations.

"You're so beautifully responsive," he praises, and I can hear the raw need in his voice.

My senses are ablaze, every touch amplified to an exquisite degree. I'm floating, adrift in a sea of pleasure that Nick orchestrates with masterful control. "Nick… please," I beg, the words tumbling from my lips as my body arches toward him, seeking more, seeking release.

His hands roam over me, stoking the fire within. "We have all day, and I intend to savor every moment."

He flicks the remote, and the vibrator surges to a higher setting, drawing a strangled cry from deep in my throat. I'm teetering on the edge, desperate for the fall, when he suddenly withdraws the vibrator, leaving me empty and aching.

"Look at you," he breathes, admiration lacing his tone. He takes my hand, pulling me toward the bed. And just as I think he's about to give me what I want, his tone changes. "But let's have breakfast first."

"B-breakfast?" I ask incredulously. My mind couldn't be further from food, and as my gaze drops to the crotch of his suit pants, the huge bulge makes it clear I'm not the only one affected.

But when he points at the middle of the bed and says, "Sit." I still follow his orders, scooting back so I can lean against the end.

Nick retrieves a plate from the bedside table and places it before me, between my spread legs. It's filled with berries, cream-covered French toast, and croissants—all my favorites—and my stomach growls. But as I reach for a berry, he catches my wrist, his fingers firm and warm.

"Allow me." He brings the berry to my lips, and I part them, taking

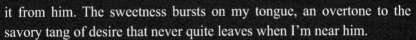

it from him. The sweetness bursts on my tongue, an overtone to the savory tang of desire that never quite leaves when I'm near him.

"Good girl," he murmurs, his eyes locked with mine. Each mouthful he feeds me is a caress, a promise of what's to come. And then his fingers swipe a dollop of cream from the plate, tracing it along my collarbone, down the valley between my breasts, making me shiver.

My lips part as he leans forward, licking the cream off my skin. His tongue is hot, his lips soft, and the scruff on his cheeks, the delicious bite making everything more intense. I arch into him, craving more contact. A buzz hums inside me, and I realize he's got the remote control for the vibrator in his other hand.

"Breakfast first, Kitten." He goes back to feeding me, but now, each bite is interspersed with a flick of the remote, sending waves of pleasure coursing through me. I squirm, bite back moans, clench around the Christmas-themed toy that fills me so completely.

"Nick, please," I gasp when I can't take it anymore, the pressure building, coiling tight in my belly.

"Are you done eating?" A smirk plays at the edges of his mouth when I nod eagerly. "Come for me," he orders, and the vibrator surges to life again. My climax washes over me like a tidal wave, leaving me shaking and breathless.

After a moment to collect myself, I notice Nicklas has not touched his own food. Instead, he brushes aside the plates. With a predatory grin, he grabs my feet and pulls me down so I'm lying on my back in the middle of the bed.

"My turn to eat," he declares, his eyes alight with mischief and something darker, more possessive. He reaches for the syrup, squirting some onto my breasts and into my belly button. Then he drapes my legs over his shoulders, and I watch, fascinated and on fire, as he dips French toast into the sticky sugar on my body.

Each swipe of his fingers is frustratingly light, teasing. He doesn't actually touch any of my erogenous zones, it's just… hmm, it's hard to explain. It's as though he makes the air move enough to feel like the ghost of a touch, without the pleasure of it actually happening.

Fucking tease.

"Nick!" I whine, bucking beneath him, eager for more.

"Yes?" he replies once he's sated in one way, though clearly hungry in another.

"Get on with it," I snap. "I want your cock inside me. Stop being a tease."

Chuckling, he places a kiss on each of my inner thighs before getting up from the bed, retrieving something from the back of the room. "I want to try something new today," he says as he returns with coils of midnight colored rope.

"You want to tie me up?" I ask, my voice breathy. "Like… like…"

"Do you know what Shibari is?" he asks.

The word dances through my mind; conjuring images of intricate and artistic bondage that I've only seen online. "Yes," I gasp, immediately intrigued.

That's all the permission he needs. "Kneel for me," he rasps, slapping the middle of the bed with his free hand. "Right here."

I get on my knees, eager to follow his every command. "Is this fine?" I ask, unsure if I should do something with my arms or my… my thoughts are cut off as the vibrator inside me buzzes to life again, making me mewl in pleasure.

"Perfect," he growls, crawling onto the bed.

The midnight blue ropes glide over my skin, cool and smooth, as he expertly loops them around my wrists. Each movement is deliberate, almost methodical, as he pulls the rope tight, binding me securely but not painfully. I can feel the strength in his hands, the way he controls the tension, ensuring that the knots are firm but not constricting.

I watch him in silence, my breath catching as he winds the ropes around my torso, creating a pattern that crisscrosses over my chest. The pressure is gentle, but it's enough to make me feel contained, held in place by his will. His touch is confident, every knot precise, every pull of the rope deliberate, as if he's weaving his control around me with each pass.

Running my fingers over the rope, I admire his work. "Let your hands fall to your side," he rasps as he moves behind me.

Again, I do as he says, feeling more than seeing him tying my wrists to my ankles, forcing me to arch my back at an almost unnatural angle. It feels weird, and I almost lose my balance a few times, but he's quick to steady me.

My heartbeat quickens as he ties the final knot, securing the intricate web he's created. The ropes dig slightly into my skin, a constant reminder of their presence, of his presence, of how he's taken complete control. I'm aware of every sensation—the texture of the ropes, the way they press against me, the way my body responds to the restraints.

I close my eyes, letting myself sink into the feeling, trusting him completely. In this moment, I am his, bound and vulnerable, but there's a strange comfort in it, a sense of safety in the way he's tied me, in the way he looks at me—like he's claimed me, but with care, with intention.

"Trust me," he whispers, moving around to my front. "I'd never let anything happen to you." His lips find mine, and he delves his tongue into my mouth, stroking mine.

Just as quickly as the kiss started, he ends it, leaving me panting. A single string of saliva hangs between us, and I look at it, watching it snap as he turns away and gets off the bed. "I do," I say, finally finding my words.

"Beautiful," he murmurs, stepping back to admire his work. In his gaze, I see more than lust—I see adoration, reverence.

Much to my dismay, Nick's still dressed. "Why aren't you naked yet?" I pout.

"Because I'm not ready to fuck you yet," he answers simply. "The last time we were in here, I hurt you. And I'm so fucking sorry—"

"It's okay," I say. It's ironic that I now am all too eager to reassure him of what I that day refused to say.

"No, it's most certainly not okay," he growls. "But if you trust me, I want to build your tolerance," he explains, brushing my hair away from my shoulders.

"I trust you. You know I do."

He steps away, only to return with a small box and a flogger—the tails made of soft suede. Then he brushes the strands over my ribs, down my stomach, trailing the tease of pain and pleasure. His other hand finds the remote, and suddenly the vibrator buzzes to life again, a background rhythm to the new sensation.

"Nick!" My hips jerk reflexively, seeking more contact, more of everything he's offering.

The flogger comes down with a gentle thwap against my thigh, a test, a question. Do I like this? My gasp is answer enough. Again, he strikes, a bit harder, on my other thigh, and I moan loudly.

"Good, Kitten," he croons. "Let's find your limits."

Each strike builds upon the last, a crescendo of stinging kisses that paint my skin in shades of pink and red. The vibrator continues its relentless hum, a counterpoint to the sharp slaps of suede. It's a dance of sensations, and I'm lost in the rhythm, adrift in a sea where only pleasure and pain exist.

"Look at you, so responsive, so eager," Nick murmurs, pausing in his ministrations. He traces the marks he's left, a proprietary glide of fingertips that sets my nerves alight. "This is trust, Carolina. This is us."

I can't form words, can only nod, my eyes heavy with lust and something deeper—something like devotion.

"More," I whisper, a plea, a demand.

"More it is," he agrees, and there's a shift in his demeanor, a darkening of his gaze that tells me we're crossing into new territory.

Switching tactics, he sets aside the flogger and picks the small box up. There's a clink of metal, and I glimpse the glint of nipple clamps just before he attaches them, a jolt of pain that zips straight to my core. I cry out, not in protest but in revelation—the sweet spot between hurt and heaven.

"Shhh, you can take it," he assures me, adjusting the tension until I'm squirming, teetering on the edge of something monumental.

"Please," I beg, not sure what I'm asking for—to stop or to never stop. Both—neither.

His tattooed hands run up my thighs, making me squirm while fighting not to fall. Although I love being tied up like this, it's hard work not to lose my balance. Especially with all the sensations he's drawing up in me simultaneously. The sting from the nipple clamps, the euphoria from the vibrator buzzing deep in my pussy, and then the… whatever the ropes make me feel. I'm so overstimulated I can barely tell one sensation from the other.

I'm so lost in my thoughts I almost miss Nick undressing, which would be a waste. Like he has all the time in the world, his tattooed hands undo his cufflinks, pocketing them. Then he unbuttons each button on his dark blue shirt before shrugging it off.

Next, he unbuckles his belt, and I suck in a breath as the air swooshes when he pulls it from the loops. It's such a small sound, yet it makes my core clench. So does the sound of his zipper being lowered, and the ruffle of his pants falling to the floor. He's not wearing his briefs, so his cock is free and erect, jutting out from his body and pointing straight at me.

"Like what you see?" he rasps, fisting himself as he strokes from base to top.

"Y-yes," I moan.

"Mhmm, so do I, Hellcat. So do I," he groans, squeezing his cock harder. "You have no idea how beautiful you are right now."

His words wash over me, making me preen. All I want to do is obey him, make him look at me the way he is right now, like I'm the only other person in the universe. "Nick," I cry, overwhelmed. "I-I... I lo—" I never get to finish confessing my love to him.

"Now's not the time, Hellcat," he rasps, slowly inching closer.

CHAPTER 25

The Breeder

What? That's definitely not the reaction I expected.

"Your pleasure is mine to give," he says, his tone possessive. And then he's moving onto the bed, positioning himself between my thighs. "Do you want to be filled with more than just toys?"

"Yes!" It's a shout, a confirmation, a surrender.

One hand grabs my hips while the other dives between my legs, quickly removing the vibrator. The head of his erection nudges at my entrance, and I'm unable not to rub myself against him. If it wasn't for both his hands that are now keeping me steady by holding my hips in a bruising grip, I'm sure I'd fall.

Then he enters me; one powerful thrust that fills me to a point of exquisite fullness. We move together. "Oh my God!" I cry, feeling so… everything. I'm feeling everything. From the clamps that tug at my nipples with every motion, to his huge cock bottoming out inside me.

"Mine," he growls, each stroke a claim. "Say it, Carolina. Say you're mine."

"Yours," I pant, the world narrowing down to just him, just this moment. "Oh God, Nicklas, yours."

"Yes, you fucking are."

Thrust!

"Mine to breed."

Thrust!

"Mine to use."

Thrust!

"Mine to fucking love."

Thrust!

His voice is a melody of darkness and desire, and I cling to it, letting it carry me through the waves of pleasure that crash over me. "Please," I whimper, so close to the edge, to the precipice of release.

"Come for me, Carolina. Now," he commands, and I shatter, my climax ripping through me with the force of a winter storm, leaving nothing untouched.

"Nicklas!" I scream his name.

My vision distorts, black circles dancing at the edge as my entire body seizes, clenching so hard tears form behind my closed lids. It feels like I'm floating, like I'm… fuck, I can't stop coming. My orgasm keeps going as he thrusts into me over and over, guttural and feral growls falling from his lips.

I try to reach for him, needing to touch him. But of course, I can't. The damn ropes that I loved not too long ago are now a hindrance, keeping me from what I want. "P-please free my hands," I beg.

"Give me… fuck. Your cunt is gripping me so tightly," he groans.

When I open my eyes again, I look into his, and they're almost completely black. All I see in them is the depth of his feelings for me, and my own reflected back at me. It's so beautiful I choke up.

Still with his cock inside me, Nick shuffles me to the side. Then he reaches above me, his hand disappearing under the pillow. I'm just about to ask what he's looking for but then I see it, the blade he must have hidden there before I got up.

I try not to wince as he cuts the ropes away, but his movements are jerky and rushed. More than once, he knicks my skin. I want to ask him if he couldn't just pull one of the ropes to free all the knots, but the look on his face is so intense I decide it doesn't matter.

Once the ropes are gone, he removes the nipple clamps, making me cry out in pain as the blood finally rushes back. "Ouch!" I never thought that would be the part to hurt.

"Are you comfortable?" His dark voice reminds me my arms are free, and I hurriedly reach for him. My fingers trail over his face, like I'm blind and need to memorize his features with my hands.

Everything feels more potent as I skim over his eyebrows, down his cheeks, over his scar, and lastly, I touch his soft lips. "Kiss me," I demand huskily.

Not needing to be told twice, he bends and claims my lips in a soul-deep kiss; one that makes my toes curl with every swipe of his tongue. While we kiss, he moves me to my back, and I eagerly wind my arms around his neck, clinging to him.

When he tries to pull away, I dig my nails into his neck in disapproval. I feel possessed, like if he lets go, I'll stop breathing. I know it's not rational by any stretch of the imagination, but it's how I feel. And I'm not ready to stop breathing yet.

Nick starts to fuck me again, with slow and long strokes. Each time he bottoms out inside me, he hits that glorious spot that both makes my breathing falter and quicken all at the same time.

Every minute with him is filled with contradictions, but I embrace each and every one. If I could, I'd climb inside him and stay there forever.

"Carolina," he rumbles when I finally let him break the kiss. "I love you so fucking much."

"And I love you, Nicklas Knight," I whisper, worried he's going to interrupt me again. When he doesn't, I repeat the words louder. "I love you, Nicklas. You're my everything."

"Forevermore," he vows.

"Forevermore!"

I blink when he lifts the knife, letting it dance across my skin before he brings it to the spot just above his heart. "You'll always be a part of me," he growls.

"What are you—" I cut myself off. My eyes widen and my nostrils flare as he digs the tip into his flesh, my initials taking shape with every precise movement. It's both terrifying and exhilarating to watch him mark himself for me. "Nick…" I start, breathless, not sure whether to plead or praise. But the sight of my name etched into his flesh steals the words right out of my mouth.

"Carolina," he says, catching my gaze with unwavering determination. "You're mine, forevermore. And now, anyone who sees this will know it."

"Why would anyone see you shirtless?" I hiss, not happy by that prospect.

Even with blood dripping from his cuts, he laughs. "Good point."

I rear up and cup his face, angling it so he has no choice but to meet my gaze. "No one is going to see that. Swear it."

"I promise," he rasps. "No one but you. Not if I can help it."

As much as I want to hear him correct the last part, I appreciate that he isn't lying to me. The truth is that there's no way to tell if anyone will ever see it, so, yeah, his words are more than good enough.

Breaking our eye contact, I lower my mouth to his cut, my mouth sealing over the C and the K and my tongue swiping across the open wounds. His cock jerks inside me, reminding me it's still there, as hot and hard as ever.

Carolina Knight—it might not technically be my initials yet, but they will be soon enough.

"Fuck!" he groans as he moves his hand to the back of my head, holding me to him. "Drink my blood, Hellcat."

And dammit, I do. Well, I don't exactly drink it, I lick it. Then I lift my head, claiming his lips so he can taste his blood as well.

"Say it again," he commands as he begins to fuck me again.

I don't need him to clarify; I know what he wants to hear. "I love you, Nicklas." My voice is a whisper, but it feels like a shout in the silence that follows.

"Fuck," he growls, sealing the declaration with a kiss that's all-consuming, devouring any lingering doubts. Our connection deepens with the mingling taste of blood and passion—a bond forged in our dark desire for each other.

Nick pushes me back down, throwing my legs over his shoulders as he fucks me in hard, punishing pumps. Oh God, he's so deep like this, hitting the perfect spot inside me. It doesn't take long until I'm shaking with another orgasm.

"Yes. Nick… fuck! Yes! Yes!" I scream as he follows, his own release hot and deep within me.

We collapse in a tangle of limbs and ropes, breathing hard. In the aftermath, our eyes lock, and I see it—the trust, the connection that's grown stronger with every shared secret, every explored kink.

The ring of his phone shatters the moment, a sharp intrusion. Nick pulls away, his dark eyes clouding over with anger at being disturbed. He snatches up the device from the floor, his body tensing as he listens to the urgent voice on the other end.

"Are you sure? He's dead?" he asks. His face paling beneath the harsh lighting of the room. His fingers dig into the phone, knuckles white, a stark contrast to the usual confidence that radiates off him like heat from a flame.

I try to listen, but I can't hear anything but his voice. "Nick, what's wrong?" My voice is barely above a whisper, but it cuts through the tension, reaching for him.

"I'm on my way," he snaps before ending the call.

He doesn't look at me as he reaches for his clothes, quickly dressing. "What happened?" I ask, my heart pounding in my chest.

"Jack's been hurt," he snaps, and the words are a physical blow, knocking the air from my lungs. "There was… it turned bad. I have to go to him."

I nod, understanding the gravity of a Knight wounded. No, it's more than that. Jack's his brother. "Is he…" I can't finish the question.

"Alive, yes. But it's serious. I need to fix this." His voice is ice over steel, the domineering man I know reasserting himself over the worry that had cracked his façade.

"Okay." It's all I can manage, a simple acknowledgment of the storm about to break over us. There's no room for hesitation, not when family, when blood, is on the line. Especially for a man like Nicklas, who'd burn the world down before he'd let harm come to those he claims as his own.

I quickly get off the bed, wrapping the sheet around my naked body. Then I run back to the bedroom, grabbing the closest clothes I find in the closet. It's a dark gray and sleeveless pantsuit. Although I'd love a shower, there's no time. So I settle for washing my face and squirting toothpaste into my mouth with one hand, while getting dressed with the other.

As I look for a hair tie in one of the bathroom drawers, I come across the pregnancy tests and spare plugs. For a second I consider grabbing one of the plugs to keep Nick's seed inside me, but then I decide against it. For one, by now, most have probably already seeped out. And for two, I don't want the day his brother got put in the hospital to be the day we conceive.

Besides, not wearing one since he fucked me on the table in his meeting room last night has felt almost freeing.

After gathering my hair on top of my head in a messy bun, I find a pair of ankle boots. I'm in the middle of zipping them up when Nick joins me. "You're not coming," he growls.

"The hell?" I exclaim, shaking my head. "I'm coming, Nick. I want to be there for you."

"It's not safe," he insists, the dominant edge we both crave slipping into his tone despite the situation. But this time, it doesn't stir desire; it stirs defiance.

"Neither was letting you buy me, but I did it—and I'd do it again," I counter, my voice stronger than I feel. His touch has awakened parts of me I didn't know existed, and now I can't just turn off the intensity of what pulses between us.

"Damn it, Carolina," he growls, pacing away. Each step he takes is filled with a predator's grace, but also with a desperation I can't bear to ignore.

"Nicklas," I say, following him. "You carved my name into your skin. You bound me to you. Now let me prove that I'm worthy of that. I can handle anything if it means supporting you."

He stops, the tension rolling off him in waves. I see it then—the way he struggles to balance his need to protect me with the respect he has for the woman I am becoming, the woman he is shaping me into.

"Please." My plea is quiet but fervent.

"Fuck," he swears again, pinching the bridge of his nose. He turns back to me, the decision clear in his eyes even before he speaks. His hands are surprisingly gentle as they cup my face, a stark contrast to the possessive, all-consuming lover from moments ago. "We'll go together. But you stay close to me, understand? If anything happens—"

"Nothing will," I interrupt with a conviction I partially borrow from him. "Because together, we're unstoppable."

As we prepare to leave, I am aware of every inch of my body, each place he's touched still tingling with remembrance. It's a reminder that no matter what the outside world throws at us, inside, we've created something untouchable.

CHAPTER 26

The Santa

I find myself pacing back and forth in front of the hospital, waiting for news about Jack. I could go inside, but I keep telling myself it's best if I wait and talk to Sergei first.

The anxiety coiling in my chest tighter than a noose around my neck. Even from out here, the sterile scent of this damn hospital invades my senses, amplifying my unease. The Rolex on my wrist is driving me nuts, I swear I can hear the incessant *tick, tick, tick*.

"For fuck's sake!" I roar, tearing it off and throwing it against the wall.

I can feel Carolina's gaze on me, but I can't bring myself to look at her just yet. My fears, my vulnerabilities, are on full display, and I can't afford to show weakness. Not now. Not in front of her.

Finally, the doors slide open, and booted footsteps echo. I turn my head, my heart lodged in my throat, and my eyes lock with Sergei's. "Nicklas!" Sergei exclaims, his voice rough with urgency and pain. "It was an ambush."

My composure shatters like a dropped wine glass, and I stride toward him, my hands outstretched as if to steady myself. Carolina's hand on my arm is my lifeline, her presence a comforting reminder.

"What happened?" I growl. "Tell me everything. Now!"

Sergei takes a deep breath, wincing as he speaks. "We were at the warehouse... I thought it was secure, I swear. But they were waiting for us. I... I don't know how. I'm so sorry."

"Focus," I bark, my voice harsh. "How is Jack? Is he..." I can't bring myself to finish the question.

"He's alive... for now," Sergei pauses, his gaze flickering to Carolina before returning to mine, "he's been shot... multiple times. We were out-manned. I managed to get him in the car and drove us here as fast as I could."

"It's not your fault," I cut him off, my nails digging into my palm so hard I think I break the skin. "How... how bad?"

Sergei hesitates, "He's lost a lot of blood. Umm, they got him in his chest and abdomen. The bleeding... I don't know, man. It was bad. Really fucking bad."

"Where is he?" I demand, my voice a low growl.

"Inside with—"

"Show us," I snap, already striding toward the entrance.

I barrel through the sliding doors of the hospital, Carolina's hand tight in mine. The crisp scent of disinfectant hangs heavy in the air, but it's the underlying hint of iron—the smell of blood—that has my stomach turning in knots. Not because I'm squeamish, but because it could be my brother's.

Fuck!

Following Sergei, I barely look around until I spot Marco immediately. He's a tower among men with his broad shoulders set like a barricade before the operating room.

"Room's secure, boss. No one gets in or out without our say-so." His voice is steady, but there's an edge to it that tells me he's ready for war.

"Good. Keep it that way," I command, as I turn to look at Carolina. She's a pillar of strength beside me, her resolve evident even in the gentle pressure she applies to my hand—a silent promise that she's here with me, for every breath, every beat of my racing heart.

Time loses meaning as we wait. Doctors and nurses become blurs of white and blue as they rush in and out of the operating room. Each time the door swings open, my heart lurches, half-expecting the worst. Carolina's touch, light on my forearm, is the only anchor keeping me tethered to sanity.

The voices are a cacophony of medical jargon, but beneath it all, there's a current of determination that I can't help but cling to. "He's fighting," I hear one nurse say, and something inside me clenches—because that's what Knights do. We fight.

"Nicklas," Carolina whispers, her voice slicing through the haze of my thoughts. Her eyes, usually so bright, now mirror the storm brewing within me. But it's her unyielding stance, the way she faces this chaos head-on that fuels the fire in my chest. "Maybe we should move."

"Fuck no," I reply, letting her see the truth in my eyes—I'm not going anywhere. Not when my brother's life hangs in the balance, and certainly not when she's standing by my side, being my rock when I need it most.

"I just meant over there," she says, pointing at a row of chairs lined against the wall. "So it's easier for them to get in and out."

Marco murmurs his agreement, assuring me he's staying in position.

"Fine," I grind out, letting her drag me over to the chairs. I pick the one closest, so when I crane my neck, I can still see the door Marco is guarding.

With each passing hour, the tension builds, wrapping around us like a vise.

As the night stretches on, I can't sit still any longer and instead, I begin pacing the length of the hall. It must look ridiculous as I walk backwards, refusing to take my eyes off Carolina. She's slumped in her chair, her head resting against the wall as she sleeps softly.

Suddenly, the doors burst open behind Marco.

The doctor's grim face is the first thing I see as he approaches, and my heart hammers against my ribcage. The sharp scent of antiseptic fills the air as he stops in front of us, his expression unreadable.

"Mr. Knight?" His voice is steady, but there's an undercurrent of urgency that sets me on edge.

"Tell me," I demand, my throat tight with barely contained panic. At my words, Carolina startles awake. When her eyes find me, she jerks up from the chair and rushes to my side.

"Jack's condition is severe," the doctor begins, and Carolina's hand finds mine, her grip like a lifeline. "He sustained multiple gunshot wounds. One bullet caused a cardiac arrest. We lost him for a minute on the table, but we brought him back. He's stable now, but critical."

Fuck! Dead even for a moment—it's unthinkable. Fury and fear churn inside me, a storm ready to break free.

"Can we see him?" Carolina's voice cuts through my haze of rage.

"Follow me." The doctor turns on his heel, his white coat a blur as we trail behind him.

The room is a cacophony of beeping machines and flashing monitors, each one tracking the thread of life still tethered to Jack. Tubes snake from his body, and there's a mechanical hiss with every labored breath he takes.

"Jesus, Jack," I mutter, my voice a low growl. Looking at his pale face, too still and quiet, it's like seeing a ghost. This isn't the brother I know—the one full of fire and fight.

I feel Carolina's eyes on me, but I can't tear my gaze away from Jack. "Nicklas, he's strong. He'll pull through this," she whispers, her voice a balm to the raw wound in my chest.

I nod, but I don't trust myself to speak. My mind is a battlefield, thoughts of vengeance warring with the cold dread that's settled in my bones.

"Look at me," Carolina urges, and I finally turn to her. Her blue eyes are fierce, a challenge and a promise all at once. "We're in this together, remember?"

"Forevermore," I say, echoing our earlier vow. It's not just about me anymore; it's about us, about what we're building together. And I'll be damned if I let anyone tear that down.

"Good," she says firmly. "All you need to do is focus on Jack getting better. He needs us to be strong for him. I'll take care of everything else."

She's right. Jack needs me to be the immovable force I've always been. No matter what, I have to protect him, protect us. And when this is over, Carolina and I will have our family, our future—no matter the cost.

I can't sit down. Can't stay still. Everything's too much and not enough at the same time. The people—my people since we've shut down this wing of the Knight owned hospital—walking around the halls annoy the shit out of me. Jack's room is a cacophony of electronic beeps and sighs from machines that are keeping him alive. It is too depressing.

There's nowhere for me to go.

Every time I leave Jack's room, I come back within a few minutes. I know there are things for me to do, but I can't seem to focus enough to actually do it.

I'm pulled from my thoughts as I hear Carolina's voice ring out. I get up from the chair and stride into the hallway.

"Dr. Morris, I expect updates every hour." Her voice slices through the chaos, sharp and commanding. I glance over, watching her confront the lead doctor. She's a force to be reckoned with, her blonde hair like a halo in the harsh fluorescent light, her figure rigid with authority.

"Of course, Ms. Sterling," the doctor replies, his eyes flicking nervously toward me.

"It's Mrs. Knight," she corrects him. "And good. I want an hourly update on the transfusion and everything else. Also, do you have enough blood on hand? Or do we need to look for donors?" she continues, her thoroughness surprising everyone in the room, me included.

"Absolutely, Mrs. Knight," Dr. Morris assures her before scurrying off.

As soon as he's gone, she turns to Marco. "Do you have an update for me?"

What the hell?

Marco steps up, his broad frame tense with unspoken questions. "We've secured all entrances and exits, no one gets in without clearance."

Nodding, she places her hands on her hips. "Expand the perimeter. I want eyes on every floor, every ward. If someone so much as sneezes out of turn, I expect to know about it," she orders, her gaze steely.

"Understood," Marco acknowledges with a nod, a small smile grazing his lips.

Sergei leans against the wall, his face pale beneath the grime and blood. "Carolina, I—"

"No, I'm not discussing this with you again," she admonishes, pointing at him. "You need to get yourself checked over. You could still have bullets inside you. Come on, Sergei."

Their compliance fills me with an odd sense of pride. Carolina, my future wife; not only is she already demanding to be called Mrs. Knight, but the way she's taking control is fucking hot. No wonder everyone is listening. It's intoxicating, how she commands respect without question. How she fights for my family as fiercely as I do.

"Nick?" Her hand touches my arm, and I realize I'm shaking.

"I'm fine," I lie through clenched teeth. My eyes are hot, the threat of tears an unwelcome weakness pressing behind my lids.

"Look at me," she says gently. But I can't. If I look at her now, everything inside me will crumble.

"Nicklas," she insists, her tone brooking no argument. Reluctantly, I meet her gaze. There's strength there, but also a softness that's just for me. It's a lifeline thrown into the raging sea of my emotions.

"Jack's a fighter. He's not going anywhere," she states with conviction.

"Damn right he isn't," I manage to say, my voice hoarse. I'm holding on by a thread, and she's the only thing keeping me stitched together.

"Let's get some air. You need to breathe." She tugs at my arm, guiding me away from Jack's room, away from the blinking monitors.

"All I need is you, Hellcat," I rasp.

"Come here," she pulls me close, and I feel her lips press against mine. A surge of longing rushes through me, desire mingling with the pain and fear that's been gnawing at my insides. Her mouth moves against mine, each kiss a brand, marking me as hers just as she's mine.

The double doors swing open, a cold draft accompanying the arrival of more people. Dad walks with an indifference that chills my blood. Ruby trails behind him, her tears slicing through the silence of the hallway like a siren's wail.

"Ruby." Carolina releases my hand, stepping toward my sister with a softness that belies her steel core. It's a contrast to the helpless rage that's keeping me rooted to the spot.

"Carolina," Ruby sobs, her usual composure as shattered as the family we're scrambling to keep whole.

"Shh, it will be okay. We're all here for Jack," Carolina says, her arms wrapping around Ruby in a protective embrace. For a moment, I see a flicker of something like gratitude in Ruby's tear-streaked face.

"Thank you," Ruby murmurs, leaning into Carolina's comfort. "For being… for being here for all of us."

Carolina nods, pulling back to lock eyes with Ruby. "We're family now. That's what we do."

Their exchange—a silent pact sealed in understanding and shared pain—cuts through the tension. My woman's compassion is boundless, her spirit unyielding. It's then that I know despite the darkness at our door, her light won't be dimmed. Not by fear, not by grief.

"Let's go check on Jack," I suggest, feeling a resurgence of purpose.

"You two go," Carolina says, gently pushing Ruby toward me. "I have a few more things to take care of."

Fuck, how I love this woman.

We stay in the hospital for two days.

Ruby spends her time glued to Jack's side, only leaving when Carolina orders her away. Usually it's because the doctors need privacy, or when she's trying to get my sister to eat or sleep.

Throughout the days, Carolina doesn't falter once; she stays on top of everything and everyone. Masterfully arranging the security rotation with Marco so everyone can get at least a couple of hours of sleep. She even takes care of Sergei, who needed to have surgery as well, though his injuries weren't fatal.

"Carolina?" I call, when I don't immediately see her after I've dozed off in one of the chairs in Jack's room.

"Here," she confirms as she steps through the door. "Do you need anything?"

The black circles below her eyes tell me she hasn't slept at all, which doesn't surprise me. Even so, her eyes gleam with satisfaction, like only someone who's thriving do. Maybe she is.

I yawn and stretch, pulling my phone out to check the time. Christ, it's the middle of the goddamn night. As I look around, I notice Ruby sitting close by, her eyes droopy as though she's seconds from falling asleep.

"Is Dad still around?" I ask, my mind reeling from the hushed conversations I've overheard between him and someone on the other end of his phone. There was something in his tone—a shifty unease I've never caught onto before. It pricks at my gut, a warning I can't shake off.

"No," she says. "He—"

"He got a call and had to leave." I whip around at the sound of my brother's croaked voice.

"You're awake," I state, not sure how I missed it when I woke up.

He nods. "I'm not sure I'm happy about that," he grumbles with a wince. "Everything fucking hurts."

I shoot him a grin as I approach. "That's because you're a fucking pussy."

"I'd rather be fucking pussy," he retorts, waggling his eyebrows.

Jack looks good, really good, actually. He's no longer so pale he could have a white-off with the sheets, and his mood seems to be good. "It's good to have you back," I say, clasping his shoulder.

"I'll go find you two some food," Carolina calls out, and when I turn to look at her, she blows me a kiss before sashaying her fine ass out of here.

Jack groans, reminding me I'm still touching his shoulder. Not the injured one, luckily. "Hey," he says, lowering his voice. "What the hell is Dad up to?"

Well fuck, if he's noticed something is up while being barely awake, it's worse than I first thought. "What do you mean?" I ask.

"He called me as Sergei and I were on our way to the warehouse. He…" Jack trails off, his brows furrowing like he's deep in thought. "He wanted our ETA. And… he asked if you were with us. It's… it makes no sense."

No… that makes no sense at all since Dad has officially passed the reins on to me, so he shouldn't be involved at all. But… what if he's unofficially still knee-deep in our empire? Could he have… no, that's a leap.

Dad might not… I mean… sure, he's cold toward Jack, indifferent at times. But he's still his son. So surely he wouldn't… would he?

Whatever is going on, it only solidifies the need to make Carolina mine in every way that counts, and that means it's time.

Time for her test.

I quickly send a text to Arthur, telling him I'm ready. I'm not, and I don't think I'll ever be. Not because of what it could cost me, but because of what I know it'll do to my hellcat.

Despite the hour, the King answers within minutes, telling me everything is already waiting for us, and that he'll be there right away.

CHAPTER 27

The Breeder

We leave the hospital, the sterile scent and the distant beeping of machines still clinging to my senses. Jack is stable, but the tight knot in my chest doesn't loosen. I think we're heading home—back to the familiar safety of our apartment, where I can collapse and finally let the worry and fear drain away. But Nick stops me just before we reach the car, his hand firm around mine.

"We're not going home yet," he says, his voice low, almost too calm. My heart skips a beat, anxiety curling in my stomach.

Before I can ask where we're going, he pulls me close, his hand cupping the back of my neck as he kisses me. It's not a soft kiss. It's fierce, consuming, as if he's pouring everything he can't say into that single moment. My heart pounds, not just from the kiss but from the unsettling sense that something is coming, something I'm not ready for.

When he pulls away, I'm left breathless, my lips tingling. "Nick, what—"

"It's time for your test," he interrupts, and before I can react, he pulls a blindfold from his pocket. The sight of it sends a jolt of fear through me. I don't want to be in the dark, not now, not when everything feels so precarious.

His hands are gentle as he slips the blindfold over my eyes, but it doesn't soothe the panic rising in my chest. The world goes black, the comforting sight of Nick's face disappearing, leaving me adrift in uncertainty. I hear the car door open, and he guides me inside, his hand never leaving mine. The door closes, sealing me in darkness and silence.

The car starts moving, and I try to focus on the familiar sound of the engine, the subtle vibrations beneath me, anything to anchor myself. But the blindfold makes everything feel distant, detached. I can't see Nick, can't read his expression or feel his presence the way I usually do. My mind races with questions; Why now? Why this secrecy?

I force myself to take deep breaths, trying to calm the frantic beating of my heart. I have to trust him. I've trusted Nick with my life before, but this feels different, more personal, more dangerous. The stakes are higher because they're not just about me—they're about us, about our future.

The car finally stops, and I hear the doors open, the sounds of people moving around outside. The air that rushes in is cold, biting, and I shiver involuntarily. Nick's hand releases mine, and I feel a pang of loss, of fear, as I wait for him to guide me out.

But the hand that takes mine isn't his. It's rougher, the grip firm but unfamiliar. My heart leaps into my throat, and I have to force myself not to pull away. I don't know who this person is, but I follow him, my steps hesitant as he leads me out of the car. The ground beneath my feet is uneven, gravel crunching with each step. The air smells damp, a mix of oil and concrete that tells me we're in some kind of industrial area.

Panic flutters in my chest as we walk. I can hear the faint echo of our footsteps bouncing off walls, the surrounding space feeling vast and empty. My senses are heightened by the blindfold, every sound sharper, every scent more potent. I focus on the rough hand guiding me, the only thing tethering me to reality in this suffocating darkness.

Finally, we stop. The blindfold is removed, and I blink against the harsh light that floods my vision. My eyes adjust, revealing a large, dimly lit warehouse, the kind of place where shadows hide secrets and danger. The space is cold, the chill in the air gnawing at my skin, making it hard to shake off the unease that's settled deep in my bones.

In front of me stands Arthur Hatt, the King. His presence is commanding, his eyes cold and assessing as they lock onto mine. Beside him, with an expression as hard as stone, is Nick's dad, Caspian. The sight of him sends a fresh wave of fear crashing over me. Caspian doesn't need words to be intimidating, he just is.

The diary entries from Sienna's diary makes coldness run down my spine, and I shiver.

Arthur steps forward, his voice cutting through the tension like a blade. "Welcome, Carolina," he says, his tone smooth but devoid of warmth. "Nicklas has chosen you, but now you must prove yourself."

My stomach drops. This is it. The test Nick mentioned—the test of loyalty, strength, and resolve. The words I want to say die on my tongue as I glance around, but I don't see my twisted Santa anywhere.

Arthur continues, his eyes never leaving mine. "The test is simple. Three men, all hooded. You must shoot two, leaving one standing. The challenge is identifying which one is Nicklas."

What? No way. He can't… the longer I look at his impassive face, the clearer it becomes that he's dead serious.

My heart slams against my ribs, the air thickening as the gravity of his words sinks in. I've never held a gun, never even touched one. And now I'm supposed to aim it at three faceless men, knowing that one of them could be Nick? My Nick? The idea of pulling the trigger, of possibly killing him by mistake, makes my knees weak.

Arthur steps aside, revealing three men standing in a line, their faces obscured by dark hoods. They're dressed identically, black suits blending into the shadows of the warehouse. My breath catches, panic clawing at my chest. I can't do this. How can I possibly know which one is him?

But I have to. There's no choice. This isn't just about passing a test—it's about proving that I belong in this world, beside Nick. That I'm strong enough, ruthless enough, to be his partner in every way.

Arthur doesn't wait for me to gather my thoughts. He gestures to Marco, who steps forward, holding a gun. My hands shake as he places it in my grasp, the cold metal foreign and terrifying. His eyes meet mine, and I see a flicker of something—sympathy, maybe, or understanding—

but it's gone in an instant, replaced by the calm, steady demeanor of a man used to violence.

"You'll need some practice," Arthur says, his voice like ice. "We won't throw you in completely unprepared."

Caspian and Arthur leave me alone with Marco, taking the hooded men with them. It's a small mercy, one that makes it easier to breathe and to think without their demanding presence scaring me.

Marco stands beside me, his presence grounding but not comforting. "Hold it like this," he instructs, adjusting my grip on the gun. His voice is patient but firm, his hands guiding mine. "Your stance needs to be firm. Feet shoulder-width apart. Don't let your emotions control your aim. Focus on the target, nothing else."

I nod, swallowing hard as I try to focus. The weight of the gun feels wrong in my hands, too heavy, too powerful. The idea that I could kill someone with a single pull of the trigger is terrifying, but I push the fear down, forcing myself to listen to Marco's instructions. This is my only chance. I can't afford to fail.

He guides me through a few practice shots, the sound of the gunfire jarring in the empty warehouse, each shot echoing off the walls and reverberating through my entire being. My hands tremble, the recoil of the gun sending shockwaves up my arms, but I grit my teeth and try again. I have to get this right. Nick's life depends on it.

I completely lose track of time as we go again and again. With each shot I miss, Marco tries his best to guide me, but the more times I pull the trigger, the more my hands shake and my resolve wavers.

"S-sorry," I stutter when I empty an entire round without hitting my imaginary mark even once. "Fuck! I don't know how to do this."

Marco sighs and rakes his hand through his hair. "You need to stop anticipating the recoil. You're working against yourself and the gun. Try again."

He reloads it for me, and while he does so, I wipe my sweaty hands on my pants. Then I take the gun back, squaring my shoulders and adjusting my stance. I use both hands to clutch the handle, telling myself to stop trembling like a leaf.

As I pull the trigger, I feel what Marco's saying; I'm tensing so much

I ruin my aim. I grit my teeth and try again.

"You're getting closer," Marco says, his deep voice a rumble. "Keep going."

The air shifts as Arthur and Caspian join us again. I don't look their way, doing my best to tune them out. But I can feel the weight of their expectations bearing down on me. I tell myself that they don't matter, which, right now, they don't.

I'm here to prove myself to Nick, not them.

When Arthur clears his throat, I know the practice is over. The real test begins now.

The three hooded men are brought back in, and Marco lines them up in front of me.

I approach the three hooded men, the gun heavy in my hand. My heart races, my mind whirling with fear and doubt. I scan them, trying to feel that connection, that pull that should tell me which one is Nick. But the fear of being wrong, of killing him, clouds my judgment. Every instinct is screaming at me to stop, to run, but I force myself to stay. I can't back down. I have to do this.

The silence is deafening as I lift the gun, my breath hitching, my hand steady but my mind spinning. I study each man, searching for something—anything—that will give Nick away. The way he stands, the tension in his muscles, the tilt of his head. But they're all so still, so quiet, and the hoods make them faceless, stripping away the familiar cues I would normally rely on.

I focus on the first man, my eyes narrowing as I try to see past the hood, past the anonymity. His stance is solid, his posture confident, but there's something off—a slight hesitation in the way he holds himself, a subtle tremor in his hand. My breath catches. It could be him, but it could also be someone imitating him, knowing that I'd look for that calm confidence.

I shift my focus to the second man. He's more rigid, his posture almost too perfect, too controlled. It's as if he's trying too hard, forcing himself to mimic Nick's natural confidence. But the way he stands, the way his shoulders are squared, it doesn't feel right. It's too stiff, too deliberate.

That leaves the third man. My heart pounds as I look at him. His stance is relaxed, but there's a tension in his shoulders, a subtle shift in his weight that reminds me of Nick. It's a barely there hint of anxiety, masked by a calm exterior. Something about it feels right, feels like Nick. But the fear of being wrong gnaws at me, paralyzing my hand.

I close my eyes for a moment, trying to drown out the noise in my head, the fear and doubt. I have to trust my instincts. I have to trust that I know him well enough to see through this. When I open my eyes again, my gaze locks onto the third man. I take a deep breath, steadying myself. This is it.

With a surge of determination, I lift the gun and aim it at the first man. My finger trembles on the trigger, but I force myself to pull it. The shot echoes through the warehouse, and the man crumples to the ground. My heart clenches, but I don't allow myself to think, to dwell on what I've just done. I have to keep going.

I shift my aim to the second man, my breath catching in my throat. He stands still, not moving an inch, and for a split second, doubt creeps in. But I can't hesitate. I can't let fear control me. I pull the trigger again. Another shot, another body falls.

The third man remains standing, his hood still hiding his face. My entire body shakes, adrenaline and terror coursing through my veins. This is the moment of truth. My heart pounds so hard it feels like it's going to burst out of my chest. The hood is pulled back, and I'm staring into Nick's eyes.

"Nick!" I cry out.

Relief floods through me, a tidal wave that leaves me weak, my knees nearly buckling. I did it. I found him. But the relief is tainted by the cold, dark reality of what I've just done, what I've just proven I'm capable of.

Arthur steps forward, his gaze still sharp, appraising. "Well done," he says, and I can hear the approval in his voice.

Caspian doesn't offer me any words, he just sneers at me like I'm offending him by merely being in the same vicinity as him.

Well, fuck him.

I turn my attention back to Nick, tears flowing down my face, distorting my vision. "Nick," I whisper, the gun falling from my hand.

Within seconds, he's on me, his lips crashing into mine, his arms holding me so tight I can barely breathe. "I knew you could do it, Hellcat," he groans against my lips.

Tears keep falling as we kiss, and I delve my hands under his shirt, needing to touch him with no barriers.

The Santa

My heart thumps with an intensity that belies my outward calm. The air is laced with tension, heavy with the scent of Carolina's fear and the lingering echoes of relief. I watch her—my everything—with a hunger that tightens every muscle in my body.

"Get out," I growl to the remaining men scattered around the perimeter. They hesitate, their eyes darting between me and Carolina, but one sharp look from me has them scurrying away like cockroaches under a spotlight.

As soon as the last man exits, the steel door slamming shut with finality, I pull Carolina closer against me. Her small frame trembles, her tears hot against my skin, but she clings to me, her lips desperately seeking mine.

"Nick," she sobs into my mouth, her hands fisting in my jacket. "I was afraid I'd—"

"Shh," I command, silencing her with another crushing kiss. My hands roam over her curves, gripping her ass, pulling her even closer. I can feel the pounding of her heart against my chest, a frantic beat that mirrors my own.

"It was just a test," I murmur between kisses, nipping at her lower lip. "I was never in any real danger. Arthur would have stopped you if you chose wrong."

Truthfully, I'm not sure what would have happened if she didn't pass the test. I never asked because I never wanted to hear the answer. Knowing my dad, he'd find a way to twist it into some kind of sadistic lesson; possibly killing the both of us just for the hell of it.

But she doesn't seem to hear me, lost in the swell of emotions, her body arching into my touch. I press her against the cold wall, my movement so forceful she lets out a small *'oomph'*. She's gasping, her breath coming in short bursts that fan across my face, her scent intoxicating—a mix of vanilla and something uniquely Carolina.

"Nick," she whispers, her voice laced with desire and relief. "Please."

I don't need any further encouragement. I'm already consumed by the need to claim her, to erase the terror that had clouded her eyes just moments before. My name on her lips is both a plea and a benediction, fueling my desire to protect, possess, and cherish.

"Carolina," I say, my tone rough with emotion. "You're mine, all mine." The words are more than a statement—they're a vow, a promise entwined with a primal claim. It's not just her body I crave—it's her soul, her future.

"Always," she breathes out, her eyes locked onto mine, a mirror reflecting back all the dark, tumultuous passion that courses through my veins.

"Say it again," I demand, my voice thick with possession.

"I'm yours forevermore, Nick," she repeats, her voice breaking on my name.

I watch, every muscle in my body tensed with desire, as Carolina leans back against the cold, unforgiving wall, her breaths coming in short, rapid bursts. The need for her burns through my veins like a wildfire. "Let me see you," I growl, my voice laced with an urgency that reverberates off the walls. I reach for her pantsuit, clawing at the fabric until it tears down the middle.

With a final tug, the pantsuit falls to a puddle at her feet, revealing the soft curves of her body, the delicate skin I'm desperate to taste. My hands are on her before I realize I've moved, dropping to my knees as if in worship.

As I press my mouth to her slick cunt, she moans my name. "Nick!" Her voice is filled with need. My tongue delves into her channel, I savor her like the rarest delicacy, eliciting gasps and whimpers that feed the fire inside me.

"You're perfect," I say against her flesh, my voice vibrating through her. "So damn perfect for me."

She writhes above me, her hands fisting in my hair, guiding me, urging me deeper, harder. And when she comes apart, screaming my name, it's more than just pleasure—it's affirmation, it's possession, it's everything.

"Fuck! I'm coming! I'm coming!" Her cry is a beacon, pulling me back to my feet, my own need a living thing inside me.

I don't give her time to come down from her high before I command, "Take off my clothes." My voice is rough with lust and love. And she does, with jerky, eager movements, stripping me of my barriers until there's nothing left between us but raw desire.

Her breath hitches, her eyes wide and wild with lust as I grab her hips and lift her up. She immediately wraps her long legs around me, moaning as I push her back against the unyielding wall. She's a tempest, a force that could either save or destroy me.

She rolls her hips, rubbing her wet slit along my hard shaft. "I need you inside me," she begs. I thrust inside her, eliciting a keening moan from her lips. "Yes, yes, God, yes!"

I fuck her against the wall, each movement a testament to our dark, powerful love, pain and pleasure indistinguishable, intermingled. "Mine," I rasp into her ear, feeling her tighten around me, her nails digging into my shoulders, marking me as surely as I mark her with every thrust.

"Yours, always," she responds, her voice a broken promise, a vow that I feel down to my marrow.

Her desperation fuels my own. The scent of her arousal is intoxicating, driving me further into the abyss of our shared hunger. I'm relentless, pushing us both toward oblivion. I slam my lips to hers, biting and licking. Our kiss isn't sweet and playful; it's dark and domineeringly perfect.

I can feel her climax building again, her body coiling tight like a spring. And when she shatters, screaming my name, I follow, pouring myself into her with possessive fervor. "Take all of me," I groan as my cum shoots from my dick, painting her insides.

CHAPTER 28

The Breeder

It's close to noon when Nick and I finally step into the privacy of our apartment. The door shuts with a soft click, and I lean back against it, feeling the weight of exhaustion settle over me like a thick blanket.

"I need a goddamn shower," he murmurs, and there's no arguing with that voice—deep, commanding, yet laced with something softer when he speaks to me.

Not that I want to argue. After two days in the hospital, and then a test that threatened to shatter my mind, a shower sounds like heaven.

I'm still not sure how I feel about the test. Relief it really was just that, a test, and that nothing happened to Nick? Or unease at not knowing what would have happened if I'd chosen wrong. The question gnaws at me, begging to be voiced. But I refuse since nothing good can come from that.

Deep in my soul, I feel that this is one question I don't want the answer to. No, it's better to focus on the victory, and then somehow move on.

As soon as we enter the bathroom, Nick switches the shower on, activating all the showerheads so the room is filled with steam in seconds. The sound of water cascading is soothing. He undresses quickly, and I watch the way his sculpted ass flexes as he walks into the shower.

Taking my time, I braid my hair so it's hanging down my back. Although it feels greasy and dry, I refuse to waste time washing it. Then I undress, but before joining him, I brush my teeth. Trying to ignore the drawer with the pregnancy tests is futile, it's calling me like a beacon. Giving in, I take one out and pee on it. Then I wrap it up in toilet paper and place it on the counter before joining Nick.

Under the warm spray, his hands are gentle, not the rough touch of the Mafia boss who rules with an iron fist, but the tender care of a man who knows every curve and contour of my body. His fingers glide over my skin, tracing paths of cleanliness and comfort. Even though he touches me everywhere, his touch isn't sexual. Not that my body understands that.

My nipples still pebble, wetness gathers in my core, and my breathing turns ragged. Just as I feel his erection digging into my stomach. We both ignore it, too content washing each other.

It might sound silly, but this is the most intimate we've been. Sure, this man has eaten both my pussy and ass, yet it's nothing compared to the way his gaze bores into mine while he washes me between my folds.

Returning the gesture, my hands run across the expanse of his tattooed chest, pausing at the scar spelling out my future initials. It's perfect.

"Thank you," I whisper, the words almost lost in the sound of the water. It's not just for this moment but for all the moments since he saw me in the alley when I stumbled upon him and Jack in the middle of an execution.

He nods, understanding, and pulls me close, his forehead resting against mine. We stand there, holding each other in the warmth and the mist, worlds away from the harsh realities that wait outside.

After the shower, I wrap myself in a towel and use my hand to wipe the mirror clear of steam. The pregnancy test sits on the counter, a silent sentinel of hope and disappointment. I peer down at it, heart hammering.

Negative. Again.

The single word echoes in my mind, a stark reminder of the timeline closing in on us. Five days left, five days to fulfill a contract I'm no longer sure I'm even still bound by. My dreams of a rich husband to provide for Willow and me have morphed into something deeper with Nick, something real.

"Carolina." His voice breaks through my spiraling thoughts, pulling me back to the present. He's watching me, those dark eyes seeing right through me. "It doesn't matter," he says firmly, stepping closer. His hand lifts, his finger tracing the initials carved into his chest. A permanent mark, a promise. "We're forever, so we have all the time in the world."

I don't know if the first part of what he's saying is true. Something tells me it isn't, and that the deadline for conceiving is as important now as it was when we started. But I still appreciate that he's doing his best to put me at ease.

My heart clenches, emotions swirling—a cocktail of love, disappointment, and desperation. Here's a man who burns the world for me, who defies his own ruthless nature to give me tenderness.

"Forevermore," I say.

"Exactly," he agrees. "Now that you've passed your test, there's no rush."

Rationally, I know that we're tethered by a connection that goes deeper than any contract and timeline. Yet, I'm still disappointed. I wanted to give him this; the one thing he's asked me for. I reach out, touching the raised skin of my initials, feeling the heat of his blood beneath.

"It will happen," I stubbornly say, lifting my chin. "I'll give you an heir before Christmas."

"I'm sure," he rumbles, the protective edge in his voice wrapping around me like a warm embrace. "But for now, how about we get some rest?"

Shaking my head, I open the cupboard above the sink and start pulling out items of makeup. It's all luxury branded stuff that Nick's bought, and I'm not sure I want to know how he's managed to get the shades correct.

I begin my ritual with a rich moisturizer, followed by dabbing on concealer to hide the dark circles haunting my reflection. My hand pauses as I catch Nick's frown in the glass.

"Why are you getting ready? We just got back and you need rest." His voice is a low rumble, confusion lacing his words like a thread out of place on one of his immaculate suits.

"I need to see my sister," I say, as I finish with the concealer and add foundation. "I want to be the one to tell her about her security detail." As we left the warehouse, Nick arranged for some of his men to guard Will at all times, which I appreciate. But she still needs to hear about it from me.

"Dammit, Carolina, we've been over this," he growls, coming up behind me, his presence a furnace at my back. "It's already done."

"She still needs to hear it from me." I turn to face him, my hands planted firmly on my hips, challenging his dominant stance.

His jaw tightens, the muscle ticking with restrained anger, or maybe it's concern. It's always hard to tell with Nick. Finally, he exhales sharply, the sound cutting through the tension. "Fine. But I'm coming with you—"

"No, you're not. I need—"

"Enough!" he shouts. "I won't jeopardize your safety for anyone. Not even your sister."

Our eye contact becomes a battlefield, a battle of wills. But I know there's no changing his mind, not if he perceives my safety to be threatened. "Fine," I agree. Then I turn back to finish my makeup, keeping it light by just adding a touch of eyeliner and mascara.

"Call her then, set it up. And Caro…" He pauses, his hand cupping my cheek, thumb brushing my skin gently—a contrast to the hard lines of his body. "… I couldn't bear anything happening to you. You know that."

"I know," I softly reply, my hand brushing across the scar on his face before I step into the bedroom.

Finding my phone, I call Will, putting her on speaker so I can get dressed while we talk.

"Hey, Will, how about lunch today? My treat," I say when she answers, my voice brighter than I feel.

While I pull on a pair of black dress pants and a Christmassy red cashmere sweater that clings to me, we make the arrangements, and I promise to pick her up within the hour. Feeling inspired by the color, I go back to the bathroom and find a matching lipstick, and as I carefully dab it on my lips, I start to feel more at ease.

Jack's going to be okay. My sister will be fine. And I... I'm happy. It feels weird to admit, but Nick makes me deliriously happy. Not in a mushy, gushy way, thankfully. Once upon a time, I might have thought that was the dream, but now, thanks to my twisted Santa, I know myself better.

After slipping on a pair of sky-high stilettos that look better than they feel on my feet, I settle a stylish beret over my braided hair. Luckily, I managed to keep it dry in the shower, and since I didn't have time to wash and dry it, I hide it under the hat.

Nick's waiting for me in the kitchen, with Marco and two other guys, and together we leave the apartment. Marco leads the way, making us wait in the elevator while he surveys the underground garage before waving us over to a vehicle that looks like a fortress on wheels.

"It's bulletproof," Nick explains as we slide into the backseat together.

"Of course it is," I quip.

The other two guys slide into the seat behind me and Nick.

We drive in silence to pick up Willow, the city blurring past us like a tapestry of chaos and life. When we reach her place, the two guys jump out and quickly help her into the car, seating her opposite us before folding her wheelchair and placing it in the back.

Despite the confusion she must feel, her smile is a ray of sun piercing through the shadows that cling to my soul. "Nice ride," Will comments. Then she looks between me and Nick. "So you're him?"

"Him?" he asks, arching an eyebrow.

As I look at Nick, I try to imagine what my sister is seeing. She's never been one to judge anyone by their looks, but there's no denying he looks intimidating thanks to his intense gaze and the scar on his face. Oh, and then there's the fact we're being chauffeured in a fucking fortress, with bodyguards behind us.

"Ruby's brother," she answers easily. "The one who got engaged to my sister without even meeting me."

Nick laughs. "That would be me, and I'm very sorry about that, Willow. Maybe I can earn your approval during lunch."

She giggles, and the two of them continue their conversation. I'm content just to listen, and only interject when I feel like it's needed. Which isn't much.

The restaurant is swanky, the kind of place I never thought I'd be able to afford to step foot in, let alone dine in. The hostess' eyes sweep over us, pausing on Nick, before she ushers us to a horse-shoe shaped booth in the back, tucked away from prying eyes.

The clink of silverware and the murmur of conversations cocoon me as Nick and I slide into the red leather booth while Will remains in her wheelchair at the end of the table. The scent of garlic and herbs wafts from the kitchen, promising a meal that'll make you forget about the world outside these walls. Nick's presence is like a gravitational pull, his dark eyes scanning the restaurant with an authority that makes my skin tingle.

"You should try the lasagna, Willow," Nick suggests with a warm smile that is both natural and unnatural on his handsome face. "It's legendary here."

"Ooh, sold!" she giggles, her eyes dancing with delight. She's always been easy to please, always seen the light in the shadows.

I watch them, my heart swelling at my sister's laughter, yet it's laced with a pang of guilt. How do I shatter this moment with the truth? That the man making her laugh is the head of the Knight Mafia? And that because of that, she's now going to be watched twenty-four-seven? Yeah, there's no easy way to say any of that.

"Are you okay? You look a bit... I don't know, lost?" Nick leans in, his voice a low rumble that vibrates through me.

"Fine." I force a smile, but my hands tremble beneath the table. "Just thinking about dessert."

"Always planning ahead," he teases, and I can't tell if he sees right through me or if he buys my act.

I open my mouth, ready to spill it all to Will when the universe decides it has other plans. A waiter, bustling by with a tray piled high with steaming dishes, clips the edge of our table. My phone skitters off the edge like a stone over ice, slamming onto the floor.

"Dammit!" I hiss, and Nick's hand shoots out to grab my wrist.

"Let me," he insists, but I'm quicker. I duck down, my fingers closing around my phone.

The sound of a gunshot rips through the chatter, a cruel blade slashing the fabric of normality. Screams erupt around us, a symphony of terror that threatens to suffocate. Instinctively, I jerk upright, my heart slamming against my ribs with the force of a caged bird desperate to escape.

"Carolina! Get down!" Nick's voice is a command, hard and unyielding, but my body rebels. My eyes dart to Will; her smile, just seconds ago so vibrant, now a fading echo on her lips, replaced by sheer terror.

"Will!" My voice is a raw scream as another shot pierces the air, its deadly whisper close, too close.

Nick's arms are iron bands trying to drag me away, but I twist in his grip. "Let me go!" I'm half-sobbing, my voice tearing at the edges. He's trying to protect me, but doesn't he understand? My sister is exposed, vulnerable, and every cell in my body screams to shield her.

"Carolina, please—" His plea cuts off as I break free, lunging toward Will.

Time slows, each moment a torture, each second an eternity. I see the panic in her eyes, the way her mouth forms my name—a silent call for help. And then the unthinkable happens. A third shot rings out, the bullet finds its mark, and she crumples like a marionette with snipped strings.

"Willow!" Her name is a prayer, a curse, as I drop to my knees beside her. She's so still, too still, her eyes wide and unseeing, her chest eerily motionless. Blood blooms like a crimson blossom against her pale sweater, and something inside me shatters. "Stay with me, Will. Please, stay with me." My hands shake as I press them to the wound, a futile attempt to stem the tide of red. Tears blur my vision, hot and relentless.

This isn't happening. It can't be happening.

"Help her!" I scream, turning to Nick, to anyone who will listen. His face is a mask of rage and sorrow, a mirror of the agony tearing through me.

He says something, but his voice is distant, swallowed by the chaos surrounding us.

"Will! Come on, talk to me." But she doesn't respond, doesn't move, and something vital within me withers.

The light, her light, flickers out, leaving me in darkness. My world, once filled with the hope of a better future—for her, for us—collapses into a void where only despair thrives.

"Please, no..." My words dissolve into sobs, my body curled protectively over hers, as if my love could somehow reverse the cold finality of death. But it's too late. My precious sister, the one I've fought so hard to provide for, to protect, is gone. And with her, a part of my soul.

"Carolina." Nick's voice is thick with unspoken pain. He reaches for me, but I recoil from his touch, lost in the abyss of my grief. Willow was all I had left in this world, and now...

Now there's nothing.

Well, almost nothing. One thing remains...

Heat ignites in my veins, a searing fire that eclipses all reason. My grief is a living thing, clawing its way out of the chasm left by Willow's absence. Marco and his men have the shooter pinned down, a writhing mass of limbs and muffled curses on the checkered floor of the restaurant.

"No! Stay here!" Nicklas' rough command barely registers over the roar in my ears.

I shove him aside, an unexpected strength surging through me, propelling me toward the man responsible for extinguishing Will's light. He struggles against the security, but my focus narrows to the cold, sharp promise of pain.

"No!" I hear Nicklas bellow, a distant echo as I launch myself at the assailant with a primal scream.

Our bodies collide, and I'm vaguely aware of shocked gasps and shouts around us. The shooter's eyes widen in terror as I straddle him, his arms flailing in a futile attempt to defend himself. I rain blows upon him, each strike a release of the tempest inside me.

"This is for her. For Willow," I snarl, my voice drenched in anguish.

I haven't noticed one of my stilettoes falling off my foot, but as I see it next to me, I reach for it. My fingers close around the nose of the shoe as I use the heel as a weapon of destruction, plunging it into his flesh with sickening ease.

Once, twice, thrice—each thrust a punctuation to my sister's stolen future.

The red pooling under him is a grotesque mirror to the blood that now stains my soul, but I can't stop. I keep going.

"Get her off!" someone yells, hands trying to pry me away, but I am unyielding, a force of nature unleashed.

"Carolina, stop!" It's Nicklas again, his arms finally wrapping around me, dragging me back into the world of the living. But I can't stop shaking, can't stop the raw screams tearing from my throat.

"Willow…" The name is a sob, a plea, a curse.

The aftermath is surreal, patrons huddled under tables, faces pale and eyes wide. Staff cluster by the kitchen, phones pressed to their ears, their uniforms splattered with reminders of violence. Glass crunches underfoot as sirens wail in the distance, the once festive atmosphere now a tableau of horror and disbelief.

"Is he…" I can't finish the question, my gaze locked onto the motionless form beneath the security team.

"Dead," Marco confirms.

"You killed him," Nick says, his voice tinted with awe. I look up at him, searching for judgment, for condemnation. But there's only sorrow and something else—a fierce protectiveness that both comforts and terrifies me.

"An eye for an eye," I whisper, my fingers trembling as I touch the sticky red on my hands, "a life for a life."

I stand there, my breaths jagged, staring down at the man whose life has just ebbed away under my hand. My stiletto, a lethal extension of my rage, drips with the consequence of my fury. There's no tremor in my grip, no second-guessing the darkness that has settled over me like a shroud.

"Carolina?" Nick's voice cuts through the pandemonium, but I feel distant, disconnected from the chaos that my actions have wrought. The restaurant is a warzone of overturned chairs and shattered lives, yet all I see is the void where Will's light used to be. "Are you okay?" he asks, his hand reaching for my shoulder.

The touch should ground me, pull me back from the brink, but it doesn't. I shake my head, a bitter laugh escaping my lips. "I'll never be okay again. The light in my life just flickered out."

It's not just words; it's a chilling revelation.

A part of me—the part that sang Christmas carols with Will and always looked out for her—has been snuffed out. In its place is a cold certainty that I will never return to who I was before this moment.

"Let's get out of here," Nick urges, his eyes scanning the room, ever vigilant even now.

"No!" I scream, turning back to where Will lies, her wheelchair on its side now. I barely register a fleeting thought wondering why she didn't get out and hide under the table. I know why; shock. "I'm not leaving her."

"Marco can—"

"I said no."

Nick looks at one of the guys who was meant to protect us, and signals for him to come over. "Get her wheelchair," he orders. Then he steps over to her, and with more care than I've ever seen him handle anything or anyone, he picks her up, cradling her lifeless body against his chest. "Can we leave now?"

Nodding, I follow him mechanically, stepping over debris, my senses dulled to everything but the weight of emptiness within me. I don't hear the sirens approaching or the murmured prayers of the survivors. I don't feel the December chill as we exit the restaurant. All I feel is the hollowness where my sister's laughter once lived.

"Stay with me, Carolina," Nick says, his voice a lifeline I'm not sure I want to grab.

Can this man, bound by blood and violence, truly understand the abyss into which I've fallen? Does he grasp that, in seeking vengeance, I've birthed a new version of myself—one that might match his own darkness?

"Nick…" I start, but words fail me. How do I explain that the woman he knew—the one who plotted to trap a rich husband, who dreamed of a brighter future is fading fast, leaving only the raw edges of a soul torn apart?

"Shh," he soothes, pulling me close. "You don't have to say anything."

But silence is its own torment, and as we flee the scene of my transformation, I can't help but wonder if the void inside me is not a pit but a womb, gestating a new life forged from loss and retribution. And whether Nicklas Knight, the man who commands empires and demands loyalty, is ready for the woman I am becoming.

As we drive away, the city lights blur into streaks of color, bleeding into the sky. They speak of life going on, of a world oblivious to the fracture in my universe. And somewhere deep inside, something primal stirs—a recognition that survival requires adaptation, that sometimes creation is born from destruction.

"What should we do with the body?" the guy—I don't know his name—asks.

I pretend not to hear them as I sit in the backseat with Will's head resting in my lap. If I don't focus on the bullet hole or the blood, I can almost imagine she's sleeping. But… she isn't sleeping. She's dead—gone to a place where I'm not ready to follow.

"We should cremate her," I reply, barely recognizing my own voice. "That's what she wanted."

"Now?" Nick asks, and I'm startled by the question.

Is that even possible? What am I thinking, of course it is. "Yes, now." I reply. "I want it all taken care of today. And we need to tell Dr. Hargrove, and I need to call the—"

Nick clears his throat. "Can… Ruby would love to help if you'd let her. And I'm sure she would want to say goodbye."

I nod stiffly. Even with the time I spent with Ruby at the hospital, I can't say I care much for her. But Willow did, and she would have wanted Ruby's help… I think. "Okay," I agree.

Closing my eyes, I pray for darkness to take over, or a hole to open up and swallow the car. But of course none of that happens. And maybe that's for the best because no matter how bleak everything looks right now, I'm not ready to say goodbye.

As I open my eyes, I look at Nick. He's so much more than what everyone thinks; to me, he's everything.

I've already embraced his darkness, so I can do the same for my own. Right?

CHAPTER 29

The Breeder

Nick's voice is low and steady as he speaks on the phone, his words piercing through the haze around me. "Ruby, Willow is dead. Carolina wants the body cremated immediately." The words hit me like a blow, and I feel myself slipping away, drifting into memories that come rushing back, unbidden and relentless.

I'm seven, and Will is just a year old, her tiny hands clutching my fingers as she giggles, her eyes bright with wonder. I remember the way she used to follow me everywhere, toddling after me on chubby legs, her laughter filling the air like music. We're in the garden, the sun is warm on our faces, and I'm showing her how to pick flowers without breaking the stems. She looks up at me with such trust, her little face glowing with love and admiration, and I feel like the whole world is perfect at that moment.

The memory shifts, and now Will is eight, and I'm fourteen.

We're running through the fields behind the house, the tall grass swaying around us as we chase each other. She's fast, so fast, and her laughter is wild and free, echoing in the open air. I catch her, finally, and we collapse together on the ground, breathless and happy, staring up at the sky as the clouds drift by. She's my little sister, my shadow, and in that moment, everything feels simple and right.

"Carolina." Nick's voice pulls me out of my trip down memory lane. "Do you want... umm, Ruby's asking if you need any help with Willow's things?"

Do I? Yeah, I guess I do. I'm not leaving my sister, so someone has to gather it all. "Yeah, I do, actually." My tone doesn't sound like mine as I mention that Will's room at Ability Acres needs to be emptied, and that they need to know she's not coming back.

"I'll take care of it." Ruby's voice rings out from the speaker on Nick's phone. "Is there anything else you need?"

Rather than answering, I just shake my head as another memory surfaces, and I let it pull me away from the horrible present.

Will is eleven, and I'm seventeen. We're at the lake, and while I'm sunbathing, she's swimming. "Look, Caro," she shouts excitedly, wiggling her legs beneath the water. "I'm swimming like a mermaid." The sun sets behind us, turning the water into a shimmering gold, and I remember thinking how beautiful she looked, how full of life and promise.

But then the memories start to darken, the happy moments fading into the background as the accident looms closer in my mind. I try to hold on to the good times, the times when Will was free and happy, before everything changed. But the weight of what's happened now, the reality of her being gone, pulls me back into the present, into the crushing grief that's settled in my chest like a stone.

Nick is still talking, but his voice is distant, almost drowned out by the ache inside me. I stare at the wall we're parked next to, trying to process it all, trying to hold on to the memories of who my sister was before everything fell apart. But it's hard. The pain is too fresh, too overwhelming, and all I can do is sit here, lost in the past, wishing I could go back to those moments when we were both so young, so full of hope, and nothing could touch us.

The crematorium is quiet, the air thick with the scent of burning wood that clings to everything, filling my nostrils as I step out of the car. Nick moves ahead of me, cradling Will's body in his arms with a tenderness that feels out of place in a world so dark. I follow him in silence, my legs carrying me forward even though I feel disconnected from everything, like I'm walking through a fog.

We enter the back room, the light dim and cold, reflecting off the stone walls that seem to close in around us. The air is heavy, oppressive, but he moves with purpose, his face set in that unreadable mask. An attendant appears, bowing slightly as he greets Nick, his words laced with respect, even deference. It's clear he knows who Nick is—what he is—and he treats him with the cautious reverence that people like him command.

The attendant offers his services, speaking in hushed tones, but I barely register the conversation. I'm too focused on Will, on the stillness of her form wrapped in the soft white fabric.

I don't know how long I sit on the cold stone floor, my back pressed against the wall as I stroke my sister's hair, but it feels like hours. Time seems to stretch and warp, each second dragging out into an eternity. My fingers move automatically, brushing through her locks like I used to when we were younger, back when things were simple and happy. But now, there's nothing—no tears, no pain. Just a vast, empty numbness that swallows everything.

Nick joins me after a while, lowering himself onto the floor beside me. He wraps his arm around my shoulders, pulling me close, trying to offer some comfort in the only way he knows how. But I don't respond, don't speak. I can't. There's nothing left to say, nothing that could make this any less real.

Instead, I begin to sing softly, my voice barely above a whisper as I cradle her head in my lap. The words come from deep within me, songs from our childhood, lullabies that our mom used to sing to us before bedtime. I sing them now, for Will, for myself—trying to fill the emptiness with something, anything, that could bring her back to me, even for a moment.

But the only sound is my voice, soft and broken, echoing off the cold stone walls. Nick holds me tighter, his presence solid and unyielding, but I can't bring myself to look at him. I just keep singing, my hand moving through Will's hair, wishing that I could hold on to these last moments before she's truly gone.

I can't do this. I just can't. The thought chokes me, but tears don't come. They're trapped, like everything else inside me—my grief, my rage, a scream that's got no voice.

"Carolina?" Ruby's voice cuts through the haze of my numbness. I look up, catching the red-rimmed gaze of my sister-in-law to be. "Oh God!" she cries as her eyes dart to Will. Her eyes are bloodshot, and I see the concern etched into her usually immaculate features. It's a stark reminder that I'm supposed to feel something, anything, but there's only emptiness where my heart should be.

"Hey," I manage, my voice sounding foreign to my own ears—flat, lifeless.

"Nick told me what you wanted. I've brought everything." She gestures to the suitcases behind her, her words trailing off as if she's unsure how to navigate this conversation.

"Thank you," I reply robotically.

"What do you want to do with—"

"Everything burns," I say, interrupting Nick, my tone leaving no room for debate. It's not a request; it's an order.

There's a flicker of surprise in Ruby's eyes. "Are you sure you don't want to go through—" she starts, but I cut her off.

"Everything, Ruby," I interrupt, my voice sharper than I intend. "Willow's gone. What's left is just… stuff."

The scent of burning wood lingers in the air, wrapping around me like a shroud. Ruby moves to the suitcases, opening them one by one and emptying their contents onto the cold stone floor without another word. Clothes, books, the small trinkets of Willow's life—they all make a pile that seems so insignificant now.

I notice the attendant slinking closer, careful not to look at me as he carefully sorts through Will's things. He makes a small pile where he places a few things such as beauty and hygiene products. "I'm sorry, but we can't—"

"Burn them," I insist.

"But—"

Nick clears his throat. "She said to burn it all, so you'll fucking burn it all."

The man nods, and I'm irrationally angry at him for making me repeat myself. But my anger dissipates as he scrambles to put all of Will's things back in the suitcases, disappearing with them once they're full again.

When it's time, Nick carries Will's body again, and I hold her hand for as long as I can.

I stand frozen, my breath catching in my throat as the attendant opens the heavy metal door of the cremator. The heat rushes out, hitting me like a wave, but I barely notice it. My eyes are locked on the dark, gaping mouth of the machine, where flames flicker inside, waiting to consume everything.

Moving forward, Nick cradles Will's body in his arms with a gentleness that makes my chest tighten. The suitcases are already placed in the metal tray used for the cremation, so Nick carefully places Willow on top of her makeshift pyre. The tray glides out smoothly, almost silently, as if this is just another routine task for the machine.

I step closer, feeling the heat intensify as I reach out to touch her one last time. My fingers brush against her hair, and I want to scream, to tear her away from this horrible place, but I can't. I have to let her go.

Nick looks at me, his eyes searching mine for something, maybe permission, maybe strength, but I have none to give. I nod, just once, and he gently pushes the tray into the cremator.

The heavy door of the cremation chamber clanks shut, sealing Will's body from view. The roar of the flames is immediate, voracious, and something inside me cringes at their hunger. I stand motionless, my gaze fixed on the steel door as if I could still see her through it. There's a smell in the air that's not quite burning wood, not quite anything I can name—a scent that will haunt me forever.

"Carolina," Nicklas murmurs beside me. His hand finds mine, a lifeline amidst this storm of sorrow, but my fingers are ice despite his warmth. I don't look at him, I can't. My eyes remain locked on where my sister lies beyond sight, being reduced to ashes while memories play hide and seek in my mind.

We're six and twelve, running through a field dusted with snow, our laughter crystallizing in the frigid air. Willow tumbles, her small frame swallowed by a drift, and I dive after her. We're angels in the snow, wings flapping wildly, the cold forgotten for the joy of just being us—alive and together.

"Though I walk through the valley of the shadow of death, I will fear no evil: for thou art with me." I whisper the scripture, the words spilling out like a balm over the crackle of destruction.

That verse is—*was*—Will's favorite. At her insistence, we recited it at our dad's funeral, and again at Mom's. So it seems only right that I speak the words now.

Nick squeezes my hand, grounding me to the present, to this new… not-funeral where the verse belongs to Will herself. "Though I walk through the valley of the shadow of death, I will fear no evil: for thou art with me," he repeats, his voice low and reverent.

Ruby also echoes the verse, her head bowed.

A tear betrays me, carving a hot path down my frozen cheek. I'm a statue, an effigy of loss, yet that single tear feels like a fissure in a dam holding back an ocean of grief.

As the fire dances, my thoughts drift to Will—the gap in our years never mattered to us. She was more than a little sister; she was my confidante, my charge, my reason to keep going when life got too tough to bear. And now, with her ashes and these flames, I'm unmoored, adrift in a sea of grief I can't even begin to navigate.

"Goodbye, my little angel," I breathe out, my voice catching on a sob I refuse to release. I imagine her bright eyes, her smile that never dimmed, not after the accident, not ever. She was pure light—a light that's now fading into embers and smoke.

I know I have to find a way to live in a world without her. But not today. Today, I burn with her.

Through the hours it takes to cremate Will's body, and the subsequent waiting time for everything to cool back down, Nick remains at my side. His hand never leaves mine. We don't talk, but our connection transcends words; I know he's here for me, that he loves me just as much as I love him.

Even though I can't feel the grief I know is locked down inside me, his love reaches me, and I know I'd crumble without it.

The attendant appears, his movements somber as he respectfully gathers what remains of Willow into a simple urn. He hands it to me; it's heavier than I expect, and suddenly, the weight of her life, its abrupt end, bears down on me. My arms tighten around the vessel as if I could shield it, protect it one last time.

"Are you ready?" Nicklas asks softly, guiding me toward the exit. His touch is gentle, but there's an unwavering strength in him, a rock amidst my storm.

"Never," I answer truthfully. But we walk out together, the urn cradled in my arms like a fragile hope.

Inside the bulletproof vehicle, the silence hangs thick, only the hum of the engine and the faint whisper of tires on pavement breaking it. Ruby turns to me, her green eyes searching for something in my eyes. "What do you want to do with the ashes?" she asks, her voice is careful as though she thinks her question is going to make me shatter.

No words can do that to me, I'm already in as many pieces as one can be.

"When she was six, Will once told me she wanted to be buried with the mermaids in the Hudson River," I say, my voice a ghost of itself.

A sad smile touches Ruby's lips, and even Nick lets out a quiet chuckle. It's a bleak sort of humor we share, but it's something—a flicker in the darkness.

"Mermaids, huh?" he says, meeting my gaze in the rearview mirror. There's warmth there, an ember that might ignite if I reach for it.

I momentarily wonder where the nameless security guy is, but as I notice a car driving right behind us, I guess I have my answer.

"Yep. She said she'd race them and win every time." I clutch the urn a little tighter, imagining Willow's triumphant laughter echoing through the currents of the river.

"Then that's where we'll go," he declares, his voice firm yet tender.

One day, I think, one day I won't be this hollow shell. One day, I'll feel again, laugh again. And maybe, just maybe, Nicklas will be there beside me, his possessive nature not a cage but a cocoon from which I'll emerge, reborn. But for now, I hold on to the urn, my sister's final wish, and the stories of mermaids dancing in the depths of the Hudson River.

The Hudson stretches before me, a wide expanse of water that sparkles even under the gray December sky. I'm standing at the edge of a high overlook, the railing cool and unyielding beneath my hands. The urn is heavy in my grip, a weight I'm both reluctant and desperate to release.

"Are you ready?" Nick asks from beside me, his body a solid presence in a world that feels like it's fracturing.

I nod, not trusting my voice. The wind whips around us, carrying the scent of salt and city grime, an odd mixture that somehow fits this moment perfectly. My heart thuds painfully against my ribs, each beat a staccato reminder of what I'm about to do.

"Whenever you're ready, Carolina," he murmurs, and there's a reverence in his tone that tugs at something inside me—a raw ache that's been growing since the flames claimed my sister.

Taking a deep breath, I unscrew the lid of the urn. The ashes are lighter than I expect, a soft gray dust that looks nothing like the vibrant girl Will once was. Memories flood me—her laughter, her stubbornness, her dreams—and for a moment, I'm drowning in them, the pain sharp and all-consuming.

"Goodbye, Will," I whisper, my voice breaking on her name. "Go find your mermaids."

With a flick of my wrists, I tilt the urn. Ashes cascade into the wind, a cloud of what was once life, now set free over the churning waters below. Some part of me expects to feel closure, but there's only emptiness, a hollow space where my sister used to be.

"Beautiful," Nick says softly, and when I glance at him, there's a sheen of moisture in his eyes that mirrors my own unshed tears. His hand finds mine, fingers intertwining as if he knows I need to be anchored to something, anything.

"Goodbye, Willow," Ruby echoes hoarsely.

As I look at Ruby, I feel like I should say something. Will considered her a friend, which is all I need to know there's more to the Mafia princess than what meets the eye. I consider striking up a conversation, but then I decide against it. I don't bear her any ill will, I just... don't care about her. I don't mean it in a cruel way. There's no underhandedness to my thoughts, it just is.

We stand together, watching the last of the ashes disappear into the river's embrace. It's a raw, intimate moment, shared grief that binds us tighter more than any physical chain could. And despite the void inside me, despite the desolation, I can't help but feel a perverse gratitude for Nicklas' presence, for his silent strength.

CHAPTER 30

The Santa

The silence engulfing us as I usher my hellcat through the door to the apartment is a living thing, pulsing with sorrow. She doesn't speak; her eyes are glassy, haunted orbs. I can see the weight of grief pressing down on her shoulders.

"Let's get you to bed," I murmur, my voice roughened by the day's emotion. It's an unspoken command, and she merely nods, allowing me to guide her to our room.

I shuffle her over to the bed where she obediently sits down. While I undress her, she looks straight ahead; not at me or anything specific. I get the sense that she isn't even seeing what's in front of her.

As I undress her, she lifts her arms when I ask for it, her hips when I need to pull her pants down. But other than that, she's completely immovable. Seeing her like this breaks my damn heart. This isn't the Carolina I've come to know and love, this… this is an imposter; her shadow-self.

Once she's tucked under the duvet, her breaths evening out in the dim light, I leave her side. The need to act—to do something—is burning through my veins. Willow's cremation was supposed to offer closure, but instead, it's opened a festering wound. Then again, who can get closure in the span of just mere hours?

Fuck!

My study awaits, shrouded in shadows. I don't bother with lights. Instead, I allow the darkness to envelop me, a mirror to the turmoil churning within. Reports lay scattered across the desk, and I pick through them with cold precision, the lights coming from the windows allow me to read each paper carefully.

My mind races; every scenario it conjures up is more brutal than the last. Someone dared to aim at my inner circle, at my family. They'll regret it.

I'm pacing the study, a predator caged by his own fury, when Marco slips through the door, a specter against the shadows. His presence is both a balm and an agitator to my frayed nerves. "Nicklas," he begins, his voice as steady as ever, "we've taken care of the loose ends."

Flicking the light on, I snap, "I want details." My eyes are fixed on the city's lights that dare twinkle, as if mocking me.

"The police are already in our pocket, so we know they won't dig deep. The restaurant staff have been handled—memories erased with crisp bills. Cameras, phones, anything that could have caught something, it's all ash now," Marco reports methodically.

"Good." My jaw clenches, the simmering anger threatening to boil over. I trust Marco, but trust isn't enough. Not this time.

Willow was innocence personified, and her death screams for vengeance. Carolina will want it—demand it. And I, well, I want to give her anything her now stained heart desires.

"Find out who did this," I order, my voice low, lethal. "I don't care how deep you have to go or whose blood needs spilling. They took one of mine. I want them brought to me."

Marco nods once, the ghost of a grim smile touching his lips. He knows. There's no line I won't cross, not anymore. "I'll give the order," he says before slipping back into the night from whence he came.

"And call the three," I shout after him.

It doesn't take long before my most trusted men file in; Lee, Dominic, and Sergei. They're stone-faced, ready for war, and hungry for retribution. The air crackles with tension as they wait for my command.

"Someone made the mistake of thinking they can touch what's mine," I begin, voice ice-cold, every word a sharpened knife. "Willow Sterling's death wasn't just a tragedy; it was a message. And I intend to reply in kind."

They stand rigid, their silence a testament to their readiness.

"Pull in every favor. Crack open every secret. No mercy. We find who's behind this, and we end them," I continue, my resolve steel-hard. "But I want them alive."

"Understood," Lee says, his hand already on his gun.

"Nobody fucks with the Knights," Dominic adds, his dark eyes gleaming with fury.

"Blood will answer blood," Sergei vows, his Russian accent thickening his promise.

"Get to work," I dismiss them, each man dissipating like wraiths on a mission of death.

The moment I'm alone, I allow myself a single breath, letting the beast of rage rest, but only for a heartbeat. Carolina's face flashes across my vision, her grief-stricken eyes fueling my resolve. Whoever did this didn't just aim at Willow. They aimed at us.

I move over to the window, looking at the city as it sprawls out before me, a network of shadows and secrets that belong to me. It's a chessboard, and I am the king—Knight—poised for a deadly game.

My fingers drum against the window, the glass as cold and unyielding as my resolve. I'm missing something, I know I am. There's more to all of this, I can feel it in my very marrow. It's like a jigsaw puzzle where you know what piece is missing, even where it fits. Yet you don't know exactly what's on it.

What the hell am I missing?

The harder I try to think about it, the more my thoughts scatter. Mental images of blood and bullets assault me, but the more I try to latch on to each thought, the farther away it seems.

Carolina's face flashes in my mind, her eyes haunted with grief that cuts deeper than any blade I own. That pain—her pain—fans the flames of my rage, igniting a dark promise within me.

I will rip apart every alley, every high rise, every hidden corner until

I unearth the bastard who dared to shatter her world.

My thoughts are a whirlwind, but suddenly they screech to a halt; I need her. The need to see her, to ensure she's safe and here and mine, propels me from the room, and I find myself moving through the apartment with purpose.

The bedroom door creaks open, and it's like walking into a void. Empty. She's not here. Panic claws at my chest, a fierce growl building inside me. I charge from room to room, my heart a thunderous beat in my ears until I find her.

I chuckle to myself when I finally find her; she's lying naked on the marital bed, an ethereal figure bathed in the dim light. My breath catches; she's so vulnerable, so beautiful it hurts to look at her. Her blonde hair fans out across the pillow like a halo, her soft curves illuminated by the moonlight seeping through the windows.

I can't move, can't think. All I can do is watch her sleep, feel the possessive pull tighten around my soul. My gaze roams over her, protective instincts warring with a darker, more obsessive yearning.

Fuck, I'm torn between the urge to shield her from the world and the desire to claim every inch of her. "Mine," I whisper to the silence, a vow that is both promise and curse.

A curse because I suspect her sister is dead because of me, because I forced her into my life. Even as I think that, I regret nothing. Does that make me a cold asshole? Maybe. A ruthless knight, definitely. But I'm her Knight, and I proudly carry the scars on my chest to prove it.

Carolina stirs, a soft sigh escaping her lips, and I realize this moment is a crossroads between madness and salvation. I'll choose her every time, even if it means painting New York red with vengeance. Because she's the beacon guiding me through the darkness, the reason my world still has any light left in it.

"Nick?" Her voice is a whisper in the dark, laden with need. She's awake now, gaze heavy-lidded but focused on me with an intensity that burns through my resolve.

"Go back to sleep," I say, attempting to maintain control over my urges, but my tone is laced with the dangerous edge of a man on the brink. "I'm here."

"Make me feel, Nick. Please." Her plea scrapes against my restraint. Her tone is pure desperation; raw and painful.

I close the distance between us in two strides, my hands framing her face. "You want to drown out the pain?" I ask, searching her eyes for any sign of hesitation.

"I need you to make me feel," she repeats, and I'm undone.

As quickly as possible, I get rid of my clothes before joining her on the bed. She pulls me down to her, and our lips meet in a collision of shared agony and yearning.

Her fingers trail fire across my inked skin, drawing me further into the depths where only she and I exist. I groan as she begins stroking my rigid cock, pumping it hard and fast. "Carolina!"

"Touch me," she begs. "Please, Nick. I need… I need to feel something."

Deepening the kiss, I push my hand between her legs, cupping her cunt. She isn't wet yet, which tells me more than anything just how fucked her mind must be. I roll her clit slowly with two fingers, and I can feel the exact moment she becomes turned on.

Throwing her head back, she moans loudly, her hips chasing my hand as I pull back. "Don't stop," she pouts.

"Never," I vow as I kiss my way down her body, lavishing each tit in nips, licks, and bites before I continue my journey south.

I don't stop until I'm inhaling her arousal and her small landing strip grazes my nose. Her breath hitches in anticipation. I want to take my time with her, to make this about more than just the physical. My hellcat wants to *feel,* and I want her to feel me *everywhere.*

As I bury my head in her cunt, sucking her clit between my teeth, I feel the tension in her body, the way she's holding on to something, and I know it's more than just grief. It's everything—everything she's been through, everything she's feeling or stopping herself from feeling.

She lifts her hips, urging me on, but I'm going to do this at my pace. So I place my hand on her pubic bone, pressing down so she can't move. "Feel me," I rasp. "Feel what I do to you." I inhale deeply, taking in the faint scent of her, something uniquely hers, something that always drives me wild.

I flatten my tongue, eagerly licking the length of her cunt, tasting her cream. Then harden my tongue, focusing on her needy nub while pushing two fingers into her slick channel, moving them in and out so slowly I know it's driving her insane.

"Nick!" she complains, her fingers tangling in my hair, and I can feel the shift in her, the way she's letting go, giving herself over to the moment.

I focus on her entirely; the way she tastes, the way she moves, and every little sound she makes. I want her to let go of the dark thoughts in her head, even if it's just for a little while.

"Come for me, Hellcat," I rasp, moving my fingers in and out of her faster, adding more pressure to her bud.

Her feet dig into the mattress beneath us, and she tightens her hold on my hair, pulling me closer to her opening. "More," she demands. "I need… I need… Oh, fuck! Nick!"

I continue to lick and finger her through her orgasm, curling my fingers inside her so I hit the spot that has her mewling incoherently. I don't stop until her trembles and moans lessen, and then I greedily thrust my tongue into her opening so I can drink her nectar.

"Fuck," I curse as I rut into the mattress like a feral animal. I can feel the wet stain underneath me, but I don't fucking care. Not when I have my mouth on her sex and my tongue inside her cunt.

As she pants, trying to get her breathing under control, I lick her pretty cunt one more time before I make my way up her body, biting each of her nipples before I lie down next to her and claim her lips.

I fucking love knowing she's tasting herself, so I stroke her tongue harder, faster. The kiss is scorching. Grabbing her thigh, I throw it over my hip, angling myself so the tip of my cock rubs between her drenched folds.

"Are you ready for me?" I groan.

"Yes!" she moans. "Fill me with your big cock, Nick."

Entering her, slow and deep, I watch as she unravels before me. A gasp escapes her, and it's the most beautiful sound I've ever heard. My name falls from her lips like a benediction, fueling my desire to worship her.

Once I'm all the way inside her, I stay there for a moment, not moving until she's ready. Or at least that was my intention. But my hellcat rakes her nails down my back, urging me to move, and I oblige with a hunger that matches hers.

She cants her hips, meeting me thrust for thrust. I'm so deep inside her that I can barely stand it. My head is resting in the crook of her neck, and I can't resist biting the soft skin, which draws a guttural moan from her.

"Yes! That's it… hurt me," she mewls.

I continue to fuck her as I move my head back, looking into her blue eyes. "What do you want me to do?" I ask. "Use your words, Carolina. There's nothing I won't do for you. All you have to do is tell me."

Her eyes widen slightly. "I think…" Trailing off, she licks her lips. "I want you to cut me."

I wasn't expecting that, but I'm not dumb enough to question her. If this is what she wants, I'm the luckiest guy in the fucking world. There's nothing I want more than to see my hellcat bleed for me. As if to prove my point, my cock jerks, becoming impossibly harder inside her.

"Look at me," I command. Her eyes snap to mine, and there's a silent exchange of vows in that gaze. Normally, no words are needed when our bodies speak volumes, but I need to make sure she knows what she's asking me for. "How do you want me to cut you?"

Her brows furrow, creating a small divot between them as she thinks it through. "I want… umm, I don't know. I just… I came in here because I was dreaming about it when I was alone in our bed, and I woke up so wet I wanted to try it for real."

Before I can say anything, she reaches underneath the pillow, pulling out the knife I used to carve her initials into my chest. She must have found it in the drawer I hid it in after cleaning it.

"And I want you to use this."

I take the knife from her, holding it up in the air so the blade glints in the light. "And you're sure?" I ask, thrusting into her again.

"Yes," she sighs needily. "Beyond sure."

"Where do you want my cut?" I rasp. I let the tip of the knife glide over the swell of her tit. "Here?" I move it to her cleavage. "Or here?"

Then I trail it down her body to the place just above her hip bone. "Or maybe you imagined it more like here?"

The sound she makes is like a purr, reminding me why all my names for her are of the feline variety. "Yes. There." She wiggles her hips, pushing back against the knife.

I make the first cut. It's shallow, more symbolic than anything, but it elicits a sharp intake of breath from her. The sight of crimson on her porcelain skin is intoxicating, pushing me further. I cut her on the other side.

"Are you *feeling* this?" I groan, pausing so I can thrust into her once, twice… five times.

"Mhmm," she confirms with a moan. "I feel you everywhere."

Without pulling out of her, I twist us so she's on her back and I'm positioned between her spread legs, hovering above her. "Do you want more?" I ask, my voice husky.

She winds her legs around me, digging her heels into my ass to get me deeper in her greedy cunt. "I want everything you have to give," she pants. She gyrates her hips and bucks, fucking herself on me.

I grip the knife tighter, letting the tip skim the area between her tits before adding more pressure, watching as her blood rushes to the surface of her split skin. Needing to taste the red essence, I lean down, licking the length of the cut. I moan; it's a guttural sound, as the coppery taste explodes on my tongue.

"Fuck!" I throw the knife to the side, hearing it clang against the floor. "I need to fuck you. Hard."

Her eyes are dazed as she looks up at me. Lifting her hand, she runs her thumb across my lips, and when I look down, there's a bead of blood on the tip. I close my mouth around her digit while I mercilessly slam into her, and bite the soft skin.

Then I claim her lips; her tongue delves into my mouth, our saliva mixing with her blood. The taste is potently delicious, spurring me on further. I feel like a man possessed as I piston my hips. The only sound in the room is our heavy breathing and our skin slapping together over and fucking over.

"Hellcat," I groan out, feeling the familiar coil of heat in my abdomen. I quicken the pace, chasing the edge with her. "My cock is fucking perfect for breeding you. Can you feel how thick and swollen I am? Just. For. You!"

"Nick… I'm—"

I press her thighs up to her shoulders, fucking her even deeper than before. Her moans intensify as she clenches around me. Leaning back, I admire the sight of my hardness sliding in and out of her tight heat.

"Come on my cock," I command, and she does, her body surrendering to the onslaught of pleasure. She comes so hard, squirting, that it feels like her body is both trying to push me out and suck me in deeper.

"Oh, Hellcat, you're so fucking perfect. Your cunt was made for me," I groan, loving the sensation of all the wetness she's expelling. "Are you ready for my cum?"

"Yes!" she screams, still contracting around me.

I climax so hard my vision distorts. My cum is flooding her drenched channel, and I keep my cock deep inside her, making sure not a drop of me is spilling out.

We're a tangle of limbs and soaked sheets, the coppery scent of blood lingering in the air. In this moment, boundaries cease to exist. We are one, bound by shared scars and a love forged in the darkest corners of our souls.

CHAPTER 31

The Santa

Sleep eludes me as the hours trickle by, and although I feel like I should get up and do something, I can't bring myself to leave Carolina. She's fast asleep in my arms, snoring softly.

When she first fell asleep, she was tossing and turning and whimpering like she was stuck in a nightmare of sorts. But for the past couple of hours her breathing has evened out, and she seems peaceful in her sleep.

Not for the first time, I hear a noise that seems out of place, but when I check my phone, there's no update from Marco or any of the others. It's probably just my imagination playing tricks on me.

As much as I hate doing it, I untangle myself from Carolina's sleeping form and shrug on my clothes. Then I leave the room as quietly as possible. The need to do something to find whoever is really behind Willow's death is stronger than my need to stay with my hellcat.

Though I haven't told her that I suspect someone else is pulling the strings, I want to find the fucking puppeteer. Not just because no one crosses me and lives, but also because I'm eager to give her the gift of closure, of knowing all ends have been tied.

Walking through the dark halls of my home, I run my hand down

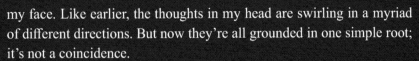

my face. Like earlier, the thoughts in my head are swirling in a myriad of different directions. But now they're all grounded in one simple root; it's not a coincidence.

The ambush on Jack and then shooting Willow…

One might be a coincidence but two is a pattern.

The reports in my study don't offer any more info than they did earlier, but something gnaws at my gut. I feel as though the answer is right in front of me, yet I'm *still* not seeing it clearly. With a final glance at the papers that don't offer any answers, I head for the kitchen, needing something to drink.

Padding soundlessly down the hallway, I navigate the familiar shadows of my home. The kitchen's just ahead, its appliances gleaming faintly in the moonlight filtering through the windows. I reach for a glass, filling it with water from the fridge. It's when I turn, sipping the cool liquid, that my world tilts.

Marco, my right-hand man, lies sprawled on the tiles. Unconscious or worse. The glass slips from my grasp, shattering against the floor, splintering like the calm before the storm.

"Shit." My voice comes out in a snarl.

Adrenaline surges as I kneel beside him, checking for a pulse. It's there, weak but steady. No time to figure out what happened—there's only one thought that consumes me; Carolina. I spring back through the hallways, every second stretching into an eternity. She's alone, unprotected. My chest tightens, muscles coil ready to strike at anything that threatens her safety.

Bursting into the room, the sight that greets me ignites a primal rage within my veins. An intruder stands over the marital bed, a shadow with malicious intent, while my hellcat sleeps, oblivious to the danger looming over her.

"Get away from her!" The words come out as a growl. I launch myself at the bastard, tackle him mid-air. We crash to the ground, a tangle of limbs and fury. His surprise is to my advantage.

I'm a dark storm of fury as I pin the intruder to the ground, my hands itching to end his pathetic life. Every muscle in my body screams for vengeance, but there's something I need more than his blood—answers.

"Who sent you?" My voice is a blade, sharp and deadly.

"Nick…" Carolina's voice quivers behind me, but it steadies into something harder, colder. I don't turn to look at her; I can't risk losing my focus on this bastard beneath me.

"Tell me!" I demand, pushing the pressure point under his jaw with ruthless precision, promising silent death if he doesn't comply.

"Okay! Okay!" He chokes out the words, eyes wild with fear. "It was Caspian!"

The name slices through me like ice, the betrayal by my own flesh and blood igniting a firestorm inside my chest. "Caspian? My dad?" I growl, disbelief warring with a rage that threatens to consume everything in its path.

I sense Carolina moving behind me, hopefully she's covering herself up. Not that this fucker will survive the night, but that doesn't mean I want him seeing what's *mine*. That fucking settles it. I squeeze tighter around his throat, restricting his air until he becomes unconscious. Then, just for the hell of it, I kick him hard in the side, hearing a rib or two break.

Spinning around, I look at the love of my life, who has wrapped the sheet around her naked form. "Get dressed," I bark. When she arches an eyebrow, I soften my voice and add, "Please."

I fucking marvel when a smile spreads on her face. This woman has been my rock in the hospital, passed the family test with flying colors, and then been to hell and back, all of it happening within a span of three days.

Yet, she fucking smiles.

I thought I knew what strength was before knowing her, but now I know that isn't true. She's strength personified, and I'm lucky to even be in her presence. While I ponder that, I drag the intruder into the kitchen, which is closer than the room I usually reserve for torturing people.

I have him halfway onto the table when Carolina joins me, now dressed in a pair of black jeans, a tight black long-sleeved shirt, and knee-high boots. She looks more like someone that's about to step onto the catwalk than watch while I torture the truth out of a stranger.

"I'm ready," she announces as she finishes braiding her long hair.

Her blue eyes flash with barely contained anger, and I fucking love that she's no longer cold and distant.

"Whatever for?" I question with a wry smile. "You do know there's no dress code for torture, right?"

"Yeah, but…" Pausing, she rolls her eyes. "I figured we might have to leave to do… I don't know. Chase… someone? And I wanted to be prepared."

I haul the intruder all the way onto the table. "Fair enough," I agree, which it is. Not only has she passed her test, she's the one he tried to attack. If my woman wants to see him burn, or chase him just for fun, I'll give that to her.

"What can I do to help?" she asks, and when I ask her to go to my study and get some rope, she practically runs out of here.

The man is still out for the count when she returns, and while I ask her to go check on Marco, I tie the man to the dining table. It's not exactly savory, but I don't care.

As soon as he's secure, I join Carolina who's pulling Marco into a sitting position. He stirs, and before even opening his eyes, his hand shoots out toward her. "Marco!" I growl, batting the limb away.

"Hey big guy," she coos—fucking coos—ignoring my attempt at shielding her behind me. "It's just me. Well, us. Me and Nick." She continues to ramble on, but it seems to help.

Marco groans and lowers his hand. His eyes slowly open, and I see the exact moment he registers it's just us. "Where is he?" he growls. "The fucking coward attacked me from behind." He rubs at the back of his head.

Carolina hisses, "He attacked you from behind?" sounding incredibly offended on Marco's behalf.

While she gets up and pours some water for Marco, I catch him up on what happened; how I was getting a drink, and then that the intruder went straight for Carolina. "I don't get how the hell he got in," I finish.

Marco shakes his head. "The alarm never went off, and he didn't use the elevator."

Shaking my head, I replay the intruder's words over and over in my head. Yeah, even if it wasn't my dad, it was an insider. It's one thing to scale the fucking outside walls and climb the building unseen, it's an entirely different matter to know where the bedrooms in my home are.

"He said my dad's behind it," I growl, tasting the words and damnit if it doesn't sound right.

"Why?" Marco questions, taking the water from her outstretched hand. "Why would he leave you in charge just to—"

We're interrupted as the intruder groans, and as one, all three of us turn to watch his eyes flutter open. Next, is my favorite part; watching his confusion turn into fear as he realizes he's bound tightly.

I get up first, pulling Carolina with me, taking her hand as we step closer to the table. Marco follows quietly, crossing his arms over his chest. He wobbles slightly, but it's not enough to negate the grim expression on his face.

"Only a coward attacks someone from behind," he growls menacingly.

I lean in closer, my voice low and dangerous. "You're going to tell me everything, aren't you?"

"P-please," the man cries. "I've already told you who sent me. W-what more do you want to know?"

Letting go of Carolina, I reach under the table, gripping one of the knives hidden on the underside of the surface. "I just told you," I sigh, showing him the knife in my hand. "I want to know everything."

The man's breath quickens, his eyes darting around the room as if searching for an escape. But there's none.

"It's only a matter of how much pain you want to endure before you talk," I say, my tone casual, as if we're discussing the weather. I press the knife against his cheek, just enough to draw a thin line of blood. He flinches, a whimper escaping his lips.

"Please… I'll talk," he gasps, his voice trembling. "It was Caspian… he gave the orders."

"That's old news," my hellcat hisses, taking a step closer. "How did you get in?"

"He… he told me how," the intruder stammers, his eyes wide with fear. "He knew the layout, the security details. Everything."

My grip on the knife tightens, rage boiling beneath the surface. Dad betrayed me. I should have known. I should have seen it coming. But instead, he's been plotting against me, pulling strings behind the scenes. And this man, this pathetic excuse for a killer, thought he could waltz into my home and take what's mine.

Pressing the knife deeper into his face, I elicit a pained cry from him. "Why?" I demand, my voice a low growl. "Why would he do this?"

"I don't know," the intruder sobs. "He just… he just said it had to be done. He didn't give us a reason. I swear."

"Us?" I echo. My blood runs hot and cold simultaneously; fury like I've never known before threatens to consume me whole.

"Yeah, man," he cries. "I wasn't the only one."

I'd already deduced as much. "Do you know who the others are?" I snarl.

"N-no."

"Call the three," I growl to Marco. "I want them here within the hour."

"Right away," Marco replies.

While he makes the call, I do my best to get my temper under control. But judging by the screams coming from the intruder, I'm not entirely successful. When I look down, I realize I'm still pressing the knife against his cheek, and that by now, I've pressed so hard the skin has split completely.

Removing the blade from his mangled skin, I glance over at Carolina. Her eyes are locked on the man, but her expression is unreadable. I know she's listening, taking in every word, but I can't tell what she's thinking.

I turn my attention back to the intruder, my anger simmering just below the surface. "You've made a grave mistake," I say, my voice deathly calm. "And so has my dad. You've both crossed a line that can never be uncrossed."

Finished with the call, Marco steps forward. "They'll be here," he confirms. "And I've arranged for double protection on Jack at the

B. LYBAEK

hospital."

I nod at the man who's always at the ready when I need him. "He's all yours," I say, flipping the knife and offering him the handle. "Have fun."

Marco grins. He knows what needs to be done. There's no room for mercy, no place for leniency. This man will suffer, and through his pain, we'll send a message. No one betrays me and walks away unscathed.

As Marco takes over, I step back, letting the reality of what's happened settle in. Dad's betrayal, the intruder's confession— everything has changed. This isn't just about power anymore. It's personal. And I'll make sure that he pays for what he's done.

"Wait!" Marco halts his movements at Carolina's demand. "Did Caspian make my sister a target?" she asks, her tone chillingly sharp.

The intruder whimpers as he shakes his head. "N-no. That was an accident."

"An accident?" I growl, already knowing what he's going to say next.

"We were sent there to kill Carolina, but—"

Carolina lets out an inhuman scream and pulls the knife from Marco's hand. Before I can react, she plunges it into the man's eye socket. She doesn't even flinch at the squelching sound, or the intruder's scream.

CHAPTER 32

The Santa

The elevator ride down to the garage is steeped in tension, the silence so thick it's almost suffocating. I grip the steering wheel hard, knuckles white against the leather, while my other hand holds Carolina's tightly. Her fingers tremble slightly, but she doesn't let go. Marco, Sergei, Lee, and Dominic are stone-faced, their eyes forward, minds set on the task ahead. This isn't just a mission. It's personal.

As we drive through the dark streets, the city blurs past us, the only sound is the low hum of the engine. I can feel the fury simmering inside me, a deadly calm before the storm. Dad's going to pay for his betrayal.

When we finally reach the estate, the air feels heavier, thick with the promise of violence. As soon as the car stops, we're out, weapons drawn. Carolina is right beside me, her eyes wide with fear but resolute. She isn't a fighter, not like the rest of us, but she holds the gun with a grip that betrays her determination. She's scared, but she's here. With me.

We kick down the front door, and hell explodes around us. Gunfire erupts, the sharp crack of bullets splitting the air. Men rush at us from every corner, Dad's soldiers, desperate to protect their boss. But they're no match for us. We move like a well-oiled machine, every action precise, every shot lethal.

Marco is a force of nature, his knife flashing as he cuts down two men with brutal efficiency. Sergei and Lee cover our flanks, a deadly combination of fists and bullets that leaves a trail of bodies in their wake. Dominic is right behind them, his shots precise, every pull of the trigger a death sentence.

I'm in the center of it all, the chaos fueling my rage, pushing me forward. A man lunges at me, but I'm faster. I block his attack, driving my elbow into his throat before slamming him into the wall. He crumples, and I'm already moving on, focused on the next threat. Carolina stays close, her breath ragged, eyes darting around as she tries to keep up.

Despite the fear in her eyes, she doesn't look away. Her blue eyes scan the room, taking in every movement as she holds the gun in her hand, her knuckles pale, but she's ready to do what needs to be done.

I do my best to protect her, making sure she doesn't need to use it. I refuse to let my world taint her beautiful soul more than it already has.

We fight our way through the mansion, every room a battlefield. The sound of gunfire and screams reverberates through the halls, the stench of blood and sweat filling the air. It's a warzone, but we thrive in this chaos. We were born for it.

A man charges at Carolina, his knife gleaming under the dim lights. She freezes, eyes wide, and my heart lurches. But before he can reach her, I'm there. I grab him, spinning him around. The fucker's quick, and before I can secure his arm, I feel the knife slice along my upper arm.

Roaring in anger more than pain, I grab hold of his arm, twisting it until I hear the satisfying crack of bone, then slam him to the ground. He doesn't get up.

"Nick… oh my God! Are you okay?" Carolina wraps her delicate fingers around the cut.

I already know it's shallow. "I'm fine," I promise. As I glance at her, she nods. "Just a scratch."

We push forward, the opposition thinning as we cut through Dad's men. Finally, we reach the basement door, reinforced but not enough to stop us. I kick it open, the wood splintering under the force, and we descend into the darkness.

The basement is colder, the air damp and stale. Shadows cling to the walls, but there's no mistaking the figure at the far end. Dad. He's standing with his back to us, hands clasped behind him, as if he's been waiting, expecting this confrontation.

The room is silent, the chaos above fading into a distant hum. I can feel the tension rolling off my men, their eyes locked on him, waiting for my signal.

"Dad," I say, my voice echoing in the dim space.

He turns slowly, a cruel smile on his lips, as if this is all some twisted game. "Nicklas," he replies, his tone almost mocking. "I knew you'd come, son."

The sight of him, the man who's caused so much pain, ignites a fire in me, hotter than before. This is it. The final confrontation. Carolina steps closer, her hand brushing against mine, a silent reminder that we're in this together.

Dad glances at her, his smile widening. "Ah, the lovely Carolina. I see you've dragged her into this too. How predictable."

The Breeder

Caspian's eyes land on me, and the way his lips curl into a sneer makes my skin crawl. His voice drips with disdain as he says my name, as if even acknowledging me is beneath him. I can't help it—I hiss in disgust, the sound escaping before I can stop it.

My hatred for this man, for everything he's done, burns hot inside me, almost choking me with its intensity. "Why?" I demand, my voice sharp, cutting through the thick air of the basement. "Why did you have Willow killed?"

Even though the guy back at the penthouse swore that my sister's death was an accident, I need to hear it from Caspian.

He tilts his head slightly, as if pondering how to best twist the proverbial knife. "Willow?" he repeats, mockingly. "Oh, that was an unfortunate mistake. The hit wasn't meant for your dear sister, Carolina. It was meant for you."

The words hit me like a blow to the chest, knocking the breath from my lungs. I stagger back, my hand instinctively clutching at my heart as if I can physically hold it together. My mind reels, struggling to process what he's saying.

Will... she died because of me. Because someone thought she was me. The room spins, and I feel like I'm falling, spiraling down into a pit of despair.

Caspian watches me, and I see a flicker of something dark and cruel in his eyes—a twisted satisfaction in my pain. "You were wearing that ridiculous hat, hiding your hair," he continues, his tone cold and devoid of any remorse. "My men were confused. They thought she was you. Fools, the lot of them."

His words are like shards of glass, slicing through me, leaving me raw and bleeding. Will's face flashes in my mind, her smile, her laughter—memories that are now tainted with the knowledge that she died because of me.

My sister, who was everything good and pure in my life, taken away because I didn't want to wash my hair. The guilt is overwhelming, a suffocating weight that crushes me from the inside out. I can't breathe, can't think, can't do anything but drown in this sea of sorrow and guilt.

"But really, Nicklas, this is all your fault." Caspian's voice drags me back to the present, and I force myself to focus on the man before me—the man responsible for all this pain. "You've been neglecting your duties. You've become pussy-whipped and weak." He spits out the last words like a curse.

My head snaps in Nicklas' direction, but I shouldn't have worried. His face is showing less emotion than a stone. I guess his dad's words aren't hitting the way they were intended.

"At first, I thought it was your brother's influence. So naturally, I tried to have him taken out. But like the damn pest he is, he proved

"What the fuck?" Nick roars.

Caspian nods. "First I had to find someone who could be the scapegoat for the theft. But when you insisted on going with Jack, I had to call off my best men. I couldn't risk losing my only worthy heir." He lets out a scathing laugh. "If I'd known just how unworthy you really were, I wouldn't have bothered."

I look at Nick, and the expression on his face tells me he knows exactly what Caspian is talking about. "You betrayed Jack and Sergei," Nick says, his tone cold.

"Indeed," Caspian replies easily. "Well, betrayal is such a distasteful word. I did what I had to."

"Why?" I ask when Nick looks like he's frozen, unable to ask more questions. "Why would you want Jack dead?"

Caspian shrugs like it's no big deal. "He's a waste of space, not worthy of the family name. When Nicklas went with Jack to catch the thief, I thought my cover would be blown. Thankfully, none of the people I hired sang. I guess that means they weren't entirely useless."

The fuck.

I don't know if Nick's dad can see the confusion on my face, or if he just likes hearing himself talk. Either way, he continues.

"After you left my home with your useless brother, I had to improvise. The guy I'd hired to take Jack out offered up one of his own men as a fall guy. That's the one you tortured for information, son. And I dare say I was impressed with your technique when I saw the body—"

"Why the fuck would you do any of this?" Nick roars.

When Caspian steps closer, Nick moves so his body is angled in front of mine. His dad's eyes narrow as he regards me with pure contempt. "It's all because of you, Carolina. You're nothing but a distraction, a pretty little thing that led my son astray. I had such high hopes for him, but he's thrown it all away for you." He sighs deeply.

As he stops talking it's quiet, the only sound to be heard is the shuffling of feet and our breathing.

"You ask why, Nicklas. But there's no why, only what had to be done. As I've already stated, you were neglecting your duties. Too busy playing house to take the Knight business seriously. Hell, you didn't even notice the Russian spy I planted in your territory. One of your men did."

He takes a deep breath, straightening to his full height and widens his stance.

"You trusted your useless brother with jobs he had no business even knowing about." Caspian turns his cold eyes on me again. "And because of *your* choices, your sister ended up as collateral damage."

His words are venomous, each one striking with deadly precision. I feel them sink into my skin, poisoning me with doubt and despair.

Nick lets out a vicious snarl. "Don't talk to her," he warns. Taking my hand, he squeezes it, and I think I fall even more in love with him at his show of support.

My heart breaks all over again, shattering into a thousand pieces. The pain is unbearable, but I can't let it show. Not here, not in front of this man. I force myself to stand tall, to keep my voice steady as I say, "You're wrong. Nick is stronger than you'll ever know. And he's not yours to control."

Caspian's laugh is cold and hollow, echoing off the walls of the basement. "You think you know him, girl? You don't. You're just a temporary distraction, something he'll toss aside when you're no longer useful."

I bite down on my lip to stop the tremble that threatens to expose my fear. Caspian's words are meant to hurt, to break me, but I refuse to let him win. "You're the one who's weak, Caspian," I spit, my voice trembling with suppressed emotion. Tempted as I am to lash out, to mention some of the things I read about this man in Sienna's diary, I keep my mouth shut.

His expression darkens, and for a moment, I see a flash of rage in his eyes. But then it's gone, replaced by that same cold indifference. "Believe what you want," he says dismissively. "It won't change anything. Nicklas will realize soon enough that you're nothing but a liability."

I clench my fists, squeezing Nick's hand harder with one hand while my nails dig into my palm on the other as I fight the urge to spew some truths of my own. But before I can say anything, Nick takes a step forward. His eyes are locked on his father, a storm brewing in their depths.

"Say what you want about me, Dad," he spits. "But to try to have your own son killed is low."

Caspian just shrugs. "He's weak as well. All my children turned out to be a disappointment."

"If all the apples are rotten, maybe it's the tree that's the problem," Nick volleys, his voice low and dangerous. "Not that it matters now. You're done." There's no hesitation, no doubt. He's made his decision.

A sneer twists Caspian's lips. "Finally ready to do what needs to be done, son?"

Nick doesn't respond. He raises the gun, his hand steady as he takes aim. For a moment, time seems to freeze. The air is thick with tension, the silence deafening. I can't breathe, can't move, as I watch the man I love prepare to pull the trigger.

Caspian smirks, his eyes gleaming with twisted pride. "Go on, then. Do it."

And then, in a heartbeat, it's over. The sound of the gunshot echoes through the room, loud and final. Caspian crumples to the ground, his lifeless body hitting the cold concrete with a dull thud.

The silence that follows is suffocating, heavy with the weight of what's just happened. My heart is pounding in my chest, my breath coming in shallow gasps. I can't take my eyes off his body, can't shake the feeling that something inside me has been irrevocably changed.

Nicklas lowers the gun, his hand trembling ever so slightly. Is it wrong that when he turns to me, I hope to see the same pain and turmoil I feel being reflected back at me?

Regardless, it isn't there. All I find in the depth of Nick's eyes is cold determination.

I collapse against him, burying my face in his chest, letting the tears I've been holding back finally fall. Willow is gone, and nothing will ever bring her back. But Caspian is gone too, silenced forever. And maybe, just maybe, we can finally start to heal.

CHAPTER 33

The Breeder

The early morning sun, weak and pale against the gray December sky, barely penetrates the thick clouds as we step out of Caspian's house. The cold air bites at my skin, but I barely notice it. Nick's hand grips mine tightly, his warmth a stark contrast to the numbness that's settled deep within me. I feel disconnected, like I'm floating outside my body, watching everything unfold as if it's happening to someone else.

Nick murmurs something to his men, and they nod, understanding the unspoken orders. They stay behind to deal with the aftermath—the blood, the bodies, the evidence of what we've done. But Nick doesn't linger. He's already guiding me toward the car, his arm wrapped protectively around my shoulders, pulling me close. I can feel the tension in his body, the anger simmering just beneath the surface. But all I can do is follow, my legs moving on autopilot, my mind too overwhelmed to process anything.

I'm a stone, unfeeling on the outside, but inside I'm drowning. Shock, grief, guilt—they all collide in a chaotic storm, each emotion clawing at me, threatening to tear me apart. Willow is gone, and it's my fault. Caspian's words echo in my mind, taunting me, reminding me that my sister died because of me. The realization is like a knife to the heart, twisting deeper with every breath I take.

Nick says nothing as we drive back to the penthouse. The silence between us is heavy, suffocating, but I'm grateful for it. I can't talk, can't even think straight. The city passes by in a blur, the bright lights of New York muted by the fog in my mind. Everything feels distant, unreal, like I'm trapped in a nightmare I can't wake up from.

When we finally reach the penthouse, Nick leads me inside, his movements gentle but firm. I follow him up the stairs, barely aware of my surroundings. The walls seem to close in on me, the familiar space suddenly foreign and suffocating. I'm shaking, but I can't stop. My hands are trembling uncontrollably, and I feel like I'm going to shatter into a million pieces.

Nick says nothing as he starts running a bath, the sound of water filling the tub almost soothing in the oppressive silence. He undresses me with a tenderness that makes my heart ache, his fingers brushing against my skin as he removes the blood-stained clothes.

I feel like I'm watching it all from a distance, detached from my own body. When he's done, he lifts me into the bath, the warm water enveloping me like a cocoon. I sink into it, the heat seeping into my bones, but it does nothing to thaw the coldness inside me.

He climbs in behind me, pulling me against his chest, his arms wrapping around me. I lean into him, my head resting on his shoulder, my eyes fixed on the water as it turns pink, then red, the blood from Caspian's men, and from Nick's cut, washing off my skin. The sight should horrify me, but I feel nothing. I'm too numb, too broken.

But then, slowly, the tears start to fall. At first, it's just a trickle, a few drops sliding down my cheeks. But then the dam breaks, and I'm sobbing uncontrollably, my body shaking with the force of it. The grief, the guilt, the pain—it all pours out of me, raw and unfiltered.

Nick holds me tighter, his hand stroking my hair, his lips pressing against my forehead in silent comfort.

"I'm sorry," I whisper, my voice choking with tears. "I'm so sorry, Nick…"

He doesn't say anything, just holds me as I cry, his presence grounding me, keeping me from spiraling completely into the darkness.

The water turns darker; the crimson spreading through the tub like a stain that can't be washed away. But Nick doesn't flinch, doesn't pull away. He stays with me, his strength my lifeline in this sea of despair.

When my sobs finally subside, and I'm too exhausted to cry anymore, he empties the tub and refills it with fresh water. He washes away the blood, the dirt, the remnants of the night's horrors, all while whispering soothing words I can't quite hear. I feel hollow, emptied out, but the numbness has lessened, replaced by a deep, bone-weary exhaustion.

Nick helps me out of the bath and dries me off with a towel, his hands gentle as they move over my skin. He leads me to our bed, the soft sheets welcoming me as I collapse onto them. I curl up, pulling the sheet over me, trying to find some semblance of warmth, of comfort. Nick slides in beside me, his body pressed against mine, his arm draped over my waist.

I close my eyes, the weight of the day finally dragging me under. Sleep takes me, but even in my dreams, I can't escape the memory of Caspian's cold eyes, or the knowledge that Willow died because of me. The darkness surrounds me, but Nick's presence is a faint light, keeping the worst of it at bay.

But for how long?

CHAPTER 34

The Santa

As soon as Carolina falls asleep, I sneak out of bed and get dressed again. After checking in with Marco, who stayed back to take care of the bodies, I make my way to my office and immediately open my laptop. While I look for my group chat with Jack and Ruby, I mentally go over how to tell them everything that's happened.

Try as I might, there's no rehearsing the words I'm about to spill. So instead of wasting my time doing that, I hit the call button.

The laptop screen glows with the familiar faces of Ruby and Jack. Ruby's in a small, dark room, her face lit only by the harsh glow of her phone. The shadows accentuate the bruise forming on her cheek, and my chest tightens with a cold, familiar rage. Jack, on the other hand, is propped up in a hospital bed, his skin pale even against the white sheets. Seeing them together on the screen, yet worlds apart, brings a tightness to my chest that I can't shake.

Jack is the first to speak, his voice weak but laced with the same cocky bravado he's had since we were kids. "You look like shit, Nick. Long night?"

I manage a smirk, but it doesn't reach my eyes. "You could say that. But it's over now."

Ruby leans forward slightly, and even in the dim light, I can see the guarded look in her eyes. She's waiting, always bracing herself for the worst. "What's over?"

Taking a deep breath, I steady myself. I've always been the one to protect them, to shield them from the worst of it. But there's no protecting them from this. "Dad's dead."

The silence that follows is heavy, almost suffocating. Ruby's face doesn't change much, but I see the flicker of something in her eyes—relief, maybe, or something darker. Jack, on the other hand, closes his eyes, a slow exhale escaping his lips, like he's been holding his breath for years.

"It was him," I continue, my voice cold and steady. "He's the reason you're in that hospital bed, Jack. The reason Willow's dead. He betrayed us all."

Jack's eyes snap open, a flash of anger crossing his face. "That son of a bitch. I knew he was twisted, but this…" He makes a sound of disgust. "Fucker!"

Ruby's voice cuts through the tension like a blade. "And you took care of it?"

I nod, meeting her gaze head-on. "I did what had to be done."

There's a beat of silence, and then Ruby leans back in her chair, crossing her arms. "Good. He deserved worse than whatever you did to him."

My eyes drift to the bruise on her cheek, the ugly mark marring her pale skin. The anger inside me flares again, hot and uncontrollable. I grit my teeth, the taste of bile rising in my throat. I don't want to push her, not when she's already on edge, but I can't let this go.

"Ruby…" I begin, my voice lower, more measured. "About your marriage. I can get you out, make it disappear. You don't have to stay with Michael."

Her eyes flash with something fierce, a strength that's always been there, just beneath the surface. But there's something else too—a defiance that I recognize all too well. "No, Nick. I'm done with handouts. I'll deal with my life on my own terms from now on."

Her words hit me harder than I expect. She's always been strong, but here's a finality in her voice, a determination that leaves no room for argument. It's a moment of clarity, a glimpse of the woman she's become—no longer the little sister I need to protect, but a force of her own.

I nod slowly, swallowing the urge to argue. "I respect that."

Jack shifts in his bed, wincing slightly as he adjusts the pillows behind him. His voice is quieter now, more thoughtful. "So, the old man finally paid the price. Guess the family curse got him too."

The Knight family superstition, the one that's haunted us since we were kids—three heirs to secure the future, because only one survives. It's a dark joke, one we've always half-believed, and now it feels more real than ever.

Jack grins, though it's a shadow of his usual smile. "Well, I guess I've already died once, so I'm in the clear."

"Don't joke about that," Ruby snaps, her voice sharper than usual. She's always hated the superstition, hated the idea that our fates were somehow cursed before we were even born.

Jack shrugs, but there's a sadness in his eyes that he can't hide. "Just trying to lighten the mood, sis."

Since my siblings aren't asking questions about what Dad did or didn't do, I decide not to elaborate. If they ask, I'll answer. But if not… why taint them?

I clear my throat, trying to shift the conversation away from the darkness that's settled over us. "There's something else we need to discuss. Dad's estate."

Ruby's eyes darken at the mention, her expression hardening. Jack just looks tired, like the mere thought of it drains him of what little energy he has left. I can't blame them. The estate is a place filled with nothing but bad memories and ghosts of the past.

"As the eldest, it all belongs to me now," I continue, the weight of tradition pressing down on my shoulders. "But I want your input."

"I don't want anything from that place," Ruby says quickly, her voice cold and final. "I don't care if you burn it to the ground."

Jack nods in agreement. "She's right, Nick. That place is cursed. There's nothing good there."

I knew they'd say that, but hearing it still stings. The estate is more than just a house—it's a symbol of everything we've inherited, for better or worse. But I also know that Carolina and I need to move in there. It's tradition, and in our world, tradition isn't something you can just ignore.

"I understand," I say quietly. "But Carolina and I... we'll have to move in. It's what's expected."

Ruby looks at me with a mixture of pity and anger. "You don't have to, Nick. You can break the cycle."

"Maybe," I reply, though the words feel hollow. "But some things are bigger than us. I'll figure out what to do with the place." I'll have to talk to Carolina about it later, figure out how we can turn that cursed place into something we can live with—if that's even possible.

The silence after our discussion about the estate is thick, laden with the unspoken weight of our shared history. We've always been bound by blood, by the legacy of the Knight family, but tonight, something's shifted. I can feel it, in the way Ruby's eyes flicker with a new resolve, in the way Jack seems more distant, more resigned.

Ruby is the first to break the silence. She adjusts her position in that dark room, the glow from her phone still casting shadows on her face. There's a subtle change in her posture, a confidence that wasn't there before. "Nick, you know, for the longest time, I've been running… from everything. But I'm tired of running. I've made my decision. I'm going to face my life, my way."

There's a knot in my chest that tightens with every word.

Though I've always done my best to protect my sister, I know I've fallen short many times. But now, she's stepping out on her own, and as much as it hurts, I know she needs to do this. "I understand, Ruby. Just know that I'm always here if you need me."

She smiles, but it's tinged with sadness. "I know. But it's time I stand on my own."

Jack shifts in his hospital bed, the lines of pain etched deep into his face. He's been through hell, and it shows. His voice is softer, more reflective than I've ever heard it. "I guess we all have our paths to walk. Just make sure you don't lose yourself along the way, Ruby. Don't let this world chew you up like it did Dad."

Her jaw tightens, and for a moment, I see a flicker of the old anger that used to drive her. But then she softens, her voice gentle but firm. "I won't, Jack. I'm not Dad, and I'm not going to let his mistakes define me."

Jack nods, and I can see the approval in his eyes, but it's laced with a bittersweet understanding. "Good. We've had enough of that."

There's a beat of silence, the three of us lost in our own thoughts, our own memories of what we've endured to get here. Being a Knight has always been a heavy burden, and tonight, it feels like we're finally starting to shed some of that weight.

But even as we find closure in these moments, there's an unspoken acknowledgment between us. We've been through too much together to walk away clean. We're all marked by the same blood, the same pain, and while we might be heading in different directions, those marks will always tie us back to each other, even if we never say it aloud.

Jack's voice breaks the silence again, but this time it's lighter, almost teasing. "You know, Nick, if you're moving into the old man's place, you better make sure you don't let it turn you into him."

I chuckle, but there's no real humor in it. "Don't worry about that. I've got Carolina to keep me in check."

Ruby's smile is small, but it's there. "She's good for you, Nick. Don't lose sight of that."

"I won't," I promise, and I mean it. Carolina's the one thing in this world I won't let slip through my fingers.

Another pause, this one longer, as if we're all searching for the right words to say. But nothing comes. There's nothing left to say, really. We've said our goodbyes, even if we haven't spoken them aloud.

"I'll check in on you, Jack," I say finally, my voice gruff. "But take care of yourself, okay? Don't rush getting back on your feet."

He smirks, though it doesn't reach his eyes. "Yeah, yeah. You know me, always taking it easy."

Ruby's voice is soft as she adds, "And Nick… take care of yourself, too. You've carried us all for so long. It's okay to let go a little."

I swallow hard, nodding once. "I'll try."

The call ends with a series of quiet goodbyes, and then the screen goes dark. The room feels emptier now, the silence heavier. We're all going our separate ways, and though we didn't say it, the truth is clear.

CHAPTER 35

The Breeder

Two days pass in a blur, and I barely move from the bed. My heart feels shattered, and every time I try to pick up the pieces, they slip through my fingers. The weight of grief, guilt, and Caspian's words crush me—*you're making Nick weak*. The last thing I ever wanted was to be a burden to him, to be the reason he falters.

Nick stays with me as much as he can, his presence both comforting and suffocating. Every time he's near, the guilt gnaws at me harder. Caspian's voice echoes in my mind, and I can't shake the feeling that I'm failing, that I'm dragging Nick down when he needs to be strong.

But finally, Nick's had enough. He comes to me with that determined look in his eyes, the one that leaves no room for argument. "Get up, Carolina. You need to get dressed."

There's no room for refusal. I drag myself out of bed, my limbs heavy as I pull on clothes that feel foreign against my skin. The warmth of his hand is steadying as he leads me out of the apartment, down to the car.

We drive in silence, the tension thick between us. I know where we're going before we arrive—Caspian's estate. The place that now belongs to Nick, the place that holds so many memories, none of them good.

Nick's voice breaks the quiet. "I spoke with Ruby and Jack. They don't want the estate. They have no interest in it." His eyes flicker to me as he continues, "But I need to know if you want to live here. We can make it our own. Wipe away the past, shape a new future."

As soon as we step inside, my mental images of pools of blood and bodies are put to shame. The house is clean, too clean, and the overwhelming smell of bleach wraps around me, making my nostrils flare.

Despite the scent, the air is heavy with history, with the ghosts of everything that happened here. I feel like I'm suffocating under the weight of it, but I force myself to keep moving, to keep looking.

We walk through the rooms, and I take in every detail. The dark, oppressive decor, the outdated furniture, the way the walls seem to close in on me. But as I walk, I start to see it differently. I imagine brighter colors, open spaces, a place that could be filled with warmth instead of the cold shadows of the past.

By the time we finish the tour in the basement where Nick killed his dad, something shifts inside me. I turn to the man who owns my heart, my voice steady for the first time in days. "Let's do it. Let's make this place ours. We can erase the old memories and create new ones."

Nick's relief is palpable. He nods, and together, we start to talk about what we could do—tearing down walls, bringing in light, making it modern, making it ours. It's the first time since everything happened that I feel a glimmer of hope, a spark of something better. Maybe, just maybe, we can take this place that was filled with so much pain and turn it into something new, something good.

"There's something we have to do first," I say, pulling on Nick's hand when he turns to walk back upstairs.

"What's that?" he asks, curiosity lilting his words. "If you want, we can destroy the basement, and—"

Shaking my head, I lick my lips. "No, that's not what I want." I tear on the buttons of my coat, throwing it to the side at the same time as I kick off my shoes. "I want to make it ours."

He smirks knowingly. "It's already ours, Hellcat," he deadpans.

I roll my eyes and pull my sweater over my head before hooking my thumbs into my pants, slowly pushing them down my legs. "Well, if you don't want to mark it with me, I'll just do it alone." I cup my heavy breasts, squeezing the flesh in my hands.

"Fuck no," he growls. Within seconds, he's on me, shoving me back against the wall. His lips claim mine in a hard kiss while he ruts against me. "All your orgasms are mine!"

I lick his tongue with mine, tugging at his hair as I deepen the kiss. I kiss him with an intensity that's so hot I'm almost surprised the basement isn't catching fire. "All yours," I reply before biting down on his bottom lip. I don't let go until the skin breaks, and he hisses when blood forms. "So stop holding back and give me some."

Pulling back, he lets out a surprised chuckle. "Holding back?" he questions, his dark gaze trailing over my naked body. "I think you need a reminder of your place, Hellcat."

I'm teetering on the edge of something reckless, something that screams danger in a way that sends shivers down my spine. The light of the basement reflects off the cold, intimidating walls, casting shadows that dance with our movements. I know what I want, need, even as my heart pounds against my ribcage.

"Do you need a reminder?" he asks, his voice a low growl tinged with a possessiveness that should frighten me, but instead ignites a fire deep inside me. It's a call to the wild part of my soul, the part that yearns for this man.

Without hesitance, I drop to my knees before him, gazing up into those dark eyes that see right through me. "I think I do," I purr.

My fingers work deftly, freeing him from the confines of his tailored pants. The air between us crackles with electricity as I wrap my lips around him, taking him deep.

"Fuck," he curses, threading his fingers through my blonde hair, guiding me with an unyielding grip. His hips push forward gently at first, then with more insistence. I revel in the feeling of him, hard and pulsing, the salty taste of his skin on my tongue. This is where I belong, here at his feet, worshiping him in the most intimate way.

"You're mine, Carolina," Nick rasps, his voice laced with dirty promises as he watches me with intense eyes. "All mine. I'll protect you, own you, in ways you can't even imagine."

A moan escapes me, vibrating around him, and I feel his body tense. There's pleasure in submission, in knowing I hold his ecstasy in my mouth, but there's also power here, in the way he surrenders to the sensation, in how he grows even harder.

"Good girl," he praises, his tone dripping with a toxic love that wraps around me like a vise. "Take me deeper, show me how much you want this. Show me you understand what it means to be mine."

His words are a spell, binding me to him, and I obey, pushing past my limits to accommodate him fully. I cup his balls, fondling them carefully while I let him fuck my mouth. The sounds he makes has my clit pulsating and my core clenching around nothing. I move one hand between my thighs and begin fingering myself.

"What did I just say?" he growls, and when I look up at him, his dark gaze is ablaze. "Your orgasms belong to me, Carolina. So get those fingers out of your cunt."

"But I—"

"Now!"

With a huff, I do as he says, secretly loving the way he commands me.

"Look at me," he commands, and I lift my gaze to meet his, lost in the depths of his desire. "You're so fucking pretty like this," he rasps.

I don't try to answer since there's no point. Instead, I dart my tongue around his shaft, loving his primal groans, and the way he shudders, especially when I add pressure to his nuts.

"God, yes," he groans, his hand tightening in my hair, his body quivering on the brink. "You were made for this, for me."

Suddenly, he pulls his cock from my mouth and grips my shoulders, pulling me up from the floor. Heat courses through my body, a flame stoked by Nick. The coldness of the basement wall presses against my skin as he turns me around, pressing me face-first against the unforgiving surface.

His breath is hot on my neck. "Spread your legs for me," he growls, and I obey without hesitation, shifting my stance to grant him better access to my core.

He trails his fingers down my spine, igniting an insatiable need that pools deep in my belly. "Nick," I gasp, feeling the head of his cock nudging at my entrance.

He doesn't ease into me; instead, he claims me with a single, powerful thrust that has me biting back a scream. The raw intensity of it, the way our bodies crash together—it's more than just sex. It's possession and love, each movement writing our story on these cold, stone walls.

"Mine," he pants, punctuating the word with another deep drive that robs me of thought. "You're mine, Carolina. Every inch of you."

The dominance in his voice sends a shiver down my spine, but it's laced with an undercurrent of something deeper, something that tethers me to him in ways I can't comprehend. His hands roam over my body, claiming every curve, every edge, as if he's branding me as his own.

"Everything," I breathe out, the word barely audible above the sound of our frantic coupling. My nails scrape against the wall, searching for purchase in a world spinning out of control. "I want to be your everything."

"You already are." His affirmation is a snarl, possessive and fiercely protective. "I'll destroy anyone who tries to come between us. You hear me? Anyone."

I nod, a simple gesture that seals my consent, my willingness to belong to this man who embodies danger and desire in equal measure. As he moves within me, I feel the edges of my being blur until there's no Carolina, no Nicklas—just us, entwined and inseparable.

His lips tracing the shell of my ear. "Give yourself to me. Let me fill you up with my jizz. I want to watch it drip out of your cunt and onto the place my dad took his last breath."

Well… shit. Wrong as it might be, I want that too.

"Nick, please… fuck me harder!" The plea escapes me as I teeter on the brink, desperate for release. I'm lost in the sensation of him, the unyielding strength and the tender care with which he handles me.

"Come for me," he commands, his voice rough with his own need. "Let me feel you clench around me."

And I do. I shatter, waves of pleasure crashing over me, washing away all doubt, all fear. I'm his, wholly and completely—and he's mine. Nick follows me over the edge, his release hot and potent inside me.

Rather than giving me time to recover, he roughly pulls me over to the spot where Caspian died. "Squat down," he orders, and I do. We both watch between my legs as juices leak out of my pussy and onto the cold floor. "That's so fucking hot," he rasps.

"This place is ours now," I say, a wicked grin splitting my lips as I reach down, smearing the liquid over the floor.

Nick takes my hand and pulls me flush against him. "I love you so fucking much," he growls against my lips.

"Forevermore," I vow. "I'll love you forevermore, Nicklas Knight."

CHAPTER 36

The Santa

I'm standing in the middle of the penthouse, the soft glow of Christmas lights painting Carolina's face with a golden hue. It's a rare sight—her guard down, breathing slow and easy as snowflakes dance beyond the windowpane. Our world, filled with danger and demands, fades away. Right now, it's just us and the silent whisper of our shared solitude.

This is exactly what I wanted to achieve when I arranged for the tree and the decorations to be done while she was sleeping. What can I say, like my namesake Saint Nick, I had my elf do all the heavy lifting.

Totally worth it.

"Merry Christmas, Carolina," I rasp, brushing fabric and hair out of the way so I can kiss her bare shoulder.

My hellcat looks amazing as she stands in front of the Christmas tree, wearing a silky, deep red robe that clings to her curves, barely tied at the waist. The fabric flows around her like liquid, highlighting every movement, every step whispering against the floor.

Underneath, I catch glimpses of matching lace—a delicate bralette and matching shorts that tease more than they reveal. It's sexy, effortlessly so, but there's a comfort to it too, a casual confidence that

"Nick…" My name quivers in the air, heavy with unspoken emotions. "It's perfect."

"Put it on," I command softly, stepping closer to clasp it around her neck. The cool metal rests against her warm skin. Her breath hitches, and I feel the tremor run through her body as my fingers brush her nape.

"Thank you," she whispers, eyes glistening. "It's really perfect."

"Only the best for my goddess." The words slip out before I can stop them, but they're true. I've given her a kingdom of shadows, and now I crown her sovereign of our dark domain.

"Nicklas Knight, you are full of surprises." Her laugh is a melody that dances with the flickering firelight.

The warmth from the fireplace licks at my skin, but it's nothing compared to the heat that flares within me as Carolina reaches for two inconspicuous boxes wrapped in red and gold. Her hands, delicate yet capable, pass them to me with a shy smile that belies the audacity of her actions this past month.

"Your turn," she says, her voice a sultry whisper carrying the weight of secrets. Come to think of it, she's used that tone ever since her shower yesterday morning.

I take the first gift, the size and heft not revealing much. The paper crinkles under my fingers as I peel it away, anticipation coiling in my gut. It's not like me to be nervous—Knight men don't do nerves—but with Carolina, everything is different.

The lid pops off, and there… "Is that lube?" I ask on a choked laugh.

She nods proudly. "Yep."

I playfully waggle my eyebrows. "So I'm getting your ass for Christmas, is that it?"

Still beaming, she hands me the other box. "Open this one."

It's the same kind of box, just smaller. As I remove the lid, I'm taken aback. On a bed of crinkled paper lies—a plastic stick, its digital screen screaming one word at me: Pregnant. My heart doesn't just skip; it ceases for a fraction of a second. A positive pregnancy test. My heir. Our child.

"Carolina…" The name escapes me, a breathless sound of wonder and disbelief.

She bites her lip, watching me with eyes wide, brimming with unshed tears. "I think… I think it's a girl."

A girl. A daughter. A tiny life formed from the most volatile parts of us both. Every Knight family superstition about heirs rushes through my mind, but they're silenced by the thunderous beat of my own heart. A daughter—*my* daughter.

"If it's a girl, I'd like to name her Willow," she croaks.

I can't think of anything more fitting than naming our girl after the sister she sacrificed everything for. Carolina's love for her runs deep, and now she wants to give our daughter a piece of that devotion, an anchor in this stormy life we lead.

"Willow," I repeat, tasting the name on my tongue. It fits. It's perfect. A flood of emotion washes over me, and for a moment, I'm adrift in it, lost in the vibrant blue depths of Carolina's gaze.

"Is that okay?" Uncertainty creeps into her tone, and it grounds me, pulls me back to shore.

"Of course it is." I reach for her, my movements decisive, my touch firm yet reverent. "This is the best damn Christmas gift I could have ever received."

Her laugh is watery, joy mingling with relief. Then, I pull her close, our bodies flush against each other, the reality of the gift nestled securely between us.

I'm a man who's walked through life with iron in my soul and steel on my tongue. But today, the sight of my hellcat and that small piece of plastic shatters every ounce of armor I've ever worn. Her eyes snap up to mine, ocean-deep and spilling over with tears. I drop to one knee, the lush carpet cushioning the impact.

"Carolina Sterling," I say, and everything else falls away. It's just her and me, and the promise of a little girl named Willow. "You've stormed into my life like a hurricane, tearing down walls I didn't even know I had."

Her hand flies to her mouth, a dam trying to hold back a flood. I reach out, taking her other hand in mine, feeling the tremor that runs through her delicate fingers.

"Today, you've given me more than I ever thought I needed. You've given me a future, a family." My throat tightens around the words. "Marry me, Carolina. Not because of obligation or power. Not because I say so…" That makes her snort. "…but because you've stolen my dark heart and made it yours. Because I love you, now and forevermore."

There's a sharp intake of breath, and I watch as a single tear escapes, tracking down her cheek like the first snowflake of winter—delicate, pure, transformative. "Are you really asking me?" she chokes out.

"I am," I confirm. It takes everything in me to allow her the option to say no. Ah, who am I kidding, that's never an option.

"Yes, Nicklas, I will marry you."

The proposal may be traditional, but what comes next isn't. We're not a couple forged in the softness of whispers; we blaze in the darkness, igniting with each touch, each word.

I yank on her hand, pulling her down to me, and when her legs give out, I cradle her, gently laying her down on the floor. "Thank fuck for that," I growl before fusing our lips together in a deep, hungry kiss.

While our tongues dance, my hands roam over her curves, staking my claim. She eagerly spreads her legs, making room for me as my hand dives beneath the waistband of her shorts and cups her cunt. "Always so eady for me," I rasp when I find her already wet.

As I take my time undressing her, she pushes my briefs down, squeezing my rock hard cock. "I want you," she moans when I've removed all her clothes and I slide two fingers into her tight channel. "But I—"

"What do you want, Hellcat?" I groan, thrusting into her hand.

She bites on her bottom lip. "Now that I'm pregnant, I want you to fuck my ass."

"Oh, I think that can be arranged," I growl, my cock twitching in her grip at the mere thought. I've wanted to claim her delicious ass since the night I met her. "Turn around."

She obeys, getting on all fours, arching her back and presenting herself to me, and the sight nearly brings me to my knees. I run my hands along her spine, down to the dip of her lower back. She shivers, her breath hitching as I roughly spread her cheeks and press one finger against her asshole.

"You want me here?" I ask, my voice thick with want.

"Y-yes," she moans, pressing back against my finger, seeking more.

With a chuckle, I reach for the lube she so generously gave me, lathering two fingers and her puckered opening in it. Then I begin to slowly work my fingers into her opening. It takes some coaxing before she relaxes enough for my first knuckles to slip through the ring.

"Fuck!" she cries, her breathing labored, and I know she isn't enjoying it yet.

"You're doing so good," I praise. "Just a bit mo—"

"Just do it," she hisses. "Shove your fingers all the way inside me."

Despite her words, I take my time. I lean forward and bite her soft ass cheek, eliciting a deep moan from her that makes it easy to get to my second knuckles.

"Almost there," I soothe, slapping her ass so it jiggles.

"It… it… I don't know if it hurts or not. I can't tell anymore," she whines.

Using my free hand, I pinch her clit, rolling it until she's moaning for more, even moving back toward me, taking my fingers all the way inside her ass.

I give her a few moments to get used to the intrusion, and then I begin to pump my digits in and out. Her breathing intensifies, but before long, she arches her back and moans loudly. "You like that?" I rasp. "Because I love the way my fingers look in your ass."

Adding a third finger makes her buck and keen, and my fourth finger has her lowering to her elbows while wagging her ass.

"Oh my God!" she cries, her ass contracting around me.

Letting go of her clit, I push three fingers into her cunt, fucking both of her holes in perfect tandem.

With every thrust of my fingers, I map out her pleasure, and it feels like I'm re-learning the language of her body. With the double penetration, she quickly comes undone, and it only takes a few more pumps before she's screaming out her climax.

"Fuck! Yes! Just like that! I... I... Fuck, Nick, I'm coming."

"Are you ready for my cock?" I ask. She's still shuddering from her orgasm.

"Yes. I want your cock filling my ass," she cries.

I grab the lube and squirt a generous amount over my length. Then I grip her hips, pulling her closer. "You're mine," I rasp, unable to keep the tremble from my voice. "Look at me." She complies, her gaze locking with mine over her shoulder as I press the tip of my hardness against her entrance.

With excruciating patience, I ease forward, giving her time to adjust to the fullness, the stretch, the intensity of our connection. She's tight, heat engulfing me, and it takes everything not to lose myself in the sensation.

"Oh... this is so..." Her voice shakes, and I still, letting her acclimate.

"Shh, I've got you," I soothe, brushing a kiss on her shoulder. "Breathe with me."

We inhale together, and as she exhales, I push in further, both of us gasping at the depth. The possessive edge claws at me, wanting to mark every inch of her as mine.

"It feels so good," Carolina confesses, her words laced with a raw honesty that clutches at my heart.

I set a slow rhythm that soon has her moaning my name like a sacred chant. The sound of it is sweeter than any Christmas carol, more intoxicating than the finest whiskey.

"Harder," she begs, and I comply, the pace building, her body meeting each of my thrusts.

"Fuck, Carolina, your ass feels incredible," I groan. As I begin to fuck her harder, she sucks her bottom lip between her teeth. I raise my hand, gently tugging at the skin until she lets go. "If you want your lip bitten, I'll do it." The words come out as a possessive growl, which I guess she likes with the way her ass tightens around me.

I continue to fuck her while leaning in so I can claim her lips, doing exactly that; biting down on her lip, and when the skin breaks, I lap the blood up before snaking my tongue around hers so she can taste her essence in my mouth.

I'm so lost in her that I can barely stand it. Every sense is filled with her, and I know it won't take long before I erupt. I move one hand to her clit, furiously rubbing it until she clenches harder around me.

"Yes! Yes! Ye—" Her words break off into a crescendo of pleasure, her climax triggering my own.

I groan her name like a benediction, pouring my hot jizz into her tight ass. As her hole contracts around my cock, I keep coming, and keep coming. I shudder and roar her name, still fucking her with all my might.

Once I'm completely spent, I collapse onto the floor, pulling her into my arms and throwing her leg over my hip.

It's early evening when we finally finish our Christmas meal, both of us high on the day and everything it brought with it.

"I don't think I can squeeze down another bite," Carolina sighs, patting her belly.

A knock echoes through the penthouse, interrupting us. "Finally," I sigh. When I notice her worried expression, I clarify, "It's just Arthur."

After I fucked her the second or third time, I finally got around to explaining that Arthur was the one who set the deadline for the conception, and that whether I contacted him or not, he'd probably stop by for an update.

"Right, right. I forgot," she mumbles, her hands shaking slightly.

I get up and stride over to Carolina, positioning myself at her back with one hand on her shoulder. "It'll be fine," I say reassuringly. "It's just a formality."

Feet scuffle along the floor at the elevator entry as Marco lets Arthur in, and then the door opens to reveal the King, his imposing frame filling the doorway. His piercing blue eyes scanning the room—assessing, always assessing.

"Arthur." My voice is steady, masking the undercurrent of tension that prickles at the back of my neck. "Good to see you."

"Nicklas," he greets, stepping inside with a nod. His gaze lands on Carolina, dipping to where her hands are steepled together around her stomach. "Carolina." He inclines his head with a respect that's hard won in our world.

"Good evening, Arthur," she replies, her tone matching his formality.

I offer him a glass of whiskey, which he happily accepts. "We have news," I say when I'm back behind my kitten.

"Well?"

"Carolina's pregnant," I announce, my chest swelling with pride even as I watch for his reaction.

"Indeed?" Arthur's eyebrow arches slightly. He sips the whiskey, his gaze never leaving mine. "Congratulations are in order, then. To both of you."

"Thank you," Carolina murmurs, clutching the fabric of her sweater.

"The timing couldn't be more perfect," Arthur continues, setting down his glass with deliberate care, "especially now that Knights seem to be dropping like flies." He winks playfully at Carolina.

"Yes, what a shame," she deadpans.

I wasn't sure how Arthur was going to react to the news of Dad's death, but he couldn't seem less interested if he tried. "Well, thanks for the update, Nicklas," Arthur says. "We'll talk again I'm sure. But seeing as you have things under control on your side of the pond, I don't see any reason to stay longer."

"Great," I confirm, watching as he drinks the last of the whiskey.

"You have my permission and approval to marry Carolina." He throws it out so casually I'm not sure I heard him correctly.

"I passed the test," she says, straightening her back. "Are you now saying that didn't mean anything?"

Arthur smirks. "Not at all. When I arrived in late November, I couldn't care less who my cousin ended up with, if any. But you've impressed me, which is why you get my approval. Do with it what you please."

With those words, he spins on his heel, heading toward the door.

He pauses briefly, looking at me over his shoulder. "Don't forget about the Hunter."

"How could I forget," I grunt, not too happy about the deal Arthur apparently has with the nameless killer for hire.

Arthur chuckles. "Just don't get in his way. He has free access to New York City in February."

Then the King leaves the same way he came in.

My hellcat looks up at me, confusion written all over her features. "Was the test for nothing or not?" she asks, annoyance creeping into her tone.

I bend down and place a kiss on her cheek. "Not at all. The test technically just gave you permission, but not his… approval." That word sounds all wrong because, honestly, who cares? "But since he's the King, his approval is supposed to carry some weight."

Snorting, she gets out of the chair. "He might be our King," she says, winding her arms around my neck. "But you're my dark Knight. Now and forevermore."

EPILOGUE

Ruby

The chapel is colder than I expected, the chill creeping into my bones as I stand in the shadows, hidden behind a marble column. The scent of old wood and faded incense lingers in the air, mixing with the soft murmur of guests gathered for the ceremony.

It's December thirty-first, the last day of the year, and I'm here, unseen, watching Nick marry Carolina.

I wasn't going to come. I didn't even respond to the invitation, unsure if I could bear it. But something drew me here, an invisible force I couldn't resist, even if it's just to watch from the dark. I can't stand beside them, smiling and pretending everything is fine. But I need to witness this moment in their lives, even if they don't know I'm here.

Nick looks… different. More at peace than I've ever seen him. He stands tall at the front, his usual stern expression softened as he gazes at Carolina. The way he looks at her—it's like she's the only person in the world. I've never seen him like that before, so open, so vulnerable. It makes me ache, a sharp reminder of the kind of love I've never had. The kind of love I never will have.

At the front, near the aisle, there's a picture of Willow, her bright smile frozen in time. It's a large portrait, blown up so no one can miss it. The sight of her face knocks the breath out of me, a wave of grief crashing over me so suddenly it nearly doubles me over.

I miss her so much, more than I can put into words.

Willow, with her laughter, her endless curiosity, her way of making everything seem brighter. I didn't get to know her for long—our time together was brief, stolen in the midst of all the chaos. But it was enough. Enough to love her. Enough to feel this void now that she's gone.

The vows are soft, intimate, and they carry through the quiet chapel like a whispered secret. Carolina's voice trembles just slightly, but there's strength there too—a determination to see this through, to stand by Nick no matter what comes.

Nick's voice is steady, the words rolling off his tongue with the kind of certainty I've always envied. They talk about forever, about promises that won't break, about a love that will last. It's beautiful, really, but all I can think about is how far away that kind of love feels for me.

I don't have love, not even a shred of it.

What I have is a man who bought me like a piece of property, a man who wears cruelty like a second skin. My dad sold me to him, traded me away ten years ago for power and wealth, and left me in the hands of a monster.

Every time I think of him—his cold eyes, his twisted smile, the way his fingers dig into my skin—I feel a surge of hatred so fierce it almost scares me. But it's not just hatred. It's fear. Fear of what he'll do next, of the darkness that lurks behind his every word, his every touch. I need to get out, but I don't know how. And every day I stay, I feel myself shrinking, disappearing into nothing.

When Nick offered to free me, I almost said yes. But I can't. My freedom won't ever mean anything if it's given to me just like it was taken away from me. And besides, I don't need saving. I need to find a way to save myself.

But standing here, hidden in the shadows, I feel so far away from that. So far away from everything I want, everything I need. All I can do is watch, wondering if I'll ever have what Nick and Carolina have. Or if I'm destined to stay in the shadows, watching as the people I love find happiness, while I wait for the curse to catch up with me.

Or maybe the presence haunting me will finally show itself, and end me before I can take my next breath. Hmm, no, still nothing.

I've felt the presence of someone following me for almost a week now. Though I've never seen this person, I know they're there. I can feel it in the air, hear it in the too quiet footsteps. I haven't been alone since Christmas morning.

There's a small chance I'm getting paranoid and it's just my mind playing tricks on me, but I don't think it's that. I'm used to being followed by people; first at my dad's command, later at my husband's. I know what it feels like to be shadowed.

I let out a small sigh, wondering, not for the first time, if it's the curse catching up with me.

The Knight family curse—three heirs to secure the future, because fate always takes two. We've heard it our whole lives, how one of us is destined to survive while the others fall. Jack's already died once—he jokes about it, but I see the truth in his eyes.

He knows the curse is real, knows it's already marked us.

I feel it too, this creeping sense of inevitability. It's coming for me, I'm sure of it. The curse, the fate that's waiting in the wings, ready to claim its next victim. I feel it in my bones, this knowledge that I won't survive for long. Maybe that's why I'm here, hidden away, watching from the shadows. Maybe I'm just waiting for the end, for the curse to take what it's owed.

Nick and Carolina kiss, sealing their vows, their fates intertwined in a way that feels almost sacred. The chapel is silent, the kind of quiet that feels heavy with meaning. And all I can do is watch, wondering if I'll ever have that. Or if I'm destined to stay trapped in this marriage, suffocating under the weight of a life I never chose.

But I push those thoughts away, focusing instead on the warmth in Nick's eyes as he looks at Carolina. There's so much love there, so much devotion. I can't help but feel a pang of envy, but also… hope. Maybe it's not too late for me, either. Maybe there's still a chance for something more, something real.

Or maybe it's just a fool's dream, and I'm the next one on the chopping block. But for now, I'll stay here, hidden in the shadows, watching and waiting. It's what I've always done best, after all. And if the curse comes for me, if my husband finally breaks me, I'll be ready.

I have to be.

Made in United States
Troutdale, OR
12/04/2024

25873374R00199